LORD LANGCLIFFE'S KISS

"Where are we going?" Riordan asked.

"To the village," Cambria answered.

"And how will this little stroll punish me?"

"We shall walk through all the shops with you looking like a man in love. You have my permission to spout whatever nonsense an enraptured man might say. I promise not to laugh."

So, she meant to make a fool of him for her own satisfaction? Little did she know how willing he was to act the lovesick swain. He slid his arm over her shoulder, his fingers playing with her ear.

"Not that caveman nonsense, Riordan," Cambria hissed. "Just give me fond looks, and I'll rest my fingers on your arm."

He laughed. "Anyone who knows me would never believe such a feeble courtship as that." He stopped before a large window. "We'll have to give everyone something to talk about." He turned her and rested his hands on her shoulders. Leaning down, he touched his lips to hers.

She knew she should go along with it, but she couldn't help stiffening. He gave her shoulders a little shake. "Close your eyes and pretend you like it."

As she obeyed, she could feel his breath as he drew closer, and, this time, he didn't stop with a fragile touch. This one came in waves. A warm touch, then lifting only to come back with a slanted kiss and a sound deep in his throat that stirred her insides. She could feel every eye in the village on them, knew that no one ever behaved this way in public, not even in London, but she couldn't pull back, could only lean into the kiss. She was surely *melting* . . .

BOOK YOUR PLACE ON OUR WEBSITE AND MAKE THE READING CONNECTION!

We've created a customized website just for our very special readers, where you can get the inside scoop on everything that's going on with Zebra, Pinnacle and Kensington books.

When you come online, you'll have the exciting opportunity to:

- View covers of upcoming books
- Read sample chapters
- Learn about our future publishing schedule (listed by publication month *and author*)
- Find out when your favorite authors will be visiting a city near you
- Search for and order backlist books from our online catalog
- Check out author bios and background information
- Send e-mail to your favorite authors
- Meet the Kensington staff online
- Join us in weekly chats with authors, readers and other guests
- Get writing guidelines
- AND MUCH MORE!

**Visit our website at
http://www.zebrabooks.com**

LORD LANGCLIFFE'S LADY

Donna Davidson

Zebra Books
Kensington Publishing Corp.

http://www.zebrabooks.com

Dedicated to

Pat Teal, Agent
For her warm friendship, advice, and encouragement

Thanks to
Gregory L. Alt, mentor
Dale McCann, critic partner, friend
Allan Davidson, historian husband
and to daughters
Ann Alt, final reading editor
Coral Davidson, for a delightful supply of characters

Prologue

A scratching at the door sent the Duke of Langcliffe's heart pounding as if he were a stripling once more, waiting eagerly for his love's arrival . . .

He sent a last glance around the room he'd arranged to please her. Food waited on the table before the blazing fire. A rose from the garden rested on one of the two plates, along with a gift—a ruby set in intricate gold, hanging from a heavy gold chain—wrapped in an exquisite silk scarf he had brought back from the crusades. The enormous bed dominated the room, *as well it should.*

Henry Langcliffe lifted his goblet and took a bracing swallow of wine. "Come!" His roar filled the room.

The door opened just far enough for his aging servant to slip inside. Shoulders hunched as if expecting a blow, he murmured, "M'lord, they are here."

Fury filled Langcliffe. *"They?"*

"Miss Thorne is accompanied by her father."

Langcliffe slammed down his goblet.

The servant flinched.

Good. At least someone feared him these days. "Let them enter."

Roxanne slipped in first, her dark, adoring eyes flitting nervously toward him. Like a deer entering a clearing, unsure of itself, she moved forward just far enough to let her father step inside behind her.

"Sir Thorne," Langcliffe drawled, barely acknowledging Roxanne's father. Instead, he strode across the room, grasped Roxanne's hand to draw her to the table. "Welcome, my dear. Let me take your wrap." His fingers trailed across her neck as he lifted the garment. He was pleased to see her sensuous shiver as her face lifted to give him a shy smile. At ten years and five, Roxanne's earthy beauty affected him as no other. Strong features, high cheekbones, rosy complexion, and lush mouth, she was every man's dream. Tall for a woman, a welcome match to his large frame, she moved like warm honey as he seated her in the chair.

Thorne took a stance behind his daughter's chair. "We have to talk,"

Langcliffe's brow rose at Thorne's insolence. *"Have to?"*

Thorne's fingers tightened on the back of the chair, but his gaze met Langcliffe's without fear. "I'm worried about Roxanne's future, your grace, should anything happen to you."

"You expect *something* to happen to me?"

"You have returned from the crusades to find a hostile household. Two attempts have been made on your life already, and everyone knows who's behind it—the father of your wife's two young bastards—and your own son siding with his mother."

A brave man, thought Langcliffe, to speak of such things. Perhaps he would *not* slay him. Langcliffe nodded, giving Thorne leave to continue.

"Should you fall at their hands," Thorne said, "the first thing they will do is turn on Roxanne. Is that what you want, to see my daughter and whatever children result from this union turned out penniless, perhaps banished? Or dead?"

Langcliffe watched Roxanne's face as her father spoke. No matter that theirs was a love match, Roxanne felt real terror at her father's words.

"What do you suggest, Sir Thorne?"

"Grant her some land. Not in a will that would not survive

you, but send the documents to the king. Have it made a royal charter—he would do it for you. Make sure Roxanne and her children inherit.''

He gave Sir Thorne an admiring look. ''Down to the last son, eh, Thorne?''

Thorne nodded. ''That should do it.''

Roxanne spoke. ''No, Henry, that will not do.''

The men turned to stare at her.

''Be silent,'' Thorne said harshly. ''This is men's business.''

Ignoring her father, Roxanne sent an imploring look toward Langcliffe.

''You want more?'' Langcliffe asked, somewhat disappointed at this first sign of avarice.

Shaking her head, she pleaded in a quivering voice. ''What if there are no sons? I do not want my female heirs to be left out as though they don't matter. Who needs protection more than a female?''

''Ah,'' Langcliffe said, his faith once more restored by her soft-hearted request. ''But what if she should remain single?'' It was impossible, of course.

''Let a daughter remain unmarried until she is . . . say twenty-five . . . then she must marry. If she does not, then the land will revert to the Langcliffe heirs.''

''The Thorne name must survive,'' Sir Thorne insisted. ''Let no marriage be allowed unless the husband assumes the Thorne name.''

Agreeing to the proud demand, Langcliffe nodded, ''Very wise. The males, by right of primogeniture, will inherit first, then the eldest female, but only if her husband takes the Thorne name. That way the land and the name stay intact.''

Smiling, he sat down and took her hand in his. ''What land would you have, then?''

She blushed. ''I'd like the lake and the old Roman baths . . . with a little land around them. I want the right to use your road to reach my land. You keep the land surrounding mine—to keep me safe—but I want the right to forage for food and firewood on your land since you will have the woods and the orchards.''

"Granted," he said easily. Her request, while womanly practical, deeply touched his heart. She had chosen places that had witnessed their courtship. They had met at the baths, kissed first near the lake, and spent long hours strolling through the orchards.

"We shall call my property Lakeview, and your land shall be called Thorne's Well."

Sir Thorne growled his approval.

"And should my heirs attack yours," Langcliffe said fiercely, "then this entire estate becomes Thorne property."

"Oh, no . . ." She was horrified.

Her protest made him even more determined. "Let me worry about the details, my dear. Your father will take the documents to the king himself. Nothing will be left to chance—no Langcliffe will ever harm a Thorne."

Chapter One

Riordan Langcliffe, Earl of Langcliffe, replaced his pen in its holder and leaned his muscled forearms on the broad oak desk. "Alistair, if you're going to argue over every decision I make, you'll be out of my employment before your first week is over."

Alistair, a younger, moodier replica of his uncle, strolled slowly around the perimeter of the vast library, thumbing the gold-embossed titles on leather-bound books. Dark hair fell over his forehead as he dipped his head at the rebuke, but the look he sent Riordan—black-eyed and intense—was stubbornly unrepentant. "You might at least consider an alternate opinion, Uncle Riordan."

Riordan returned a disbelieving grin. "I'm the one who has amassed an obscene fortune, Alistair. You're the one who got sent down for sneaking a pig into the headmaster's rooms. Whose opinion should be considered . . . yours or mine?"

Alistair stopped, his face flushed. "It seems so heartless, though, buying up Johnstone's vowels just to get his property."

"Is that right?" Riordan leaned back to signal his willingness to listen. He waved at the chair opposite his desk. "Explain your position."

As Alistair's long legs brought him across the room, Riordan asked himself once more what idiocy had possessed him the day he'd agreed to subject himself to this . . . redeeming of his nephew.

He knew the answer. *Family . . . emotion.* The weakest link in a man's armor.

All through history, the story was the same. A man could build a fortress with walls thick enough to safeguard his holding, sink everlasting wells, and store enough food to withstand any attack. He could train armies who gave no quarter, soldiers with steadfast hearts and loyalty capable of withstanding pain and deprivation. A man could amass a fortune large enough to control kings and countries alike.

And lose it all over *emotion.* A wounded comrade, a weeping mother, a dying father, a child in need, the weakness of loving a woman.

After shoring up his own defenses, here he was, trapped in a promise given to a hero-worshiping youth. Alistair had been trotting along behind Riordan since he'd first escaped the nursery and found his uncle's arms preferable to the pinching fingers of his nurse. And now, because Alistair once more needed rescue, Riordan was to be *irritated* to death with transforming a youth controlled by London's fads into a man of judgment, a project that had very little hope of success.

Alistair dropped gracelessly into the chair opposite Riordan's desk. "Why don't you hold Johnstone's vowels for a while and give him a chance to redeem them? Everyone would think you a fine fellow."

"And I'm not considered *a fine fellow* now?" Riordan knew the answer to that, but he was curious none the less.

Alistair swallowed hard, but he looked Riordan straight in the eye. "They say you're no better than a money lender, that if your aim weren't as sharp as your business dealings, you'd be ousted from polite society."

Riordan chuckled, more amused at his nephew's shaky bravado than the depiction of his own character. "That's one I haven't heard."

Incredulity rippled over Alistair's features. "You really don't mind?"

"No."

"I wish I didn't care what people thought about me." He leaned forward. "Is it *money* that gives you the confidence?"

Riordan shook his head. "Experience."

"So, I just have to live a little longer?"

Riordan studied the frowning young man in the chair opposite. Every instinct rebelled at opening old wounds, but Alistair's innocent idealism needed a sharp jolt. "I was fourteen when my father killed himself. He left me a chain of neglected, mortgaged estates and a long line of circling, blood-scenting creditors."

Alistair nodded eagerly. "Whom you sent packing in short order."

"No. I hid behind locked doors with my mother, terrified at seeing those people who had once been so obsequious suddenly so violent." He, paused to let Alistair's disillusionment sink in. "I hated being ineffectual, *weak.*" Riordan looked into Alistair's eyes. "D'you know why I was weak?"

"You were young."

Riordan leaned forward, his voice forceful. "No . . . because I was *ignorant.* A pampered young aristocrat is ill-prepared for situations like that, much less for governing his own estates."

Alistair's face cleared. "So someone taught you . . . guided you."

"My guardians were my mother and her brother."

"Gawd . . . Grandmother and Old Mouldy?

"Exactly." Riordan could still taste the old bitterness. "My mother was hysterical, thought I was too young to know such things. She convinced Moulton to dismiss any solicitor who wanted to instruct me."

"But what about the circling creditors?"

"They came in for the kill. Moulton panicked. All our property began toppling off the auction block, and I couldn't do anything to stop it. We had nothing left except the town house and Langcliffe Hall, yet Mother maintained her place in society, charging things and entertaining lavishly."

Alistair looked horrified. "How did you ever get control?"

"I taught myself. I studied my father's old dog-eared volumes on estate management and investments. Once I had a glimmering of what it was all about, I questioned men who understood the system."

"*Then* you convinced Old Mouldy that you could handle it?"

Riordan chuckled. "I didn't waste my time. I marched into the latest solicitor's office—Rountree, when he was newly appointed—and told him he could either work with me or know that his days were numbered. Rountree took one look at my face and agreed.

"What a mess," he murmured. "Over the next few months, we were hampered by half-finished transactions, lost documents, uncollected debts . . . I don't think we ever got all the facts."

"What did Grandmother and Old Mouldy do?"

Riordan's lips twitched. "Mother screeched that we were doomed and demanded that Moulton *'do something.'* Moulton, who only wanted to fish his days away, fled to his country home to escape her noisy drama."

"But the creditors were happy."

"No, they panicked as well. They were back, pounding on the town house door and refused my mother further credit. She set up a wailing that could be heard across the square."

Alistair shuddered. "How did you stand it?"

"I'd already learned one important lesson . . . that only a cold, clear head and an unfeeling heart would carry the day."

Nodding with satisfaction, Alistair's respectful eyes gleamed. "So," he said, leaning forward, "how did you get *rich?* How long did it take?"

"It took years. First I leased out the town house and we moved to Langcliffe Hall. Mother rebelled and went to live with your mother at Singleton Hall—and soon came scuttling back, whining even louder over the tyranny of your grandmother, who still firmly ruled the roost."

Alistair sighed. "That sounds about right." He shifted in his chair, far more interested in the rest of Riordan's story. "And then?"

Riordan's eyes grew cold. "I had to be brutal. I cut off unprofitable renters and servants, no matter how long their connection to Langcliffe. Mother hated it, but I cut off her credit. There were no more luxuries, no more *anything* I did not personally approve."

"Good grief!"

"I bought seed and planted," Riordan said, half amused at the memory, "then cursed myself for investing in so slow a return. I closed up most of the hall, and Mother and I lived in the rest. After the crop was in, I was wiser and brought in sheep."

"That's where you got money to begin buying properties?

"No, but we managed to eat . . . and it gave me money to gamble."

Alistair's eyes widened. "I thought you hated gambling."

"Needs must, Alistair. I had to do something quickly or lose Langcliffe Hall. London is littered with drunken gamblers who think nothing of tossing away fortunes, both monies and property."

Alistair's face darkened in sudden understanding. "Like Johnstone."

Grimly, Riordan nodded. "Sometimes I managed properties and kept them . . . sometimes I sold them for a profit. Then I invested in canals and shipping and financed new building in London." It took years, Riordan reflected. In time, he restored dignity to their name, and had long since allowed his mother to open the town house and fritter away a fortune each season, living the totally useless life she loved.

Nodding with pride, Alistair quoted, "A damned midas in our midst. A legend, and you're barely thirty."

And feeling older by the minute, Riordan thought. "You said you wanted to make your own fortune. You wanted to work with me, find out how it's done. Are you still willing?"

"Yes."

"Why?"

"Why?" Propelled into action, Alistair stood and began

another restless stroll around the room. "I want to be wealthy like you."

"Why?"

Alistair stopped by the window overlooking the front of Langcliffe Hall. Grasping the bottom ledge, he sent his gaze skimming over the vast grounds. "I want to look out of a window and see my own land. I want to see gardeners trimming my hedge, rolling my lawn. I want a drive so long you can't see the house from the road."

He turned his back to the window. "I want a room like this, with the smell of leather reminding me that my books are valued, protected."

He stepped forward, on the move once more. "When I walk into a ball, I want people to step aside, not so they can notice me while I'm walking by, but because they're half afraid of me as they are of you." Stopping before Riordan's desk, he ran long fingers once more through his dark hair. "I don't want women admiring my good looks, then reminding themselves that I have nothing to offer."

"They think that? You're my heir. Someday, all this *will* be yours."

"No," Alistair replied harshly, dropping into the chair once more. "I'd be a fool to depend on that. Nobody believes it anyway. One of these days, you'll marry and start your own nursery." Alistair stretched out his long legs and contemplated the shine on his Hessions with a frown. "Even if you *don't* marry, as you claim, what kind of man am I to stand around doing nothing, expecting you to take care of me like a mewling child?"

He looked up. "I want to see my mother in a nice gown, sitting in a London parlor riffling through invitations. I want to know that *I* made that possible. Instead, we live in poverty at Singleton Hall, the only property my father hasn't wagered away, and that's only because the place is entailed."

He sat upright, facing Riordan once more. "Sorry. You asked a simple question, and I've rambled on like a madman."

"Not so mad as you might think, Alistair." *Damn.* Now that he'd seen this vein of strength and purpose in his nephew, he would only set himself up for the pain of seeing the youth fall as soon as he got back to London.

Riordan pushed the untidy stack of Johnstone's papers forward. "Here . . . Johnstone's vowels . . . this is your first project to manage."

Shocked, Alistair picked them up, riffling through the notes as if seeing them for the first time. Placing them neatly back onto the desk, he looked at Riordan. "Surely, you'll advise me?"

"I'll answer your questions, but I won't make your decisions. I give you free rein to handle it however you wish. My only requirement is that you make a healthy profit—selling it or managing it. That profit will be yours to invest in the next project you manage. You keep whatever you earn, and you take the consequences for your own actions."

Squinting, Alistair asked, "Consequences?"

"Every action has a consequence, Alistair. If you were to give these vowels back to your friend, Johnstone, you would gain an instant lack of respect from your friends, while dealing a blow to Johnstone's dignity. No one appreciates being beholden—it's an instant enemy maker."

Alistair gave the notes an uneasy glance. "Once I take these, I suspect the friendship is over, anyway."

"Well, then, good riddance. Just don't offer it back for a small sum more than he wagered. Because he lost *property* and property is priceless."

Alistair frowned. "Priceless? Surely not Johnstone's. The place is falling down around him. Not only that, but his mother lives there." He smiled. "I went out there with Johnstone once, and she kept thinking I was her son instead of Johnston. Followed me around giving me treats and kissing me on the cheek." He frowned. "Of course, he only goes out when she gets her quarterly allowance. Poor dear . . . you couldn't evict a batty old lady from her home." He glanced up to affirm his statement, gasping at the truth in Riordan's eyes.

"Don't go maudlin on me, Alistair. Her son evicted her when he wagered his home."

"He's my friend. How can I explain this?"

"You are already a *fine fellow,* Alistair. Now's the time to decide if you meant the things you just said. Do you truly want to be like me?"

His jaw clenched, Alistair nodded. "I'm just asking for advice."

"Then," Riordan said, "I'll give you two basic rules. First, never explain, never apologize. The only reason to discuss business is to acquire information or to give instructions to minions." Riordan paused. "Or to train one's heir."

Flushed with pride, Alistair nodded. "You said *two* rules . . ."

"Distrust emotion," Riordan said, reaching for his pen. "It's the surest road to making foolish decisions."

"Like my father. That's what makes him weak."

Riordan's head snapped up. "Your father is *not* driven by emotion."

"But he *is.* He must follow his feelings or decline as an artist."

"D'you *really* want the truth?"

Alistair brought his hands up onto the table, tightly clasped, braced. "That's why I am here, am I not? If I am to learn to be successful, it seems equally important to see how *not* to do it."

"Very well then. Your father is not an artist, Alistair. An artist *creates.* Your father destroys, he uses, wastes, and throws away, but he *creates* nothing. He excuses his self-indulgence by claiming artistic emotion, when its only a weakling's ploy to avoid responsibility. No," Riordan said firmly, "the emotions I speak of cause you to do something for another that will bring injury to yourself."

Slumping, Alistair's gaze dropped to the floor. Damn, Riordan thought, he didn't have to *bludgeon* the boy with the truth. He knew from his own life how it felt to discover a father's weakness. "Alistair," he said, "you're not the only boy to see his idolized father fall off his pedestal."

Alistair shifted in the chair. "I suppose not."

"Sometimes it makes us better men."

Alistair looked up. "You're speaking of yourself."

"Yes. When I was young I loved my father. I went everywhere with him. He taught me how to fish and hunt. When my mother didn't want animals in the house, he said a boy needed a dog, that we had servants to clean up after them. He was my champion.''

''What happened?''

Riordan looked out the window. ''My mother explained it after our family broke up. She said, *'Thorne women led him into debauchery—drinking and gambling—and he was never the same after that.'* She was very bitter.''

Alistair perked up. ''Thorne women?''

''Neighbors of ours.'' He gave a dismissing shrug. ''It's an old story. The year after your mother married, my mother took me away, and we left him there at Lakeview.''

''Did you hate him, then?''

''No, but I was only ten. As I grew older, my mother told me what happened. It was painful for me because I was so young, whereas you've already begun your own independence.''

''But I've grown to adulthood thinking my father's way is all right.'' He frowned. ''You think I won't be able to change, don't you?''

''I won't lie to you, Alistair. You might find my way of life too hard. You're popular with your friends; you may not be able to give that up. Gambling is part of that life, and so is drinking yourself senseless. People rationalize, they find reasons for doing what they *like.*''

''Then, damn it, tell me *how.* How do *you* stay strong?''

Riordan rubbed the bridge of his nose. This was harder than he expected. ''All right . . . here are a few tricks I use to keep myself in line. When I'm gambling, I don't drink—''

''I've heard that.''

''I don't say I *never* drink, but never when I need my brain sharp.''

Alistair grinned. ''I'll be like you. What a stir that will make when I start acting just like you.''

Riordan bit back a smile. ''All right, here's the tricky part. When I'm gambling and find myself getting euphoric over it, excited . . . that's when I stop. I just stop playing and leave.''

''What do people say?''

Riordan leaned forward, his voice intense. ''At that moment, you're busy mastering yourself. Caring what they say gives your control to them.''

''Right,'' Alistair mused, his face intent. Riordan thought he'd like to be there when Alistair assumed his new persona . . . or at least tried to.

''Riordan,'' Alistair said, ''you said the second rule was *distrust emotion* . . . but, what use has emotion if we can't trust it?''

Riordan smiled faintly. ''To gull young girls into marriage, I suppose.''

''Like my mother?''

''Don't judge Lily too harshly, Alistair. My sister was a dreamer just as you are. She thought a curly-haired gentleman who wore all the right clothes and spouted poetry would make her happy. But like all young girls, she wasn't sensible enough to think of how it might affect her children. Everyone knew your father gambled, and everyone knew he didn't make a decision without consulting his mother. Both of those flaws have made Lily a very unhappy person. And she's too proud to let me help her, so you have the unhappy task of suffering for it.''

''She let you send me to school.''

''I earned that honor by buying up your father's vowels.'' He hardened his heart against the shock in Alistair's eyes. *''And,* I'll warn you now that should you begin drinking and gambling like your father, I will cut you off. You'll no longer be my heir.''

''I understand that.''

''Good.''

Riordan turned away as the sound of crunching gravel, and jingling harnesses echoed through the open window behind him. He stood and turned to look down as voices drifted up through the window. Two petite ladies made their way daintily out of a large, crested coach. ''What the devil? My mother's here, and she's brought a guest.''

Alistair moved alongside Riordan, leaning forward for a

better look. He grinned at Riordan. "Another damned virginal offering."

Riordan's head jerked sideways. "Where the hell did you hear that?"

"From you . . . every time you go to London, Grandmother brings another girl around, and you start swearing." Clearly determined to stand up to his idol, he gave Riordan a cheeky smile. "Just thought I'd give you a leg up since I knew the drill."

Riordan's lips twitched, but his thoughts were on the sight of luggage—mounds of luggage—being plucked from the coach like a ripe harvest of trouble. "It's the beginning of the season," he muttered, turning away. "What could be important enough to drag her all the way out here?"

Riordan sauntered down the marble staircase. Below him on the black and white checkered floor, servants scurried back and forth with military precision, carrying bags and trunks toward the back staircase. One footman took the yapping little dog from Lady Langcliffe's thin arms, and another footman wrested an identical terror from the guest's.

Blast it all, where did his mother find these girls, these perfect little reflections of herself?

He sent an expert glance over the newcomer. Another blonde like his mother, he noted, with wings of lustrous hair looped over each ear. Prettier than most. Dainty bosom like his mother's. Oh, well.

His mother looked up, her blue eyes glowing. "Riordan, my dear, come and meet Priscilla Norton who has generously agreed to keep me company for a few days. Her father is Lord Norton from the Cotswold Nortons, and will be coming to get her on his way back to London."

"Miss Norton," Riordan said smoothly with a bow over her outstretched hand, "Welcome to Langcliffe Hall." He turned to his mother and kissed her cheek. "You're looking well, Mother."

"Thank you, darling," she said, already looking toward the kitchen. "Shall I speak to the cook about dinner?"

As if he could stop her. "Of course."

"When I saw your coach," Riordan said, detaining her, "I wondered if something was wrong." Best to get her objective out in the open.

Her expression cleared. "No, it's good news, actually. Phillip died."

He was ashamed to be struck silent for even the barest second. "I see," he managed. *Who the hell was Phillip?*

"When did this happen?" *And why was it good news?*

"Almost a year ago. And did they send a notice to the papers? Not at all . . . just one more indication of their low origins!"

"And this disturbs you?"

"Of course. We must foreclose immediately."

"Of course." He assumed an interested expression and held on.

"Send the vicious nest of vipers packing, it's far overdue."

"How long has this . . . nest of vipers been bothering you, Mother?"

"How long?" She frowned. "Since the last crusade, as you know."

"Well," he said faintly, "it's certainly time to put an end to it."

"Good. We shall see you at dinner. Come, Priscilla." Every candidate Lady Langcliffe adopted got the same treatment: following her around as she directed the servants so they might see how Riordan's mother liked things done. Priscilla nodded and followed obediently.

Riordan frowned . . . poor Mother, more absent-minded every year.

Lady Langcliffe waited until they were relaxing in the parlor after dinner to accost Riordan. "When can you evict them, darling? Lakeview always was my favorite property, and reclaiming the Thorne property makes it perfect."

Alerted by her choice of words, Riordan asked, "You want to reclaim Thorne's Well?"

"Of course. I told you Phillip Thorne died."

"Lakeview?" he murmured, then stopped himself as violent emotions churned inside him. *Lakeview, his childhood home*, the last place they had all lived together as a family. He could still picture driving away, and his father growing smaller and smaller as they left.

What a mess. His mother still thought they owned it, thought she could at last gain her retribution by claiming *Thorne's Well* . . . the home of the enemy. He studied her face, so animated, so excited. How cruel to just blurt out the truth now, to snatch away her triumph.

No, he would let her have her moment and go through the motions of doing her bidding. Once he had the proof of sale in hand, he would gently break the news that Lakeview no longer belonged to them.

"Phillip," he mused, joining the conversation, "he was the older brother, right? He lived in London, he had some job there."

"He went off to be a solicitor. It's just like the Thornes to choose such a lowly life when he was already a landowner."

"And there was a little girl. She cried when I left. She hung on to my hand and forbade me to go." He remembered his own tight throat, how he hated to leave her so bereft.

Bits of the story surfaced in his mind. The infamous Thorne women. The despicable Langcliffe ancestor who had caused the trouble in the first place, all for the love of a woman. But had the Langcliffe men learned from their forefathers, from the constant agitation? No, down through the ages, they'd still been attracted to the blasted Thorne women.

As had his father.

Too bad that they *didn't* still own Lakeview and the hold on Thorne's Well. He would gladly hand Thorne's Well over to her like a gift, finally negating his youthful inability to stem her tears. "I shall go tomorrow."

"Absolutely not! I don't want *you* going. Send someone else." She stopped then, suspicion blossoming on her petite features. "Have you been seeing those women? I told you to stay away from there."

He bit back a laugh. "Perhaps you'd like to go along as chaperon . . . and keep me safe?"

Her lovely brows rose in indignation. "You are not setting foot in the valley until those women are gone."

Alistair grinned. "I'll go with you, Uncle Riordan."

Lady Langcliffe's hands flew up. "Lord save us," she shrieked, "don't let the boy go!"

Riordan replied with a wink at Alistair, who looked rather fascinated by the thought of loose women on their property. "I wouldn't dream of it. I'll consult with Rountree tomorrow."

He asked gently, "May we speak of something else, Mother?"

She patted a delicate yawn as if suddenly exhausted. "I think I will retire, dear, but perhaps you might show Priscilla the rose garden."

Chapter Two

Rountree removed his spectacles to swipe a large handkerchief over his face. Blotting his curly red beard, he frowned. "This is strange, Langcliffe. We've looked through every box. We have nothing on Lakeview, not even the old ledgers your father kept on all his other properties."

Riordan closed the last box and carried it to join the others against the wall. "There's only one other place it could be . . . Moulton's house."

"I thought we took everything he had."

"We took everything he *gave* us, but the paper we need might be stuffed in some dusty vase. Or," he added with a moue of distaste, "wrapped around fish entrails and buried in his rose garden."

"Perhaps your mother knows—"

"Knows what?" Lady Langcliffe stood in the doorway eyeing Riordan's dusty clothes with distaste. Her pointed glance slid past Rountree. "You have servants for this sort of work."

Riordan ignored the gibe. "We can't find the Lakeview papers."

She looked alarmed. "Lakeview? Why do you need them?"

Curious, Riordan studied her face. Guilt? Had she, in one

of her capricious moments, destroyed everything to do with Lakeview? "If we are to turf out the Thornes and reclaim their property, we must have them."

"Can't you do it without the papers?"

"Mother," he said gently, "it's possible that Lakeview was one of the properties that was sold."

She leaned against the door jamb. "Oh, dear. I suppose I shall have to tell you." She paused. "Uncle Moulton has the records," her words laced with dismay, tinged with anxiety. She looked imploringly at Riordan. "You see, I *kept* Lakeview for myself. After all I suffered, it was only fair."

They still owned Lakeview? Riordan's brows rose. "Who manages it?"

"Manages?"

"Who oversees repairs, collects rents, pays the vicar, *manages* it?"

"Oh," she said, her face clearing. "Moulton has replaced the vicar twice since then. The vicar sends regular reports."

Riordan wasn't about to let it alone. "But does he *do* anything?"

Her chin rose. Through tight lips, she replied, "I won't have him sending succor to the enemy, Riordan. They already forage on our land. If they want anything else, they can beg their paramours."

Ignoring her old refrain, Riordan kept to the subject. "I'm not talking about the Thornes. What about our tenants, the people in the village?"

"What has that to do with anything?" She turned and marched away.

Riordan watched her stiff-gaited retreat. Still obsessed after all these years, she could not discuss Lakeview with any detachment. He looked at Rountree. "Mystery solved, Rountree. Shall we go to Moulton's house?"

Rountree pushed his spectacles upward. "I wouldn't miss it."

* * *

Riordan stretched as the coach began slowly moving. Already, his muscles twitched at the prospect of the next four hours. "I wonder if it's going to rain all the way to Moulton's house."

Rountree glanced at Riordan's long legs. "We can stop at every inn, my lord. You can get out and prowl around the stables—"

The door jerked open, and Alistair tumbled onto the bench beside Riordan. "Whew! I didn't think I would catch up." He slipped a book and a package of sandwiches from his pockets onto the bench. "I'm begging sanctuary. The minute you left, Grandmother started badgering me."

"Wants you out of my clutches, does she?"

"Time to resume my *gentlemanly* ways, she says." He squirmed out of his coat, turned the dry side out, and tucked it behind his head. "I don't understand. She doesn't mind spending your money, but she's unhappy with the way you spend your time."

"She thinks I get a little too close to the work."

"Adding ledgers . . . things like that?"

Rountree chuckled. "Try digging ditches or carpentry work. Your uncle can put on a roof with the best of them."

Alistair shuddered, "Why would you do such a thing?"

"Most of the places I won were wrecks, Alistair. I hired craftsmen, but I couldn't afford a full crew to help them."

"So, you actually *worked* on them?" Then he looked worried. "Is that what you expect me to do?"

"You should at least know shoddy work from good."

Alistair retrieved his book. "That's why you've got me reading this?"

Leaning back, Riordan closed his eyes. "You'd better get busy."

Hours later, Alistair looked up. "D'you know all this stuff about planting and fertilizer and *drains?*" Clearly, Alistair thought it leagues beneath him.

Riordan nodded. "I shall quiz you on it."

Alistair gasped. "You're serious."

"Yes."

Alistair sighed and looked out the window. Eyes brightening in relief, he reported eagerly, ''We're here.''

Riordan glanced up and smiled at the sight of Moulton's residence. Moulton always took the most comfortable path through life. He lived by a lazy stream, a small tributary of icy water that yielded a steady supply of fish. His house, a two-story, thatched-roof cottage, sat on a wooded rise just above seasonal flood lines. Dark smoke curled up from the house. Too complacent to have the chimney swept, Moulton would one day choke to death from the black stuff that lingered inside the cottage . . . or succumb to the ague after endless days sitting on damp ground beside the stream.

The coach stopped. Riordan exited first, stretching the kinks out of his stiffened muscles. He hated being confined in a small space. Even in his study, he often paced to expend the endless energy that drove him. As the others stepped out, the footman hopped off the back of the coach and ran forward to pound on Moulton's front door.

Umbrellas unfurled as they approached the cottage. Rain-water dripped down in a staccato rhythm all around the roof— with no portico to protect visitors. Nor were the servants in a hurry to see who awaited without.

Finally, Moulton's housekeeper opened the door and peered at them as if dumbfounded. ''Lord Langcliffe, is it? And young Alistair?'' She nodded at Rountree and stepped back to let them in. ''Go on upstairs and refresh yourselves, there's guest rooms one up, as you know. Lord Moulton's in his study. Just knock on the door.''

They trooped into Moulton's study together. The older man stood, astonished, but pleased at the intrusion. A tall, drooping gentleman, he appeared inches shorter than Riordan, while in truth, he topped Riordan's six feet by an additional inch or two. His graying blond hair was long and shaggy, but his blue eyes twinkled with delight at seeing them.

Riordan hoped to make the return trip that day, so got straight to the point. ''We've come for the papers regarding Lakeview.''

A guilty flush heightened Moulton's cheeks. ''M'sister told you about it, eh?'' He waved them to chairs. ''Told her it wasn't right, but the woman will have her way." Moulton turned away. "I'll get the papers."

Alistair coughed in the murky room. That set Rountree on a sympathetic coughing fit, while they both wiped their eyes. Riordan strode to the window and, after several hard yanks, opened it with a protesting squawk. Fresh air blew in, and set the flames dancing in the fireplace.

Upon his return, Moulton gave the open window a faint scowl, but said nothing. He plunked a stack of papers on the table and sat down to untie the string.

Riordan joined him, picking up each paper in turn. "Damn it, Moulton . . . you leased out pieces of Lakeview?"

Moulton shrugged. "M'sister needed money."

"I provided all the money she needed," Riordan declared, resuming his searching. "Where are the documents for Thorne's Well? Phillip Thorne died, and Mother wants to take back our land."

Moulton dug through and found them, his lips twisting in amusement "Phillip may be dead, but there's a sister. According to the original papers—with King Richard's seal, I might add—she can inherit if she marries before she's twenty-five. I've been keeping track for you. I thought she might let it slip by, since she's almost twenty-five. However, she's betrothed to the vicar, so I think you're out of luck."

Alistair laughed. "Don't worry, Riordan will think of something."

"Unfair, Uncle Riordan." Alistair strolled away from the window overlooking the Langcliffe Hall drive and threw himself into a chair. "You send that dried up old stick to snoop around the fallen ladies of Thorne's Well, while two healthy men remain locked up with a pile of ledgers."

Riordan allowed himself a smile, but finished adding a column. "Rountree has my *carte blanche* to tempt Miss Thorne's vicar-fiance out of the country."

"How could the vicar, or any man, allow himself to be

plucked out of his home and willingly jaunt off to live with
foreigners?''

Riordan looked up. ''What would it take—money or otherwise—to make you agree to such a scheme?''

''Me? . . . nothing would.''

''Ten, twenty thousand? For just a year or two of your life?
What if it was something you'd wanted to do, but couldn't
manage it on your own? Or what if, in your case, your mother
would benefit?''

Alistair leaned his head back and studied the high ceiling.
''All right, I'll grant you that point.'' Then he cocked his head
to look at Riordan. ''Is that why you're doing this . . . revenge
for your mother?'' He paused with a thoughtful frown, ''Or is
the land valuable? Are you after a profit?''

Riordan shook his head. ''It's a small bit of land in the
middle of Lakeview. Even if I got my hands on it, I couldn't
sell it because it would then be part of Lakeview, and that's
entailed.''

''Why didn't the Thornes sell it back to the Langcliffes?''

''They can't sell it, not even to us.''

''Why do they even *want* such an awkward little piece of
land?''

''It's a good question for our present day, Alistair, but back
then, owning land separated a man from the serfs, and it would
never be given up. Then, too, they had the best part, which the
Langcliffes didn't like.''

Alistair's gaze sharpened. ''The best part? The water?''

''Not that—the river and the lake mark the boundary between
them on one side—but the Thornes own the Roman hot baths.
Many a fable about miracle cures came down through the
years.''

Alistair grinned. ''Sounds like that's what you're after, Riordan, a long hot soak for your old bones.''

Riordan acknowledged the hit with an absent smile. ''I shall
give my mother the house she loved, with no Thornes living
down the road to mar her enjoyment. If she wishes to feel
triumphant or vengeful or any other emotion that might occur
to her, then she may do so with my blessing.''

Chapter Three

With a secret smile, Cambria Thorne touched the invitation in her pocket and sauntered through the front garden to the vicarage door. Just inside the vicar's study, her betrothed heard her half boots on the slate garden path and called through the open window, "Come in, Cambria."

She plucked a rose bud from a bush—then gasped as a thorn pricked her finger. "Blast!" she swore, then shook her head at letting her language slip. Being raised with an older brother had its drawbacks, and a collection of swear words at-the-ready was one of them. Although, she thought, whipping off her glove and popping the wounded finger in her mouth, she would give anything if she could only have him back.

Opening the door, she paused to put her glove back on. John's housekeeper, the ever-scowling Mrs. Locke, came rushing to the foyer.

Sailing past her with a false little smile, Carmbria waved her rose in greeting. "John said to come in, Mrs. Locke. How are you today?"

Locke bobbed her head just enough to pass for an acknowledgment. Even the most optimistic would not mistake it for friendliness. Every aspect of the stick-thin woman, from her crinkled gray hair to her glittering black eyes, made Cambria think of a coiled serpent ready to strike.

But then, Cambria thought, what could you expect from a person with a drop of Langcliffe blood in her? Of course, Locke's connection to the wretched Langcliffes was a dozen generations back, so she couldn't help her natural enmity . . . or prevent her sour disposition.

John stood just inside his study. He wrapped his arm around her shoulders and kissed her gently on the forehead. "Good morning, darling."

Cambria wished he were less stiff with her, but stickler that he was for the *proper thing,* he immediately put a distance between them. But then, she taunted herself cheerfully, wasn't that the reason she was marrying him? In becoming the vicar's wife, she hoped to sluff off the infamous Thorne identity and don the respectable title of *vicar's wife.*

Reaching inside her pocket, she pulled out a small paste board card. "It's the invitation to dinner tomorrow night," she said, unable to wait for him to read it. "My aunts sent their apologies for such short notice, but they have to get back to London the next day."

John took the card gingerly, his fingers touching only the edges.

She couldn't ignore his reluctance. If he was going to postpone their wedding one more time, she must know now. "You said you wanted to announce our wedding date, John. It was your idea to marry next month."

Looking up from the card, he gave her a faint smile. "We can't let you lose Thorne's Well, Cambria. Your birthday is only three months away."

"But if that weren't a factor, would you want to wait?"

He shrugged guiltily. "I'd like my brother to get to know you better."

"John," she whispered, "would you rather not marry me at all?"

Not liking to be pushed, he cleared his throat with an important air. "Not at all. It's just that with more time, my brother would be more enthusiastic." He paused. "He seemed to soften up when he came to visit."

She chuckled, remembering the rather thick-brained, condescending earl. "Your brother thought I *owned* the valley. I explained, but he couldn't seem to get it straight." She sat down, patting the adjoining cushion in invitation. "Perhaps, if he met my aunts in person, saw that they're nothing like the gossips say." Gently, she reproved him as he sat beside her. "Even you haven't given them a chance. You've refused all their invitations. If you don't come to dinner, you'll miss them again. They're hurrying back to London for my cousins' first season."

"You'll like my family," she said hopefully. "Ellie is a cheerful little sunflower and Amelia is a shy violet."

He looked amused. "Have you allotted a flower for your aunts?"

"Oh . . ." She resisted, but perhaps a dose of the truth might prepare him for her aunts. "Honeysuckle or night-blooming jasmine." It was true, they moved like courtesans and couldn't converse with a man without touching him. They twined themselves into a chair and tipped their heads in unconscious flirtation. She dared not tell John that he was the first man who didn't think *her* own voluptuous form was a blatant invitation, and that Thorne blood exuded some invisible man-attracting essence.

"They're very friendly," she said finally, "You'll find them most affectionate, and sometimes that's misinterpreted."

He didn't look convinced. "Enough to ruin their reputation?"

"No," she said bitterly, "that particular responsibility lies at the door of Lady Langcliffe. She spread her lies here in the village and then trotted off to London to poison the *ton*. Everyone knows the Thorne legend, so they believed her. Of course," she added, "since most of the *ton* are, in fact, *truly* guilty of immorality, my aunts are still invited everywhere."

John's response was tepid at best. "I think your loyalty is admirable, Cambria." Then, sensing the anger that she could not hide, he quickly said, *"I've* never heard the Thorne legend."

Gritting her teeth, Cambria forced herself to explain. "My ancestress, Roxanne, was Henry Langcliffe's mistress, and we've borne the stigma ever since. She lived secluded with Lord Langcliffe for many fruitful years. Upon his death, a feud erupted between his legal son and those children borne of Roxanne." She grimaced. "I wish it could just be forgotten."

Cambria decided not to tell him the rest, that the Thorne clan had always considered the Langcliffe family despotic, cruel, acquisitive, and led by their . . . lecherous tendencies. The Langcliffes declared the Thornes exotic, sensuous, prolific troublemakers without a moral in sight. She sighed. "I'm surprised the ladies didn't come tattling to your brother while he was here. He'd forbid the marriage for sure."

John's chest puffed out. "Darling, what kind of person would I be if I judged you on gossip? I think it admirable that you have risen above your ancestry. Even the biblical fallen woman was allowed to repent."

She hurried to stop him. This theme was his favorite, and sometimes she wondered if he wanted *her* or liked the idea of his own beneficence. "Just to keep the record accurate, John, *I* have nothing to repent."

He turned red. "I didn't mean that, my dear, not at all." He quickly changed the subject. "Your aunts are widows, are they not?"

Cambria nodded. "Diana, Lady Waterson and Talia, Lady Maxwell. Diana will insist that you fill your plate twice and her daughter, Ellie, will ask you embarrassing questions. Talia will put pillows behind your back and her daughter, Amelia, will watch your face to see if you're hiding some discomfort or if anyone hurts your feelings."

He caressed her cheek. "And you are the best combination of them all. I am very fortunate to be marrying you."

Locke marched in and gave them a disgusted look. She dropped the mail on John's desk and left with an audible huff. Cambria smiled faintly as John drew his hand away from her face, consoling herself with the thought of dismissing Locke immediately after their summer wedding.

"John," she said, intending to plant the idea in his head, "I don't think Locke and I will work well together—"

He didn't like it. "Locke is a God-fearing woman, Cambria. After we are married and she can see how well you adjust to your new position, you will gain her respect. You must remember that she is older and has grown up seeing your aunts carrying on."

Her temper rose. "My aunts are exemplary women, and never had affairs as many people do in the *ton*. In their society, widows have a certain freedom, and so they may flirt, but that's all."

A pained look crossed his face. "Let's speak of something else."

"Of course." She should never have argued with him. Her temper was her worst trait, and if she was to be the wife of a vicar, she must gain more self-control. She rose to pick up the mail for John. She riffled through the small pile. "Your brother wrote."

John left the settee to stand beside her, surprising her by opening another letter first. He rounded the desk to sit in his chair and, leaning back, read every word with rapt attention. When he finished, he secured the edge of the letter partway, under his lamp, with the writing still visible. "It's Reverend Porter. He's translating scriptures into Indian dialects. The East India Company doesn't like missionaries in their areas of control, but if he gets firmly established and does such an important work, it will mean real strength to resist them. He's asking me to come again."

It was sad, really, that John couldn't follow his dream and serve as a missionary, but his stiff-necked brother held the purse strings and thought John's dream a foolish waste of money.

"John," she asked, too curious to hold back the question, but not sure she truly wanted the answer, "if your brother would finance it, would you join Reverend Porter?"

A dark flush gave her the answer, but he softened the blow with a proviso. "I would go, but I would take you with me."

Smiling gently, selfishly grateful that she wouldn't be

expected to leave her family to follow him to India, she turned to leave. "I must go." Another time she might have stayed to help him. She often acted as clerk for John, including reports to Lord Moulton, Langcliffe's representative, listing the needs of the community. She had yet to see any reply to those pleas . . . typical Langcliffe behavior. Just as Diana had predicted, her childhood friend, Riordan, had clearly followed his mother's attitude of disdain for everyone in the valley.

John nudged a wax-sealed letter toward her. "Drop this off at the Saracen's Head on your way home, would you? It needs to go out today."

Cambria stared in horror at the innocent letter lying on the edge of his desk. "The *inn?*"

John nodded absently as he scratched away at his next bit of correspondence. "I asked Locke to do it, but she wants to finish counting the linen, or something. She suggested that since it's on your way home . . ." His voice trailed off while he finished his task. He looked up at her face, drained and pale, she knew, and frowned. He stood and reached for her hands. "You look fagged, my dear. Perhaps you would rather just go home?"

Yes, right after I wring Locke's neck. Cambria took the letter. "Not at all. As you said, it's on my way."

"Very well." He kissed her cheek. "I'll see you tomorrow night."

She turned to leave, her thoughts far more engrossed in her present dilemma than the dinner party. Just the thought of going near the inn made her ill, but she dared not tell her betrothed that. She was surprised that Locke remembered the incident from her childhood. To everyone else, no real harm was done, but just thinking of it made her shudder.

She'd been barely ten and her friend, Sarah, only nine. Rolling hoops on the village footway, they'd lingered near the Saracen Head's courtyard to show off a bit for a couple of London lords who seemed to be admiring their skill. The lords, taking snuff and sneezing loudly, walked toward them, smiling and talking behind their hands. On a lark, the men told everyone afterward, they threw Cambria into the coach, but before they could release her, she had "screamed and kicked up a silly fuss."

"She misunderstood," they claimed, but Cambria remembered their hands on her arms and legs, their wet mouths on her neck, remembered how they wouldn't stop when she begged them to let her go. Remembered how helpless she felt, how *terrified* when she couldn't make them stop.

"Just a little Thorne bitch," they said inside the coach. They knew the legend, they said, and seeing the way she looked, they knew it was true. "Thorne females ask for it," they claimed. "They were bred for it."

Thanks to her friend, Sarah, screaming like a banshee and pounding on the door of the coach, the alarm was sounded. After the servants came and ripped open the door—saving her—she wanted only to wash off the feeling of their ghastly touch. But *worse* was the feeling that somehow it was her fault. She had spent the rest of her life making sure she wouldn't cause such a horror to happen again.

All of her plans had one single objective: to secure her place in the small community as John's wife—before her birthday— a *safe* place where she could control her own destiny. Perhaps after that she might go to London with John, protected by the mantle of his respected position, and experience the places Phillip had so enthusiastically praised. Just imagine all the book stores and the plays . . .

Tucking John's letter in her pocket, Cambria brushed past the flowered settee and slid sideways to avoid the tiny collectibles on the round table. Glancing at her tall reflection in the mirror above the fireplace, she checked the lace fichu at her throat, pleased to see that no part of her neck was uncovered. Now if only she could leach out the auburn lights in her hair and disguise the voluptuous curves beneath the dark gray dress.

As she reached the foyer, her footsteps faltered. A spectacle-wearing man with a curly red beard stood just inside, impatiently trying to get past Locke without giving his life story to the woman. "I'm here to see the vicar on important business, none of which is any concern of yours."

Locke's chin jutted forward. "The vicar likes his visitors announced."

Cambria stepped back into the study. "John, you'd better come and rescue some poor soul who wants to see you. Locke's got him trapped in the foyer." As John rose from his chair, Cambria strolled along the hallway toward the increasingly loud confrontation. Ignoring Locke, she caught the stranger's attention. "The vicar is coming, sir."

Immediately, his gaze veered to hers, studied her as if he should know her. Then he gave her a courtly bow, his head lifting with an enigmatic smile. "You must be the vicar's betrothed? Your beauty precedes you." Then, before she could discover *how* he knew her, he turned to greet John. "Reverend Adley? May we speak in private?"

Cambria was tempted to request his name, but after rescuing the gentleman from Locke's inquisitive clutches, she could hardly give him the same treatment. Dousing her curiosity, she hurried outside where a far more disturbing matter awaited at the other end of the village.

Looking ahead, she examined the street in front of the Saracen's Head. No coaches waited in the front, but then, vehicles usually passed under the arch and went into the interior courtyard. She could slip past the courtyard and enter by the less-used front door.

The heavy oak door screeched as she pushed it open. Cambria stepped over the sill and let her eyes grow accustomed to the near-darkness. The smell of ale wafted into her nostrils, along with the rank odor of stale cheroots and dirty sawdust. It was quiet, though, with only a trio of elderly village regulars having their afternoon pint in the corner. She nodded at their friendly wave and looked around, unable to find a servant.

The inn's grimy, dark-paneled interior was a disgrace to their charming village. While the other shopkeepers toiled to make the village a flower-garden showplace, the Saracen's Head resembled an unkempt old man. A door opened somewhere beyond the common room and footsteps came closer. Ah, a servant. Cambria stepped forward to catch his eye, but he didn't see her. Instead, he slipped behind the long bar and bent over

. . . to pick something up or move items around, evidently, for he puffed and moaned, and things scraped on the floor.

Sending a cautious look toward the silent hall from whence the servant arrived, she walked quickly toward the opening to the bar. "Sir," she said, looking down at the busy servant, "I have a letter that needs to go on the next coach—" She broke off as he lifted a large case of dusty bottles and carried them to the far end. Waiting for him to complete his difficult task, she followed him in a few steps.

Behind her in the hallway, a door opened, loud laughter followed. She began to panic. Her heart raced and she couldn't catch her breath. Could she slip around the end of the bar and out the door before they arrived? Fighting the impulse to sink down and hide, she forced herself to begin her exit—but not in time.

Three men turned into the common room. Brightly dressed gentleman with flushed faces and heavy boots tramping on the dirty sawdust. "Ale!" the leader bellowed into the air. The others echoed, "Ale . . . ale!"

The servant rose to stare at them.

"Beefsteak," the leader roared, and their echoed replies bounced off the walls like the beat of a drum, "Steak . . . steak."

Cambria scurried through the narrow opening and turned away just as the next braying demand reached her ears: "Women!"

She was caught. Strong fingers clutched the back of Cambria's dress. "Ahh," her captor growled. "What have we here? A nice buxom wench to while away the afternoon?"

Cambria struggled to loosen his hold, but he flung his arms around her, his hot mouth nuzzling her neck.

Behind the bar, the servant yelled at them, and Cambria prayed he would come to her rescue. Instead, he rushed back into the hall. The three old gentlemen stood as well, but only stared at the violence transpiring before them.

Cambria fought wildly, surprising her assailant with her strength. Angered, he backhanded her hard enough to stun her, inducing a high-pitched ringing in her ears. With his prey weakened, he held her at arms's length—and stopped to stare at the rest of her. "Gawd!"

Cambria towered over him by half a head, but his hands were like steel, forcing her to endure being undressed by lascivious eyes. Spots flickered before her eyes as her childhood horror mixed itself with *this* man's hands on her. *So helpless.* She couldn't faint, she must not. She struggled, kicked at him as his friends gathered around, silent as they ran hot glances over her torn dress.

One whistled under his breath. "She's a beauty, Crowley."

"I'll have her first," the leader snarled to warn him away.

"I'm a lady," Cambria gasped, her voice barely audible as she blinked to stop the room from spinning, "betrothed to the vicar." Her face stung where his fist struck her, and her head ached fiercely.

"And I'm mad King George." Crowley's hot breath grazed her ear.

A kinder voice intruded. "Let her go, Crowley. I think she means it." He stepped forward, reaching for Crowley's grasping fingers.

"Stow it, Parish, *look at her.* Does she seem like a lady to you?"

"Yeah, stow it," the third man said, pulling at Parish.

"Ask the innkeeper," Cambria implored. "He'll tell you who I am."

Crowley grabbed her wrist and began pulling her toward the hall. "Tell Bass I've taken his barmaid upstairs—"

A roaring filled Cambria's ears. *No one was going to do this to her.* Her fist flew up and blasted Crowley in the nose. Blood spouted like a waterfall, drenching Crowley and Cambria alike. Crowley's hands flew protectively toward his injury. Loosed at last, Cambria stepped back and dealt his nose a harder blow, just as her brother had taught her after her childhood attack.

The drunken oaf doubled over with pain, cursing loudly. His friends' laughter met his every curse.

"Whoa!" Bass, strode toward them, enraged. "What are you men doing?" He looked at Cambria's dress. "I'm sorry, Miss Thorne . . ."

"As well you should be." With one hand holding her bodice closed, Cambria shoved her now-bloody letter at Bass. "A lady should be free of assault in a public place."

Bass looked around the room, skewering the three old villagers with angry eyes. "What were you doing while Miss Thorne was being attacked?" He waved his fist. "Get the hell out of here." They scuttled out of the inn, *tattling old men who would spread the tale with glee, defending themselves by blaming someone else . . . Cambria.*

She fought the urge to run through the village, to race the elderly storytellers to the vicarage. Glancing down at her torn dress, she knew she must *not*. Such a spectacle would only fuel the village gossip.

Locke would salivate over this scandal. Even though Cambria had painstakingly earned the villagers' respect, old stories would resurrect themselves, grow like toadstools overnight.

John—loyal John who had discounted the gossip and defended her—would be shocked at the old men's prevarication. His unbending brother would be horrified, demand he break off the engagement.

Go home, Cambria thought, gulping back tears, go home. John would hear the story and would come to see her. He would believe her. If all else failed, she knew John would not disappoint her.

Chapter Four

As Cambria trudged slowly home, every footstep jarred her battered head, every breath hurt her ribs where Crowley's arms had crushed her against him. The dirt road had never looked so long, nor had her legs ever seemed so unfit for the task.

When she reached Lakeview, the deserted Langcliffe house, she veered off the road to lean against a shady tree. Still two-thirds to go, she thought, and all of it uphill. Idly, she surveyed the unwooded area around the old sprawling Langcliffe mansion. It was time to send her servants down to clear away the weeds before they grew brittle in the summer heat. She was foolish to worry over the absent enemy's domain, but a spark from a hiker's pipe would streak straight toward the house, and all that history would be gone.

She pushed away from the tree, shocked at how all her pains came screaming back to life. Don't stop now, she told herself, you might never get going again. Just make it to the river and then rest once more.

Or, she mused hopefully, perhaps John would catch up to her soon. Even now, John might be heading for the stables, rushing to her rescue, panicked over his precious wife-to-be.

He would stop on the road, saying, "Why didn't you come to me, darling? Oh, your poor, swollen face . . ."

That lovely daydream took her all the way to the river.

She walked onto the old wooden bridge, and, holding the railing, she faced the noisy waterfall. Both the spray misting her upraised face and the sound of tumbling water soothed her edgy nerves. Like a mother's open arms, this entrance to Thorne's Well comforted her. She loved this spot. She'd mourned her brother here, had healed here.

After the death of their parents in her second year, her aunts had spent much of their time at Thorne's Well, playing mother to Cambria and Phillip. After widowhood struck them each in turn, they came often for long, extended visits.

Phillip, fourteen when their father died, had let Cambria "assist" him as he took over the estate. When Phillip left for London, she put all she had learned to work. If he could make the hated sacrifice of living in the city, she could certainly make sure he didn't regret his trust in her.

The last few times he'd come home, he brought his young law partner, Mark Glendover, devising plans to make Thorne's Well a profitable concern. But, before he realized his dream, London had killed him. Long hours spent hunched over a desk in drafty, cold rooms weakened his health and took his life before he could manage to come home for good.

Gingerly—for now even her neck was beginning to stiffen—Cambria turned, resting her back against the railing to watch the river make its way down the hill, slowing as it widened into the lake. On her left was Langcliffe land, almost twenty years of untamed woods crowding the water all the way down to the village. On the right lay her own hillside of wildflowers that never failed to take her breath away.

She'd learned to fish downriver, not at the busy Phillip's direction, but under the tutelage of her neighbor, Riordan Langcliffe, an impressive five years her elder. In the lake, she'd learned to row a boat, skip rocks, and swim in her shift. When Riordan's father traipsed over to soak in the old Roman hot baths, he brought Riordan, who was far more interested in her kitchen than with her. She didn't care. She followed him like a cheerful little puppy, never let him out of her sight. *Little did they know how their lives would change, how they would never be friends again.*

Cambria forced her legs to move. Keeping to the shady wooded side of the road, her half boots scuffed in the dirt as her legs grew heavier with each lagging step. Like an old lady, she thought, hoping that her old-lady days would, indeed, find her still trudging up this road.

If one continued straight ahead instead of turning right toward her home, the narrow, overgrown road would lead all the way to Pick Hill.

She stopped at the sound of a fast-moving vehicle behind her. John, she thought, smiling. Now everything would be all right.

Turning, her smile faded . . . then grew again. Her childhood friend, Sarah, came wheeling along the road in her pony cart, her oversized straw hat flopping over her face and her tummy once again swelling with child. "Cambria," she called, whipping off her hat, "why didn't you come to me instead of traipsing out here all alone?" She heaved herself out of the cart and hurried over to hug her, then appalled, stared at Cambria's face. "We're just across the street from the inn. I would have driven you home."

Cambria clutched at her torn dress with a shaky laugh. "I didn't want anyone to see me like this." She looked at Sarah's thick middle. "Does Sam know you're driving around in your condition?" The red-haired, freckle-faced Sarah had shocked her gentry parents by falling in love with the young village blacksmith. When they refused to sanction the match, she'd promptly threatened to get herself with child, forcing an acquiescence from parents who knew the headstrong girl never backed down.

"Does Sam know?" Sarah laughed. "He's the one who told me what happened. He wouldn't have done that if he wanted me to stay home." She draped her arm around Cambria's waist and nudged her into the cart. Once they were both settled, she turned to her, her voice soft with concern. "What did those men do to you, Cambria?"

As Sarah snapped the reins to move her horse forward, Cambria related the simple facts. "Who told Sam?" Cambria asked. "The old men?"

"Yes. They're making it sound like it was all your fault for being there. Did you really bloody that man's nose?"

"Yes," Cambria said, "twice."

Sarah sighed happily. "Bless Phillip for that."

As the road turned, Sarah grinned. "Shall I keep you posted on the village news? I know you'll be worrying over what they're saying." She grinned. "You shouldn't, but you will."

Cambria nodded. "Thank you, Sarah. Did you get the fruit I sent yesterday? I supposed you were craving it like always."

She grinned once more. "Yes, but you needn't bother. I've been helping myself to it all along." Her face sobered. "I've got to get back to the children, but I'll wait until you get inside the door."

Waving, Cambria slipped inside, then leaned back against the door, waiting for enough strength to face her family. In one way, she longed to let them fuss over her, let Diana tend to her hurts, and feel Talia's arms around her. Even more, though, she longed for solitude, for the comfort and privacy of her bed. She didn't want to relate the story, to dwell on the details, to listen to their outraged voices. She didn't want them asking her what the devil she was doing going into the inn all by herself, because then she would have to admit she'd made a foolish mistake, that she'd known better, but had put herself in danger . . . again.

She looked around the foyer. No one in sight. Holding her torn dress closed, she headed toward the stairs. Behind her, footsteps approached. Carefully, to keep her pain at a minimum, she turned back to look.

Her aunt, Diana, a tall, junoesque blonde, walked briskly from the back hall carrying a large vase of flowers. She glanced over the blossoms and smiled. "I was beginning to worry, Cambria. Why are you so late—?"

She blanched.

Not taking her horrified gaze from Cambria, she moved toward a low table against the wall. Tenderly lowering the vase toward it's intended destination, she let it drop the last few inches. It hit the edge of the table and crashed onto the floor. Without blinking as water poured over the tiled floor, Diana moved toward Cambria, hand outstretched. "Your face . . . what happened?" Diana's fingers slid lightly over Cambria's cheek, and like a fluttering butterfly, flew next to examine her ruined dress. "Are you hurt, Cambria? What happened to your dress? Is that *blood?*"

"Diana, It's not *my* blood. Let me change, then I shall explain."

"No. I want Talia to see this." Her arm around Cambria's waist, Diana firmly guided her to the conservatory. Talia lay on a chaise lounge with a knitted robe over her long legs, a Minerva novel resting just below her marvelous bosom. She cocked her head sideways as they entered, her auburn hair haloed by the sunlight coming through the window. In an instant, she rose and rushed across the room, clucking like a mother hen. "Come sit down, darling. What happened?" Talia practically carried Cambria to her lounge, snatching up her own soft robe to cover her.

Cambria told the tale briefly. Just as she'd dreaded, they pressed for the rest, every action, every word. Diana, whose attitude had taken on a militant air, wanted to rouse the servants and storm the inn.

"Don't bother, Diana. Bass threw the men out."

Frustrated, Diana settled for second best. "You're not to go to that village again, Cambria."

Talia's husky laughter filled the conservatory. "Leave the girl alone, Diana. A girl who punched Lord Crowley in the nose can take care of herself. Cambria," she said, "there's hope for you yet."

With a huff of disagreement, Diana helped Cambria off the lounge. "Up you go. First a bath, then I'll take care of that cheek. *And,*" she said archly, "a tonic for the headache you're trying to hide from us."

* * *

Cambria awakened to a darkened room. Outside, night had fallen and was beginning to pick itself back up. *She'd missed John's visit.*

Not only that, but she was famished and her head hurt, as Phillip used to say, *like the very devil.* The glass on her bedside table stood empty, and Diana had taken the laudanum away.

There was no help for it, she would have to make a trip to the kitchen. She turned over—and yelped as she rolled onto her sore cheek. How could it hurt *worse* now? Gingerly, she sat upright, noting at once the delicate balance required to keep her head from pounding.

As she slid off the bed, her reflection in her dressing table mirror stopped her cold. She leaned forward, unable to believe what she saw. *Horrible.* She resembled a barmaid she'd once observed whose bruised face sported red and purple blotches, a visual badge, it seemed, of her lowly occupation. Red-rimmed, bloodshot eyes betrayed a nighttime bout of tears, while beneath one eye swelled a charcoal half-moon. *Disgraceful.*

Grabbing her robe from the end of her bed, Cambria slipped into it as she made her way down the stairs, frowning at the sound of voices in the family dining room. She opened the door and spotted an opened letter in the middle of the table. Her aunts' guilty faces stared at her.

She leaned against the door jamb. "What is it?"

Diana replied. "Reverend Adley came yesterday. He wanted to speak with you, but I'd given you a sleeping potion." She sounded defensive, as if denying him access needed justification. "He left a note."

Cambria moved forward, her gaze affixed to the paper as it passed from Diana's hands to hers. The pressure behind her eyes increased with each second as she reached for the note.

> *Dearest Cambria,*
> *I rushed to see you as soon as I heard of the trouble at the inn, only to discover that you had been sedated and were asleep for the night. I must go now, but will be back for your dinner party. The gentleman whom you saw at the vicarage bore an important message, and it*

*was necessary that I leave with him. Nevertheless, be
assured that my thoughts are with you.*
    Love . . . John

She looked up. "You read it, didn't you?"

Faint nods answered her. Diana braved the first speech.
"Rumors came from Locke that the vicar has packed up and
moved out. If John's note is truthful, then he just took things
for an overnight stay."

Cambria looked closely at her aunts' faces. Sympathy, com-
passion, a touch of pity. No regret, however, over the possible
loss of John. Cambria shrugged as if it didn't matter, but in
truth, hurt settled deeply within her. "Locke is part Langcliffe,
what can you expect? Phillip would have told me to go on as
if nothing were amiss. John *will* be back."

She received another note the next day shortly before noon.

My Dear Cambria,
    *I am being somewhat detained while I contemplate a
most important matter. I may be late to dinner. Please
do not delay serving, but go ahead with the calm assurance that I will be there eventually.*
    With fond affection . . . John

With unspoken agreement, they continued allotting name
cards to places at the table. Amelia sighed and Ellie looked
murderous, but after their mothers issued warning looks, they
remained silent. Her family's tenderness toward Cambria
increased, while she clung to her composure as if suspended
over a deep, yawning chasm.

Two hours before the guests were expected, another note
came. Diana and Talia brought it to her room as she was
dressing.

Dear Miss Thorne,

I am in a quandary and wish you were able to advise me. I have been approached by a patron who wishes to remain anonymous. He is sending a group of single clergymen to India and, after unearthing my desire to serve with Reverend Porter, wishes to sponsor me in that important work. I cannot take you, but trust that you would have advised me to go.

I must leave in the morning. I rely on your sensible nature to forgive my going without a personal farewell.

Yours in friendship . . . John Adley

Fighting back tears of humiliation and loss, Cambria let Talia take the note from her fingers. She was *not* going to weep in front of her aunts, not when this moment spelled tragedy to everything that she held dear . . . and they would only consider John's departure a blessing.

Cambria reached for anger. If her aunts began telling her that this was *all right,* that now she could come to London as they'd been begging her to, that she still had three months to find a husband, she might begin throwing things.

She'd never wanted to go to London, but she could not tell them why. Indeed, what would she say? "I'd love to see the sights, but I don't want men like my childhood attackers to recognize me as a Thorne. It's all right for you to have suffered all these years with a ruined reputation, but I'm too cowardly to face it." In truth, she could not imagine anything worse than a city full of Crowleys. *Except losing Thorne's Well.*

She would have to grow up now. Toughen up. Even the safest man one could imagine—a vicar with the highest ideals, who never gave the slightest hint of aggression or lechery— had left her defenseless. She had stood up to Crowley, had she not? Surely, she could show a little more backbone and face London, especially when her need was more imperative.

She would not fall apart. She would not look for someone else to rescue her. She would take charge, do it herself, using whatever means she had to employ. Out of the depths of her deepest sorrow came a resolve, an oath, a vow she would follow from this moment. *She would forge ahead with all the power within her, never wavering, until she saved Thorne's Well.*

Cambria crossed to her small desk near the window. Opening the drawer, she lifted the list of dinner guests and rang for a servant. When he appeared, she crossed to the door and handed him the list. "Send runners to these people and tell them the dinner is canceled."

As he retreated, a sudden wave of emotion poured over her, almost bringing her to her knees. She held on to the door knob and closed her eyes. *Dear God, she was going to have to marry a stranger . . . in less than twelve weeks.* She let it pass by her, let it go on its taunting way. She suppressed the wave of panic, hid it lest it weakened her resolve.

Desperate for something to distract her, she turned back to Diana. "You'll be back in London tomorrow. Can you stop the order for wedding invitations in time?"

Diana nodded. "I'll send a messenger tomorrow morning, but we won't leave you here like this, Cambria."

"But, the girls' season . . . you have already sent acceptances. They'll be distraught if they miss even one event."

Diana shook her head. "You'll come back with us. A busy schedule will keep your mind off your troubles."

Cambria curled her fingernails into her palms, pressing hard enough for the pain to steady her. *Oh Phillip, why aren't you here to stop this?* Blast, she was *not* going to cry. "I'll have to close the house, arrange for things to be done, attend to the servants."

"We'll wait," Diana replied firmly. "I cannot imagine what your mother would say to our leaving you alone now."

Cambria's throat ached at the tender thought, but she hung on to her composure. "I must have time to plan how I am to go about this. As things stand, I have very little chance to attract a suitable husband. I have no dowry. Even now, I'm at the point of letting most of the servants go."

Diana's gaze sharpened. "What do you mean?"

Cambria explained in a low, controlled voice. "Phillip's been gone for a year. We had a little bit saved, but, as you know, Thorne's Well generates no income. I expected to be married before I completely ran out.''

Talia looked stunned. "No dowry at all?''

"Worse yet,'' Cambria said, "any husband of mine will have to lower himself to forage on Langcliffe land.'' As they stared at her, she added, "As I understand it, a gentleman looks for a wife who can add to his fortune, not drain it off. Owning Thorne's Well means very little because it cannot be sold.'' She paused. "If I'm out of the running before they meet me, what kind of husband will I find?''

Diana waved an impatient hand. "The men will flock to your side when they see how beautiful you are. After all,'' she said softly, "you have the Thorne looks. Once we get you out of those dresses . . .''

Cambria's gaze dropped to Diana's neckline, an invitation to trouble if she ever saw it. Talia was worse, for she always wore gowns that resembled silky bedclothes. Cambria looked fondly at them both, loving them for their years of care. She was a wretch to be so ungrateful.

With that thought, she couldn't hold it all in. Fury erupted. "How could John have done this, just walked away? We'd made plans together. We'd even named our children. He *knew* I would lose my home.'' She gave a harsh laugh. "The first chance he got, though, he . . .'' Her lips trembled, which made her even more furious to be wasting emotion on him. "After all his talk of overlooking my tainted family's past, he left me because of vicious gossip. *Despicable man . . . selfish coward.*''

Her control slipped further, and she could hear herself babbling. "And now I'll have to make do, take the first offer that comes my way, someone slovenly, fat with rotted teeth . . . or someone like Crowley.''

Talia's arm slid over her shoulders. "I'm sure you can find a perfectly good husband, Cambria. Tell me what you're looking for.''

Cambria sniffed. "Someone proper, someone gentle and respectful of women. A man who doesn't drink or fight or swear. Someone who will be willing to live quietly at Thorne's Well, be grateful for what little I have to offer.'' She could feel Talia shaking. How sweet, she thought, that she should be so concerned.

"Are you sure," Talia asked in a choked voice, "you don't want him gelded as well?"

Cambria couldn't help herself. She laughed. A small, embarrassed one to be sure, but it snapped her out of that horrible, *wasteful* self-pity.

Talia looked into her eyes. "Cambria, darling, you've lived alone out here too long. It's time you came down to see the rest of the world."

Cambria took a strengthening breath. "I know it, Talia. I know I have to go to London, but I'm serious about wanting something to offer, since I don't have a dowry." She hesitated. "I want you to listen to an idea that Phillip and his law partner, Mark Glendover, talked about. I suggested it to John, but he didn't like the idea of being in trade."

The door burst open. Ellie and Amelia rushed in, colorful young butterflies in their London gowns. Ellie had been out picking wildflowers, for one was now stuck in her mussed blonde hair. Amelia, as usual, was neatly elegant with her own dark locks tied back with a pink ribbon to match her dress. Just imagining herself hoping to attract a husband surrounded with girls like her cousins made her realize how difficult was the task before her.

"Why aren't we having the dinner party?" Amelia asked. "Did John cry off again?"

Diana quickly explained, then tried to shush their spate of indignant remarks. Ellie, however, would have her say, the more dramatic, the better. "So now the dreaded Langcliffes will come and take your land." Since this had been Ellie's most popular subject since Phillip's death, no one took umbrage at so ill-timed a remark.

Amelia had her own concern. "Is your heart broken, Cambria? Shall I get you some camomile tea?"

Diana turned on them. "If you want to stay here, you must let us finish our conversation." Then she turned back to Cambria, surprising her with an intense interest. "What venture were Phillip and Mark planning?"

"Opening the hot baths to the public. The patrons would be housed in the east wing and be served meals in our formal dining room. The hot springs would be the attraction, of course. Phillip thought we should advertise them as medicinal, hint at miraculous cures." She paused. "If we all got involved, it would be a family concern."

"Smashing," said Ellie with a huge grin, but Amelia's shock held her silent. Cambria expected arguments from her aunts. Instead, they exchanged identical glances as if the idea excited them as well.

Diana, as usual, went straight to the heart of the matter. "You would have to open the project almost immediately so the word could get around. How would you attract people to the baths?"

The last was the weak point of the plan, and she hated to admit it. "I thought you might advertise it around the city for me."

Once more, the sisters exchanged glances. They were surprisingly willing to listen. Talia calmly took point again. "Very astute of you."

Encouraged, Cambria explained her plan. "We would not invite everyone, but only a select few—by invitation—as men's clubs do."

Ellie smiled. "Like Almacks. Who will be your patronesses?"

"I need advice. Should they be ladies . . . or gentlemen?"

"Both," Talia said. A growing enthusiasm laced through her words. "Diana and I will be on the committee, of course. As for the men, they must be mature, extremely upright and respected . . . whom do we know?"

Stunned by their effusive participation, Cambria watched in awe as they spun into an organizing frenzy. Diana waved her fingers. "Lord Ragsdale. After remaining so annoyingly single, he's looking for a wife and hasn't once flirted with me. Of course," she said as if affronted at the very thought, "he might be looking at the younger set rather than someone his own age, but still, he's been *looking* at me all these years."

"He'll drive you crazy, Diana. He shuns society, and all he

ever thinks of is making money." Talia waited for Diana to recant her choice.

When Diana remained quiet, Talia shrugged her lovely shoulders as if telling Diana she could suffer if she wished. "I know," she added after a thoughtful moment, "I shall choose the Duke of Havenshire."

"Oh, no . . . he's always giving you sermons on a lady's behavior. You'd think he was your father rather than a man we've grown up with."

"You get your choice, Diana. I should be allowed mine."

"If you choose him, *no one* will be allowed in."

"Exactly. That very fact will drive everyone crazy. Out of self defense he will have to relax his vigilance."

Cambria had to intervene. "If these gentlemen are so utterly proper that they don't approve of *you* two, how on earth will you get them to work with you?" In unison, the aunts sent brow-raising, *disbelieving* looks her way. Ellie and Amelia broke out in laughter.

Cambria gave in. "All right, then, but I shall head the committee." She would need to retain some control of this runaway project.

Talia and Diana shared a cautious look. Diana nodded, her managing ways in full bloom. "We must begin at once, while everyone is still in London. By late summer, you will know if it will succeed. You'll need workmen to enlarge the baths for the elegant expectations of the *ton.*"

Panicked, Cambria squeaked, "Enlarge?" No one was listening.

Talia tipped her head. "What about accommodations, Diana? The inn is too crude for ladies."

"Ladies and couples will stay here, the gentlemen at the inn."

Cambria moaned, "You must remember that I can't afford all this."

Diana gave Talia a long, meaningful look. "Shall we fund these expenses, invest, so to speak?"

Talia nodded. "If we pay for the original expenses and have it all done now, it could be opened very quickly."

Relieved at their solution, Cambria leaned back in thought. "I shall write to Mark. Perhaps he still has their plans."

Talia's brows arched. "Now there's an idea, Cambria. Young Glendover might make you an excellent husband. He's only a younger son, but his family's name is respectable."

"Talia, don't be silly. We're like brother and sister."

"Love can grow," Amelia offered. "He's a rather handsome gentleman and not much older than you."

"Or," Ellie said cheerfully, "he might hate the whole idea."

Alistair pulled an ottoman between Riordan's and Rountree's wing-backed chairs before the midnight fire. Dropping down onto his perch, he leaned eagerly forward. "So, Rountree, did you see any Thorne women?"

Rountree caught Riordan's nod of permission. "I spoke with Miss Cambria Thorne. *Splendid* woman." A heavy sigh followed. "Poor thing, I met her on her way to meet a terrible fate." The sentence dwindled away.

Alistair groaned. "Don't stop *now,* Rountree."

Rountree shook his head slowly as if confused with the vagaries of fate. "Shortly after I saw her in the vicarage, she was accosted by a trio of inebriated lords passing through on the coach. In case the thought occurs to you, rest assured I did *not* arrange that. The proprietor of the inn, Bass, promptly tossed them out on their ear. I believe you know one of them . . . a Lord Crowley?"

Riordan whistled. Crowley? Thrown out of an inn?"

Rountree chuckled. "Right after Miss Thorne bloodied his nose."

Riordan laughed. "I'd liked to have seen that."

"It was hard to believe, though, after meeting the young lady."

"Why? If she frequents an inn—"

"Oh, no. She was delivering a note to go out on the coach. She's a very proper young lady. She doesn't look proper at first glance, but after speaking to her, one immediately changes his mind."

"Doesn't *look* proper?"

"It's not something one can explain, Langcliffe. She's extremely innocent and properly dressed. She just seemed to exude a rather . . . it might be the way she looks, or the way she moves . . ."

Alistair soaked up the tantalizing implication of that for a moment, then his soft heart took over. "She's all right, though?"

Rountree nodded briskly then, all business, turned his attention to Riordan. Raising his eyebrows, he gave a long, whistling sigh. "Never thought a *vicar* would be such a hard nut to crack."

Alistair sighed. "Because he didn't want to leave his love?"

Rountree laughed. "No, he wanted a larger allowance."

Chapter Five

"Mark is here," Cambria turned from the window and hurried out to greet him. "He must have hopped in a coach the minute he got my letter."

As they all flew out the front door, a high-perched phaeton drove smartly halfway around the graveled circle and stopped. They waved as the jaunty, sandy-haired young gentleman hopped down.

Grinning, he clutched the front of his coat. "M'heart can't take all this beauty in one place. Give me a drink fast, or I'm not going to make it." The vest in question must be the current fashion, Cambria thought, with its embroidery emblazoning every color in the rainbow.

Ellie sighed. "He's splendid!"

Mark motioned toward his luggage, now in the hands of busy servants. "I found the plans you wanted. They were at the office."

Cambria smiled. "Thank you, Mark. We're anxious to begin."

Mark made his bows to Diana and Talia, then stopped before their daughters. "Ah, the lovely ladies Ellie and Amelia. And with your hair up, no less. The last time I saw you was winter before last. You were racing sleds down the hill to see how far you could go out onto the frozen lake.''

As Cambria led them back into the house, Ellie flashed her dimples to enchant Mark, then broke into a pout. ''Is it true? Can Lord Langcliffe take Thorne's Well away from us if Cambria doesn't marry?'' The topic still fascinated the dramatic Ellie, and Mark was a likely candidate to enlighten—or frighten her—and she didn't seem to care which.

''I'm afraid so, Ellie. But Cambria won't go without a fight—''

Talia interrupted. ''If there's any fuss, it will come from the old lady. She's a troublemaker, born and bred.''

Hot on the scent of excitement, Ellie asked, ''What was she like?''

''Insanely jealous. It was amusing to keep her stirred up.''

Mark looked surprised, as well he should, for both Diana and Talia preferred a quiet, unruffled state of affairs. ''You deliberately incited her?''

Shrugging, Talia smiled lazily. ''Tit for tat.''

''Don't get them started,'' Cambria warned, leading them upstairs. ''They'll wear you out with their stories, and it's time to go up for tea.''

''Well,'' Mark said, ''I'm just sorry Langcliffe doesn't live at Lakeview. He's rather a legend in financial circles, and I would like to meet him.''

''What does he look like?'' asked Ellie.

Mark paused to think. ''I suppose ladies might find him interesting. He's so formidable in the business world, that I've never thought about how he looks. He's taller than I am. Black hair, dark eyes. He's very cool, never lets his temper explode, but he's wounded two men in duels, not over a lady's favor as is usual, but over insults to his family.''

Cambria was confused. ''He's a business man?''

''He has money invested in building projects all over London. Sometimes he buys up property lost at gambling halls. Ruthless, really. He brought his family back from ruin. Doesn't care who's in his way.''

''He gambles, then.''

Mark frowned and slowly shook his head. "Very seldom. He's become a gambler's broker of sorts. Gamblers go to him when they've won property and would rather have cash. Langcliffe sends his crew out and turns it into something more valuable. Sometimes he keeps it, sometimes he sells."

Amelia joined the conversation. "Does he have a wife?"

"Or a mistress?" asked Ellie, ignoring her mother's dark scowl.

Mark looked trapped, but, too much a gentleman to raise an indignant brow, he managed a reply. "He . . . enjoys the company of ladies, but is not married. The question whether he will or will not marry lies on the betting books at Whites."

As they entered the parlor, Mark moaned in delighted anticipation. The low table between two facing settees was, as usual when her family were visiting, heaped to overflowing. Ellie pestered him with questions while Amelia filled his plate and poured his tea.

Mark smiled at the quiet Amelia. "Cambria's note said you girls were having your first season this year. Are you enjoying it?"

Amelia nodded, her enthusiasm overcoming her natural shyness. "We had to leave London to come out here, but we did get to attend a musicale. We went to Gunters Tea Shop, and to Hatchard's book store."

Ellie grinned. "Amelia and I bought *novels*"

Mark tweaked her nose. "Naughty girl."

When tea was over, Mark looked across at Cambria, finally, and commandeered her attention. "May we speak in private, Cambria?"

She rose immediately. "Of course. Shall we walk down to the bridge?" With apologies to the rest, they made their way outside.

Mark didn't waste any time once they started down the drive. "How are you, really, Cambria? Heartbroken over John's leaving or furious?"

She didn't hesitate. "Definitely furious."

With a satisfied nod, Mark murmured, "You still have to marry."

"I know. I'm going to London to find a husband."

"But you don't want to go."

Cambria was surprised at his remark. "Why do you say that?" It was true, of course, but she thought she'd hidden her distaste for the venture.

"Phillip and I used to argue over his letting you remain out here without seeing a broader horizon."

"I'm sure my aunts will be happy to hear another voice pleading for their cause, just to make sure they can pry me out of the valley. However," she added with a confidence that was growing stronger every day, "I intend to throw my whole heart into the business of finding a suitable husband."

"Good," he replied absently, distracted as they turned onto the main road. "I've located a builder for you, someone Phillip and I planned to use. Would you like me to employ him? Watch how he's spending your money?"

Relieved, she nodded. "Will you have the time to do so?"

He looked apologetic. "Not a lot, but I'll come out when I can." Nervously, he cleared his throat, about to embark on a difficult subject, she could see. She braced herself.

"Cambria," he said slowly, seriously. "I just want you to know that if you find yourself without a husband in time to save Thorne's Well, I'll be glad to step in and do the honors."

She stared up into his dear face. Did he have some affection for her, or did gallantry demand such a sacrifice? "Will you tell me why, Mark? I'm sorry to ask when you haven't offered to tell me, but it's important."

He threw his arm over her shoulder and moved them forward, and in that action she had one question answered. This was not a lover's caress—not that she had ever experienced such a wondrous thing—but the same old casual brotherly manner she had always known.

"We've never veered in that direction, and I'm not sure why. But if you married unhappily just to keep the land, I'd never forgive myself."

His face took on a stubborn look, as if he'd practiced an argument and wanted to spell it out so there would be no misunderstanding. "I do want you to go look for a husband whom you could love first. Don't just fall back on my offer because it's easier and because it's more comfortable.''

She reached up and grasped the hand resting on her shoulder. ''You know me too well, Mark, for that's exactly what I am tempted to do. I'll look even harder just to make sure I don't cheat you out of your freedom.''

''What will you tell your family? Or do you want to keep it secret?''

Cambria hid a blossoming smile. She wasn't about to confess her family's intentions of dragging him to the altar whether he was willing or not. ''We'll tell them everything. It's useless to do anything else. You've never seen that pack with their curiosity in full cry.'' They walked to the bridge and reminisced, recounted stories of Philip to comfort each other. Through it all, his generous offer stayed with her, giving her ease. *Then a little voice set her nerves ajar with a message that made far too much sense.*

Complacency was a dangerous frame of mind when the clock was ticking down the days until her birthday. If she didn't stay alert, pressing ahead under her own power, not relying on the buffering crowd around her, she could still lose it all. In a strange way, they were a danger to her, softening her, dulling the edges of her resolve. It was not their loss, but hers. If she misplaced her focus and lost the land, they would sympathize and simply absorb her into the periphery of their lives. She must never sink into a soft, feather-tick frame of mind and let him rescue her.

Even her heartfelt hope of sloughing off the Thorne reputation must take second place to the task before her—*forge ahead until she saved Thorne's Well.*

Noise . . . never-ending, *constant* noise. Hammers pounding, wagons coming up and down the driveway, workmen yelling. Cambria loved it.

From her bedroom, she watched a load of planks make its way up the makeshift road. They were widening the enclosed walkway from the house, installing skylights, and adding dressing rooms to the baths.

Progress, however, demanded its price. Deeply entrenched ruts displaced ground that had once nurtured delicate ferns. The building's wall that once bounced sun warmth down upon a bank of fragrant lilacs now had a gaping hole overlooking debris tossed out by busy workmen.

At the newly dug saw pit, a swirl of golden sawdust flew into the air, settling gently on the sawyer above and coating the sawyer in the pit. Cambria was fascinated with their precision rhythm, so vital to keep the double-handed saw from bending and binding as the top man pulled up and the bottom sawyer pulled down in turn.

Over the last two weeks, wonderful disruption and chaos had filled her days. And, wonder of wonders, *she'd finally gotten a taste of London,* if one could call one rushed trip to the modiste and the shops a true test of the sprawling city. Diana chaperoned the girls through two days of social events while Talia took Cambria shopping. Cambria, pin-pricked and blushing at having a dozen strangers discuss her figure while she stood on a pedestal like a slave on the auction block, returned home alone, wondering what the devil she'd ordered.

She would know soon, for tomorrow they were making another swift trip to the city. She was going to attend a musicale in the afternoon and dance at a ball in the evening before rushing back. Her heart thudded at the thought, but her resolve would carry her through. *Never waver.*

Cambria snatched up her list of tasks to be done and headed for the library. Her family had arrived last night and would be eager to relate the latest stalking successes of Diana's choice, Lord Ragsdale or Talia's prey, Lord Havenshire.

Talia looked up. "Cambria, you should have been there. Havenshire never relaxes. I swear, I don't know how his man dresses him, for I doubt his knees even bend. It's a shame. He's handsome to a fault with that marvelous thick hair. If I didn't know better I would think his man uses curling papers on it, but he wouldn't allow even that subterfuge.

"Let me tell you how our interview went." She took a quick breath, checking to be sure of their rapt attention. "I gave him my helpless routine, and Havenshire pulled that annoying look of disbelief. I touched his hand as though I didn't know what I was doing, and, at last, his upper lip beaded up like he'd run up a hill.''

Ellie and Amelia laughed, a tribute that speeded Talia's tale. ''I suffered over my poor niece who had no male to advise her—you, Cambria—and he puffed up like a frog. I mentioned our first committee meeting here next week and told him who else was on the committee.''

A meeting . . . here? Cambria gasped at that piece of news, but Talia never missed a beat. ''Havenshire approved of Ragsdale, but frowned over three ladies, and I asked his advice as to who should be the committee chairman. He volunteered for the job so fast I almost fell off my chair, but, instead, I let a little tear of gratitude roll down my cheek.''

She grinned. ''I cannot wait until he sees the baths. Ragsdale is coming as well. They'll want to see our progress. We shall let them enjoy a session in the hot baths. Let them congratulate each other for rescuing us.''

''I thought the men were to stay at the inn,'' Cambria asked.

''The committee? Certainly not. They will be privileged, of course, so they can feel superior. They won't be charged, but if they bring guests, they must pay.'' Talia tossed her head. ''I'm not a complete fool.''

Cambria infused a hasty bit of firmness into her voice. ''Did I mention that I expect denial power over the committee's decisions?''

Diana eyed her warily. ''Of course, Cambria.''

Talia lied without blinking. ''I never thought otherwise.'

Cambria adjusted her lacy shawl over her shoulders and sighed happily as the boulanger ended and Mark walked with her to the edge of the crowded dance floor. ''There,'' he said with an I-told-you-so smirk, ''I saw you having a wonderful time. Aren't you glad you came to London?''

She nodded. ''I didn't realize how protected ladies were. Shopping is even safer than home, with trailing footmen and maids.'' She looked around. ''Even here, the gentlemen behave so well.''

Mark reached for her fan and examined it for the name of her next partner. ''I cannot read this. Do you remember who has the next dance?''

She shook her head. ''They just swarmed us when we came in. I thought I would be sitting on a chair hoping someone would notice me.''

Mark chuckled at her foolishness as a blond, broad-shouldered man with a tanned face came strolling purposely toward them. Bowing, he said, ''B'lieve this is my dance, Miss Thorne.'' Looking next at Mark who stood so protectively next to her, the young man bowed his way. ''M'name's Paul, Viscount Marchant.''

The Honorable Mark Glendover returned the courtesy, then murmured into Cambria's ear. ''Ellie's my next partner. I'd better find her before she gives the dance to someone else.''

Cambria smiled and waved him off. Marchant took her hand and headed for the dance floor. As they waited for the set to form, he hurried into speech. ''Feel lucky to get this dance with you, Miss Thorne. Was wondering when you'd get to town.''

''You were expecting me?''

He nodded. ''If I'd known you'd look like this, I would have gotten here earlier. Maybe signed up for two dances.''

Did he have her confused with someone else? This conversation made no sense. ''Did my cousins tell you I was coming?''

''No, Havenshire did. Everyone's been looking forward to meeting you. The heiress of Thorne's Well, and all.'' He looked down, realizing that he'd blurted out his interest in her fortune before he'd stuffed her full of compliments. ''He said you were a looker, but he didn't say . . .'' He broke off as his gaze streaked over her form as though he'd been served a double portion and didn't know what to do with the extra.

''I see,'' she murmured, partly insulted over being weighed in like a slab of mutton, but gratified that her baths were hiking her value up before she even got into town. ''How very nice to have friends waiting. I've never been to London before, and I was afraid of what I might find.''

''I don't know whose idea was the smartest,'' he admitted frankly, carrying on his own conversation without listening to hers. ''The ones pestering Havenshire for a subscription, or the ones hoping to get into your good graces instead.''

He gave a great sigh as the music began. ''B'lieve we better dance. Don't mind me if I don't talk much then. If I lose track of the steps, I'm done for.''

Cambria enjoyed the young man's meandering conversation. She waited until they were once again standing next to one another while the others went down the line, then began her list of inquiries. ''Tell me about your family, Lord Marchant. Do you have brothers and sisters?'' He bobbed his head and began spilling out his family history.

As they took their turn down the line, she reviewed what she'd learned. Marchant was the eldest son of a poverty-stricken family, and he was definitely looking for a woman of substance. She, it seemed, would do.

At their next opportunity to talk, she posed another question. ''What activities do you enjoy in London, Lord Marchant?

His eyes gleamed. ''I'm a *Corinthian,* Miss Thorne. Sportsman, you know . . . horses and racing and boxing. Stood up to Gentleman Jackson once.'' He frowned as a thought came to him. ''Don't mind a fast coach ride, do you, Miss Thorne?''

''Oh, no,'' she assured him. ''My late brother, Phillip, used to have a phaeton, and I loved it. The faster the better.''

His chest swelled with the sweet sound of that. ''How about your stables? Any prime blood at home?''

Without thinking what she was doing, she touched his hand and gave him a helpless look. ''Not since my brother died. I just don't know how to pick out a good horse.''

Marchant puffed up until she thought he might explode. ''Any time you need advice, Miss Thorne, just ask me and I'll whisk off to Tattersolls and find you a sweet pair of goers. Do you like a matched pair? Most of the ladies do, and . . .''

Cambria let him carry on, her smile pasted firmly in place. What had she just done? She'd pulled one of Talia's tricks, and it had come so naturally that she didn't know she'd done it until it was too late. Stunned, it took her a moment to realize something else.

Marchant's reaction.

She'd never seen anything like it. A loaded musket couldn't have had a greater impact on the man. Her brain was racing . . . ashamed and excited all at once. She'd promised herself she would do all in her power to find a husband, but . . . this?

Yet, she argued, it hadn't been like lowering her neckline to entice a man to do her bidding—and heaven knows, they were low enough, thanks to her aunts' instructions to the modiste—for she had dodged that stratagem by wearing shawls to cover up the far too seductive gowns, to her aunts' combined dismay.

A thought occurred. London was *fun.* All this time she'd let the disapproval of Thornedale stunt her growth. Let her own sense of unworthiness box her in. The games ladies played, that her aunts played, were harmless . . . innocent . . . and *fun.*

Her little ploy with Marchant did no harm. It was just a touch of a hand and a helpless look. She'd gained his surrender without seduction. This little trick of Talia's was like a hidden weapon that presented no invitation other than to come to the aid of a helpless damsel.

If it brought her closer to her goal, then so much the better.

Marchand deposited her beside Talia before she realized the dance was over. She looked down at her fan to see who was next, when a shy voice interrupted. "Anthony Hale," he announced, pointing to her fan. "Have you received permission for the waltz?"

"Yes, have you?"

He bit back a smile, his shy manner falling away when he saw how *new* she was. "Gentlemen do not have to ask, Miss Thorne, only the ladies." He offered his arm, and they strolled onto the floor.

"Why is that, Mr. Hale? In fact, why must anyone ask permission?"

Tugging at his neckcloth, he looked off into the distance as if searching for the answer. "Men do not need the protection ladies do."

The music began. With a surprisingly firm hand for someone so shy, he swirled her around the floor. After enjoying the heady movement, Cambria returned to the confusing question. "Protection from what? Why does their approval make a lady safer?"

She watched his face. An expressive face, she thought, far too revealing. He opened his mouth twice to answer her, then seemed to choke on the words. Finally, he murmured softly. "I think it's a humbug, Miss Thorne. They just want to boss people around."

She laughed in delight.

Then deciding to try out her newfound system for charming the gentlemen, she sighed heavily. "I can see that I'm going to need a great deal of advice, Mr. Hale."

Standing a little taller, he looked at her fondly. "M'mother said I should dance with you . . . because of the subscription, you know. Don't like to disappoint her, so I did." He turned a shade rosier. "Next time we dance, it'll be my own idea."

She sighed. She was becoming just like Talia and Diana, with no regrets whatsoever. Given a choice between the sanctimonious ladies of Thornedale and her indecorous aunts, the aunts won every time.

She relaxed. "Tell me about your family, Lord Marchant. Do you have any brothers and sisters?"

Chapter Six

Riordan stopped his gray stallion at the top of the hill. To the right lay the road up to his old home, *Lakeview,* and beyond that up the hill, *Thorne's Well,* the home of his mother's enemies. Straight ahead, below him, the village, *Thornedale,* awaited his inspection.

An unsettling feeling—the ache of remembering, of wanting something beyond one's reach—twisted inside him. *Damned emotions.*

Why the devil had he come?

He needn't be here. Rountree's watchman, Toby, worked as stableman at the Saracen's Head. Another watchman was footman at the Waterson's London house. Rountree's exacting investigation of the family—five females, two widowed and three single—told him they hadn't a chance against him. Rountree had efficiently dispatched the vicar over a month ago, thus leaving the heiress blessedly single, never dreaming what a poor choice for a husband she'd made . . . and luckily lost. Should all go well, Riordan could turn Thorne's Well over to his mother at the end of July.

He nudged the gray forward, sauntering past the unsightly Saracen Head's Inn where the Thorne girl with the handy fives had bloodied Lord Crowley's nose. As Rountree's report indicated, the coaching inn brought in passengers who, smitten with the flowered beauty of the rest of the village, carried the tale to others. Artists came to paint the village, hikers included it in their rambling routes. Even the Langcliffe-Thorne saga attracted gawkers who hoped for a glimpse of the infamous Thorne women.

Riordan moved slowly down the street. According to legend, this village had not changed significantly down through the ages. although it had been rebuilt several times. His ancestor, the poor, lovestruck Henry, had planned this arrangement of buildings for love of Roxanne, whom he wanted to please. The village *nestled,* winding sinuously around the bottom edge of the wooded hills upon which perched Lakeview and Thorne's Well.

The stones comprising the village road looked fresh scrubbed, free of traffic, except for a cob pulling a farm wagon slowly down the road. A pair of ladies crossed the street, their parasols bouncing with every step, a family sat amongst a group of tables outside a shop. At the foot of the village, the church spire rose above its ancient place of worship. Beside the vicarage, a cemetery lay thick with flowers left from a Sabbath visit. They were not dying but instead comprised a glorious, *growing* field of flowers. The village was exquisite, a witness to English villagers' cleverness in attracting needed custom.

Then it hit him. He'd been thinking of *their* town, *their* woods, *their* history, when the truth was, *this valley was his.* He remembered coming with his father, a child's clear memory. They went everywhere together, through the woods, the river, the lake, even to Thorne's Well.

Is this why he'd come? To make real the shadowy Thorne's Well, to solve the mystery of a father who loved his son, then let him go?

He sent his horse trotting back up the hill. Turning left onto the lane to Lakeview, he let the horse saunter slowly while he surveyed the neglected woods. Aging larches, beeches, oaks, spruces, and pines fought for room and sunlight. Rare seedlings grew on rotted logs or struggled for life near the roots of older trees. *Abysmal neglect.*

Just ahead sat the house. He'd always loved the way the old gothic edifice sprawled in its L-shaped majesty. The overall effect was of several cottages snug up against each other with the corner chapel reflecting the extra flavor of religion held by the ancestor who rebuilt it in the previous century. The chapel tower dominated the building with its admixture of tracery and stained glass windows.

In his youth, he had transformed the echoing tower into an imaginary hold under siege and often had to be reprimanded for pouring down icy water—boiling oil not being available— upon the imaginary enemies, consisting of his sister, Lily, and the long-suffering servants.

He sensed before going inside that the heart of the home had long since departed. It was not just the lack of growing things around the house—for the grounds around the house had been recently turned over, leaving a vast expanse of brown dirt—but the *empty* feeling that pervaded.

Dreading the disappointment he might expect, he entered the house, noting at once the lack of locks or even door handles. *Gutted,* he realized as he stepped over the sill. Had he thought he would walk in here to find the house he'd left behind? His throat ached with regret. What a waste.

What a shame upon his family.

He walked through each room, dredging up memories long since forgotten. The sound of his mother's pianoforte in the parlor, the smell of his father's coat as they shared the enormous chair, his special cushion at the dining room table, the hearth where his dog slept during the day, his bedroom where it slept at night.

At the top of the stairs, he looked down upon the home he had loved. Once the Thornes were gone, he would restore this house so his mother might walk through these rooms finally at peace.

* * *

Cambria leaned over the railing of the old wooden bridge. She found her usual calmness in the sound of water splashing over the falls above. Then she heard a horse approaching. *She turned—and froze.*

A stranger sat atop a powerful gray stallion down the road toward Lakeview, and at her turning, halted the enormous beast. The first thing she noticed were his powerful thighs as he nudged his horse a few feet closer, then stopped once more. He leaned forward and rubbed his hand on the restive horse's neck, and the muscles in his forearms stretched tautly as he gave the animal a stroke of approval. It took her a second or two to realize that he had removed his coat and draped it across the saddle, and his shirtsleeves were rolled up to just below the elbows. He sat upon his horse with an easy strength, as if holding all that muscle and bone and sinew upright were no effort all.

His expression was familiar—*stunned*—but, unlike the louts who passed through on the coach, there was a piercing intelligence, pleasure, and fascination upon those features as his gaze stroked her face and form, just as his large hand stroked his yielding mount.

Then she made the mistake of looking into his eyes. *Sorcerer's eyes,* glowing black as ebony, and just as capable of holding her steady as he did the compliant stallion. Did she know this man? Why did she feel she had always known to expect him here upon this road, capturing her gaze, speaking to her without words?

Riordan watched the play of emotions on her incredible face. At that moment, he longed for the skill of an artist to be able to render on canvas the strength of character, the innocent bewilderment, the unconscious seductiveness. He'd caught her in a fleeting moment when her barriers were down and her emotions showing—sculptured cheeks flushed vibrant rose, deep eyes glowing like a stormy ocean, full lips and open with surprise—dangerously unaware of how alluring a picture she made.

Or how dangerously aroused he became just looking at her. His gaze broke loose from her face, only to find yet more snares awaiting. Had there ever been such a color as that hair? Even pulled back in a spinster's bun of thick, auburn-streaked sable, it framed her face with the subtle richness and energy of a Gainsborough watercolor.

He blinked and let his view broaden, taking in the very essence of her. She was poised to flee, yet clearly entangled as he was in the magic of their meeting, wanting a moment more to take it all in.

She was tall for a woman, full-bodied, yet disguised, unaware of her power . . . perhaps not caring or perhaps not wishing for such attention.

She made a soft noise, dismay . . . fear.

He broke the silence with a soft question. "Have I frightened you? If you wish to go, I'll wait here until you are safely away."

Cambria gasped at the sound of his voice, so low and powerful. She stepped back as reason rushed in. This was no casual stranger riding through the woods to enjoy its beauty. This man took charge, *commanded,* and because she had bemused him, he was letting her go. Danger sparked between them as she hesitated, as if her delay revealed a message in itself.

Hurry.

She fought the urge to run. Chilled at turning her back on him, she turned and strolled sedately back toward Thorne's Well, feeling the potency of his gaze with every step.

Riordan watched her go—and suddenly his thoughts began clearing, as if a low ground fog suddenly swirled and lifted. He'd thought her a servant, but he knew better.

She was the little girl who'd wept at his leaving. Cambria Thorne, *compelling* as Rountree had described her. Only in a secluded village like this, could such a woman remain unclaimed so long.

Cambria *Thorne*—and just like Langcliffes down the ages, he had wanted her in an instant, had momentarily lost his power of reason, had sat upon his horse staring at her as a man bewitched.

Damn. He'd met a Thorne female and been stunned by his attraction to her, momentarily, of course. Still a little shaken, he took a cleansing breath and slowly let it out, feeling as if he'd been bitten by a particularly virulent, man-killing asp . . . and lived to tell the tale.

How interesting that this stunning creature represented the only barrier to acquiring Thorne's Well. Adversaries after the same prize.

He smiled in anticipation as he gave Cambria time to escape, then sent his mount ambling over the old wooden bridge. No wonder, Riordan thought, his ancestors worked themselves into a frenzy over a small piece of land that presented no actual threat to them. Like a thunderous prelude to a beautiful symphony, the noisy waterfall heralded the beginning of Thorne's Well. Hidden beyond the Langcliffe woods like some mystic tale of old, Thorne's Well seemed almost magically charmed. The music of nature, warbling birds and leaves dancing to a quickening wind, seemed to pick up in tempo as he neared the Thorne dwelling.

He shook his head at such fanciful musings. A simple storm was brewing, and he must turn it into a dance of the winds. He shivered as the brisk wind suddenly bore the icy threat of a storm. He rolled down his sleeves and slipped on his coat. He would make his introductory bows to the Thornes, hiding his disgust of them, and retreat before the storm hit.

A polite quarter-hour visit for now, occasional visits later, and the mystique of the Thornes might be dispelled. Eventually, the shadows would be gone, and with it, the unwelcome outpouring of emotion over this place.

His thoughts broke off as he rounded a turn and beheld the home Henry had built for his beloved Roxanne. Damn, he *remembered* this house. He remembered stalking it as a child, a warrior hiding in the bushes while he reconnoitered the castle he would storm and conquer.

Although it had the look of a miniature castle, complete with turrets and arrow slits, no moat and drawbridge ruined its beauty with an unfriendly edge, but instead a meandering flower-lined road beckoned one closer. Along the circular drive were several tree-shaded benches, enticing to a foot traveler, and an inviting gazebo sat beyond a rose garden, tucked under a cove of well-trimmed willows. Cunningly seductive.

At the entrance to the house itself, a portico extruded out over the front door, wide and deep enough to harbor a coachful of guests who awaited entry. Protected by this later addition to the house, rain-beleaguered ladies might trip lightly from a coach without ruining their bonnets and gentlemen need not worry over the shine of their boots. Even a storm would not be allowed to discomfort a guest of the Thornes.

As for storms, Riordan could feel the pressure of this one growing. Glancing at the sky, he nudged his stallion to a halt under the portico.

The door burst open and the doorman rushed out. ''Hurry, my lord. Let me get your horse to the stables before the rain hits.'' Riordan had to agree. He couldn't leave his mount out in the weather just because he did not wish to accept any favors from the Thornes. He dismounted and handed the reins to the servant. Immediately, another servant appeared, adding his own plea. ''Come inside. We've a nice fire inside to warm you.''

Again, he paused. Go, he told himself, why did he hesitate? Had he thought to conduct his first contact with the Thornes out on the drive? ''Thank you,'' he murmured, and, walking into the foyer, the most powerful feeling hit him. *The house opened its arms and welcomed him.*

He'd been inside this house before.

Warmth. The fragrance of vanilla and chocolate, baking bread, hearty meat and vegetables simmering. Roses lovingly arranged on the ornately carved table against the wall, waxed furniture glowing.

The soothing sound of ladies' gentle laughter.

He stiffened as unwanted, turbulent emotion struck hard in his midsection. His mother's vitriolic hatred poured through him, his own jealousy at losing his father to these women. He felt ill, wanted to bolt out the door. He couldn't think. Even his vision seemed cloudy. *Damn, what was wrong with him?* He'd faced the enemy before, sometimes with a pistol in the hand of his opponent. Would he cower before helpless females?

He forced himself to look up, to don the social mask he'd

perfected so long ago when his father shamed the family with his suicide.

Five ladies came strolling down the stairs, two mature ladies and three younger. The Thorne family, just as Rountree's extremely detailed investigation had unearthed, complete with names and descriptions.

Immediately, he picked out Cambria, more mature at twenty-four than her cousins. She was dressed in the same dull dress, covered to the neck and completely out of style. Had she hoped to disguise the magnificently lush, long-legged Thorne figure, she should have worn a tent.

Perhaps that wary, touch-me-not glare she bestowed upon him might slow a man down. He knew, however, that scowl's purpose . . . to disguise the attraction she'd felt for him in the woods. He *knew* she'd been struck with the same physical jolt he had. While he was immune to its power, of course, he might turn that interesting fact to his own advantage.

His eyes drifted upward. Another young lady, Cambria's cousin, Ellie, evoked a smile. Such elfin mischief dancing on those dainty lips. Golden, shimmering with energy, she would enliven any company.

He identified Amelia as well. Blushing, avoiding his gaze, delicate, refined to her fingertips. Her rosy cheeks matched her soft pink dress. A gentle girl, fragile in her feelings, but fierce in her loyalty.

The aunts . . . heaven help a grown male who thought he could remain untouched by either one of them. How had Rountree described them? Talia, the sleepy-eyed enchantress and Diana, the more energetic protector of the family. Both clearly exuding that Thorne charm without conscious thought, he suspected, but fully capable of deliberate seduction. *As his father had learned, to his sorrow.*

He sent out his sensors to test the air. An almost crackling energy filled the foyer . . . not just Cambria's hostility, but a watchful, *distrustful* feeling. Someone, then, knew who he was and didn't want him here.

Talia moved toward him as the others drifted onto the floor, her hand outstretched as she approached. "Lord Langcliffe, welcome back to Thorne's Well. Are you opening Lakeview?"

When Cambria gasped, Riordan smiled. Just as he'd suspected, Cambria had *not* known his identity when they met in the woods.

Riordan bowed. "I am considering opening the house, Lady Maxwell."

"You remember me? How charming."

"One could never forget you, but how did you recognize me?"

Talia's husky laugh pealed forth. "You used to run tame in the house Riordan. I am surprised that you have forgotten. I believe it was cupboard love, though. You spent half your time pestering the pastry chef, and the other half trying to escape from Cambria."

His gaze flew to meet Cambria's hotly flashing eyes. "I'm sorry," he said, making his bow to her, "I do remember a little girl, five or six years old, who clung to my hand and begged me not to leave. Strange," he mused with twitching lips, "I remembered her as a servant's child."

Pure outrage crossed her face. A deep flush of anger enhanced her loveliness as she made her curtsy. "And I seem to have forgotten you completely, Lord Langcliffe."

Talia chuckled.

Masking his pleasure at Cambria's anger, Riordan turned to Diana. "Lady Waterson, how lovely to see you again after all these years."

She gave him a gracious smile with no warmth. "Lord Langcliffe."

So, he thought, Diana and Cambria were the hostile females.

Ellie stepped forward. "I wasn't born yet." She offered her hand. "I would have remembered you." Riordan gave Ellie his most courtly bow and was rewarded with an unabashed grin. Amelia hung back, but as he turned to her, she made a quick curtsy and studied the tiled floor.

Above them on the stairs, two male voices drifted down. Ladies Maxwell and Waterson immediately took on a new glow. If he hadn't seen it, he wouldn't have believed such a transformation. Turning slightly toward the stairs, they stepped back to create a space directly in front of them. As if drawn into a funnel, Havenshire and Ragsdale made their way to their allotted spots, not fawning as Riordan might expect, but attempting to appear aloof from the ladies' charms.

What the hell were these pillars of society doing here? In all of the land, no two men were more respected, more admired for their integrity. Was this the secret of the Thornes? Like mate-eating spiders, they enticed the finest specimens, then destroyed them? What had he stumbled upon?

He'd met these men, but only in passing. Although a wealthy landowner, Havenshire's interest lay in the academic. One might put a dean's robe across those broad shoulders and a pair of spectacles framing those steely gray eyes, and the image would be complete.

Opposite in appearance, Ragsdale's habitual, blue-eyed smile and casual manner gave the false appearance that he might be compromised. Yet more than one person had made the mistake of such an offer. No gray yet touched his sandy hair as it had Havenshire's. His tall frame looked sturdy as a large tree. Like Riordan, he was a canny investor and, like Riordan, he had faced insults at dawn and survived.

How very entertaining. How very deadly these ladies were to have enticed these men to their web. How gratifying he'd been inoculated, not only from the dreaded smallpox, but from the wiles of such women.

But then, his cynical mind taunted in rebuttal, as a youth he'd consorted with these Thornes on a regular basis and today had been lured into the house without a single peep of protest.

Diana took over introductions, and the older men gave him a cautious greeting, as most men did. Riordan's sense of humor stirred as they smothered their curiosity over his presence.

Talia tucked her arm in Riordan's and strolled toward the back of the house. "You are just in time for dinner, Riordan."

He stiffened—he could not dine with these women who ruined his father's life—but before he could protest, Talia gave his arm a tug. "No formality between old friends, dear boy. We still eat in the family dining room near the kitchen, just as we always did. Not when formal guests are here, of course, but you are hardly that, are you?''

This was a nightmare, Riordan thought, *he could not stay.* Then the thought struck him . . . he would have to endure this in order to achieve the insight he was determined to gain for himself. He must not be at odds with any of them. This was no fragmented family at odds and welcoming dissension, but a snug, harmonious group whose decisions would be affected by the opinions of other family members.

Cambria strode ahead into the comfortable room and glanced over the table, her intelligent eyes examining the dishes and silver. She spoke to a servant who hurried to add a place while she frowned, obviously mentally rearranging the seating to accommodate Riordan's unexpected arrival.

Her lips lifted upward, invoking Riordan's curiosity. "If I take the time to follow protocol at this table, the soup will be cold. We'll pretend we are a well-worn family without a care about such things. Just choose the chair in front of you, no matter where you're standing.''

Clearly, Lord Havenshire and Ragsdale had never been subjected to such informality, nor had they ever eaten next door to the traditionally dungeon-like kitchen. Riordan had the sneaking suspicion that the kitchen at Thorne's Well would be as great a pleasant surprise as everything else.

As everyone slid onto their chairs, the high-ranking aristocrats quickly adjusted and sat down without a frown crossing their faces. Riordan had to admire their unruffled *savoir-vivre*. Riordan was not surprised to see Diana seat herself beside Lord Ragsdale and Talia slip in beside Havenshire. Biting back a smile, he looked up—and met Cambria's equally amused face. Something shifted between them in that infinitesimal second of shared humor. *Careful.* Drifting close to this particular fire might prove disastrous. *He would do better to fan her anger than to court her good will.*

Ellie and Amelia flanked Riordan on either side as the older diners sat across from them. Cambria sat at the head of the table with an empty place at her right. The place of honor saved for someone? But, who?

Ellie frowned. "Where's Mark?"

Cambria intercepted the question. "Mark will join us as soon as he finds his other boot. The hounds got upstairs, evidently, and decided to play hide-and-seek with his footwear. He begged us to go ahead, said if he didn't find it soon, he would be down without it." With Ellie's curiosity satisfied, Cambria signaled the waiting footmen to began serving.

The soup arrived . . . hot.

Then he remembered, very clearly, sitting at this table. He liked to eat here because the food was served hot, so different from his own home where the food cooled before it could make the trek to the dining room on the floor above. He finished every wonderful drop.

"Oh, please," a male voice moaned from the doorway, "don't tell me the soup is gone." Immediately a footman left the room and returned with a tureen. As Cambria made introductions, Mark Glendover's eyes filled with unspoken curiosity. He let his questions lie quietly unasked, and, by the time his soup was replaced by the next course—roast venison and jugged hare—polite chatter filled the room.

Cambria looked at Riordan, her lips twitching with mischief. "Perhaps we should thank Lord Langcliffe for this course since it came from the Langcliffe estate."

Attention swung to watch Riordan's reaction.

He was perfectly willing to banter with her. "Poachers, are you?"

"Oh, no," Cambria replied. "It's part of our ownership of Thorne's Well. Foraging rights. The fruit is from your orchards." She gave him her first smile. "Of course, we have had to replant when the old trees died from neglect. Since then, we have maintained them ourselves."

"Cambria," Diana murmured, "desist." Cambria's head dipped, but not with regret. Nor without reason, Riordan thought, for if Moulton had ignored the property completely enough to bring the appalling neglect Riordan had discovered, Cambria was due a passing jab at him. Still, he had no intention of explaining or apologizing.

"Please thank your cook for such excellent treatment of Langcliffe property."

Mark Glendover laughed, and Ellie joined in. Cambria looked surprised at his pleasantry and was clearly longing to resume the small battle. He wished they were alone so they might do just that.

"I noticed you had workmen working on the old Roman baths," Riordan said in idle conversation. "Are you restoring or repairing?" I ask because I do a number of old building restorations and am always fascinated by how they may be improved."

He was surprised when he silenced the room. Cambria's guilty flush lent suspicion to her answer. "A little of both."

When he didn't push it further, the Thornes relaxed. Whatever they were worried about had not come to light. *Devious,* he thought, just as he'd expected, but why should his innocent question elicit such a response?

Too many of his questions remained unanswered. What were all these people doing here? Were any of them suitors for Cambria's hand?

Rountree's report had identified young Glendover as the family solicitor who was managing the work going on at the baths. He had been to Thorne's Well twice, both brief visits, with no hint at romance. However, Rountree's system was clearly faulty, for here Glendover was, sitting at the place of honor at Cambria's right, young and personable and certainly eligible for marriage. Riordan shifted in his chair, uneasy to have been so complacent about such a crucial matter as this.

He needed answers . . . but cautiously, in due time. He turned first to Ragsdale. "I understand you are one of the investors in the Bude canal project. I'm considering it myself."

Ragsdale's face glowed. "Are you, indeed? If you approve, I must be content with my investment."

"I'm waiting now for the core investors to accept my money."

Ragsdale laughed. "They're careful past the point of common sense." He paused, clearing his throat in preamble to speech. "Langcliffe, I will be going to Bude, arriving two weeks from tomorrow. The directors are hosting an examination of the new system—''

Riordan grinned. "Ramps on rails instead of locks. Have you seen how it's working?''

Ragsdale smiled at Riordan's enthusiasm. "Not yet. If you want to meet me there, I will take you about as a guest and give the directors my personal approval of your investment.''

Wholly gratified by Ragsdale's endorsement, Riordan immediately accepted. "Thank you. I'll meet you there.''

Havenshire asked, "Where's the canal going? What's it hauling?

Riordan smiled. "Calcium-rich sand to fertilize the poor soil of northeast Cornwall and northwest Devon. It's coming inland then turning south to Launceston, river-fed from the Bude, the Deer, and the Claw.''

Ragsdale looked impressed. "You live up to your reputation for thoroughness, Langcliffe.''

"And you likewise, Ragsdale. In fact, I was surprised to see you here. My understanding was that you seldom have time for social life—or are you on the scent of yet another investment?''

Ragsdale would not be drawn. "I believe you take the honors for avoiding society, Langcliffe, yet here we are, both spending the evening at Thorne's Well. Credit must be given to the hospitality to be found.''

Cambria chuckled. "The very same cupboard love that drew Langcliffe here before.''

Riordan's spirits lightened. Here he had the challenge of a mystery and a battle of wits with a beautiful woman. He must consider himself fortunate that their interchange would prove so interesting. So far, though, he had learned nothing about why her guests were gathered here. He turned to Glendover. "Do you get out to Thorne's Well often?''

Glendover answered easily. "Phillip's family members are gracious enough to consider me one of them.''

Another bland reply with no substance. Riordan needed more. "Will you be staying long?''

A look passed between Glendover and Cambria, worried, it seemed, over what they should reveal to the interloper, Langcliffe. "Yes," Glendover replied finally, "I'm on holiday. I'll be here two weeks. I'm overseeing the repairs to the baths."

Two weeks, Riordan mused. If, as he was beginning to suspect, they were considering marriage, he'd arrived just in time.

He turned to another guest. "And you, Havenshire?" Riordan said, skirting the edge of intrusion. "As a renowned leader of the *ton,* you must be here for pleasure."

Havenshire wasn't fazed. "I'm here on a quest, Lord Langcliffe. Lady Maxwell has challenged me with a difficult task, and I am here to do my duty." He looked at Talia's shocked expression and allowed his stern visage a faint smile. "She's always in trouble with the more pious ladies of the *ton.* I'm here to educate her in more fitting behavior."

Talia looked incensed, while Diana's serious expression dissolved into laughter. *Bizarre,* thought Riordan, to see Havenshire *tease* such a woman. Was that why he and Ragsdale were here, simply in response to the call of two beautiful women?

Ellie decided to join in the conversation. "Lord Langcliffe, when did you begin managing the Langcliffe properties?" Diana gave Ellie a warning look, but the little imp ignored her. It might be best if he did the same, but he hated to back down with Cambria so keenly interested in his reply.

"I was fourteen when my father died and eighteen when I took over the actual management."

"Perhaps that explains it," Ellie said, insulting him with utter innocence. "Will you be moving into Lakeview?"

"My men are coming out to examine the house, and then I will decide." That had not been true until this very moment. He hadn't planned to touch the house until after the Thornes were gone. However, after seeing Glendover so dangerously resembling a suitor, he needed an excuse to spend time here in the valley.

Ellie wasn't through. "Will you spend the season in London?"

"No. I spend most of my time at Langcliffe Hall." Riordan decided to turn the focus. "Do you enjoy traveling to London for the season?"

She looked confused. "Traveling to London? Oh," she said, realizing what his remark meant, "you think we live here at Thorne's Well and travel back and forth to London? No, we live in London and occasionally travel out to Thorne's Well to visit Cambria."

He nodded as if not surprised, but in truth *he was*. All these years, he supposed that the aunts lived here as one large sprawling family. The London report said Cambria had gone with her family to order a few clothes, attend two functions, and come right back again. No doubt, with her year of mourning over, she wished to cast off her dark clothes. Or was Cambria's clothes-buying trip in honor of a blossoming romance?

By the time they arrived at the final remove, Riordan's taste buds were in ecstasy, his stomach full, and his intention to never return for future meals a matter for some regret. Evidently, his cupboard love for the Thorne household had not completely died.

At meal's end, the entire company rose with the intention of spending the evening up in the parlor. Past time for him to escape. "I must be leaving," he began. "Could you ring the stables—"

"You cannot leave in this storm," Diana said briskly as they moved out of the dining room and into the foyer. "You'll stay overnight, of course."

Talia agreed. "We absolutely forbid your leaving,"

He had intended only the briefest of visits. Remaining overnight was out of the question. Riordan strode toward the front door and opened it. Outside, rain poured down. Inches of water covered the graveled drive. Riordan's heart sank. What choice had he? Only a monster would subject his mount to this all the way back to the wretched inn, and only an idiot would leave a warm house and court a bad case of the ague.

"You'll end up sick," said Glendover, affirming the obvious.

Riordan looked toward his hostess, Miss Cambria Thorne. She must issue the invitation, and he could see it was the last thing she wished. She looked at the rain, then turned toward the stairs. Her reply trailed down behind her. "I couldn't do that to a poor, undeserving horse. Come on up."

* * *

When they reached the parlor, with its well-worn, vastly comfortable chairs and settees, Riordan began wondering why no one even hinted toward the obvious question—why had he come uninvited?

The ladies took turns entertaining the rest, each surprising him with her expertise. Talia sang in a voice that evoked visions of satin sheets and perfume while Diana played the pianoforte. Talia played the harp while Diana sang a series of charming English lullabies. With each, he found himself sinking further and further into a daze of well-being.

All he needed, he thought, with a private jab at himself, was a bit more room beside the two sleeping hounds; he could curl up by the fire and sleep peacefully through the night.

The young ladies were next. Cambria played a set of country songs while Ellie and Amelia harmonized. Afterward, Ellie strolled across the room to sit beside him on the settee. As Cambria continued playing, Ellie began another spate of questioning. No one looked at them, but everyone listened carefully to his answers. Her last one shocked them all. "You've been so nice. I thought we were enemies."

Riordan couldn't speak, for his first reaction was denial. He felt no animosity toward Ellie or her cousin. Cambria evoked no hostility within him. Even his ingrained hatred toward the aunts had been diluted by their graciousness. He recoiled inside when he realized what had happened.

He'd been seduced . . . not to a bed, but by another kind of seduction. Human warmth. Pleasant, affectionate conversation between family members, extended to him and Glendover and the stiff-lipped lords. Food more pleasing than any he'd ever tasted. Smiles. Laughter. In a matter of hours, he'd felt the tug of that silky undertow.

Before he could form his reply, Cambria's playing slowed, and she turned sideways on the cushioned bench. "Langcliffes, I understand, always come in sheep's clothing."

A hot fury arose from deep within him. How dare she level such a claim against a Langcliffe when his father had been seduced by one of her aunts? He was sure his expression had not changed, but something had. A cold, apprehensive feeling filtered through the room. One of the hounds raised his head as if sensing something amiss, then lay back down . . . but not to sleep.

Ellie broke the harsh silence. "So why did you come?"

Chapter Seven

"Why did I come? Curiosity brought me here," he replied, finding his equilibrium at last. *And,"* he added, looking directly at Cambria, "rather mistakenly, perhaps, to renew our acquaintance."

Riordan watched Cambria fall silent, a deep flush infusing her cheeks. She'd gone too far for good manners, past her witty disapproval of him.

This wasn't what he wanted. He stood and crossed to her, not caring that everyone watched. "I'm thinking of adding a conservatory to Lakeview, and I recall what wonderful success you've had with yours. Would you mind showing it to me?" No one objected to his request. Indeed, a feeling of relief emanated from the others in the room.

Riordan held out his hand, as any gentleman would do, to aid her rising. Cambria's head snapped up, fresh suspicion replacing her chagrin. She looked at his hand long enough for him to understand that she was the one making the decision to go with him, that he had not compelled her to do anything against her will.

She lay her hand in his, surprising him yet again. No soft, pampered hand was this, but firm and capable. He wrapped her hand around his arm and ushered her out. "I cannot remember where the conservatory lies. You will have to tug me along, lest I end up in the butler's pantry."

Turning toward the back of the house, she allotted him a small smile . . . but that was all. It made him impatient. He didn't want her silent. "Has finding a little blood on your claws rendered you speechless?"

He'd confused her. She frowned. "Blood? . . ."

"Your sheep's clothing remark. You drew blood, you bested me, made me lose my control and snap at you. Surely, you're not stopping with one successful hit when I'm sure you have much more to say to me."

Her mouth dropped open.

His voice softened. "It's the feud, don't you think? Even though we were childhood friends, we've been indoctrinated to dislike one another, and it's difficult not to show hostility."

She stopped before a heavy door, her expression furious. *"Childhood friends?* You said you remembered me as a servant's child!"

He grinned. "Teasing you, I'm afraid. An old habit with us, if I remember correctly. You had quite a temper."

"Only because you were always baiting me, Langcliffe."

"Hah," he crowed, "you remembered as well!"

Her chin rose, and she dropped her hand to open the door. "Of course, but you'd just insulted me and made me angry."

"Mea culpa," he murmured, following her into the conservatory. He noted her twitching lips, but her refusal to soften made him curious.

As she closed the door to keep the moist heat contained within, Riordan looked around the vast conservatory. Thorne-like, the room was lush with growing things . . . trees laden with fruit, bushes heavy with unseasonable tomatoes, seedlings destined for a summer garden.

She led him to a sitting area near the far wall with a wonderful view of the rose garden outside, but remained standing. He could see that she would have loved to pace angrily, but refused to betray her raging displeasure. "We used to be friends, Cambria," he said, his voice muted by the sound of rain pounding on the glass walls and ceiling. "Tell me why you're so angry with me."

Cambria hesitated. Should she take the chance and anger so powerful a man as Langcliffe? She could not resist. "Perhaps you're right."

"Ah," he replied gently, clearly pleased with having pried open her bottled complaints.

She couldn't wait to puncture that great condescension. "However much the feud has primed our prejudices, my anger toward you is not based on the actions of your ancestors—but on your own."

He stared at her . . . his expression shocked. How the devil could such a man as Langcliffe look so *innocent?* It only made her more furious. "I do not consider you an innocent boy grown up and coming back to visit, not when your sins scream to the tops of every tree in the valley."

He recoiled, surprised, shocked at her venom. But, she consoled herself, had he not asked for the truth? Had she not waited years to say these words to this betraying man? And she had much more to tell him.

"There's nothing so despicable as cruelty to those who are helplessly dependent on you. This land used to be prosperous. Langcliffe tenants thrived, their children fat and healthy. Then, typical of the *ton,* you lost interest, not caring that their cottages fell to ruin, that they were punished by your factor for feeding themselves on your rich, productive land."

She watched his eyes darken. Some inward battle raged within him, and she braced herself for the explosion.

It never came. Silent, he waited for her to finish, which she was perfectly willing to do. "Your tenants all moved away, carried their pitiful possessions in wagons and on their backs. Went to work in the mills . . . Need I explain what happened to them?" She gave a bitter laugh. "They should have waited, for not long after that, your factor stripped the house and left. Your tenants could have moved in and lived very happily all this time, had they only known you weren't coming back."

She waited once more, watching his jaw clench. "Have you nothing to say, Lord Langcliffe?"

Never explain, Riordan thought. He'd never broken that sacred rule, and the very fact that Cambria was pushing him to the edge of a deep ravine with no place to go made him furious. He could remain silent, keep his vow and walk out of her life with his pride intact. Let her anger be silenced by the very real results of his subsequent actions.

And lose his necessary connection to these people. His watchman, Toby, had done his best, but what Riordan really needed was a maid installed in the house to provide reports. But that would never happen—servants who worked at Thorne's Well never wanted to leave—and if Cambria needed help, the villagers jumped at the chance to make extra money. Rountree had to pay Bass just to get Toby installed at the inn.

Gritting his teeth, Riordan forced himself to speak. "I never explain my actions to others. I will, however, make an exception this one time. I warn you that you probably won't believe me."

She raised her chin and waited.

He took a deep breath. "There are many elements to this matter that are too private to divulge, but the pertinent fact is that until a short time ago, I believed this property had been sold." There, he'd done it.

Disbelieving, her eyes flashed. "Every quarter, the vicar has sent pleas for aid to Lord Moulton. Have you been ignoring him as well?"

Damn, she was like a dog with a bone—or more like an enraged bear with his leg in her jaws. "Moulton used to have that responsibility. As I explained, I was unaware of this situation."

"That's *it?*"

He clenched his teeth, but the words slipped past. "I have said too much already."

"But now I suppose you've come to set things right?"

"Yes," He tipped his enraged face close to hers, "I'm setting up a kettle of soup at the entrance to the village, and all the hungry people of this valley are welcome to come feed themselves."

She laughed and stepped back. "When you do, I shall stand beside you and ladle it out."

He scowled fiercely to keep from laughing, but she'd punctured his anger so adeptly, the laugh exploded anyway. Still grinning with the mischief of the child-Cambria he remembered dancing on her lips, she watched him warily as he pulled his frown back onto his face. Damn, this female had the power to infuriate him. Determined to keep this serious, he growled, "Have you any other grievances?"

Reluctantly Cambria shook her head, donning sobriety once more. Laughter had united them for a moment, but old hatreds, like mold under rocks, soon flourished back into their natural form. "You see, Lord Langcliffe, I've heard you are something of a scavenger feeding on carrion, that is, on others' losses at the gambling table. *Ruthless* is the word, I believe. I hear you are a brilliant investor and wealthy beyond belief. So, even if your excuse were true and you didn't know you owned Lakeview until now, you must still allow my skittishness at finding a reputed predator on my doorstep."

Cambria watched his eyes grow cold, his tone equally icy. "I find no fault with your condemning the neglect of Lakeview, since you saw it firsthand. However, giving vicious gossip the same credence makes me wonder how fair a hearing I will ever receive from you. I can see now that I should have saved my breath telling you my version of the facts, Miss Thorne. Next time you accuse me of a crime, be warned that I may not bother to defend myself."

"Fair enough," she returned, shamed by his assessment and hating to admit it. How often had she and her family suffered by others blindly believing every damning story they heard about the Thornes?

And yet, she thought with growing fury, who had started the stories in the first place? Lady Langcliffe, the woman who had nurtured this man beside her, the woman who molded her childhood friend into the hard, grasping man he was today. "I stand corrected in the matter of gossip, but be warned that I shall be watching your future actions."

"Unfortunately," he replied, "once I direct my men in correcting the neglect of the last several years, I will only be back occasionally, and so must deprive you of that particular pleasure.''

The door flew open. ''Mother says not to linger too long, Cambria. They're ready for the committee meeting.'' Ellie withdrew and the door slammed closed.

Riordan gave Cambria an inquisitive look, hoping she might tell him about it. She looked away, as if that would douse his curiosity. ''Perhaps I should go now.'' She hesitated, then became effusive. ''You must be tired, let me have a servant take you to your room.''

Riordan gave her a smile that told her he knew what she was doing. ''We'll discuss the conservatory another time, shall we?''

''Yes.'' With great relief, she rang for a servant.

He bowed and left immediately. All the way to his room, and all through his evening ablutions, he mulled over the mistakes he'd made. He'd been far too arrogantly sure of himself. He had let circumstances determine his actions. Let a mere female force his hand. Lost himself to emotion. Tonight he'd wavered, been seduced before he'd recognized the danger. Is this how his father began his long slide downward?

More dangerous than that, he found himself more exhilarated, furious and amused with Cambria than any other woman he'd ever met. It wasn't just the pleasure of looking at her or the steady core of lust she incited, but the vibrant sparks their minds sent crackling into the air. Not another woman in his acquaintance would stand up to him like that—indeed, he knew no *man* who would dare to speak to him in such a manner— yet her fierce arguments and her brilliant logic garnered his admiration. Even now, he looked forward to their next encounter.

He should be frothing at the mouth over being detained as a personal watchman over Mark and Cambria. The very fact that he was not irate made him realize just what a serious danger Cambria presented.

* * *

Cambria made her way quickly up to the library. The four committee members sat at the long table, embroiled in a heated debate. They ceased only with the greatest reluctance, as she took the chair at the head of the table. Diana pointed to a small pile of documents in the center of the table. "Lord Havenshire brought us the list of rules from Whites, and Ragsdale had a copy from Brooks. We have Almack's list and," she said, sorting through the stack, "something from Bath."

Havenshire handed Cambria the men's offering as she sat down. Immediately fascinated, she read through quickly. "What might we offer that would interest a member of these men's clubs?

Havenshire replied, "A gentleman might catch up on the newspapers or enjoy a bit of gambling. Business and matters of state are often conducted in such establishments."

"If you wish," Ragsdale said, "you might set aside a room for gentlemen that would serve the same purpose."

Diana objected. "The ladies won't like that."

"What does Almacks offer the ladies?" Cambria asked.

Talia laughed. "Gentlemen."

"Talia," Diana scolded, "it's more than that. It's a feeling of being select, a mark of acceptance, a gracious way of life. Dancing and music—"

As the evening wore on, she was surprised that people like her aunts—pleasure-seeking dilettantes—could work so hard or find a sensible mixing of common sense and cunning out of all the possibilities they discussed. Nor had Lord Havenshire and Ragsdale, for it seemed to surprise them as well. By the time the finer points were refined, the four participants were no longer at arm's length, with the gentlemen treating her aunts like empty-headed idiots, but were cheerfully arguing on as equals.

As Cambria suspected, the sun would accompany her to bed, not the evening stars as she had hoped. Longing only to close her aching, sleep-deprived eyes, she washed quickly, threw her nightgown over her head, and dove for the pillow. One second, and she would be asleep.

That's when—like a slumbering child carried upstairs to bed—her store of submerged thoughts woke up and wanted to chat. Wanted to mull things over, wanted decisions. Just the thought of confronting her newest problem—Riordan—filled her chest with a torrent of purest panic.

Yet, blast it all, did she have the sense to concentrate on the man's infamies? Did her brain caution her against the very fact that upon Langcliffe's discovering he owned Lakeview, he came trotting down to their house and began asking questions? Did it stop to contemplate the fact that a man who made a living repossessing other people's properties was on the verge of winning Thorne's Well on a default? Did her brain want to admit that no matter how she found great exhilaration exchanging insults with Langcliffe, he was still a man raised by the woman who spread lies that, in essence, impacted her own life for the worse?

No, casting a shadow over all the confusion in her life was her first meeting with Riordan Langcliffe. What had possessed her to stand there, alone in the woods, staring at a stranger? What was wrong with her that she was so bemused by a man's physical appearance? Was she to be like her aunts, after all? Was there some latent disease in the family that, like a spigot, turned on dreamy contemplation when she should be trying to escape?

She turned over and pounded the pillow. *No,* she was not like her aunts. She'd been startled, surprised by a well-favored Langcliffe. A wretch who offered the poorest excuse for neglecting Lakeview. But, she thought with a grin . . . that agonized explanation . . . she'd never seen a man's face turn brick red before. Had he a smoother, well-rehearsed answer ready, she wouldn't be wondering now if he told the truth.

Not that it mattered.

She didn't like the way she felt around Riordan. He was too powerful, too forceful . . . and she found forceful men frightening.

The point was, Riordan was just as she found him, a man

who made her uneasy. If she must think about him at all, she should be deciding what the devil was she going to do about him.

She flipped over again, miserably wide awake.

All she *could* do was brace herself for his next move.

Chapter Eight

Riordan strode across the Saracen's Head courtyard and handed a note to his watchdog, Toby. "Give this to Peck. Come back in two weeks." The young man tugged at his knitted cap and trotted toward the stable. An intelligent servant, Toby was prized . . . always present, but never visible.

Bass, the owner of the Saracen's Head, strolled up beside him. He was tall with an easy smile and the crinkling eyes of a man who enjoyed life. Graying hair denoted his age, but his movements were quick and efficient. A man with his eye on a coin. "Will you be paying for Toby while he's gone, Langcliffe?"

Riordan laughed. "You're a hard man, Bass. I not only pay Toby's wages, but put coins in your hand as well. Now that I've sent him away, you still want your bit?"

Bass shrugged. "The fact is, my men have gotten used to having a lighter load. Now that he's gone, they'll be grumbling at the extra work."

Riordan liked Bass. The man was a reprobate, but once he'd gotten the hint that Langcliffe was keeping an eye on the lovely Miss Thorne for romantic reasons, he'd gone all mushy and agreed to the charade. "I'll tell you what, Bass. I'll keep paying

Toby's fee if you put a new tick on my bed and wash the linens. Your inn is a disgrace. I can't even see out of the window, it's so dirty.''

"Well," Bass said, shuffling his feet while he considered the bargain, that'll mean more work for my maids . . ."

"Bass," Riordan warned him, "have you thought about how long it's been since someone collected money for your lease? About fifteen years since my father's old factor left town."

Bass's eyes widened. "Gawd, Langcliffe, you're not going to ask for back rents, are you? It wasn't our fault no one was minding the village."

"No, I was just totting up the reckoning lying on the books—"

Bass waved his words away. "Don't worry, Langcliffe. When you come back today, your room will be right and tight."

Riordan smiled. "Good. And while you're at it, clean out your top floor. My crew will be needing a place to stay while they're working on Lakeview, and they're used to something more civilized than your place."

Riordan took off across the courtyard, leaving a stunned innkeeper behind him. He strode across to the blacksmith's shop and wandered into the huge barn. His stallion should have been shod by now. He found the horse eating contently in the last stall.

"How are you doing, boy?" He lifted a hoof. Well done, he thought, relieved to find good workmanship available in the village.

Riordan began saddling the stallion, but the blacksmith, a broad-chested, handsome young giant, came hurrying over to stop him. "Here now, let the boy do that, your grace."

Riordan had to smile. The blacksmith should have seen him in his struggling years, when he put his hand to every job at Langcliffe Hall . . . and found he enjoyed the labor.

"Will you wait a minute, Langcliffe? When my wife heard you were on your way up to Thorne's Well, she asked me to send along a note." He trotted back toward the shop and disappeared inside. Like all the merchants, the family lived upstairs over the shop. He'd barely been gone a minute before his wife rushed out. He turned back toward the blacksmith shop, while she rushed toward Riordan.

"Lord Langcliffe," she called, moving along with the grace of a waddling duck. "Will you take this to Cambria for me?" As she grew closer he could see a flurry of freckles across her cheeks and her red hair straggling out of a hasty bun.

He smiled. "Aren't you little Sarah, Cambria's friend?"

She returned the smile and touched her middle lightly. "Not so little, your grace, but I am Sarah. It's good to see you again, all grown up and back in town. Will you be staying?"

Not willing to tell anyone of his plans, he shrugged his shoulders. "That'll depends. The house might not be worth restoring."

"Are you and Cambria enjoying your reunion?"

"It's been more of a grand battle so far, as you can imagine. She's parted my hair with a stool over the shape of Lakeview."

Sarah nodded. "She's had a bad time lately, and she's trying to be brave about it. The truth is, she's too tender-hearted for her own good. And now she's got the village gossiping, which makes it worse."

"Gossiping?"

"You've heard about the incident at the inn, haven't you?"

"Yes. But why should that cause gossip? It wasn't her fault."

Sarah looked at him strangely. "I guess you don't know what happened after you left, do you?" At his look of confusion, she led the way out into the paddock behind the building where they could talk in private. "About five years after you left, something similar happened to her. She and I were rolling hoops . . ."

Riordan listened with growing horror. Sarah's voice grew tight as she described Cambria's difficult recovery after the incident. "It changed her, Riordan," she said, slipping into their old childhood habit of first names. "For the longest time, she wouldn't even leave Thorne's Well. She just kept to her land and sort of *hid*. Phillip didn't know how to help her— other than teaching her how to defend herself, should it ever happen again—so he let her remain secluded."

"She's not timid now—more tiger than kitten, if you ask me."

Sarah nodded. "When Phillip went to London to bring in money for the estate, she shook off her old fears and seemed like herself again. Not laughing so much, mind you, but then, we weren't little girls any longer, either of us. Things change, people grow up. Life's never what you plan."

"You're still friends, I gather," he said, fingering the note.

"Oh, yes. She comes down and plays with my babies, and I go up and steal your fruit." She chuckled. "It seems an even trade." She looked at the note in his hand. "I've invited her to an afternoon party. She knows half of the ladies have taken a stand against her, and so she's holding off. If I got her into town, she'd get her back up and do something about it. She thinks she's a cowardly mouse, but you should see her when she's mad . . . oh," she said grinning, "I guess you have, haven't you?"

Her head turned as a door banged and a sturdy little boy came looking for her. "I have to go, Riordan. I'll see you again, won't I?"

Of course." He watched her hurry toward her little son. Memories from a happier time came tumbling into his mind. But, as Sarah said, things change, people grow up, and life was never what one planned.

He mounted his horse and headed out toward Thorne's Well.

He'd pondered last night how best to conduct his probe into Cambria's affairs. It seemed clear to him that Mark and Cambria were more than friends, but he hadn't seen any evidence of actual romance from the way they acted together. There were no lingering looks, no hands touching as they moved from room to room. In truth, Mark's interest seemed far more caught with the younger cousin, Ellie. Of course, Ellie, a natural flirt and forward to a fault, had not perfected a smooth, lady-like way of interacting with gentlemen.

He needed to take the young people out of the house without watchful eyes proscribing their behavior. He'd concocted a plan—a rather flimsy one to be sure—but he thought they'd be interested enough to agree.

Cambria looked out toward the rose garden and the house beyond. Beside her in the gazebo, Mark sipped his lemonade and sighed with satisfaction. "You do realize, Cambria, that just a taste of life here at Thorne's Well would be enticement enough. If you find a suitor you like, be sure to bring him out to feel the magic of the place."

She smiled. "I'll take your advice if the time does come." She blushed and cleared her throat nervously. "I've been wondering if you'd like to kiss me, Mark." Seeing his startled look, she hurried on. "It seems to me that kissing would be part of marriage, and if we don't like it now, it might make a difference."

"You're such a dunce, Cambria. Don't you know men like kissing girls even if they don't have the slightest intention of marrying them?"

"But girls who seem like their sister?"

He sent an ogling, evil-villain look over her figure. "Surely you don't think I'm blind to your charms?"

Playfully, she nudged his arm. "Kiss me and let's see."

He placed his glass down on the floor and turned toward her. Tipping her chin up with his fingers, he leaned forward. She liked the way his lips felt. Soft and pleasant, and his breath was fresh, tasting like the peppermint leaf floating in his lemonade.

He leaned back and looked down into her eyes. "What do you think?"

"I didn't mind it at all, It was very nice. Friendly, warm, and cozy."

He gave her a strange look. "Not a brain in her head."

"Didn't I do it right?"

He gave her another quick smack, then tweaked her nose. "You did just fine, Cambria. Don't worry about it." He picked up his glass and looked inside with a frown. "Empty. I guess we'd better get back to work."

Letting his mount amble slowly up the drive, Riordan watched Glendover and Cambria wander through the rose garden. They could have been an old married couple or neighbors, but not a pair waiting anxiously for the joys of marriage. Not in love, at least, but perhaps with Thorne's Well at risk, the alliance took precedence.

Marriages were often contracted purely for land or money or titles, leaving to chance the development of sincere affection. He often thought that humble people such as Sarah and her blacksmith husband had a better chance of happiness. She seemed perfectly happy, and, if he hadn't been mistaken, her virile young husband had patted her posterior with a definitely tender leer before she came out to talk to him. His mind mulled over that moment, while a strange ache went through him.

He'd been alone by preference for most all his life. His mother was a matter apart, eliciting a love stemming from need. *Her need,* that is, for he always felt more like parent than child.

But could he ever love like Sarah and her husband? Would he like to have that casual, friendly hunger for a spouse punctuating his days and nights? And, he thought with sudden impatience, why the devil was he dwelling on such thoughts now?

He halted before the Thorne house. As before, he'd barely dismounted before a servant came running out to hold the horse. Upon spotting him, Cambria's smile lessened, but Mark Glendover gave a friendly wave.

Riordan strode forward "Hello, Glendover. It's a beautiful day, isn't it? Hard to believe that storm last night." He bowed to Cambria. "And the lovely Miss Thorne." He could not resist. "So like the roses in her garden."

She took the challenge. "Prickly, you mean?"

He feigned innocence. "Heavens no. I refer to your beauty, of course." His grin belied his protest, as she was perfectly aware. What was it about the girl that made him revert to such adolescent jabbing? He reached in his pocket and brought forth a note. "Your friend, Sarah, gave this to me."

Taking the note, Cambria stepped aside to read it through quickly. She chuckled at Sarah's irreverent attitude toward the local gentry as she urged Cambria to come down and do battle with them.

There were over a dozen families who had leased parts of Lakeview over the years, creating a strata of society that hadn't existed before. Sarah's family had been one of the first. Those ladies had formed themselves into self-proclaimed arbiters of behavior, using the Thorndale Improvement Society as their weapon of choice. They had even allowed the shopkeepers to join so they would have someone to look down upon.

If ladies were to wear a number denoting their rank, Thornes, as land *owners,* would have stood second just below Lady Langcliffe, only without a title. Primed by Lady Langcliffe's gossiping lies, the local ladies turned their backs on the Thorne family *en masse,* thus stepping up one illusory notch.

To a small girl who didn't understand, being suddenly snubbed by the other girls—except Sarah's family—had been devastating. Then, when the incident at the inn happened in her youth, things worsened. Instead of impersonal snubs, her every word and action received the greatest *suspicious* attention.

When Phillip left for London, and she was forced into more contact with her neighbors, she found it comforting when spoken to with politeness. Once John singled her out, respect crept into their manner. She knew that, given the slightest excuse, some of them would pounce once more, but to be totally accepted for the first time since childhood somehow became vitally important. After the recent incident, the ladies had evidently fallen into opposing camps over her suitability.

Somehow, having what seemed to be worst happen—another disgrace of sorts—shook up all her insecurities, surprising her by revealing things truly important to her and sifting the opinions of her enemies to the bottom of the list. But Sarah deserved a reply. She tucked the note in her pocket, resting her fingers on the paper for just an extra second.

She looked back at Riordan. "May we offer you refreshments?"

"No." Riordan replied, bemused by her expressive face as she read Sarah's note. He only hoped his own news would capture that same attention. "Rather, I've come to beg a favor."

Cambria looked suspicious, but not Glendover. He stepped forward. "What do you need, Langcliffe?" They both paused as the front door opened, and Cambria's cousins came strolling out to join the group.

Riordan made his bows to Ellie and Amelia, then included them in the conversation. "I've sent for my crew to clean out the woods and take a look at the house. I looked through the interior this morning, and it seemed like the most practical solution might be to just torch it and start over. I like the old place, though, and hate to do it. I've come to ask you to walk over and see what you think."

Mark looked horrified. "Good grief, Langcliffe, you're not serious. You wouldn't burn it down."

Amelia agreed with Mark. "Surely something can be done to save it."

Ellie looked excited, but as she stood there, clearly imagining the importance of burning down the house of a duke, she gave him a worried frown. "Wouldn't that catch the woods on fire?"

"No," Cambria assured her. We've always kept the land around the house clear of dry brush to prevent just such a thing."

Riordan moved closer to Cambria. "I noticed that the earth had been spaded when I rode by yesterday. I'm indebted to you." He expected her to snap back a long list of tasks she'd ordered done on his behalf, for after her dig about his fruit trees, she was certainly willing to do so.

Instead, she simply nodded. "Are you serious about Lakeview?"

"Would you mind?"

"I suppose it just shocks me. It's such a beautiful old house, and it's been there forever." She began moving toward the open door. "I think we'd all enjoy the walk down to Lakeview. The adults are running up to London tomorrow to make purchases for the baths, but Ellie and Amelia couldn't go. This might be just the thing to cheer them up.''

She glanced down at her leather slippers. ''We'll need to get our parasols and our boots.'' She stepped into the house. ''Come in and say hello to the others. Havenshire and Ragsdale have not arisen yet, but my aunts are downstairs.''

As Riordan moved alongside her, he kept an eye on Glendover, looking for traces of jealousy at their somewhat private conversation. Glendover, however, seemed to be the target of the cousins' attentions, letting them herd him into the house without a glance toward Riordan and Cambria. *Interesting.*

The girls scurried up the stairs to change their shoes, and Mark led Riordan back to the ground floor dining room. The aunts were sitting at the table studying bits of colored fabric. ''Hello,'' Talia said, standing to kiss Riordan on the cheek.

Diana stood as well, moving toward the dish cupboard for a cup and saucer. ''Have some tea, Riordan. What brings you here this morning?''

Glendover answered for him. ''He wants the girls and me to go down and look his house over. See if we think it's worth restoring.''

Talia motioned Riordan toward a chair. ''If you're remaining in the valley, you must stay with us.'' Riordan heard Diana's soft gasp, clearly sharing Riordan's resistance to his bedding down at Thorne's Well.

Grinning to invite amusement, Riordan turned to Talia and drawled the one answer that would put an end to her hospitality. ''My mother would have a fit if she saw me here at your table, Lady Maxwell. If I moved in, she'd come to Thorne's Well and scratch your eyes out.''

Talia laughed, choked and laughed again. Diana joined her. ''Ah, Riordan,'' Talia said, gasping for breath, ''you have your father's wonderful sense of humor.''

He fought back a red haze of fury. How could she bring up her familiarity with his father here in front of him? ''Thank you,'' he managed, sitting down and reaching for his cup. Staring across at the opposite wall as if lost in fond remembrance, he nursed the tea in small sips for several minutes, a sick feeling in his gut.

Every moment he spent in this unreal, convoluted intrigue made him wonder if he would ever be the same again.

Chapter Nine

By the time they reached Lakeview, Riordan could see that his suspicion about Glendover and Cambria was correct. They walked together the entire way, casually consulting each other's opinions in a subtle, probing manner, just as business associates do before making an alliance.

He made another discovery—that he would rather be digging a ditch than dealing in this *personal* business. What the devil did he think he would do if he found out they were intending marriage? Glendover wasn't going to be enticed off to India. If he committed himself to a betrothal, he was too honorable to cry off, especially when he knew the consequences for Cambria. Riordan supposed he could arrange some forced disappearance for the man, just long enough to get past Cambria's birthday. Afterward, he would make it up to him. Send him some other prize he might value.

As they made the trek to Lakeview an idea that occurred yesterday began to percolate in his brain. "Let's divide up," Riordan said as they reached the house. "That way I'll get a variety of opinions, not just one agreement as we go along." He looked at Glendover. "Why don't you and Ellie start at the top and the rest of us will start down here."

Ellie grinned. "I'll beat you to the attic." Riordan held back a grin as Glendover took the challenge and loped up beside her as if they'd been together forever. Ellie and Mark . . . dry tinder waiting to be ignited.

Riordan turned to Cambria and Amelia. "Where shall we begin?"

"The kitchen, of course." Cambria took Amelia's arm and pulled her close. In a rogue's voice, she growled, "He'll be sorry he ever asked us."

"The floor slates are broken," Riordan pointed out inside the kitchen. "And the cupboards are rotting from rain pouring in the broken windows."

Amelia frowned and crossed to the huge kitchen fireplace. "This oven is wonderful, Langcliffe. You should be thinking what can be saved, not what's spoiled. Cupboards are easy, they can be torn down and new ones installed. Only," she scolded, as if he'd made the mess himself, "you'd have to fix the windows first."

Riordan and Cambria shared shocked expressions at the shy Amelia giving orders like a little general. Silently, they moved to the side and let her have her way.

"Ice room," Amelia murmured. "The floor needs scouring, of course, but no repair needed." Sticking her head through the next door, she paused a little longer, wrinkling her nose. "Fish room. This will need a soda wash . . . perhaps a dose of lye."

"Bugs," she announced at the door to the larder." Riordan half expected the guilty little intruders to flee the scene. The pantry and pastry closets got merely an approving nod. At the last room, the game larder, she mused, "Too bad you can't torch just one small room." Finished with the kitchen, she marched into the next room.

"Good grief," Riordan muttered to Cambria.

"Thorne women are very domestic. It's our *peasant* blood."

He let that go untouched. "What do you think of the house?"

"I've always liked this place. I used to play at decorating it in my mind, paint and paper, colors I'd choose."

"Can it be saved, though?"

Her nose crinkled. "How rich are you?"

He laughed. "Rich enough."

"Then you should restore it." She grew quiet. "Will you do it?"

He nodded. He'd already sent for his crew.

"Will you live here?"

So, that's what she's worried about. "You'd rather I didn't?"

Before she could reply, Amelia stuck her head through the door. "Are you two coming?" Obediently, they followed, but Amelia's brisk pace soon left them behind once more.

In the parlor, Riordan asked, "How did you envision this room?"

Dreamily, she turned slowly around. "Green watered silk, gold and ivory . . . delicate furniture, French, I think." How revealing, he thought, to see her stiff distrust fall away when she forgot he was there.

"And this room?" he asked in the next.

She trailed her fingers along the wall. "This was the music room, was it not?" At his nod, she drifted into a trance. "Something romantic . . . velvet draperies, thick carpets, comfortable furniture a man might fall asleep on while his wife makes soothing music."

How typically Thorne.

A dozen fully-inspected rooms later, they found Ellie and Glendover upstairs in a bedroom, leaning out the window side by side. "Someone's coming," Ellie said. She and Glendover moved back to yield the view.

Riordan leaned out, just spotting the rider galloping up the road, looking born to the saddle. *Alistair?* Riordan's heart sank as he saw his nephew's grin at seeing Riordan at the window. He'd instructed Alistair to come only if Lady Langcliffe were causing trouble.

"Hello the house," Alistair called. Riordan waved in reply.

Cambria looked over Riordan's shoulder. "Who is it?

"My nephew, Viscount Singleton."

Her face bemused, Cambria said, "He looks just like you."

"Handsome devil, you say?"

"No . . ." Her eyes full of laughter, she gave his face a

frowning once-over, "I think it's that unruly mop of hair hanging in his face. Perhaps the idiot grin."

He smiled—then couldn't look away.

For an instant, it seemed to Riordan that they were the only ones in the room. She stared back at him as if in a daze, her lips parted and her bewildered gaze locked with his. He wondered if she knew how much she revealed, standing so still, blinking like a doe caught in the glare of a dozen hunters' lanterns. She was more than wary, he thought with sudden comprehension, almost frightened of their mutual attraction. Had the vicar's defection left her skittish ... or was it her commitment to young Hale?

As for himself, *damn,* this had to stop.

Alistair dismounted in the driveway. Tying his horse on a knarled stump, his eager gaze darted quickly over the others watching from the windows. "I'm coming up." He headed at a youthful dash toward the door.

With unspoken agreement, they met him on the stairs. Before Riordan could say anything, Alistair defended his presence. "I have some messages for you, Uncle Riordan. It's like bedlam when you're gone."

Then he turned toward the others, smiling at the ladies. As Riordan made introductions, he could see Alistair's intelligence at work as he met each one. His brows rose in appreciation at meeting Cambria. He answered Ellie's grin with a boyish one of his own, and at meeting the shy Amelia, he hurried to put her at ease.

After Alistair and Glendover exchanged greetings. Alistair looked around. "What are you doing here, Riordan? The place is a wreck."

"We're the torch brigade," Ellie returned cheerfully. "We're deciding if the house is fit or if it needs a hot farewell. *I* think it needs it."

Glendover coughed, somewhat embarrassed at Ellie's assertion. "I don't, and I don't think Langcliffe means to torch it ... not really."

Clearly wishing to give them privacy, Cambria murmured politely, "We'll all start back toward the house. You two may catch up when you wish." She looked toward Alistair. "You're welcome to tea, Lord Singleton."

Alistair's brows rose in delight. "We'll be right behind you."

"Alistair," Riordan said when they were alone, "what's amiss?"

Alistair slumped against the bannister. "Grandmother has some argument going with Rountree—about what I don't know—and nothing will do except to set the matter before you."

"She can't come here. There's no place for her to stay. The inn's unfit, and, as you can see, the house is an empty shell."

"She already left to visit my mother. Then she's coming here."

Damn. "Well, go back and tell her how things are."

Alistair gave a huge sigh. "Can't you just send her a note to stay away, Riordan? I told her I was going to town for a few days just to get away to warn you."

He looked so forlorn, Riordan could not force him to go. "I could use you here, Alistair, if you wouldn't mind staying."

Alistair's eyes lighted. "Splendid."

Alistair trotted downward, but stopped suddenly, grinning at Riordan. "I forgot to tell you. I leased out Johnstone's house. For a boy's school. Troublemakers who have been sent down. I shall receive rents and a percentage of the business."

"Very good." Inwardly, he groaned. Already it sounded like a nightmare in the making.

Alistair grinned at the praise. "I made such a bargain that they had to keep Johnstone's mother there in her own apartment. Don't be angry, Riordan," he said quickly. "I just couldn't leave her to her son's mercy."

"Don't apologize, Alistair. I told you I would let you make your own decisions. What about her food, the things she needs?"

Alistair's face cleared. "That's the best part. The renters know Johnstone. They don't like him, so they made a clause in the agreement forbidding his entering the property. So, if he can't get to his mother's money every quarter, she'll do all right."

Riordan could see problems peeking out of every corner but didn't intend to say so. They stepped out into the sunshine. Down the road, the others dawdled slowly, waiting for them to catch up.

Eagerly, Alistair caught his horse's reins and hurried to catch up with Glendover. "Whatever made you go into law?" he asked.

Riordan smiled at the youngster's insatiable curiosity. He would probably keep Glendover busy answering questions all the way back to Thorne's Well. Thank goodness Glendover didn't seem to mind. The young cousins, Ellie and Amelia, however, didn't like being ignored and flanked the young men to siphon off their share of attention.

Cambria surprised him by drifting back to walk alongside him. "He's a charming young man," she said in idle conversation. He could tell she was distracted and wondered if she, too, were nervous about the awareness that simmered between them. It was strange, he thought, the variety of emotions she evoked in him . . . and maddening that she evoked any at all. However, he could not deny the fact that the very moment she began to walk beside him, he felt . . . how would he describe it? . . . *content?*

The roar of the waterfall sounded faintly in the distance. Behind them, the clatter of horses approaching quickly stopped the company, turned them all around to see who came up this private road.

Two rather castaway gentlemen with decidedly poor seats sawed at the mouths of their long-suffering horses until the poor creatures halted. Alistair, an avid horse lover, groaned in sympathy. Cambria issued a disgusted sound and moved to stand beside her cousins, clearly repulsed by the gawking interlopers.

"Lord Langcliffe!" one stranger called.

Riordan looked closer, and realized he knew them . . . unpleasant fellows hanging on the edges of society. "Potter, Jones."

Jones, short and balding with bandy legs, dropped the reins and slid down to the ground, heading toward Riordan as if seeing a long-lost friend. Potter secured his mount to a nearby tree and hurried to join them. "Have you come to see the baths, Langcliffe?"

Riordan frowned *The baths?* The only baths nearby were the Thornes' old Roman baths, and these particularly repulsive males would never be invited there. A niggle of unease shook that assurance, though, when he recalled that suspenseful moment at dinner when the Thornes seemed so relieved to have dropped the subject of the baths.

"This is my holding," he began, "but—"

"Never say *you* own them? I thought the Thornes did."

Glendover's expression was one of impending thunder as he marched up to stand beside Riordan. Riordan glanced over at Cambria, not surprised to see the color draining from her face. Feigning a muddled comprehension was not difficult as Riordan turned back at the two men. "You're to be guests of the Thornes?"

Potter laughed. "Hardly that. Just thought we'd have a quick glimpse before they start the subscription. Once old Havenshire starts deciding who's good enough, a second son like me won't get near the place."

Ah, the committee. Feeling as if he were side-slipping through a bramble bush, Riordan nodded. "How did you hear of it?"

Jones, a slow, plodding speaker, explained. "It hasn't even opened, and already people are queuing up to be admitted. What do you know about the subscription rules, Langcliffe? You being a neighbor . . ."

As calmly as he could manage, Riordan pursed his lips in contemplation. "Havenshire and Ragsdale seem a reasonable sort, but rather strict. We haven't discussed the matter."

"Well, a person has to get past the rest of the committee, and three Thorne females might have ideas of their own. Not the usual sort, you know." *The women were on the committee?* Of course, that's why Cambria had been called away the other night.

Grinning at Riordan, Potter nudged his friend. "Bet you don't have to stand in line, eh, Langcliffe?"

"Right," said Jones, smirking at the thought.

Glendover stepped forward and grabbed Jones by his neck-cloth, while, incensed, Riordan stepped toward the smirking Potter. "What do you mean by that remark, Potter?"

Potter shuffled backward, his eyes skewing back between Glendover and Riordan. "Well, you know ... the Thorne ladies."

"I do know the Thornes, and I take great insult at your disrespect."

Potter raised his hand to ward him off. "No insult intended."

"Too late for that," Riordan announced. "This is private property, Potter. *My* private property. If I ever see you two even in the village down the hill, you'll be the sorriest bastards who ever walked."

Potter scrabbled away, along with the just-released Jones. While Potter untied his horse and mounted, Jones turned around in circles searching for his horse. Spotting it at the edge of the woods, he scurried through the low brush, his knobby knees pumping up and down. Glendover began to chuckle while Riordan watched in silence. *Fury poured through him.* He'd been rhapsodizing over Cambria's charms while she was deceitfully hiding her plans to open a commercial enterprise in the middle of his property.

He let the cold fury seep into his blood, let it chill his heated body and clear the cobwebs from his smitten brain to the point of pure clarity. What else should he expect from the niece of the fallen Thorne women?

He forced a shuttered expression onto his face. An old friend, this expression, well-used at the green baize table and a faithful ally in difficult negotiations. He would do nothing to show his displeasure, but only that which would gain a firmer foothold toward his goal. Cambria must be quaking in her shoes by now, wondering what he would do.

He turned to look at her. She, too, had her mask in place. Good. If she produced one tear, he would be tempted to throttle her. He strolled toward her. "I was surprised to hear about this enterprise, Miss Thorne."

She didn't back down. "That sounds a wee bit like a grievance."

"Not at all," he replied smoothly. "I only found it strange that the explanation was avoided last evening when I asked about the baths."

Her eyes sparked. "Are you saying we deliberately deceived you? You have no right to question. We may do whatever we wish at Thorne's Well."

His teeth ached to argue with her, but he forced himself to back down. "I expressed myself poorly, Miss Thorne. And, it seems, I assumed too much after your graciousness last night."

She hated losing the wind from her sails. Stiffly, she asked, "What was it you *assumed?*"

"Why," he said innocently, "that we would forget the feud, that we would be friendly neighbors. I cannot imagine why you would deliberately hide something that I was to discover anyway." Exultant, as his logic left her speechless, he added, "Unless you think I would be angry over your operating a business in the middle of my property."

Disbelieving eyebrows rose sharply. "Don't tell me you *approve?*"

Knowing the business would not exist after the end of July made Riordan expansive. "Why not? I, too, have my hand in several profitable ventures. This is very enterprising."

Still suspicious, she said, "Such geniality makes me wonder what you really want."

"I shall demand a subscription for the wear and tear on my road."

Her eyes narrowed at such easy acquiescence. As several tumblers clicked in his mind, he added, "And one other thing."

Her chin rose as if to congratulate herself on knowing there was something more he wanted. "Yes?"

"I shall offer my services to you . . . to help you make this a success. I have an interest in two small hotels in London, and one rather successful inn near Bath. I like to master the workings of a project when I take it over, and have learned quite a bit that might save you problems."

Cambria's eyes narrowed. "Such as?"

"Such as tricks customers try on inexperienced innkeepers.

Working out plans for emergencies that I certainly had no idea might occur.''

"My time is very limited, Riordan. I don't think—'' She looked toward Glendover for assistance.

To her dismay, Glendover agreed with Riordan. "You might be wise to accept, Cambria. The time you spend now will save you money on the other end. He's talking about things none of us know.''

"That depends,'' Cambria muttered, "What does he want in return?''

"Cambria!'' Glendover was shocked at her rudeness.

Riordan laughed. "It's all right. Cambria has the right idea. Never give anything away when you're in business.'' He gave her a cozening look. "I was hoping you would feed me now and then.''

She was trapped, but not going easily. "We'll trade directly, then, say an hour a day?''

Riordan produced a hurt look. "If you don't wish my help, Cambria, just tell me.''

She slumped. "When would you like to begin?''

"Tomorrow. We have almost two weeks before I go to Bude. If we work hard, we should be through most of it by then.''

"I have to leave at the end of the week,'' Glendover said. "Sounds like you came along just in time.''

Ah, Riordan thought, he had Cambria just where he wanted her, cut off from Glendover for part of each day. He would recruit Alistair to orchestrate activities keeping the young people together.

Cambria glared at Riordan. Just when she was beginning to like him, he became aggressive, forcing her into something she didn't want to do. "Meet me in the library at noon.'' Having forced his will upon her, the wretch moved toward Alistair and Mark to discuss the trespassers.

The girls crowded around Cambria, and Amelia whispered, "Who were those horrible people, Cambria?''

Cambria grimaced. "Men from London. To see the baths.''

Amelia burst into tears. "Oh dear, what if more of them come? What if they ruin your business?''

Cambria stared at her. "Amelia, don't be upset. If the business fails, it won't be the end of the world. I won't be destitute."

Amelia wiped her cheeks with her sleeve. "But we will. My mother and Diana borrowed the money from a *moneylender.*"

Horrified, Cambria grabbed Amelia's arm. "But why?"

Amelia sniffed. "They promised your mother they would see you find a good husband."

"I thought they were—"

"Rich?" Amelia shook her head. "Not at all. They sold most of their jewelry to give us a season. Don't tell them I told you, though. They don't want anyone to know."

"Dear heavens."

"So, you see, Cambria, the business has to succeed."

Chapter Ten

Cambria flew down the stairs. "Is his grace here yet?"

The maid looked up, her dust cloth stilled on the porcelain vase. "Yes, Miss Thorne. He ate the lunch you ordered for him. Then I put him the library as you asked."

"Thank you." Cambria rushed past her toward the library. "Blast the man," she muttered. "Why did I let him talk me into this?" She ran a hand over her hastily brushed hair and then slowed at the door. One deep breath and she let herself in.

"Good afternoon, Riordan. You're somewhat early, you know." Better attack than defend.

He looked up from a paper he was reading—one of her lists—with an amazed expression. "I see you are quite the organizer, Cambria."

The superior, *surprised* way he said it made her blood boil.

"So sorry to give your system such a shock, Riordan. Would you like to sit down . . . perhaps a burnt feather?"

That woke him up. His eyes widened, and though he tried to keep that hateful, shuttered look on his face, his lips twitched. Looking away, he replaced the list and reached for another. "Penmanship doesn't seem to belong on your list of virtues, Cambria. I can barely read this."

She bit back a retort. Her handwriting was perfectly lovely, but not if she was working through the night, her mind far more involved in calling Riordan names than on how many candles and sheets she owned. After Riordan left yesterday— first sticking his arrogant nose in her almost-finished baths to see if they met his lordly approval—she dropped everything, determined *not* to be found wanting. Yet here he was, verbally patting her on the head like some dimwitted aunt.

"Thank you for pointing that out, your grace. What would I do without your exceptional insight?"

His head snapped up like a startled owl. "A bit touchy today?"

She gave him an innocent look. "Have I not been in everything agreeable?" She perched on the edge of a chair. "Shall we begin?"

He nodded, but did not sit. "If you're ready, then conduct me to the guest-patrons' bedrooms."

Confused, she asked, "You want to see the bedrooms?"

His brows arched at her question, as if she should know better than to voice any protest, but should just trot gratefully wherever he wished. *Well, she'd had had enough,* for not only was he a stiff-rumped pain, but she had turned into a virago she didn't like any better. She stood and leaned her hands on the table. "All right, Riordan. Either you come down off your high horse, or this tutelage is at an end. Remember, I knew you when you had scabs on your knees, and I caught more fish than you."

He stared at her, his jaw grinding his teeth a half-inch shorter. He turned on his heel and left the room. She hurried ahead to lead him to the east wing. Once there, Riordan took over. In the first room, he stopped to consider a painting on the wall. "Is that a copy of a Rembrandt?"

She stepped closer. "No. Why would we want a copy?"

He took it off the wall. "That's not the point. If you leave something valuable in a paying guest's room, eventually someone will take it home." He circled the room and exited, stopping to lean the painting against the corridor wall.

Inside the second room, she watched as he moved to the

fireplace. "This piece," he said, plucking a squat crystal vase off the mantel, "is too fragile to be left here to be broken. Someone will knock it to the floor." A Dresden statue and a small oriental rug joined the vase in the hall.

He walked into the third room and halted in shock. "You're expecting royalty?"

"I thought ladies might like this room."

"The damned place is *white*. White *lace*. Do you have any idea what a pair of walking shoes or a pair of boots will do to this counterpane?"

"Surely not, Riordan. Who would do such a thing?" She paused. "I'll leave a little note in the room asking them to be careful."

He leaned his head against the wide door jamb. "Your first lesson Cambria . . . Stop expecting to be treated with the respect you're used to. Your only goal is to please the patrons enough to make a profit."

She hated his tone. "The minute they get here, I'll do just that. In the meantime I'm not going to spend the next two weeks being bludgeoned by your consequence and bullied into doing things your way."

She watched his face, amazed as he forced his muscles to relax and don another, more cajoling mask. This time he looked almost pleasant. "Very well, Cambria. You have three days to prepare yourself."

She frowned. This made no sense. "For what?"

This time his smile was real. "I've sent for a manager and a housekeeper to run this place. If you want it to succeed, you have to work behind the scenes. Mr. Bosworth works in my Bath hotel. And," he added with a hateful gleam in his eye, "I told him to bring some guests with him. I'm going to teach you the business with *real* people."

Mark walked in with a pleasant smile. "How are things going?"

Both Riordan and Cambria snarled in unison, "Just fine!"

* * *

"So," Alistair said, guiding his mount onto the Thorne's Well drive, "what you want me to do is keep Mark Glendover out of the way."

"Yes. I swear, the man pestered us every hour yesterday."

"At the same time I'm to push Mark and Ellie together." He grinned. "That won't be hard. Ellie adores Mark. She hangs on his every word."

"Get them to practice some songs together. They can entertain the guests when they get here."

"How are you progressing with Cambria?"

Riordan grinned. "Splendid. She hates being told what to do."

He smiled once more when he approached the circular drive. Outside the house, sitting grandly in a pony cart, was Sarah and two small children, her husky little boy and a tiny, red-haired replica of Sarah.

Glendover and Cambria stood nearby, laughing with the charming little family. At seeing Riordan arrive, Glendover strode forward. "Back to the lessons, eh, Langcliffe? And Alistair . . . welcome back."

"Thank you," Alistair said, letting the servants take the horses. "Riordan tells me there's a billiards table in the library. Do you play?"

Glendover grinned. "Yes. Do you wager, Singleton?"

Alistair hesitated. "Yes, but Riordan and I aren't much for high stakes." Riordan had a difficult time keeping a straight face. He hadn't expected Alistair's clever solution. Allying himself with his respected uncle would prevent criticism of Alistair's new, stringent habits.

Glendover looked surprised . . . and pleased. "The girls haven't come down yet, so come say hello to Cambria, and then we'll go inside."

As greetings were accomplished, Riordan kept his gaze on Cambria's thoughtful face. Damn, if the keen-witted girl hadn't laid him low yesterday. What a tongue in her sassy mouth, and what a temper when pushed too far! He hadn't expected to have such a grand time.

Sarah gave them an apologetic look. "I'd better get back,

now. Nurse is rather old, and though she won't admit it, she needs her afternoon nap." As they bid her goodbye, she reached for the reins and started the pony trotting down the long drive.

Riordan frowned. "Should she be driving around like that?"

Cambria watched Sarah go, a distant expression on her face. "She came to tell me something."

"The gossiping Improvement Society."

Her head snapped toward him. "She told you about that?"

"She wants you to come down and do battle with the ladies."

Cambria smiled. "She just likes to fight." She sobered, her thoughts troubled. "She said we have a new vicar. He stopped by to look over his new post. He's on his way to London to arrange for his things to be delivered to the vicarage. Did you employ him, Riordan?"

Confused, he asked, "A new vicar? No. Has Sarah spoken to him?"

She nodded. "She says he's asking questions about the Thornes."

Damn, his mother had done it. "Perhaps my solicitor has taken care of it. I shall send him a note of inquiry."

Cambria didn't look convinced, and he didn't blame her. How the devil was he to keep Cambria lulled and complacent if his mother was going to stir things up?

Cambria began walking toward the house. "Shall we go in? I've asked cook to send in trays for us both, since I haven't had time to eat."

Once settled in the library, Riordan finished reading Cambria's lists. "Will you be serving food in the bath area?"

"I hadn't thought I should. What do you think?"

"Liquids, yes, water or clear drinks. No chocolate or milk. Food, absolutely not. You can imagine the disruption to your schedule if you had to clear the rooms and completely refill those huge tubs. The patrons would want their entire scheduled time, yet it would put everyone back for the rest of the day." He remembered something else. "And no animals allowed, not even a dowager's favorite pet."

She looked worried. "Did someone do that to you?"

"I told you about my place in Bath? Well, I let two old

ladies take their snapping little lap dogs in with them. Pretty soon a servant came screaming about trouble in the lady's bath. I came running, and before I even sent the matron in to get permission to enter, I heard this awful howling. All I could think of was dead dogs and blood flowing in the water.'' He grinned. ''One of the dogs gave birth to a litter not too long after.''

She tried to look shocked that he would discuss such a thing in her hearing, but she was a country girl, and her laughter broke loose, full-throated and utterly enchanting. *Enchanting* . . . The word stuck in his head for a moment as he stood there dumbstruck. *This would never do.* Abruptly, he stood. ''Let's go down to the lake.''

She rose, confusion tinting her cheeks. ''The lake?''

''I want to inspect your boats. Speak to your boatmen.'' As she hesitated, he realized what that confusion meant. ''Cambria, when your guests see that lake they will want to go boating. They'll want entertainment.

''Entertainment?''

Cambria hurried into the library as the clock chimed seven in the morning. No more leisurely half-day sessions. Her practice guests would be here tomorrow. She and Riordan had worked until Mark dragged them out for dinner. Who would have believed there were so many intricacies to simple things like bathing schedules, reservations, deposits . . .

The man was a menace. Without referring to any record, any list of his own, he rattled off figures and cited examples as if they were written on the wall before him. She'd never seen anything like it, not even her own brother had shown the vast comprehension of Riordan Langcliffe.

Cambria's pen stopped writing in mid word—*what a splendid thought.* Absently, she tucked her pen in the compartment of her portable writing desk and twisted the cover back on the ink well. She'd been so worried about copying her lists out for

Bosworth this morning that she hadn't fully comprehended that Riordan had unknowingly enabled her to move to London far sooner than expected.

By the time her *ton* patrons arrived, Bosworth could be left with the business, and she could trot off with an easy mind. What a delightful bonus . . . and how very satisfying it felt that Riordan had no idea that she was even going. No, until she had Thorne's Well past the point of danger, she could not relax her guard.

She yawned again, then leaned her head against the gazebo cushion to rest her eyes. She would finish her copying in just a moment . . .

As Riordan and Alistair rode up the drive, they could see papers gusting up out of the gazebo and impaling themselves onto rose bushes. "I see Cambria out in the gazebo, fast asleep if I'm not mistaken."

"I'll help you gather the papers, Riordan."

Riordan waved him away. "Go on in. I'll do it." Amused, he made his way to the rose garden. As he plucked the papers up and made a stack of them—more of her lists—he made his way to the gazebo. Dark circles underlined Cambria's eyes. Pity stirred him, and an admiration he hadn't expected to feel. *Imagine, a hard working Thorne.*

It made him edgy, feeling *anything* for a Thorne. He nudged her foot with his boot. "Wake up, Cambria."

She stirred, then seeing him, straightened up and reached for her hair. He could see her blushing as she tamed the loose ends, but when she looked up, he realized it was as much anger as chagrin at being found asleep. Stubborn and proud, she lifted her chin. "I've been working for hours. Would you like breakfast now?"

"No." What he wanted was something to stop this *soft* feeling. A brisk walk would clear his head. "Let's go inspect the orchards."

She nodded and tucked her papers under the thick cushion. "Are you worried about our fruit supply this summer?"

He didn't want to insult her, but after she'd bragged over how she'd personally planted new trees and supervised the harvesting, he wasn't expecting much of anything. "I don't think you have any idea how much people eat when they are on holiday. You have to feed them twice as much, and they want treats between meals."

He stretched his long legs, impressed at how she kept stride with him. A *tall* woman was a novelty to him. As they strode along, he realized how comfortable it was walking with her. Most women were pests outdoors, and he'd never had any patience at picnics and ladies' games. His own mother might as well be indoors in her parlor.

"Here we are," Cambria said with a smug tone that made him lose all sympathy for her. He'd never met a female with so few female graces. At least she could sound modest . . . or even apologetic.

He walked into the orchard and looked around, *really* looked at the weed-free ground, the shallow troughs that efficiently fed water to the trees. He kept going, looking for some fault, but no suckers grew from the ground or the trunks or even around berry bushes, and in many places trees played host to grafted trees of other kinds.

"I am experimenting here," she explained, "to see how other things do in this soil and climate."

He had to ask. "How long have you been running Thorne's Well?"

"Almost five years. Phillip trained me for years before that."

He looked ahead, and then to the sides. In no direction could he see the edge of the orchard. "What kind of fruit do you grow?" he asked, not so much to find out, but to mask his amazement.

"Nuts and berries, too?

"Yes."

She stopped, tipping her head in thought. "Gooseberries, cherries, and peaches in June; raspberries, currants, crab apples, and apricots in July; almonds, blackberries, elderberries, mulberries, pears, and plums in August; quince, chestnuts, and apples in September, . . . and walnuts in October."

As she ran though her list, blatantly showing off, he determined not to show his incredulity. His mind, however, *finally* began clicking into operation. "You have added on to the orchards, haven't you?"

Her lips lifted. "You have a good memory, Riordan. And, yes, they used to be much smaller. I've been clearing ground and enlarging it since Phillip left for London."

"Are you selling the food, then?"

Her smile grew. She was baiting him, of course. "No."

"Then, what do you do with all this food?"

She grinned. "I'm giving something back to your people, Riordan. The entire population of the valley help themselves to your orchard."

Riordan and Cambria met Bosworth at the door. Behind Bosworth, guest-patrons were pouring out of two large coaches. Cambria stood beside him with a horror-stricken look.

Riordan found his voice first. "Good grief, Bosworth, you didn't have to bring so many people. This will practically fill the patrons' wing."

Bosworth's long, aristocratic face turned pale. "We have another half dozen coming tomorrow. Will that be a problem?"

Sharing her panic, Riordan looked at Cambria. "The west wing. What will we need? More beds?"

Frantically, Cambria shook her head. "Airing, fires, cleaning . . ."

"Linens?"

"No . . . yes. I'll need more counterpanes."

"Dishes, knives, forks . . ."

Cambria nodded, already on the move. "The attic," she called. "Trunks in the attic."

Riordan looked around the enormous family dining room. Every chair was filled. Servants and masters hung over their food in various drooping poses, gratefully fueling their exhausted bodies. Candles lit at dawn were still burning.

Amelia stood up. "I'm going to bed. Coming Ellie?"

Ellie stuffed the last finger of toast into her mouth and rose from her chair. "Umm."

Alistair, long since asleep on one arm near his plate, did not hear them.

Mark shook him awake. "Come along, Singleton. You're snoring and keeping the rest from their food."

Cambria rose. "I think I'll just take one last look."

Riordan smiled. "I'll come with you." He stood slowly, creaking, he was sure, like an old man.

The walked side by side to the west wing, stopping at the first bedroom. "Where did you find the counterpanes, Cambria?"

She rested her back against the door jam. "Sewed them. Old draperies from the attic. What do you think, will they do?"

He draped his arm over her shoulder. "I'd never have guessed." He yawned. "I'm going to sleep all day."

She lifted her shoulder and nudged him off. "Be awake by noon. You have the first shift rowing the boat."

Chapter Eleven

Riordan glanced toward Cambria as they strolled down the sunny road toward the bridge. "How does it feel to take a day off?"

She sighed. "Like my last day of freedom."

Riordan nudged her shoulder playfully, sending her footsteps skittering to the side. He grabbed her sleeve and pulled her back beside him. "Are you saying you're not going to let your new manager do his job? I knew you were a bossy female, but I didn't know you were this bad."

"I left him alone today, didn't I?"

"Ah, but Bosworth is just reconnoitering without you there to bother him. When the patrons arrive tomorrow . . . that will tell the tale."

"He's a bit old for the job, isn't he?"

"That's to charm the old ladies. You should see them fluttering their eyes around him. In fact," he teased, "weren't your aunts fluttering their eyes at dinner last night?" As a matter of fact, they were *not* doing so, which surprised him immensely.

"No, they were trying to stay awake while you and Bosworth bored them with talk of business."

She kicked a stone in his path, smiling when he kicked it back toward her. "I remember walking down this road with you when we were children. I always remember those days as sunny, as though it never rained."

"My mother kept me home. Little dukes in training were pampered for fear they would get sick and die before making more little dukes."

She looked up at him, a smile playing on her lips. "I didn't know she pampered you, Riordan. You never said so."

He grinned back. "I wasn't about to admit it when you were allowed to do whatever you wanted. It was too humiliating. My father tried to make her change her mind, but she got upset, so he let her have her way."

They reached the bridge and stopped. She looked down toward the river below the falls. "After you left, I spent a lot of time with your father."

His heart jolted. "You did?" he said in a deceptively calm voice. "When he came visiting?"

"Oh, no. He used to sit by the river with a fishing pole in his hand. He didn't fish. He just sat there."

He searched for the right words. "What did you talk about?"

She looked at him and smiled. "You." Riordan couldn't utter a sound, but Cambria went on, "I used to think I was a very interesting girl, getting your father to listen so carefully to my every word. Now I realize that he just liked hearing about you."

Riordan let the picture linger in his mind, afraid to examine it too closely lest hidden barbs be present. Later, he thought, later he would look for the substance of this gift from Cambria.

Later . . . after he was gone. He had no more reason to linger here at Thorne's Well. He'd watched her with Mark Glendover and knew that Cambria did not love her brother's friend, but that she was willing to marry him. He'd watched Glendover with Ellie and saw that sparks fairly flew between them, but they would never acknowledge their affection.

He was leaving for Bude tomorrow. With Bosworth in place he would at last have his spy at Thorne's Well. At any hint of marriage, Riordan would be immediately notified. Thorne's

Well was three days from Bude, and, after he returned, Langcliffe Hall was less than a day's ride. He was prepared to counter whatever move Cambria made.

He dare not stay here any longer. The sensual promise of their first meeting now hovered too near, sensitized by each chance touch, enhanced each day as her smile seemed sweeter, each little twist of her lips more charming as she studied her endless lists. As he watched the dark circles fade away, replaced by a radiant confidence engendered by his successful tutelage, he knew he'd already come too close.

He'd never worked *with* someone like this. Never shared the accelerated pulse as a faint idea went from plan to success. He'd never met a man whose intellect matched his as Cambria's did. Work had always been a serious business, even grim. With Cambria, laughter was likely to break out at the most ridiculous times, usually when it ought to be suppressed.

When he'd realized that he was counting down the bittersweet days left to them, he knew it was past time to make a break.

Kicking a rock off to his own side of the road, Riordan started them moving once more, this time toward Lakeview.

He studied the house. Peck, Riordan's builder, already had his enormous crew swarming over the house. The progress had amazed even him. They had already repaired the roof and installed new windows. The walls, inside and out, were dotted with holes, evidence of their all-too successful search for dry rot. This part of the process was nearly finished, and the walls were ready for patching. The next phase would move more swiftly, probably finishing before Cambria's birthday.

He would *not* be here to witness that event.

Cambria strolled alongside Riordan, content just to be with him on this last day of their association. She could not even say goodbye, for she still felt compelled to keep her return sojourn to London a secret.

Efficient Bosworth had fulfilled her hope of freeing her to leave for London. Just as Mark predicted, she did not wish to go husband-hunting, but would far rather marry him, her good friend. They were so comfortable with each other. Far more comfortable than with Riordan.

Her throat tightened. *Riordan.* A dangerous man in ways she'd never expected. Each day when he left, she vowed she'd be stronger the next day, but the moment he came striding into the room, her Thorne blood responded. Those blasted laughing eyes and the heady challenge in his smile *intoxicated* her. How could she be so stirred, she wondered in dismay, without her mind's permission? How could just the warmth of sitting next to him make her skin tingle? How could his scent make her ache inside? She even liked to hear him breathe.

Even so—far more dangerous—was the resurgence of their old friendship. She'd never realized how childhood memories could bind people together almost like family. Or that the very feud that separated them somehow solidified that link. She'd never realized that the interchange between minds could be so exciting, as though they sometimes shared thoughts yet unspoken. She'd never expected to become friends again, but they had. She'd been so sure she could never trust him again, but she *almost* had.

Then there was her runaway imagination. Completely unconstrained, her traitor mind spun tales of them together, during sleep or wide awake, bombarding her with *what ifs*. Even as she scolded and tried to reason, it went on its headstrong way.

Only her vow saved her from her foolishness. Like a harsh taskmaster, the Thorne's Well deadline loomed up, forcing her to leave daydreams behind her and take charge of her life. *Never waver.*

Still . . . she didn't want this last idyllic day to end.

Shaking herself from her reverie, Cambria looked up to find they had arrived at Lakeview. ''Good grief,'' she said. ''It looks like an ant hill with those men crawling all over the house. Or termites. Look at the holes.'' She walked slowly around the house.

By the time she reached full circle, she realized that all this building was making her anxious, unsettled. It was happening far too quickly. All these changes *stirred up* things. It was bad enough that her own life was changing, but now the valley itself was changing. When she returned home, strangers would still be living at Thorne's Well—paying patrons to be sure—but things would never be the same.

She looked for Riordan, but he was nowhere in sight. She moved toward the front door, only to find him inside studying a note in his hand. She stepped inside. "What is it, Riordan?"

He looked up, a distant look on his face. "My mother's coming by tomorrow."

"Perhaps she wants to see the house."

Riordan came back to reality with a thud. His mother would certainly want to see the house. What was he to tell Cambria? He'd wanted Cambria to be completely out of the valley before his mother arrived to claim Lakeview. He must prevent the duchess from accidentally meeting any of the Thornes, for who knew what she might say? The aunts were back at Thorne's Well now, making the situation far too combustible.

He answered cautiously. "I shall have to stay one more day and find out what she wants. I should have her on her way before the sun sets. Can you keep your aunts from coming to the house or to the village? I don't think either of us wants them to meet."

Her eyes widened at the thought. "Yes, I will."

They moved back onto the road. "Where shall we go next? To the village? I'd hoped to see you do battle with your enemies."

She shook her head. "The merchants are serving our needs, and that's all I care about." Her eyes twinkled with mischief. "You hate to miss it, don't you? You think it won't work if you aren't directing every move."

He frowned. "Are you saying I'm domineering?"

She stepped back, grinning. "Heavens, no. Tyrannical, overbearing perhaps, but never domineering."

He moved closer. "I've been very patient with you, Cambria. Haven't you noticed?"

She backed away again, this time with a laugh in her voice. "I did, indeed. Poor Riordan. It must have been quite a strain."

He stepped forward and grasped her shoulders. "You little devil . . ." He stopped, staring as she, too, stilled at his touch.

Her laugh settled into a sigh as her gaze met his. Something sizzled between them, something compelling . . .

He pulled her closer, his eyes looking now at her mouth. He *needed* to feel the touch of her lips. He leaned down—and hearing a sound behind him, realized how many eyes were watching this same drama, were holding their breath to see if their duke would kiss the lady.

Dropping his hands, he stepped back and began the trek back to Thorne's Well, his entire system protesting its loss.

Once out of sight of the house, she broke the silence at last. "Riordan, do you think your mother will want to live at Lakeview once she sees the house again?"

Riordan's heart sank. Anything he said now would be a lie, and he did not want to leave with any more deceit between them. "I reside at Langcliffe Hall, as does my mother. She travels back and forth to London, but she spends the season in town. She's not going to bother you, Cambria. I'll send her on her way."

"What about after the house is finished? Will she come at all?"

He stalled. "Why do you ask?"

"I know you were teasing Talia about your mother earlier, but my aunts . . . they still harbor resentment toward your mother—"

He was too stunned to reply. *Easy, let the girl talk.* "Is that right?"

"Yes . . . you may have noticed Diana's reserve toward you . . . She seems to think . . . ." She sighed. "I shouldn't be telling you this."

"Perhaps it might clear the air."

"Promise *we* won't fight about it."

He raised his hand. "Truce."

She took a restorative breath. "Diana says that your father was too soft on his wife, and he should not have let her take you away. Talia says that love makes people blind to others' faults."

Riordan frowned in confusion. What was she talking about?

"I didn't make that clear, did I? You see, Diana thinks you'll be like your mother and hate us, and Talia says you were so much like your father that your mother could not change you.''

Looking down with her hands clenched together, she began again. ''I'm babbling . . . but, what I'm trying to say is that I don't want trouble starting again, and my aunts are perfectly willing to go into battle with your mother. There was so much animosity between them . . .''

The words slipped out. ''And whose fault was that?''

Startled, she looked up at him. ''How much do you remember before you left, Riordan?''

It took him a moment to find the words . . . and the willingness to give her what she wanted. ''I remember coming to Thorne's Well with my father. I remember you.''

''What else do you remember . . . any conversation about *why* your mother took you away?''

''I don't think it was any secret. My father was having an affair with one of your aunts . . . or both.''

She closed her eyes. ''Dear heavens.''

''They probably left that part out.''

Her eyes flew open. ''No, you've got it all wrong, Riordan.''

Fiercely, he ground out, ''I remember my mother's tears. She told me everything.''

''Diana was right, then. You do hate us.''

Riordan snapped his mouth shut. This hopeless conversation could only lead to an immediate rift, the very last thing he wanted on this last day with her. ''Let's leave it alone, Cambria. Each of us believes what our family told us.''

She touched his sleeve, her fingers trembling. ''But you hate us for no reason. It's not fair.''

His curiosity stirred. *Was* there something he didn't know? He lowered his voice to calm her. ''Tell me what you think the truth is.'' He waited, but she just looked at him, examining his face as if reading his mind. Then, sighing, she shook her head. ''It would do more harm than good, Riordan. Let it alone.''

''Harm? Who would be harmed? The damned Thornes?''

She snatched her hand away. Blast, he thought, as her face closed up and she walked quickly up the road, he should have kept his mouth shut and let her blurt it all out. He'd come to Thorne's Well for the truth, and if he only heard what she thought was truth—twice-told lies—he should not have cut her off with his damned temper.

He caught up with her and snaked his arm around her waist, bringing her to a stop. Turning to face him, she gave him an anguished look. "All right, Riordan—the person who would get hurt is *you*. If you want the truth, ask your mother. Now let me go."

As he stepped back, tears pooled in her eyes. "I knew you were hiding something from us, but I didn't want to believe it. Now that I know how you really feel about *the damned Thornes,* I want you to stay away. If my aunts, especially Talia, found out what you think of them, they would be terribly hurt."

"Convicted without a trial, Cambria?"

"Don't tell me you have an explanation for this, too?"

"Last time you didn't believe me. I warned you I'd never offer again."

Her voice shook. Very formally, she said, "Thank you for your help these last few days. If you wish to withdraw Bosworth, I will understand."

"Let him stay. He has nothing to do with this."

That stopped her. She nodded, then, resolute, she went on. "I shall send Alistair home with your horse, and after that we shall be pleasant when we meet. I do not wish a war between us, but I won't have you hurting my family." Without another word, she turned away, left him standing alone in the road.

Cambria kicked a rock off the road as her tears fell silently to the ground. No heaving sighs, no wrenching sobs. Just let her heartache pour out like a torrent, full force, once and for all. Suspecting that he'd kept some secret hidden hadn't made a bit of difference. Discovering that it was *insurmountable* was almost a relief, for now she needn't make any more choices. One swift fall of the sword, and it was over.

The violence of his feelings toward her aunts had frightened her. No use asking herself why he came to see them, why he bothered to help her. That questioning path would only get her lost, let her wander around in a forest full of questions when

only he knew the answers. Perhaps the next secret uncovered
would be worse. Even now, it could be coiled silently, waiting
to strike. *Retreat.* Build her walls higher just in case.

Furious with himself, Riordan watched Cambria move farther
and farther away. He could barely believe it. The blasted girl
had banished him.

Cambria's words rang in his ears. *Ask his mother for the
truth?* The last thing in the world he wanted to do was corner
his mother and try to get a straight answer. He was still reeling
over her deception about Lakeview. What other secrets might
she have?

Indeed, he thought with a sudden feeling of urgency, what
other secrets might his mother have? And, heaven help him,
did he want to know?

He watched Cambria disappear around the bend. His throat
tightened as he realized that this might be his very last glimpse
of her.

Alone on the road, disillusioned with her old friend.

Riordan turned and walked the other way.

The early morning sun accompanied Riordan on his way to
Lakeview. With a strange feeling, Riordan watched the coach
pass him on the road. Cambria's first London customers, arriving at last, and she'd been right. He had the greatest urge to
be there to see that all went well.

Today his mother would arrive—and be swiftly dispatched.
He'd posted a woodsman to sit at the bakery's outdoor tables
and watch for her. The inn's ostler's were richer by several
coins for the same purpose. After all was in place, he'd come
out to Lakeview to wait for her arrival. Peck, Langcliffe Hall's
chief carpenter, and his crew were inside wreaking a horrendous
destruction of all things damp, rotten, or broken. He couldn't
have planned his mother's arrival at a better time.

Alistair was on his way to Langcliffe Hall, subdued and
silent.

Riordan had spent a sleepless night scourging his thoughts
of any lingering anguish over his parting with Cambria. He'd

looked at the situation from a logical point of view, renewed his goals in this matter, coldly shut off any regrets. He knew exactly what he was about. Clearheaded for the first time in days.

He yawned and wandered over to a shady spot. Yawned again and let himself down to the base of the tree. So tired . . .

"Have you lost your mind, Riordan?"

Where the devil was he? He slowly pulled his drooping head to an upright position—judging by the creaking pain, something his neck did *not* like—and tried to focus his eyes. The first thing he saw was a woman's foot, tapping furiously beside a firmly planted, unfurled parasol. "Hello, Mother. I didn't hear you coming."

"I suppose you are sleeping off the aftereffects of a drinking bout, just like—"

He cut her off midword. "That's enough, Mother." He stood, ignoring the fact that he couldn't feel the toes in his right foot. Or the entire leg, for that matter. "You know me better than that."

"This is the very way your father began, Riordan. You've only been here a few days and already these women have affected you. You have been out to see them, haven't you?"

He had the strongest inclination to lie. Hell, he felt like a child again, listening to her rant on about how he must never be like his father. But, he was long past that. In truth, she should be as well. "Mother, I am responsible for our properties, all of them, including Lakeview. I cannot cower from our neighbors for fear I might become infected with some imaginary spell you claim these perfectly normal women might conjure up."

She reached up her sleeve and pulled out a lace handkerchief. Dabbing at sudden tears, she whimpered, "You're breaking my heart, Riordan." Then she frowned. "Where is Alistair? You said in your note that he was staying with you."

"He's gone back to Langcliffe Hall." He paused. "I also

told you not to come here.'' She raised her chin and ignored him.

Riordan tested his weight on his tingling leg, wiggled his toes to wake them up. ''Do you want to see the inside of the house?'' That horror should take her mind off his imaginary sins.

''Peck is making it habitable?''

He bit back a smile. ''Something like that.'' He limped carefully over the uneven ground.

''I've always loved this place. When those women are gone, it will be perfect. I shall set up my household here. It's less than two days to London, and my friends would love the old Roman baths.''

A dangerous subject. ''Mother, Thorne's Well belongs to the Thornes.''

''For now, it does, but when you get rid of them—''

He stopped her with a detaining hand. No sane man shared secret plans with an hysteria-prone woman, but something must be said to curtail her natural bent for mischief. Looking into her confused eyes, he explained. ''Miss Thorne has plenty of time to marry, Mother. If you want to live here, you must make up your mind to be peaceful.''

''*I* am to be peaceful? You're taking their side already?''

''Not at all. Miss Thorne will require the same from her aunts.''

''You and Miss Thorne have discussed this between you?

Riordan closed his eyes and asked for patience. ''She is concerned that her aunts might be difficult. She does not like contention, nor do I.''

''So this *peacemaking* is designed to make Miss Thorne happy?''

Without replying, he turned and firmly guided her down to the house. Two coaches stood waiting in the cleared area before the house. Scattered around the yard, sitting on stumps and bits of luggage, were several servants and two coachmen. His mother's companion, Hettie, sat inside the largest coach fanning her face. His mother's idea of traveling included all she needed for the smallest comfort.

Just outside the house, he gave her a hint of what she might expect should she continue her tirade. "In order to avoid trouble that might erupt if you reside here, I have considered transforming the property into orchards and game areas for our table at Langcliffe Hall."

She gasped. "But the Thornes have foraging rights, Riordan. You would never do that. Not only that," she said, waving toward the noise inside the house, "you've already begun repairs. Why, if it's to be ready in a few days, would you think of destroying it?"

He shook his head. "I still have time to change my mind, Mother. This won't be ready for several months. Come and see for yourself."

One glance at the house's interior made Lady Langcliffe stop in shock. Rooted to one spot, she sent a horrified glance around the foyer, up the staircase, and then encompassed walls and windows.

"Where are the furnishings? The paintings?

"Our old factor stripped the house when he left."

"Oh, no!"

A small anger touched him. "What did you expect, Mother? It's been abandoned for almost twenty years, and everything would have been ruined anyway." She began to cry. His heart softened at her dismay. It was a tricky business maintaining her happiness, yet holding the reins of command firmly in his hands.

Over the years, their relationship had gone through several phases. After leaving Lakeview, she'd used Riordan as a sounding board for her fury with Lord Langcliffe, detailing his sins for Riordan's young ears. Fiercely protective, Riordan reluctantly gave up his love for his beloved father, seeing him instead as the monster who had hurt his mother.

Over the difficult years it took Riordan to claw his way past her motherly skeins of protective worry, he'd become impatient, exasperated. Surprised at her ferocity against his spending limits when he finally gained control, he marveled that his mother did not *hear* what she did not *like*.

Their paths diverged then, she to whatever entertainment she might contrive, and he rabidly compulsive to ensure that poverty never snapped at their ankles again. But now—since the mystery of Thorne's Well came to light—Riordan saw yet another side of his mother. After his talk with Cambria the previous day, he could not eject the nagging worry that his mother hid more than one secret from him.

When he was a boy, he'd longed to wreak revenge on his mother's enemies, make them *sorry*. But now—like a hangman presented with the very real prospect that the condemned might be innocent—he wavered. As a man who prided himself on justice, he must be sure of the truth before he took the last damning step of giving Thorne's Well to his mother.

But not, as Cambria so naively suggested, by asking his mother for that truth. Rountree, the bloodhound, would begin that assignment as soon as Riordan's note reached him.

"Riordan," she said, "I do hope that I may have some say in how the house is decorated?"

"Once we have determined the house to be sound and the structural work is done, you may have *carte blanche*, Mother. You may begin in early August. Until then, you must not interfere with my plans here. Go to London and look through the warehouses, buy things, make plans."

He touched her elbow. *"August*. Do you understand?"

Visibly, she pulled herself together. "Of course."

As they picked their way from room to room, Riordan's mind drifted, seeing the rooms in Cambria's eyes. Then, catching himself at it, he evicted the thought. Even at a distance, she drew him.

Lady Langcliffe leaned out an open window facing Thorne's Well. "Have you succumbed to their wiles?"

Would she never let it rest? Obtusely as possible, he asked, "Succumbed to whom, mother?"

"The Thornes, of course."

"All of them?"

She turned, annoyed. "Don't play with me, Riordan."

He sobered. The entire exercise was ridiculous. He need not answer to her, nor did he have any intention of doing so. "I met them all—the two aunts and their daughters—and the heiress, Cambria Thorne.''

She casually examined her nails. "What are they like?"

"After twenty years, they have matured as one might expect. Lady Maxwell wears spectacles and Lady Waterson's fingers are mud-daubed from her seedlings or scratched from her roses." There, that should do it.

The tension in her face eased. "And their daughters . . . do they look like their mothers?"

"Not at all. They are petite, both of them, like their fathers. One is boisterous and into silly mischief and the other is a shy girl who likes housewifery."

She seemed surprised that things might have veered so far from her expectations. Then, watching him closely, she asked, "And the heiress?"

Knowing he dare not pass Cambria off as insignificant, he chose to overplay it. "I've begged her to be mine, but she won't have me."

His mother searched his face, stopping at the lopsided smile with which he'd delivered his speech. "You aren't smitten, then?"

He bypassed the question. "She's a Thorne. If I married her, the Thorne blood would mingle with Langcliffes forever. Our ancestors would turn over in their graves."

While she examined his answer for deception, he changed the subject. "Alistair said you needed money. Some contretemps with Rountree?"

Her shoulders squared and her chin arched up. "Wretched man. Why do you keep him?"

"He's a genius, mother. And very loyal." And devious and clever and intelligent beyond the scope of the usual solicitor.

"Well, *I* find him uncooperative and insolent."

"Tell me what the problem is, Mother . . . money?"

"I've run over my allowance, and he refuses to give me more without your approval."

"How much over?"

"Nine hundred." Seeing his shocked expression, her jaw tightened. "It's nothing to you. You're rich as Midas, everyone says so. Considering that you spend all your time making money like the veriest cit, you might at least see to my needs.''

''Nine hundred for *what?*''

She hunched her shoulders as if he'd attacked her. ''A few changes to the town house.'' Mulishly, she didn't like being questioned.

''Then,'' he reflected, trying to be reasonable, when every tenet he espoused, every management rule he followed, screamed in outrage, ''you should have sent the bills for the decorating to me.''

She gave him a coquettish look. ''You'll give me the money?''

''Of course. How often do you indulge?''

She leaned forward and kissed his cheek. ''Thank you darling.''

He took her arm, ''Let's get you on your way to London.''

She resisted. ''You said I might tell your workers what I wanted.''

''This place is unsafe, you cannot stay here.''

''The inn, then.''

''The inn is unfit, Mother. You wouldn't last an hour there.''

Her eyes narrowed. ''I'm too tired to go another mile.''

''If you stay overnight, I won't be here to see you off. I'm going to Bude and will be gone before you awaken.''

That didn't faze her. In fact, it cheered her up. ''Very well. Give me a draft now, and tomorrow I shall go to London.'' At his obvious relief over her capitulation, she smiled sweetly. ''In the meantime, do you have any ready coin with you?''

Riordan sat downstairs in the inn's common room nursing a glass of hot mulled cider. He'd learned the first night to avoid the liquor served here. They served nothing but heel-tap—dregs from the bottom of bottles—well-diluted and rebottled. He'd been down here for over three hours, unable to believe that his mother hadn't come running down the stairs, screaming over some obscene thing in her room.

Of course, she did travel with her own linens and mattress.

Perhaps her night might remain undisturbed. Even though she must be asleep by now, she would waste no time leaving the inn tomorrow.

He rose to go upstairs, well pleased. He'd planned the entire matter in his usual organized way and could go to Bude without a single worry.

Chapter Twelve

Strolling into the breakfast room, Cambria stopped short of the sight of Diana's drumming fingers. "Please don't tell me there's something else is wrong. Two of our kitchen maids haven't come up from the village, and Cook is throwing a fit."

"You're not going to like this any better. The butcher refuses to send up our order, as does the baker. I sent Mark down to Pick Hill to set up deliveries. Can you think why they would do this, Cambria?"

Riordan? Surely he wasn't retaliating, was he? "I don't know, and I can't go down now to find out. I'll send a note to them."

Cambria rushed down to the foyer where Bosworth was just striding through the front door. He smiled. "Relax, Miss Thorne. I've met Havenshire, and he only has two passengers in the coach. After the last two weeks, this will seem very tame, indeed."

The front door opened. Her heart lurched as the doorman bowed to the guests. "Hello, Miss Thorne," Havenshire said.

"Come meet your first guests." Like a proud new father, he made the introductions.

They were elderly ladies—two sisters—who seemed as anxious as Cambria. "What a lovely home you have, Miss Thorne. We are so excited to be first. We couldn't believe our luck to get on the list, but Havenshire is our cousin, and he slipped us in."

Cambria began to relax. "I'm sure you would have been his first choice in any case." She motioned a footman closer. "Our servant will take you to your rooms, and when you are ready, just step out into the hall and someone will take you to the conservatory for a little tea."

As their entourage passed by, Havenshire murmured, "I was just about to tell Bosworth that I have five coaches coming later, twelve people in all. Tomorrow, there will be two couples coming to the house and four men who will stay at the inn." He smiled. "Aren't you pleased?"

She gulped. "I'm simply speechless, Lord Havenshire."

Amazing man, Bosworth. He never blinked.

After Havenshire trooped upstairs, she and Bosworth looked at each other with mutual alarm. "I'll notify the kitchen," he said, hurrying away.

Cambria motioned to a footman. "Go out and tell our servants to bring in game for the table." Then she rushed upstairs to warn the maids.

The footman came to the parlor door, a look of abject misery on his face. "I'm sorry, Miss Thorne. Langcliffe's woodsmen won't let our servants hunt on their land, not even to gather wood. They shot over their heads and told them not to trespass."

Diana looked up. "I suppose Riordan's left them instructions."

Cambria shook her head. "He wouldn't have done that, Diana." Surely Riordan hadn't done such a petty thing just because she'd banished him.

"I told you not to trust him, Cambria. He's probably behind

the trouble in the village as well.'' She gave Cambria a prodding look. ''You didn't have a fight, did you?''

''Of course not.'' Blast, she should have kept her mouth shut and not made such a powerful enemy. ''I'll walk down in the morning and talk to the merchants myself.''

Diana murmured, ''I dread telling her. She was up half the night.''

Cambria froze with her hand on the door. More unpleasant news? Cambria turned the knob and entered. ''What's wrong now?''

Sarah was at the dining room table. Her infant daughter sat on her lap, her hands full of biscuits. ''Sorry to bring you bad news, Cambria.''

''The inn is full,'' Diana said angrily. ''Our male guests will have to sleep here. Lady Langcliffe, it seems, has taken over the inn.''

''She's still here? I thought she just came by to see Riordan.''

''Riordan left, but his mother stayed.''

Sarah offered a look of pity. ''He left her a bag of money. The first thing she did was demand the entire third floor. Bass didn't care, he just charged her for all the rooms. Then this morning, she paid him to put up a partition in the common room so she could have a private entrance.''

Sarah reached down to pluck one of the cookies out of the child's bulging cheeks. ''Bass thought she was leaving—what's a duchess doing in his wretched place, anyway?—but what could he say?''

Cambria sank into a chair. ''What is she *doing* here?''

''She brought the new vicar. Early this morning, she called a meeting of the Thornedale Improvement Society. Everyone went.''

Cambria braced her elbows on the table and held her head in her hands. ''Do I want to know why?''

''No,'' they all agreed.

She groaned. ''Tell me anyway.''

Talia supplied the answer. ''She wants the ladies to march

on Thorne's Well. It seems we are carrying on immoral practices out here.''

"Miss Thorne, are you awake?'' Her bedroom door creaked open.

She woke with a start. The sun had barely risen. "Yes?''

The maid sounded worried. "There are wagons spread across the road down by Lakeview.''

Cambria lay still for a moment, then a surge of furious energy filled her. "Tell Bosworth to have a half-dozen male servants on the front drive in thirty minutes. Do not awaken my family.'' The maid skuttled out.

Cambria threw back the covers. "So the duchess wants her way at Thorne's Well, too, does she? Well, she's not facing a money-hungry innkeeper or a bunch of frightened merchants this time.''

Bosworth pointed toward Lakeview. "There's a ducal coach in the yard. Looks like the duchess is here.''

Cambria wondered what the workmen would think if she marched into the house and strangled their duchess on the spot. They pulled over just short of the wagon barricade. Her servants hopped down while Cambria and Bosworth walked into the house.

Inside, men leaned over banisters and sat on scaffolding while a petite, blonde-haired lady barked orders at a large, grizzled man. "I'm telling you, Peck, to work on my bedroom *first.*''

Peck folded his arms across a broad, muscular chest. "His grace gave us a schedule, Lady Langcliffe. He was very specific.''

The duchess bristled. "My son said I might fix this house how I wished, and I'm telling you—''

"Hello,'' called Cambria. "I'd like to speak to the man in charge.''

The duchess whirled, glaring. She looked at Cambria, her

delicate face twisted in outrage. "How dare you come into my house!"

Cambria glared back. "How dare you block our road?"

The men sprawled around the room looked at each with grins and settled down for an interesting interlude. Cambria looked directly toward Peck. "Are you in charge? Are those your wagons blocking the road?"

He slid a nervous look toward Lady Langcliffe. "Aye, I'm Peck."

"By law, we have access to this roadway. I have brought servants to move the wagons, but I'd like to do it peacefully."

Lady Langcliffe marched toward Cambria. "Miss Thorne, I gather?"

"That's right," she returned. "Owner of Thorne's Well."

The duchess, short as she was, managed to look down her nose at Cambria. "Well, not for long."

Cambria ignored her. "Peck, I also need the woodsmen to stop brandishing their guns at my servants. We have the right to hunt these woods. Evidently, Lord Langcliffe forgot to advise them of this."

"Peck," warned the duchess, "you'll do nothing of the sort."

Cambria continued, "Lord Langcliffe will be very unhappy when he learns of this rudeness. As you know, he has been a guest in our house almost every day helping me get the baths organized—"

"Where you, no doubt, seduced him," the duchess screeched.

"No," she said coldly, "where I was working with Lords Havenshire and Ragsdale."

Her hand fluttered to her throat. "Havenshire?"

"They're on the subscription committee for the baths. Your wagons will be in the way of several members of the *ton* in another hour or two."

"I don't believe it."

"I don't care what you think. I want those wagons moved." Cambria looked at Peck, improvising as she went. "Lord Langcliffe and I are *very* good friends. Only a few days ago, he brought me to the house to ask my advice. Some of my ideas are probably in your plans.''

The duchess looked faint. ''He took you through my house? Why would he do such a thing?''

An idea popped into Cambria's mind. Did she dare? *Yes.* ''Why would a gentleman take a lady through his house?''

The duchess's chest heaved. ''He's asked you to marry him?''

''Nothing is official.'' Cambria stepped toward Peck. ''If you wish verification of my rights on this property, you only have to ask the villagers. Riordan will be back in a few days, but I need this done now.''

His face tight, Peck deliberated for a few tense seconds, then nodded toward a worker. ''Go tell the woodsmen to leave their servants alone.'' He waved his hand toward the rest. ''Get out and help get those wagons moved.'' Looking back at Cambria, he said, ''Anything else?''

''Yes, actually. When you're rebuilding the kitchen, don't tear out the ovens and fireplace. They're my favorite part of the house.''

Peck's tension dissolved. ''I told his grace that was a fine decision.''

Lady Langcliffe leaned on her unfurled parasol, her chin pointing at Cambria. ''You think you've won, don't you? Well, don't be too sure. Riordan is a hard man when he wants his way. He's only being nice until after July, when you and your aunts will be gone. I'm surprised he can even *pretend* to like you when he's hated the Thornes all his life.''

Cambria winced with each vitriolic word. *The ring of truth . . .*

No fool, the duchess knew it. ''When he found out your brother was dead, he put aside everything to concentrate on getting rid of you. If you don't believe me, ask his solicitor or my brother, Lord Moulton.''

''Lord Moulton? . . . Riordan's uncle? . . . the man she'd been sending the vicar's reports to?'' Moulton who knew of the neglect of Lakeview? An ache began in her throat and spread outward. *Riordan had lied?* When she'd seen Riordan's

hidden fury on the road the other day, had that been the *real* Riordan Langcliffe?

She turned to Bosworth. "Why did he send you to us, Bosworth?"

A flicker of guilt crossed his face. His voice, however, rang true. "To make the baths profitable. God's truth, Miss Thorne."

Profitable for whom . . . for the predator, Riordan? She'd been a trusting, gullible fool. How he must have laughed behind her back.

Like mother, like son. She took a deep breath. "Lady Langcliffe, don't push me too far. If you do, you will regret it."

Chapter Thirteen

Cambria opened her eyes slowly, uneasy about something . . . oh, yes . . . guilt for dismissing Bosworth yesterday. The baths had gone so smoothly with him in charge. If, indeed, his job was to make the baths profitable, she should have left him in place. He seemed so sincere, so very sure his master had only her interests at heart . . . yet, what was that guilty expression she'd seen on his face?

That made two men—Bosworth and Alistair—who protested Riordan's innocence. Alistair's face had fallen in dismay when she explained he must leave. Her cousins were not any happier. Indeed, a measure of coldness had crept into their manner with her. Talia, too, took Riordan's side.

Cambria moved through her ablutions with swift efficiency, clinging to the one cheerful thought that would chase away her gloom. *They were making money.* Lots of money. With cautious optimism, she floated down the stairs, stopping short at the sight of milling gentlemen patrons in the foyer. *What the devil?* Mark looked up with a grin on his face. Servants' arms were loaded with what looked like every rifle or musket in the valley.

Cambria stepped down beside Havenshire who held a gun of his own. "What are you doing?" she whispered.

He murmured back, "The live-out servants aren't coming . . . afraid of the duchess. She says she will remember those who crossed her." Cambria quailed at the thought of what she must do now. . . but the duchess must be stopped.

And, what about the guns in the hands of her patrons? "Surely, you aren't asking the patrons to hunt for their own food?"

He grinned. "You don't know the *ton*. They're so bored, they'll do anything for a diversion. We don't have to tell them we need the meat." He paused. "I sent for another manager, as you requested, and a housekeeper as well. They're my people, but they will serve you well."

A ruddy-faced gentleman looked up. "Wonderful place you have here, Miss Thorne. The baths are everything you promised. Didn't expect you to entertain us, but then, the whole place is a great surprise, isn't it?"

"Have you eaten?" Surely they'd fed them.

"Yes, indeed," said an older gentlemen. "Your people had it all arranged. Hauled us out of bed while it was still dark. We broke our fast at the table near the kitchen."

Another guest joined in. "I'm scheduled to go home today, but I think I'll stay awhile."

"So shall I," said another. "Hate to miss the fun."

Oh, no, Cambria thought, two more beds to prepare before the day's expected influx. "Where are the ladies, Havenshire?"

"Up in the dining room." Cambria made her way back upstairs, entered the dining room—and met accusing stares from their lady patrons.

"Why do the men get to go hunting and we don't get to do anything interesting?" This from a stout lady who had, up to this time, expressed only praise. Up early and huffy over the slight, they all wanted an answer. Havenshire was right. The *ton* wanted diversion, and the less like their usual indoor activities, the better. But what?

"That's not *quite* true," Cambria said tentatively, "we just thought the gentlemen's idea of rising while it was still dark too barbaric for ladies. So," she said, finally deciding what might work, "after tea this afternoon, put on your oldest dresses and sturdy footwear. We're going to the orchards and pick our own fruit.''

Surely they would revolt, she thought, barely breathing while they considered the outrageous notion. ''Well,'' mused one of Havenshire's cousins, ''I haven't done that since I was a girl in the country. I adored it then.'' She looked at Cambria. ''May we eat as we pick?''

Cambria stopped outside the inn. Beside her stood her largest footman whom she'd recruited for this particular errand. Eager for a chance to show his mettle as they walked to the village, he'd related every successful fight he'd engaged in since the age of eight. The thought of all that fighting jarred her frayed nerves. Entering the inn was worse.

The footman shuffled his feet, eager for something to happen. After a moment, he sighed in defeat. ''D'you want me to bring Bass out?''

''No. Go ahead and open the door.''

''Ah,'' he murmured, pushing against the heavy slab of oak.

The door screeched as it opened. Just as before, Cambria stepped over the sill and let her eyes grow accustomed to the near-darkness. The odors hit her first, ale and tobacco and dirty sawdust . . . and unwashed men. A shiver of panic streaked through her, accompanied by the kind of uncontrollable nausea she felt when drinking a nasty tonic. It went down bravely, but came up a coward.

She took a breath and swallowed hard. Bad enough that she was such a ninny that her mind wanted to go home. She'd be drawn and quartered before her stomach would disgrace her in the Saracen's Head.

She looked around, finally, first to the corner where the three old tattlers liked to sit. Empty. Too early in the morning. She forced herself to look at the rest of the travelers. A family near the window and an old man at the bar. She took another breath, this one with relief.

Behind the bar, Bass was watching her with an apprehensive expression. She raised her chin and nodded at him. He smiled in relief and strode quickly out into the room. Guiding her to a table near the hearty fire, he stood there waiting for Cambria's next move.

"Sit down, Bass. Talk to me."

Bass hesitated, looking at her footman. The poor boy was sulking after finding such tame sport. "Go behind the bar, boy. Help yourself and then wait for us at the bar." The footman strode away with a lighter step.

"Thank you," Cambria murmured as Bass took the chair across the table. "I need to speak with the duchess. Where might I find her?"

"She's at the vicarage, at the ladies' meeting."

Cambria's heart sank to the tips of her toes. *Of course she would have to run the gauntlet of the Improvement Society. Sarah would be delighted to see her facing them at last.*

Bass gave her a worried look. "D'you know how long she's going to be here in town?"

"No, I don't. I'm sorry for your troubles, Bass." It was true. For all his sins, he'd become one of her few defenders.

"And I've heard of your own troubles, Miss Thorne. Pity Lord Langcliffe isn't here. Mayhap he might halter the woman."

"I thought he was sending her home. Did he try to do so?"

"I wasn't there at that happy event, but when I saw him last, he looked too cheerful for a man who'd crossed that woman's temper."

"When was that?"

"The night before he left. Sat down here, smiling to himself." He frowned. "The duchess says he told her to do whatever she wanted."

Why couldn't she get used to hearing of Riordan's infamies? "Do you think he's really coming back?"

"He'll be back to get his report from Toby."

"Toby?"

"His man in the stable. He's been keeping track of you for his grace."

"He's had a *spy* in your stable? Keeping track of me?"

Bass shrugged. "A man can't be too careful where his woman's involved. He said he'd stop by and see how things were progressing here." He frowned. "Said he might stay, or maybe not."

She held her breath as that telling jolt hit bottom. "I hope he paid you before he left."

"Oh, he pays all right. Mighty loose with his money, if you ask me. Gave the duchess a bag full of coins. I say, give a women all that money, you're just asking for trouble." He gave her a sly smile. "Hear tell you might be the next mistress of Lakeview? Is it true?"

"Oh, no . . . you didn't believe it, did you?"

"Hoped it might be true. Knew you would settle her down, make her behave. So, are you going to? Settle her down?"

"Do you mean am I going to face her at the meeting?"

His eyes lighted. "Yes."

"I suppose I must." While she still had the courage, she made her adieus and left the inn. Once at the vicarage, she marched up through the front garden. Her footman, two pints more cheerful now than before, stepped in front of her and banged the knocker.

Locke opened the door, blocking the way like a hissing cobra. "What are you doing here?"

The footman leaned forward. "Miss Thorne to see the duchess." Cambria bit back a smile. Rather nice, she thought, to have such offices performed for her while she just stood by looking bored and important.

Locke slammed the door in his face, but, in a moment, she was back. "She'll see you in the parlor." Then she smiled at Cambria. A nasty smile of anticipation that made Cambria's skin crawl. Cambria's every instinct—cowards all—begged her not to go in, but she could not endure the thought of a Thorne backing down. "Very well."

She could hear the ladies' chatter all the way down the hall, but when Locke opened the door, it instantly stopped. Cambria braced herself. Inside awaited enemies whom she'd once thought were friends.

The first face she saw was Sarah's. She looked up in surprise and then began to grin. Cambria's spirits rose as she smiled back. Then she noticed something else. The room seemed to be divided into two camps . . . Sarah's and the duchess's with an aisle dividing them.

Sarah's group emanated the energy of relieved triumph, while the others were here to watch the blood flow. Cambria looked through the duchess's group, wondering whom she would find. Ah, Jane who even now accepted Cambria's wages for her seamstress skills. It was good lesson for her. She was toughening up. She would emblazon this difficult moment in her mind and would trot it out should Riordan ever come back with his charming lies.

The duchess, all false manners in front of her followers, dipped her head. "Good day, Miss Thorne."

Cambria came here to end the duchess's reign in the valley, but her plan to do so was not at all kind. Kinder than the duchess deserved, though, for if Cambria wanted to, she could destroy the woman. She'd grown up hearing about the duchess, never dreaming that she would be forced to use that information to defend her own home.

She would give her a chance for clemency. "May we have a private conversation? You may not wish the others to hear what I have to say."

"I'm afraid not. You're interrupting an important meeting, Miss Thorne. Say what you must, and then you may go."

So she was to be humiliated, then dismissed? *She thought not.* She strolled to a chair in back of the duchess's group and sat down, chin up, shoulders erect. "I shall stay and speak with you after the meeting."

"Perhaps you should. We were discussing what to do about you."

"Judged and condemned without a fair trial?" Cambria rose and looked around the room. "Have you ever thought, any of you, how such an action might someday put you in my place? What if the duchess decided one of you were in disfavor . . .

would you like to be judged without being able to defend yourself?''

She'd made a small hit. Avoiding each other's glances, they squirmed in their chairs. Cambria walked slowly around the group. "For instance, you, Jane." Jane looked frightened as the rest looked suspiciously toward her. "On your way home from working at Thorne's Well, you stopped to speak to one of my gardeners." The listeners leaned forward as one.

"Someone watching your animated conversation might suspect an assignation, especially since it was the second time I saw you two together." Jane shook her head, suddenly frantic as she saw her good name crumbling before her eyes. "But," Cambria said firmly, "I know that you were only getting advice for your herb garden, that neither of you would dream of immoral actions." Jane slumped in her chair with relief.

Cambria pinpointed another woman. "You, Molly . . ." That unfortunate stiffened and cringed back against her chair. "You went to visit an ailing mother last year. You were gone for quite a long time, and when you came home you were increasing." When Molly turned pastry-white, Cambria worried for a moment she'd gone too far, but she had a point to make. "Should the duchess have been here, determined to ruin you, she might have destroyed your marriage before the child was even born. Even after your little boy came into the world— looking exactly like your husband—suspicion might have done its filthy job."

Before they could react, she looked across their heads toward the duchess. "Even you, Lady Langcliffe. I learned something interesting about a longtime friend of yours . . . Lady Elton. Should I air it before these ladies, your son might hear about it and be shocked."

Cambria watched the duchess's horror-stricken face. Ah, she had her. "So," she said clearly, "you should hurry to Lady Elton's side in London and end the calamity before it gets out of hand."

She took a deep breath. "You must excuse me. I have a business to run, and I'm short-handed today." Satisfied with their stunned faces, she moved toward the open door.

Sarah rushed to her side, hurrying to keep up with Cambria. "Cambria, you were wonderful. I knew you would slay the dragon." She tucked her arm through Cambria's. "Now come home with me and tell me what you *really* meant."

Cambria sat contently watching Ellie and Mark sing a duet for the assembled guests. She missed Alistair's grinning face and his wonderful voice as did her cousins and Mark. She wondered idly if she would see him in London. She hoped not. Everything was such a mess . . . except for her routing of the duchess today. She'd left town before the day was over, leaving the inn in a flurry.

Beside her, Amelia murmured, "It's sad, isn't it?"

"That you are singing for your supper?"

"No, Cambria, pay attention. *Mark and Ellie.* They're so in love, but refuse to admit it."

Cambria made it as far as her room before giving way to her feelings. Moving like an aching old lady, she crawled facedown onto the bed. *Ellie and Mark?* Humiliation poured through her. Did everyone know? Were they all watching her with pity, wondering when she would notice?

Or were they going to let her marry Mark? Every time Mark and Ellie were in a room together, would her family be measuring their every word, every action? Eventually, she would become the villainess who took Ellie's man . . . and she would lose her family.

She rolled over. She could tell them she knew . . . release them. *No.* They would still feel guilty. It would spoil her friendship with Ellie and with Mark. It might ruin the love between the couple, drown it with guilt.

Even just telling Mark she'd changed her mind had hidden traps . . . for if she found no one, Mark would insist, as he already had.

But . . . if she already had a suitor *now.* If she called her agreement with Mark *off now,* released him to pursue Ellie openly . . . no matter what happened after that, Mark would feel no guilt. Even up to the last, finding no real suitor, she could pretend. Then if she lost Thorne's Well, Mark and Ellie would still be blameless.

But, who? She'd been sequestered in the valley with no sign of an attendant man.

Except one.

Chapter Fourteen

Splendid day, Riordan assured himself, enjoying the sound of his boots slopping up the muddy slope. Nothing like spending time with a crew of men, mucking about in rain-soaked trenches to restore one's good humor. He was postponing his departure, he knew, but submitting himself to the life waiting for him seemed akin to a dreary prison sentence. Even the prospect of secluding himself at Langcliffe Hall left him feeling restless. He'd been surprised when this depression began, but every day it got worse. He knew the reason—Cambria Thorne.

How had he, the master of indifference, let that woman get under his skin? Let her haunt his dreams and drain his zest for life?

At the top of the incline, the breeze cooled his sweat-dampened hair. Now a trip to the overhead bathing contraption, a change of clothes, and a hearty dinner with the rest of the crew. He started forward and . . . *What the devil?* . . . Bosworth sat on a stump near his tent, a coach nearby.

He sped up his gait. "What's amiss?" he called.

"I've been dismissed," he said. "There's trouble at Thorne's Well."

Riordan hurried forward, his heart pounding. "What trouble?"

"First, your woodsmen were shooting at us, the servants and me, for going after game and firewood."

"What?" he roared.

Wincing, Bosworth recoiled. "D'you want the rest, your grace?"

"Yes . . . no." He ran his fingers through his hair. Clearly this could be better conducted on his way home. "Go find my coachman. Tell him I'm leaving immediately. Tell your driver he can stay in my tent tonight and bring his coach home tomorrow. You're coming back with me."

Riordan tossed his things into his bag, topsy-turvy, with no care if they'd ever be worn again. He went to find Ragsdale to tell him goodbye.

Riordan left Bosworth sleeping in his coach and stepped down into the Saracen's Head courtyard. Raucous noise bellowed out from the inn, far louder than he'd heard during his stay here. The entire village must be inside. He strode quickly into the inn. "Bass, what's going on?"

Bass cocked his head sideways. "Can't hear you." He bustled out behind the bar and motioned Riordan to a corner table. "There, your grace, that's better. What'll you have?"

"Sit down, Bass."

Worried, Bass slipped onto a chair. "Are you just passing through . . . or are you staying?"

"Staying for now."

Bass gave him a knowing smile. "Thought so. A woman like her is worth staying for."

"What the devil are you talking about? What woman?"

"Miss Thorne, of course. Settled your mother down. Sent her scooting up to London sweet as pie."

"My mother's gone to London?"

"Yes. Course I haven't taken the wall down, but—"

"Wall?"

Bass waved at something behind Riordan. He looked around

and saw a rough wooden partition behind him blocking off the outer door. "Where the hell did that come from?"

"Lady Langcliffe . . . she wanted her own entrance."

Riordan sat still for a moment, hoping his brain might make sense of at least one part of the conversation. "How long did she stay here?"

Bass looked hunted. "Five days, your grace . . . D'you think she'll be coming back?"

A curious thought occurred to Riordan. "The *gathering* of the village here . . . This wouldn't have something to do with that, would it?"

Bass turned bright red. "No disrespect meant, your grace. The men are just celebrating having their women back where they belong." He looked down. "A long celebration. Days now, if you want the truth."

Riordan closed his eyes. Slowly he asked, "Where, pray tell, had their women gone?"

"Thornedale Improvement Society. New vicar, you see. Set great store in pleasing her grace. Cooperative, you might say."

A new vicar . . . The one Sarah had warned Cambria about. "Could you just explain the bit about the women?"

"Aye," Bass said, then paused. "Sure you don't want a drink?"

Riordan shook his head. "I dare not start."

"All right then. Her grace called a meeting. Everyone came. The women, I mean. She—her grace—got them all excited. Told them the Thornes were carrying on all kinds of wickedness at the baths. Some of them were going to march out there with torches, but their husbands threatened to lock them up if they did."

"In five short days, she convinced the entire female population?"

"Oh, no, your grace. Convincing them only took one day. But not *all* the ladies agreed with her."

Riordan leaned forward and propped up his head with elbowed hands. "Peck, I believe I'll have that drink, after all."

As Peck hurried away, Riordan rolled his forehead back and forth against the heels of his hands. Two hard days in a coach had left him exhausted. That must be why he couldn't seem to get a firm grasp on this.

Peck came back and clanged the drink down, Riordan took a long swig and leaned back to let it do its work. "Let's get back to the part where Miss Thorne settled my mother down."

Bass grinned. "Thought you might ask about her."

Riordan looked up. "My mother or Miss Thorne?"

"Miss Thorne . . . you know, your woman."

Riordan tried for a calm voice. "My woman . . ."

"Fine choice, your grace. When she came in here that day and found out your mother was down at the meeting, she was shaking all over. Brave as any soldier, she marched down and went right into the meeting. Faced them all. More than I would do."

"What day was that?"

"The day the duchess left." Bass rested his hands across his vast chest. "I wouldn't let a woman like that get away, your grace."

"You keep calling her *my* woman. Where did you get that idea?"

"Don't blame her for that. She had to tell."

"Had to tell . . . who?"

"Peck."

Riordan sat back. "She had to tell Peck that she was my woman?" Light began filtering into Riordan's brain. "To get him to move the wagons."

"You know about that?"

"I know a little . . . less than I thought." He sat drumming his fingers on the table, slowly putting the pieces together. "How did my mother talk you into building a private entrance for her?"

"Same way she got everything else . . . paid me. I can't decide if I should take it down or wait to see if she comes back."

"Take it down, Bass."

He smiled in relief. "I'll do that."

"What else did she pay for?"

"Changing the walls on the third floor. Wanted larger rooms."

Riordan groaned. "Anything else?"

Bass sighed. "One thing, your grace. When she bought my liquor, I thought she'd take it with her, but, she just left it up in her rooms. What should I do with it?"

"She bought liquor? Was she *drinking?*"

"No, she didn't like the noise. Wanted everyone to go home so she could sleep."

"And you lost all that custom?"

"Only at night." Bass grinned. "Every night she bought me out, and every day I stocked back up." He paused. "That's about it."

Stupefied to the edge of reason, Riordan stood up. He'd had enough. "My room is still empty?"

Bass heaved his bulk from the chair. "Aye. That it is."

"Bass," Riordan said, "I don't want this conversation going round the village. This is private between you and me."

Bass looked disappointed, but nodded his agreement.

Riordan went on. "My coach is outside. Tell my coachman to sleep upstairs with my crew, and then you rouse Toby. Tell him to drive Bosworth to Langcliffe Hall tonight. "Then," he added, "send my bag up to my room, along with a hot bath."

He rubbed the back of his neck. "Tell you what, Bass. *My woman* thinks this place is an eyesore. Thinks it ruins the good looks of the town. You keep my mother's liquor, and do something with this building. Plant flowers, paint it. Clean up the inside, too. When Miss Thorne likes it, you send the bill to me."

Riordan turned toward the back hallway. Behind him, Bass sighed softly. "Lucky bastard."

Cambria looked up as Sarah came rushing into the dining room. "What's wrong?"

"I need to talk to you." She crossed to the sideboard and began filling a plate. "I love your cook," she said absently, sitting down at the table. After a few bites, she looked up.

"Riordan's here at the inn. He came in last night, and he's riding out here to see you this morning."

"How do you know all this?"

"Cambria," she said, "everything Riordan does is noted, chewed over, and spit out before an hour passes."

"I don't suppose you know why he's coming, do you?"

Sarah's face fell. "Bass won't tell us anything Riordan said last night. I had to quiz the stableboy to get this much information." She sipped her chocolate. "What are you going to do?"

Cambria leaned forward, her hands twisting on the table. "I've made a decision. You have to promise not to tell anyone."

"You know I won't."

Cambria took a deep breath. "I am long overdue for getting to London, but I have two matters of unfinished business that must be taken care of before I can leave."

Sarah nodded with disgust. "The merchants. They're still afraid Lady Langcliffe will come back and ruin them. It would serve them right if you just kept shopping at Pick Hill."

"But I can't get a coach down the trail, so it keeps two servants busy riding back and forth." She paused. "Then, there's the problem of Mark."

Sarah looked worried. "Why don't you wait until after you find a London suitor. What if you don't find one?"

"You wouldn't marry a man if you knew he loved someone else."

"True." she said, still concerned. "So, what's your plan?"

"I need to convince Mark and Ellie that they don't have to worry about me. I was thinking about Riordan. If they thought he and I were getting serious about each other, they might believe it."

Sarah hesitated. "I don't know, Cambria. What if Mark talks to Riordan and finds out it's all a hum? He'll just be more worried then."

"That's just it. I'm going to convince Riordan to go along with it. He might just do it. It won't hurt him, surely, and he might be glad to see that with Mark gone, I'm running out of time to save Thorne's Well."

Sarah exhaled a long, slow breath. "Riordan's a dangerous man to be playing games with, Cambria."

"But *think,* Sarah. Mark's here now and so is Riordan. Riordan is on his way out to Thorne's Well—I don't know why, but it may be my only chance. Then when Mark goes back home, I shall tell him I don't need him any longer, and I can leave for London right away." Cambria looked at Sarah's worried frown. "I should at least try, don't you think?"

"Yes, I think you must." She paused. "What about the merchants? Will you send Riordan down to scare them?" Then she thought better of it. "Why would he, though?"

"I won't tell him that's what I'm doing. As far as he's concerned, I'm just parading him around as my new beau to impress Mark. The merchants will get the idea."

Sarah's frown disappeared. "This is like old times, isn't it?" She grinned. "How very delicious."

In a foul mood engendered by the all-night celebration of the Rose Thorne Inn, the last thing Riordan wanted to hear was the cheerful voice of his nephew. He sat back against the pillows as the young man barged in. "What's wrong, now, Alistair?"

"Bosworth said you were going out to Thorne's Well today. I thought if you were going to patch things up, I'd like to be there."

"Miss them, do you?"

"They're great fun, Riordan. We had a lot of things planned. It's not fair that Grandmother got me tossed out."

"What about the work you have waiting at Langcliffe Hall?

"My real business is to study how you handle problems, and the interesting problems are here."

"You might get tossed out again."

"I'll send a note to let them know I'm coming."

An hour later, Riordan and Alistair followed an unfamiliar coach up the long Thorne's Well drive. They stayed back, still mounted, while the passengers evacuated. Servants emerged from the house like a swarm of ants and stripped the coach in a matter of minutes. Guest-patrons disappeared into the house, met by a man Riordan had never seen before—the new manager, he supposed. The coach headed off toward the stables.

Alistair nudged his horse closer. "Looks like the business is thriving."

Riordan nodded. "Bass said it was. Despite my mother's efforts."

Servants came out to greet them and take the horses. "If you're looking for Miss Thorne, your grace, she's out in the gazebo." He turned to the eager Alistair. "You're expected in the conservatory, Lord Singleton."

As Alistair hurried inside, Riordan glanced toward the ornate wrought-iron gazebo. Cambria was sitting quietly, looking down . . . no doubt reading one of her endless lists. Even after the servant trotted back into the house, Riordan hesitated. When her temper broke loose, he'd probably end up in a rose bush with a broken nose.

As he drew closer, she looked up. "Hello, Riordan."

Where was the anger he'd expected? She was sitting out here calmly reading a novel? He replied cautiously. "How are you, Cambria?"

"Sit down, Riordan." Placing her book behind her, Cambria twisted back to her original position, sideways on the cushioned bench with one arm resting on the gazebo window ledge. "I suppose you know what happened while you were gone?"

Riordan mirrored her position, facing her only feet apart. "I've heard several versions. I'm very sorry, Cambria—"

She held up a hand to stop him. "It's all taken care of. I threw a fit and fired your manager and chased your mother out of town." She smiled politely as if he'd inquired after her health. "The business is doing fine."

"That's it?"

She gave him a surprised look. "Yes . . . why?"

He rubbed the bridge of his nose. What the devil was going on here? "You don't want to discuss what happened . . . hear my explanation?"

"Not at all. I know it's your disposition to never explain,

and I quite understand. In fact, I've decided to adopt the policy myself.''

Damn. Here he was. all primed to set things straight, and now she threw his own words in his face? Well, *fine.* When she broke down and asked him later, he would keep it to himself. ''Whatever you say, Cambria.''

''I do, however, want to ask a favor of you.''

He sat up straight, feeling more at ease. Just like a woman to wheedle something out of a man when she had him feeling guilty. ''Yes?''

''Mark and I were considering marriage, but now he's fallen in love with Ellie. They are hiding it for fear of hurting my feelings.''

Mark and Ellie? His spirits lifted. He'd been sure that had fallen through after Alistair left. Riordan studied Cambria's face, confused that she looked so calm. *So businesslike.* ''So what's the favor?''

''You seemed to like Ellie and Mark when you were here. I don't know if that's true, but in case it was, I thought you would help me.''

That made him angry. ''You're the one who thinks I hate your family, Cambria. The truth is, I've grown to like them.''

''That's hard to believe,'' she said faintly.

''Your favorite state of mind.''

She ignored his remark. ''It doesn't really matter, Riordan. The point is that it won't hurt you to cooperate, and I need your help.''

He remained silent lest he reach over and wring her neck. She could have been speaking to a stranger, for all the emotion she displayed. He took a careful breath. If that's the way she wanted it, it was all right with him. ''Can you get to the point, Cambria? What is it you want of me?''

''I want Ellie and Mark to think I'm interested in someone else, and it will have to be you. You're the only man Mark's seen me with.''

Stunned at her request, he voiced his first thought. ''I thought you already started that rumor? Why do you need me?''

"That," she bit out tightly, "was a necessity of the moment, and scarcely convincing without you here to show it's true."

"You told me to stay away, Cambria. Considering your disdain for me, why would they believe it now?"

"I never told them of our quarrel, Riordan. I didn't want to hurt anyone's feelings." She stood and bid him follow her out of the gazebo. "Mark is just here for a couple of days, so tonight I want you to come to dinner and begin the charade. Something subtle, but telling. You can be quite charming when circumstances require."

This viper-tongued woman wasn't telling him everything. No mention of her losing Thorne's Well, no wailing over losing Mark. A woman with her intellect didn't just pass over a thing like that, didn't *forget* about it. Perhaps she was in shock over the last week, worn out over the trouble with his mother. Or, he thought, *was this a plot to marry him?*

As he trailed behind her, his mind stumbled over *that* thought. Is this why she'd been so casual, so calm? "What will you tell him afterward when we don't marry?"

She shrugged. "Heavens, I will think of something." She began a leisurely stroll through the rose garden.

"Like what?"

"Oh," she said, looking off into space, "Perhaps I shall decide that you are too forceful for me. Too *domineering.*"

His eyes narrowed. That sounded too much like her previous complaints. "And, he'll believe that?"

"Yes," she said, turning back to face him. "Mark is a gentle man. That's why I wanted to marry him."

More poisoned darts . . .

"Or," she said in a dreamy voice, "perhaps I tell him I've discovered that you were just courting me so I couldn't find someone else, that you planned to wait until my birthday passes and then change your mind . . ."

She plucked a rose and held it to her nose. "Perhaps I shall discover that you are marrying me for the land and intend to toss me aside and go back to your mistress."

"I don't have a mistress," he ground out, "and I shall never subject my wife to the humiliation of adultery."

"Riordan," she chided in a humoring voice. "You're a Langcliffe. Who would believe that?"

"Of all the prejudiced, closed-minded—"

She began tearing petals off the rose. "If you want objections, what about . . . your *mother?*"

He gritted his teeth. "Tell them I'm coming to dinner tonight." He turned on his heel and left.

He'd reached the inn before he realized he'd forgotten Alistair.

Chapter Fifteen

Cambria tucked a defiant curl behind her ear. One more escape and she would chop the blasted thing off. Every sound irritated her. Her dress felt too tight and her jaw ached from grinding her teeth.

Of course, *nothing* seemed right with such a critical moment looming ahead like a great fanged dragon. When Riordan arrived, there would be no turning back. What would he say . . . or do? How would Mark react . . . Ellie? If only she and Riordan had rehearsed some little script, had agreed upon signals so they would not trip over their words.

Sarah was right, she was playing a dangerous game of deceit. Changing Mark's and Ellie's lives was no game, and she'd given that dangerous control to Riordan, to his ability to lie and charm. She gave one last tug to her new gown and left the room.

Diana caught her before she'd taken two steps into the parlor. "Talia says you've invited Riordan to dinner. You told us you'd never speak to him again. I thought we'd gotten rid of him, Cambria."

"He came by this morning. We talked. It's rather complicated."

Mark's voice called out, "Here's Riordan."

Cambria whirled, her heart pounding. *No going back now.*

Riordan came directly toward her. Lifting her gloved hand, he actually . . . *kissed* it? She looked sideways to see if Mark were watching.

He was, frowning horridly at Langcliffe. This was not what she'd planned.

"A vision," Riordan drawled, not letting go of her fingers.

She tugged, but he gave her a bland smile and, with the other hand, reached up fondly to smooth her escaping curl back behind her ear. Quickly she gasped, "Would you like a drink, Riordan?"

"Of course." Still holding her hand in that steelish grip, he led them across the room. She didn't have to peek at Mark, she could feel him stalking them, actually following in their footsteps.

Riordan, the scoundrel, was effusively genial. "Good evening, Lady Maxwell, Lady Waterson." Talia purred and kissed his cheek.

Diana, however, gaped at their locked hands and lost her smile. "Would you care to explain this familiarity?"

"Certainly," Riordan replied easily, "I'm courting your niece."

Everyone gasped. Cambria closed her eyes, wondering if she might be needing smelling salts. Where was the *finesse* she'd expected?

"Cambria," Diana said, snapping Cambria to attention, "I want an explanation this very minute."

"Don't blame her," Riordan drawled. "She's been resisting me all along, but now she's agreed to let me court her." He made room for Mark beside him and gave him a man-to-man look. "Mark knows what I mean." Riordan's smug look raised the level of curiosity to bursting.

Riordan draped his arm over Mark's shoulder. "Here he is, half in love with Ellie, but he thinks you might object, so he pretends to himself that they're just friends." He gave Mark a hearty whack on the back and, finally dropping Cambria's hand, began to pour his drink.

Poor Mark turned crimson. He stared at Riordan in perfect horror.

Cambria risked a glance toward Ellie, who looked like she'd just been dropped off a cliff and was halfway down.

Turning to face them all, Riordan took a sip and sighed as if it were ambrosia. The room watched without a word.

Mark recovered first. Looking at Cambria, he frowned. "Is it true, Cambria? Has he been chasing you? Do you want him to leave you alone?"

Everyone waited. She waited, too—for some brilliant remark to make itself known—but it never happened. She looked directly at Mark. "As you know, I had other plans, but Riordan would persist."

Riordan cleared his throat with an expansive air. "I insisted we talk this over with her family . . . set them straight, so to speak."

The wretch, Cambria thought. How like Riordan to mangle the truth.

Diana waved Ellie closer. As Ellie obeyed, Diana turned to Mark. "Is this true about you and my daughter?"

With an apologetic glance toward Cambria, Mark gave Diana a steady, confident look. "I do care for Ellie. I think she cares for me a little, but we've never discussed it."

Diana looked at her daughter. "And you, Ellie?"

Ellie bypassed her mother and looked directly at Mark with a yearning gaze. "I thought I was too silly for you, too young."

Diana's voice cut through between them. "And this is as far as it's gone?" At Mark's hopeless nod, Diana's chin rose. "I have no objection to this courtship, but, Ellie needs to meet other gentlemen. You may see each other, and, after one or two seasons, we will consider this matter again."

Mark tried to remain solemn, but a smile broke through of its own accord. "Thank you, Lady Waterson. I won't betray your trust."

"Well, then," Diana replied briskly, lowering her glass to a table, "it's time for dinner."

Cambria's heart warmed to see Mark and Ellie leaving the parlor together, openly united at last. Following them, she sighed . . . then sobered as the brash Riordan moved up beside her. "You were fairly steaming in there, Miss Thorne. Don't tell me that you were disappointed in my performance?"

She hissed back, "Did your parents find you climbing trees in some jungle, Riordan?"

He moved closer so their shoulders were touching. "Have I not, in one brilliant moment, put all the pieces tidily where you wanted them?"

She hated to admit it. "Yes."

"Had you a better plan?"

"No." Must he look so conceited?

As she sputtered beside him, Riordan held back a chuckle. After this morning's amazing display of empty-headedness, his own Cambria was back now, furious and insulting, just the way he liked her.

Still glaring at him, Cambria said, "Come by in the morning. We'll give them another performance before Mark goes back to London."

Riordan nodded his agreement. Tomorrow he'd get her alone and find out just exactly what the maddening female was really up to.

"All right," he said. "I'll come for breakfast."

As they neared the waterfall bridge, Alistair called out. "They cheered you up, didn't they, Uncle Riordan?"

"What?" Riordan kicked his horse into a gallop to get past the roaring noise.

Alistair caught up. "I said, the Thornes, they cheered you up."

"What makes you say that?"

"Admit it. When you arrived this morning, you looked like a paid mourner. Now, you seem quite cheerful." Not waiting for Riordan's reply, he became effusive. "I can certainly see why you never get close to people. I couldn't hurt the Thornes for any reason now."

Riordan was not surprised. "You may feel that way if you wish."

Alistair gave him a strange look. "You're not still—?"

Riordan interrupted. "I did warn you about consequences, Alistair."

"But you are courting Cambria . . . or is that just a trick to keep her unmarried?"

"It was her idea. So Mark would feel free to marry Ellie."

As Riordan explained Cambria's stratagem, Alistair's eyes grew cold. "If you don't care about them, why don't you just stay away? Or do you find pleasure in your masquerade?"

"Actually, I felt I owed Cambria redress for my mother's actions."

Alistair snorted. "And since it fits in so nicely with your own scheme, why not be accommodating? You're no better than Grandmother . . . just more devious." When Riordan didn't reply, Alistair spit out his disgust. "You're rich, Riordan. You don't need this land."

"You don't understand, Alistair. Leave it alone."

"I've watched how you are with Cambria. No other woman has affected you as she has, yet you would lose it for what? . . . Your mother's vendetta?

"You forget my father. You forget my mother's heartbreak. I promised myself after I left here that I would someday make it right for her."

"*Revenge* is what you mean. Get the aunts no matter who you hurt in the process? Cambria has done nothing to you. I always thought she *was* falling in love with you."

Riordan winced at that, but held firm. "I'm not after revenge, Alistair. My mother deserves to live in Lakeview with no Thornes in sight. She paid for it with her tears."

Alistair laughed bitterly. "She doesn't value the land, or she wouldn't have been leasing out Lakeview, piece by piece."

"She needed the money."

"To indulge her in her excesses. Riordan," he said. "Grandmother is after revenge, plain and simple."

"Alistair, you don't understand how devastated a wife is when her husband turns to other women, how obsessed she becomes."

"If I had to choose between your mother and the Thornes,

I'd be hard pressed not to make the same choice.'' Then he pulled his horse to a halt. ''Damn, Riordan, I didn't mean that. What a wretched tongue I have.''

Riordan pulled up alongside him. After a long silence, he replied, ''It's all right, halfling. Neither of us should have come here.''

''Why did you come in the first place? You didn't need to.''

''I thought I would discover why my father left us for the Thornes.''

''And did you?''

''I think we both know the answer to that.''

Riordan rolled over and groaned. Blast his churning mind. Blast Alistair's provocative accusations. Even as he'd been snapping back answers at his nephew tonight, he was revolting against his own reasoning. He'd run that conversation over and over in the last few hours, altering responses, chasing faulty chains of logic. Why didn't he just leave it alone?

Because he kept remembering the one thing he could not refute, a small, unimportant bit in the entire discussion. He had gone there full of gloom, and he *was* smiling when he left Thorne's Well.

No . . . not at the dinner. Before that. When he and Cambria were talking in the gazebo, he'd been filled with energy, vigor. No . . . earlier. *When Cambria wanted him back in her life.*

He flipped over and stared at the ceiling. From that *very* moment, everything brightened from dreary gray to vibrant color. How had it happened, this *need* for Cambria? *Face it, Riordan.*

He sat up and threw the covers back. Turning to sit on the edge of the bed, he stared at the low burning fire. *Face what?* . . . That everything Alistair said was true? He'd admitted that sometime in the night.

What else was there?''

Something clicked in his brain. Some wild, bursting explosion of emotion. Images flew through his mind, quickly rejected, then back again with more imagination, more color, more intensity. No . . . he was losing his mind. "It's too close in here," he gasped, striding to open a window.

Heaving air into his lungs, he calmed himself. There, he thought, that was better. He must be tired, unable to think clearly. Delusional.

Damn, that was a close call. For a moment there, he thought he'd might be in love with Cambria Thorne.

He crossed back to the fire. Throwing wood on the fire, he picked up the bellows and absently blew air on the fledgling inferno. Calmer, he let his mind wander as he left the fire to its own resources.

A chair sat near the fireplace, and he sank down onto its soft cushion, his arms relaxed on the arms. He was a man of intellect, a man who had outwitted his opponents. He owed no man anything, and no man dared renege on his debt to him. He was respected. Feared. Admired.

True, he'd let himself become embroiled in emotional matters here at Thorne's Well, and emotion—his or others—always led to confusion. However, he'd done it with his eyes wide open. He'd been on a quest to discover why his father might have chosen as he did.

True, the entire story had not entirely unfolded, but he'd already learned some painful truths. And when Rountree finished, he might find more. So far, things were sifting into their own well-fitting slots.

But then, there was Cambria.

Like a kitten's snarled skein of yarn, confusion took over his thoughts, and he could make no sense of it. Every time he tried to do so, a flood of emotion poured through him and flooded his brain.

His fingers began to drum on the chair arm. What point wasn't he facing? *His breath quickened* . . . Time?

Time was running out, wasn't it? Time before the land issue. Time before his mother came to live at Lakeview. Time before some charming man came along and married Cambria, before he took her to his bed and filled their nursery with hot-tempered little girls.

Riordan's head bowed under the weight of that image. He

couldn't breathe. His brain simply stopped functioning as it always did . . . *when he thought of losing her.* He stood up abruptly and strode back to the window. Cold air . . . he needed to breathe, to stop this panic.

Panic at losing Cambria?

So that was it? *He wanted to keep her for his own?*

Something important was happening here, but he hadn't been paying attention. The *excitement* was not new. Indeed, had he smothered the same enthusiasm over reviving his bankrupt estate, he would not be one of the wealthiest men in the kingdom.

No, his sharp bursts of brilliant insight, of *knowing* when something was right came from *opening* his mind, not closing it. The answer awaited, and all he had to do was sift out the dross to find the truth.

He gripped the window sill with both hands. *Listen.* His traitorous emotions—knowing he could never ally himself with a Thorne—still wanted desperately to take Cambria Thorne to his *own* home, to his own bed?

To his heart?

The image filled his imagination, sent blinding joy to every corner of his soul. His blood sang, and he knew he'd stepped into that magical place he'd been avoiding all this time.

He took a deep, shuddering breath.

Dear God, he loved the infuriating woman.

He leaned his elbows on the sill and let the breeze cool his face. The heartache drained away, leaving a soft, swaying rhythm that let him breathe again. The dread of existing without her softened, melted, filled all the empty places with something else entirely. Happiness, he thought, as it began to trickle through his blood, leaving a sort of *music* where it went.

Oh, his logical brain battered away at the enchanted place where he stood, but this time, he wasn't letting it come in and snatch the treasure he wanted. He'd never reached for a prize to warm his *heart,* might never do so again. But this one he would keep.

He would not hide from these protesting, practical thoughts

of his. He would argue, convince them, master them. But where should he begin?

Take an end of the yarn and pull. But which snarled end?

He began to pace. The land? His mother? His infamies regarding Thorne's Well? Cambria's distrust?

The land . . . he would just give it to Cambria. He would send a note to Rountree, let him look into it. Then, there was his mother . . . She would fight him, . . . but would he let her arguments keep them apart? A few weeks ago, that question would have been valid. But now he knew what he wanted.

At the thought of his swain-snitching deeds, his heart sank. One hint, and Cambria would be gone forever. But then, might a man's integrity be justified by telling her *later?* Perhaps as they sat, gray haired in their rocking chairs, he might tell her the truth.

And now, one last barrier.

Cambria fought him with distrust and anger. He fought her by kindling and igniting that wrath. Each of them protected themselves, each threw up barriers. Though they denied the physical lure, their minds met, entwined, longing to flirt and tease and banter. Throughout it all the link between them remained strong, thin as a web, enduring as steel.

She needed only to step into the magical place he'd found. He would entice her there. Make her want him. Keep her so busy being with him that she had no time for anyone else. She already felt an attraction, and before he left for Bude, they'd never tired of each other's company.

In truth, she had already listed her objections to their joining—that he was too domineering, that he'd court her until the time passed when she could find a real suitor, or that he'd marry her and leave her for a mistress—thus warning him in advance.

She'd even opened the gate to his courtship. For the sake of Mark Glendover and Ellie, she'd allowed him to hover on the perimeter of her life. Allowed the illusion of his loving her.

He was to stand by, pretending to be her suitor. And so he would.

Talk about the wolf in sheep's clothing . . . .

* * *

Riordan followed Cambria onto the bridge, reveling in his rather wicked thoughts as she let the waterfall mist her face. "You're looking very smug this morning, Cambria. If I were a suspicious man, I'd say you're up to some devious little mischief."

She looked sideways at him. "And if I were a suspicious lady, I might wonder why you came trotting up the hill so early this morning."

"You did say breakfast."

"You got me out of bed!"

Riordan wiggled his eyebrows with a wicked leer. "If only I had. Alas, your new housekeeper insisted on claiming that pleasure."

She ignored him. "Well, now you must pay."

"Why do I keep getting the feeling that underneath all this sweetness there is a girl who'd like nothing better than to drop me in this river with a bag of rocks tied to my feet?"

She turned to stroll down the road. "A guilty conscience?"

"Hah! You are angry." He threw his arm over her shoulder, surprised at her acquiescence as he matched his steps to hers. "I knew it."

"I will admit that in the midst of last week's chaos, I did—for one tiny moment—think you might be the villain your mother described."

"What did she accuse me of?"

"Oh, the usual Langcliffe crimes."

"You're not going to tell me."

She waved her handkerchief, a frilly, useless thing that matched another new dress. "No, it's just too tiresome."

He smiled. She could have been Talia plying her womanly wiles. "What changed your mind about my being the villain?"

"I remembered how you'd given two weeks of your precious time to see that the baths ran smoothly. Now why would a man do such a generous thing if he were going to ruin that business?"

Such an innocent question, such a deadly reply. Riordan's conscience twisted a notch. One more sin he must hide from her. Not that she wasn't hiding a flaming blaze of anger inside her, because this little act wasn't fooling him. But why was she doing it? "When I left to go to Bude you were angry about your aunts. Have you gotten over that, too?"

She stepped out from under his arm, kicked a rock . . . and it flew clear into the woods. The frilly handkerchief did a little angry dance. But her voice was sweet as honey. "How could I not, when now we're even?"

"Even?"

"Yes. *My* aunts and *your* mother. I think we're evenly matched now, don't you?" She gave him a brittle smile. "Actually, I think I'm better off."

He wasn't going to touch that one. He'd just pluck out the nasty little barb she'd thrown, and keep his mouth shut. "Where are we going?"

"To the village. I told Mark we were going to spend the day together."

"And how will this little stroll punish me?"

"We shall walk through all the shops with you looking like a man in love. You have my permission to spout whatever nonsense an enraptured man might say. I promise not to laugh."

So, she meant to make a fool of him for her own satisfaction? Little did she know how willing he was to act the lovesick swain. He groaned as if unnerved, "How could you do this to me?"

She gloated, content with his distress. She stopped at the end of the road, her eyes wide in amazement. Across the street, servants from the Saracen's Head were on their knees, planting flowers on one side of the building. On the other side, two men wielded paint brushes.

"What on earth?" she murmured.

"A bargain I made with Bass."

She looked up in surprise. "You're responsible for this?"

Riordan shrugged. "He's to fix up the place, inside and out. When you give your approval then he gets his reward."

She started across the street, eager, he knew, to see all they'd done. "And what reward would that be?"

"A man's bargain, Cambria. Don't ask." He walked beside

her, amused at her enthusiasm over the changes. As Bass came out, beaming with pleasure at seeing them, Riordan leaned closer to Cambria. "Are we to begin your little game with Bass?"

"No, he's already on my side. But," she said as an after-thought, "people might be watching."

Good, he thought. He could begin his real courtship right now. He slid his arm over her shoulder, his fingers playing with her ear.

She hissed up at him, "Not that caveman nonsense, Riordan. Just give me fond looks, and I'll rest my fingers on your arm."

He laughed. "Anyone who knows me would never believe such a feeble courtship as that. Give over, Cambria." He grinned as she relaxed and let him have his way.

Bass grinned. "So you took my advice, Langcliffe?"

"What advice?" Cambria asked.

"Keeping you, Miss Thorne. Best advice I ever gave."

Cambria hesitated, then gave Bass one of those fluttering smiles she'd copied from her aunts. "Why, thank you, Bass. Perhaps Riordan should name his firstborn after you."

Riordan tightened his fingers on her shoulder and turned her firmly away from the inn. Grasping her hand in his, he asked, "Where next, Cambria?"

"We'll just wander in and out of the shops. The butcher's right here."

Sighing as if hating it, Riordan pushed the door open. As they stepped inside, the butcher's head jerked up like a startled horse, turning pale as he looked back and forth between the two lovers.

What the devil? Why did he look so frightened?

Riordan pulled Cambria close and kissed her cheek, just as if he'd been doing it for years. He gave the butcher a casual nod. "Just getting acquainted with the village again," he said easily, strolling around the room as if fascinated with raw meat.

The butcher gulped and looked toward Cambria as if she might be dangerous. "Got a good bit of mutton here, Miss Thorne. I might send some up the hill—as a gift, of course— to celebrate your new business."

Cambria's eyes gleamed, but she hid it behind the fluttering handkerchief. "How sweet." She sighed, elated with some private thought of her own. Turning, she strolled out of the shop without another word.

Riordan's eyes narrowed. That little drama had nothing to do with convincing someone of their courtship. He had more than an inkling what his devious love was really doing. *Why didn't she just ask him?* He could knock a few heads together and get the merchants to serve her better and wouldn't have to go through this nonsense.

On the other hand, he was doing just fine right now.

Cambria felt like hugging Riordan—not really, but he'd done such a perfect job of acting the man in love—and that wonderful, *ghastly* look on the butcher's face. If she lived to be a hundred, she would never forget it.

That arm over her shoulder was another thing entirely. She hated him, of course. He was a devious, lying scoundrel . . . but when he touched her, teased her, something inside her softened. Evidently, she had the brains of a sensible person, but the rest of her was pure Thorne.

"Ah," Riordan said as they reached the bakery, "my favorite place."

Cambria hid a grimace. The last time she'd come in, she ordered a pastry and the baker *accidentally* dropped it on the floor. "Just don't forget you're more interested in me than a hot cross bun."

"Well then," he murmured, stopping before the large window, "we'll give him something to think about—then I'll go in and get my treat." He turned her and rested his hands on her shoulders. Leaning down, he touched his lips to hers.

She knew she should go along with it—to convince the baker, of course—but she couldn't help stiffening. He gave her shoulders a little shake. "Close your eyes and pretend you like it."

As she obeyed, she could feel his breath as he drew closer, and this time he didn't stop with a fragile touch. This one came in waves. A warm touch, then lifting only to come back with a slanted kiss and a sound deep in his throat that stirred her insides up to boiling. Again, he pulled back . . . not to leave her, but to heighten the pleasure with the threat of loss. Back his mouth came, this time with a low, sensuous growl as his arms wrapped around her and pulled her close.

She could feel every eye in the village on them, knew that no one ever behaved this way in public, not even in London. But she couldn't pull back, could only lean into the kiss. She was surely *melting* . . .

Then he broke away, his breath labored.

Cambria was beyond thinking. Her eyes were never going to open, and what a pity, for she wanted to look into his face and make believe that this was for real. Something this devastating surely deserved a moment of honor, a fleeting glimpse of what it would be like to have the man he *pretended* to be looking down with love in his face.

"Look at me," he said.

So she did.

His expression was dark with emotion, his eyes smokey, his mouth partly open as he clenched his jaw and held it fast. An ache began to flow though her, a yearning. She couldn't help it, she had to touch his face, feel the warmth, the rough texture beneath her fingers. As she raised her hand she could feel him stiffen, but he tipped his face down and a knowing look softened his features. Almost as if they could hear each other's thoughts, as if this moment were something apart from all the forces that kept them apart. Slowly, he turned his face, let her fingers slide over his lips still wet with the kiss.

The bakery door opened, Riordan pulled her hard against him. Two ladies walked slowly past them, gawking, she knew. Then he reached over and grabbed the closing door and ushered her in before him. "What will you have this morning, darling?"

As the baker came bustling toward them, Riordan kept his arm around her waist. "My sweetheart has been wanting a hot cross bun this morning, so what could I do but walk down here and get a dozen?

The baker gulped like a man in pain. Never taking his gaze from Cambria, he croaked, "Yes, your grace." Fumbling with shaking hands, he threw a napkin into a handled basket and tossed in far more than a dozen buns. He handed the basket to Cambria. "He gave Cambria a strangled look. "Just ask, Miss Thorne . . . whatever you want,"

Cambria turned blindly to leave the shop. She knew she was acting strangely, but she couldn't get control of herself. Dear heavens, *that kiss*. She could barely walk, and her hands were shaking. *Shaking* like some dimwitted damsel in a novel. Without a word, she handed the basket to Riordan for fear she would drop it on the pathway. Glancing quickly at his face, she saw something that upset her even more.

He was *amused*. As if he saw right through her.

As they stepped out onto the pathway, Sarah ushered her two little ones up to greet them. Riordan immediately lowered the basket to give the children a chance at the buns. Sarah grinned. "How are things proceeding, Cambria?" Then she dipped a curtsy to annoy Riordan.

Riordan gave her a curious look. "I assume by the look on your face that you had some part in this jaunt to town?"

"Of course. Have you been to the church yet?"

"No, why?"

Her grin deepened. "The vicar is furious. Someone sneaked in last night and dug up flowers from all over the cemetery."

Chapter Sixteen

If Riordan had doubted Rountree's report of near mutiny in Langcliffe Hall, his entry through the front door soon changed his mind. As one—sour-faced maids, footmen, the butler, and even the sleeping hounds—stopped their present task with an expression of joyful relief.

Upstairs, his solicitor waited with a dour visage. "I suppose the news is not good?" When Rountree hesitated, Riordan said, "Forget the diplomacy, Rountree. Just tell me."

"Very well . . . I've investigated back ten years or so, and the fact is that Lady Langcliffe gambles . . . very heavily."

Riordan grasped the back of a chair. "That's impossible. She hated my father's gambling. He put us into poverty with his weakness."

"Perhaps she took it up to get even."

He shook his head. "She would never do that."

"That's why she leased out bits of Lakeview. Gambling debts."

Confused, Riordan asked, "Where does she gamble? I cannot imagine her attending some disreputable place."

"Lady Elton's house."

"Little old Lady Elton? Why haven't I heard of this?"

"Shall I continue digging, see how far it goes back?"

Riordan sighed. "Yes. I think we'd better know it all." Looking at the work piled on the table, Riordan rubbed the back of his neck. "I've been away too long, Rountree. It will take weeks to get through this."

"There's no need for you to know every little detail. Unless," he said carefully, "you feel better checking things over."

"Not really. It's just habit. You'll need an assistant if I slack off."

"Shall I engage one?"

"An assistant?" He thought carefully. "Yes. Contact Mark Glendover. He's the Thorne's solicitor. See if you can get him on your staff. Offer him a large salary and a bonus for coming over to us." He named a sum.

Rountree whistled. "Is this a bribe?"

"No. Rather more a debt."

A few moments later, he knocked on the duchess's door.

"Come in," she called. When he entered, she rose from her dressing table, apprehension tightening her features. "How nice to see you, darling."

He kissed her cheek. "Lovely as always, mother."

"Thank you." Warily, she watched him prowl around the room.

He had no time to waste in pleasantries. "You incited a great deal of trouble in Thornedale, Mother. I don't want a repeat of that—ever."

She drew herself up. "You've been talking to the Thornes."

"The point is *your* behavior, Mother. I want you to leave them alone."

"You're not my keeper, Riordan. I shall do as I please."

"You may do as you please as long as it's within the bounds of decency. Beyond that, you will answer to me."

"Threatening your own mother," she whimpered, whipping out her handkerchief. "You're turning out just like your father."

"That brings up another unpleasant subject," he said, for once impervious to the old refrain. "You've been gambling . . . very heavily."

She exploded. "That liar! That vicious tart!" She glared at him. "How dare you believe that female's word?"

"What are you talking about?"

"Don't give excuses, Riordan. Your precious Cambria Thorne forced me out of Thornedale with her blackmail. Then she broke her word and told you." Her eyes widened when she realized she'd just confessed.

The room seemed to spin around. "How did she know?"

Real tears pooled in her eyes. "You love her, don't you? She boasted about it, but I didn't believe her. That's why you don't want any trouble."

"Moulton's papers revealed your gambling, Mother. As for Cambria," he added softly, "yes, I do love her, but your mischief caused trouble between us. If you care for my feelings, you will leave her alone."

She turned away and sat down at her dressing table. With jerky movements, she wiped almond cream under her puffed eyes, "You should have seen your precious Cambria frightening the ladies of Thornedale." She darkened her lashes with burnt cloves. "If you marry her, she will make my life a misery. Just look how she turned my small gaming pleasures into a wedge between us."

He had to admire his mother's quickness. Even in the midst of a crisis, she twisted the facts to her benefit. "I won't tell you not to gamble, but, when your allowance is gone I will not pay your debts." Then he realized something. "Rountree didn't mention any redecorating in the town house. You didn't really spend the nine hundred on that, did you?"

"I deserve some pleasure in my life, and if I choose to play a little cards with my friends—"

"At Lady Elton's where the play is deep. Shall I send Rountree to see her, advise her that I will not pay your vouchers?"

Horrified, she sobbed. "If you do that, what will they think? You'll ruin me, Riordan."

He paused. "Very well. I've asked far more than this favor from you. We'll postpone that drastic step as a compromise of sorts. You think about what I've said. Try to find some way to accept Cambria, and I will give you time to adjust. We needn't be at odds if we both try to be reasonable.''

He stood, suddenly more weary than he had been for years. ''I'll wash off my travel dust. After that, why don't you come down and play some music for me. We'll have tea and put this all behind us.''

Riordan rode into the courtyard at the Saracen's Head, almost glad to be back at the uncomfortable inn. Dusk was falling, but, even so, he could see that the vicar's flowers were thriving on Bass's property and, if he wasn't mistaken, the painting was finished. Toby came running. ''Are you stopping here on your way to London, your grace?''

''No. I hadn't planned to go up to town just now. Why do you ask?''

''Didn't you get my note? I sent it the day you left. You said to tell you if anything different was happening at Thorne's Well. They left for London. Said they were going to be gone through July.''

Diana moved close to Cambria. ''Here's Ragsdale for our dance. He said we're booked up for months. Isn't that wonderful?''

''Did he pay you and Talia back?'' Diana nodded as Ragsdale took her onto the floor.

An arm slipped around her waist, pulled her close. ''Hello, my love.'' Her breath caught as Riordan's warmth enveloped her, and all the feelings he'd sparked in Thornedale flowed over her. For just the barest second, she leaned against him, savoring the illusion of safe harbor.

Then cold reason stiffened her, made her step away. She knew better than this. ''What are you doing here, Riordan?''

The blasted man *grinned.* ''I'm here to continue our little romance . . . for Mark's sake, I believe you said?''

''*Mark,*'' she bit out, ''is now *working* for you at Langcliffe Hall, so don't tell me that's your reason.''

"You're not pleased with Mark's rise in prosperity?"

"You've enticed my solicitor away."

A smile of satisfaction crept over his features. "He can still handle matters for you, Cambria. I have no objection."

"And if you and I should find ourselves on opposite sides?"

"Why then, I shall release him to be your gallant protector." He confiscated her dance card, scribbled on it and offered it back.

She snatched it away. "You are the most devious person in the world, Riordan. You are paying him so much that he could never leave your employ." She turned and walked toward her aunts and was immediately surrounded by admirers who took her card and passed it around.

"What's this?" one asked, "Langcliffe has the supper dance?" She shook her head to deny it, then looked beyond her admirers to see Langcliffe watching with that *smug* look on his face. "And the first waltz!" Her admirers grew silent, looking at her strangely.

She took the card to examine their claims. Riordan *had* claimed those two important dances. Was he here in London to ruin her?

"How do you know Langcliffe?" one frowning gentleman asked.

"He's . . . a neighbor at home." She got a few nods over that, but still they waited for more. "We knew each other as children—"

"She used to follow me around like a little shadow," Riordan finished, ambling through the small crowd like a hot knife through butter.

"What's he doing here?" muttered one foolish man as Langcliffe passed. One flick of Langcliffe's black eyes silenced the dissenter, immediately ending all murmuring. It surprised Cambria. She'd only seen him agreeably charming or charmingly arrogant, but never *menacing*.

Aiming for peace, she quickly explained. "Langcliffe was afraid I would be a wallflower and thought someone ought to rescue me." That earned a few chuckles . . . and gave her courage. "So now that my dance card is full, Langcliffe, surely, you'll relinquish your turns?"

Before she could protest, Riordan smoothly placed her hand onto his arm. "As you can see, gentlemen, Miss Thorne is still a little too saucy. I shall take her away and return her to you with better manners." To her great indignation, the others laughed in relief of his good cheer.

With an unbreakable grip, Riordan took her strolling around the room. "We shall now promenade. I shall introduce you as my neighbor, and then I shall relinquish you to the others until the first waltz."

She was furious. "You almost instigated a small war back there. Do you intend to blacken my reputation?"

He patted her gloved hand. "They were merely surprised to see me here tonight. I have not attended a ball for over ten years." He whispered in her ear. "You should feel honored. A moment of my attention is worth more than an approving nod from Beau Brummell."

Chuckling at her shocked silence, he did as he promised. With every introduction, he marked her as someone important enough to bring Langcliffe back into society. Once around the astonished room, he handed her into the care of her first partner.

She didn't recognized the gentleman at first. The first time she'd seen him, he'd been travel-worn and drinking heavily. Lord Parish . . . Crowley's friend, the one who tried to rescue her. "I know you must wish me to Hades, Miss Thorne, but I wanted an opportunity to apologize."

Without thinking, Cambria looked quickly around, half expecting Crowley to barge in and ruin her evening.

"Crowley's not here," he assured her. "Langcliffe sent him a note. Told him if he caught him anywhere near you, in the same building even, that he would consider it a personal insult." At the end of their dance, he gave her a worried look. "I saw you with Langcliffe. Does he know I was there with Crowley?"

"I don't know. We've never spoken of it."

Parish took on a hunted expression and disappeared into the crowd.

Then as if materialized from her thoughts, Riordan bowed

before her. "Time to dance, Cambria." As he whirled with the music, a soft gasp arose from the room. She *knew* it . . . just dancing with the knave was enough to ruin a girl. And the *look* he sent skimming over her . . . as if she belonged to him. "I like the dress, Cambria."

She loved the sapphire silk but wasn't about to agree with anything he said. "It's a consolation gift for those of us on the shelf. We get to wear whatever color we wish."

Instantly insulted, he demanded, "Who said you're on the shelf?"

"At twenty-four, I'm hardly a debutante." At his confused expression, she explained. "Debutantes are like kittens, they're quickly snatched up. A creature my age will be chosen only for her mouse-catching skills."

"Mouse-catching—"

"The baths . . . now I'm worth marrying."

He roared in laughter. Heads turned, but Riordan ignored them, intent, it seemed, on gallantry. "Lovely spray of brilliants in your hair."

"It looks like I stuck my head out the window in a heavy mist." He smiled fondly, but she'd had enough. "Are you trying to ruin me? Taking two dances, one the supper dance, which Aunt Diana says is reserved for a favored gentleman." As his brows rose in feigned injury, she lowered her voice. "Why are you doing this?"

"Cambria," he said with friendly exasperation, "you continue to assume the worst of me, when you have no reason to do so. The truth is that I have decided to marry you."

Riordan spun her around while a shocked Cambria absorbed his declaration. After two minutes with her tonight, he wasn't about to give her the advantage of tender words spoken in a private place.

As he pulled her close to avoid a flying elbow, she fired back her answer. "You've *decided?* How typically Langcliffe. Next you'll be pledging your true love in the same arrogant manner."

"Is that what you want, Cambria?" Her face crimson, she refused to speak for the rest of the dance. As they exited the floor, she tried to pull away, but he wouldn't release her hand. "A gentlemen always returns a maiden to her chaperon, Cambria."

"I'm hoping Diana won't see me with you. Let me go."

"Relax," he began—

Furious, she curled her index finger around the joint of his thumb, then squeezed it back toward the wrist. Looking sweetly into his suddenly crimson face, she released it and murmured, "Next time I shall break it."

Ignoring Riordan's gasp of surprise and pain, she leaned against the nearby wall. Shaking knees and a serious question about the stability of her heaving stomach were ill-favored flaws for a woman who wanted to present a serene facade to the world.

"Damn, Cambria, where did you learn that vicious trick?"

"Phillip. He didn't believe females should be helpless." She looked pointedly at his hands, one gently holding the other. "Go wrap that around a cold glass of punch." She ducked between two couples and disappeared.

Frustrated, Riordan headed for the punch bowl and reached for the glass with the most ice floating on top. Wincing, he wrapped his thumb around the icy glass.

"Riordan." Alistair drew near, his voice full of excitement, "I got a note from the boys school, and we're actually turning a tidy profit." He laughed. "You'll never believe what's happening. Remember Johnstone's mother? Well, she's got these boys following her around now, helping with her rose garden. She takes them to the village and buys them little treats. No one can believe it, but, they hardly ever have to cane them any more." He grinned. "Trouble is, now the director wants to trot over to Bedlam and find a couple more dotty old ladies so he can expand the school."

Riordan moaned. The last thing he needed to hear now was Alistair's zany scheme—just the thought of problems lurking in this situation made his thumb pound harder. "At least Johnstone can't get her allowance."

Alistair laughed again. "He tried it one night. Climbed in her window and started looking for her money. She didn't recognize him and yelled for help. The boys came running and pounded on him until he was blubbering in the corner.'' He sighed happily. ''No wonder you love this business. This is more fun than sneaking a pig into the headmaster's rooms.'' He paused. ''Did you catch up with Grandmother?''

Riordan nodded. ''At Langcliffe Hall. I told her I was going to marry Cambria.''

Alistair sputtered and choked on his own drink. ''Why did you tell her that? To get even for the trouble she caused?''

''I thought she should know the truth. Let her get used to it.''

''You're serious.''

''Yes, but keep this to yourself, Alistair.'' Ignoring Alistair's grin, Riordan concentrated entirely on Cambria. ''You'd think she'd be ecstatic over all that attention, but have you noticed that she never quite relaxes?''

''Yes, she likes the younger men, especially if they are shy. Perhaps she's like Diana, the ultimate mothering type. Here's the one she likes best,'' Alistair said, lowering his voice. ''The tall, thin one with the look of a spaniel. He's the younger brother of Viscount Hale. His mother and sister are sitting behind us. She's the one practically clinging to her mother.''

Riordan glanced quickly around, then sent Alistair a wolfish look. ''Well, Alistair, I might as well make myself useful.'' He turned and made his bow to the little wallflower's mother. ''Lady Hale, I wonder if you might introduce me to your lovely daughter?''

Poor lady, she hadn't a clue as to who he was; nor should she, for they had never met. ''Your husband and I did business together some years ago.'' Relief flooded her features, and, in a few flustered moments, the deed was done. Little Miss Hale, a thin little brown-haired mouse, stood beside him as the present dance ended.

Waiting for the floor to clear, he asked her, ''Is this your first season?'' Blushing, she nodded. Riordan was sure she wouldn't be able to remember a single topic she'd been trained to discuss. ''Tell me about your family. Their names first, if you please.''

Such relief. A sighing smile put life back into the little wren's face. "My brother, Anthony, is here tonight. He's the next to eldest after my brother George. I'm the youngest." She'd answered his question, and she was through.

"Now, I need the names of your dogs, if you please."

She laughed at his nonsense. "Rosie and Punch." Again, she'd done her part and waited for her next cue.

"Your favorite thing to do, and your most hated?"

She took a deep breath. "I grow flowers, but I hate riding."

"And Anthony's likes, dislikes?"

She looked embarrassed, but she replied anyway. "He loves horses, but flowers make him sick. He's always had a delicate constitution, but flowers are the worst. He sort of *swells up*. Please don't tell anyone. He hates anyone to know."

"I never would," he murmured as the music began. How very interesting.

Cambria found herself watching Langcliffe as he took the floor with Hale's sister. Did he like her? Did he like that tiny, frail look? She sighed. It was bad enough that she compared every man unfavorably with Langcliffe; now she was dipping into jealousy.

Cambria went to find Talia. She felt a definite megrim approaching. Before it hit, she intended to be home in her bed.

Long before Riordan's supper dance.

Chapter Seventeen

Cambria was enjoying the contralto's second selection when Riordan, the persistent wretch, slipped onto the chair next to her, his broad shoulders taking up the space normally allotted to separate the guests.

Riordan's courting style had the finesse of a goat loose in the garden. No rules of society; no one's good opinion meant anything to the man. Once he trampled his way to her side— as he had been doing for weeks—he proceeded to batter away at her defenses.

He leaned over, his lips brushing her ear. "Convenient, the way you always sit on the back row, Cambria. Making it easier for me to find you?"

Determined to stifle the telling jolt of pleasure, she shifted away. "Such blatant conceit, Riordan. I sit here only because I am the tallest woman in the room." She paused. "Why are you here, Riordan? You cannot tell one note from another."

He pulled her hand onto his thigh. "Pursuing you, of course." His face grew serious. "We would be happy together, and you know it. Forget the old family prejudices and think about the future."

"I have no *old* prejudices. Mine are all extremely current."

He sighed. *"Touché."* Then he murmured, "Wouldn't you like to give our children an end to fighting forever? Just one contented Langcliffe family. I'll let you be the boss, Cambria. You'd like that."

Her lips twitched, she couldn't help it. She was beginning to think teasing was his most potent weapon. Tipping her head closer, she whispered, *"Thorne,* Riordan. When I marry, my husband has to change his name to Thorne."

He choked. "What?"

The woman in front of them turned, sniffed haughtily, then turned back to listen to the music.

Cambria's shoulders shook with laughter.

Riordan strode into Cambria's parlor and made his bow to Talia. "I know I'm early, but before the room fills with hopeful gentlemen, I want to show Cambria something outside." With Talia's beaming approval, he lifted Cambria out of her chair and marched her, stiff-legged and resisting, out onto the front pathway. Parked just outside the posts was a bright, cherry-red-lacquered gig drawn by a coal-black horse.

"You're not afraid of horses, are you?"

Incensed, she glared at him. *"Afraid?"*

"I've only seen you walking. What was I to think?"

"I was driving my pony cart at six, Riordan. And after you left, I was better than Phillip. I'll match my skill against yours any day."

Indeed, Riordan thought, that stubbornly raised chin and scowling face did remind him of Cambria at six, trying to best him at everything. Giving her no choice, he lifted her onto the seat. "Good. After buying this for you, I'd hate to think of it not being used."

"You *bought* it for me? Are you out of your mind, Riordan?"

Stepping up beside her, he shifted her over and handed her the reins. "Just think how jealous the tabbies of Thornedale will be seeing you drive this little gig."

Her eyes lit up at that splendid thought, but still affronted over his buying the gig, she struck a bored pose and refused to move. He gave the reins a shake and leaned back to let her deal with the horses. While she was scrambled to get control, he leaned back. "Hyde Park, please."

Riordan took pleasure in the secret smile she tried to hide. She loved action, she loved the challenge. Not only that, but she was the only woman who'd ever routed his mother. Truth to tell, he thought ruefully, she was better at it than he was. Once inside the park, Riordan murmured, "Discussion for the day, Cambria. "We shall talk about love."

She gave him a bored look. "A fool draws from a vast pool of ignorance, Riordan. Go ahead and talk. I'll think of something else."

He chuckled and draped his arm around her shoulder. Playing with her hair, he took an exultant note of her quickened breath. "Picture, if you will, the intimate situation under which babies are created."

She gasped and jerked on the reins. The horse sidestepped, eliciting another gasp from Cambria. Immediately, she got the startled horse under control and gave Riordan a furious look. "How *dare* you, Riordan."

"You're a country woman, Cambria. Procreation is not an unknown subject to you. Don't go all missish on me; not when this is so vital to your happiness." He paused. "When you consider your devoted swains, you must also envision that particular image, then wonder if, instead, the sparks between you and me are far more suited to such an activity."

Too disconcerted to concentrate, Cambria pulled the gig over under a tree and brought it to a stop. Squirming out of his embrace, she slid out her side. "Let's walk . . . and for heavens sake, change the subject."

"Very well," he said, turning onto a tree-shaded path. "My mother told me how you threatened her out of Thornedale."

Her steps halted. "Why did she do that? She was terrified when I threatened to tell you. She scuttled out of town that very day."

"My solicitor found out about it and told me. When I charged her with it, she lost her temper and blurted it out."

"How strange. *Were* you shocked about her gambling? I

half expected her to laugh and declare that she'd taught you all you knew.''

"I was shocked . . . but equally shocked at you.''

She exploded. "What did you expect, Riordan? That I'd just cringe in the corner and let her ruin my life?''

"Cambria,'' he said, half laughing, "you took that the wrong way. I'm all admiration for what you did.''

She looked surprised . . . then gave a cynical lift of her brows. "I suppose you are. A dose of blackmail probably seems tame to a Langcliffe.''

He fell silent under that blow. "What did my mother say that made you believe her . . . and hate me?''

"Oh, no. I'm not going to let you spin your lies again, Riordan. Change the subject, or I shall walk home.''

"Cambria, darling,'' he said, taking her hand, "I haven't finished the subject I brought you out to discuss. When I'm through, you will realize the implications of choosing a mate whose touch you might find offensive. Now,'' he said gently, "I'm going to explain exactly what you need to know. You may just listen or join in the conversation at any time.''

Later, blushing to the roots of her hair and totally silenced, she let him kiss her—once—under the tree. "There,'' he said, "see what I mean?''

She knew that Riordan would be waiting in the foyer. No one had told her, but the smirk on Amelia's face gave it away. She told herself she would back out, but she loved music, and they were going to hear the Philharmonic Orchestra at the opera house. Johann Solomon would perform on the violin with Muzio Clementi at the piano. Mozart, Beethoven, Cherubini, and Haydn. She could not give up such a rich feast.

When she reached the bottom stair, he took her arm. "Admit it,'' he murmured, "you're beginning to weaken, aren't you? I saw your eyes light up when you saw me.''

"My stomach was rebelling at the sight of you.''

"You were hoping I would kiss you again tonight, Cambria. You were looking at my mouth with a lustful expression.''

"I was wondering if I might be allowed to enjoy the performance or suffer through yet another outrageous sermon."

He chuckled. "I promise to not disturb your enjoyment of the music. If I do, you may torture me with one more of Phillip's little tricks."

Her eyes narrowed. "You *promise* to be quiet?"

"During the performance . . . yes." He pulled her along toward the door. "But first, we shall talk in the coach." Outwitted, she resisted, but as usual, his strength made mockery of her attempts. "Tonight," he said as he handed her up into the closed coach, "we shall discuss your secret little trip out to Thorne's Well and why you have not invited me."

She slid over to make room. "How did you find out about that?"

He closed the door. "I have spies watching you."

She laughed. "No, you don't."

Seriously, he replied, "Yes, I do. I never leave anything to chance."

She couldn't believe it . . . and yet, in Thornedale, he had done it before. "That doesn't mean you're invited, Riordan. This is just for—"

"For your prospective suitors and a few others to make it look like a house party. I can't believe your choice of suitors, Cambria. There's not one backbone between them. Can't you stand a man you can't boss around?"

Tight-lipped, she refused to answer. The truth was, she wanted a *safe* husband, one whose motives were perfectly clear. No wonder Riordan disapproved, when he was the absolute opposite in every way.

"Very well, Cambria, don't answer. In the end, you'll come to your senses." He pulled her close. She intended to stop him, but something inside her relented and curved against him. He leaned his chin against her hair as if she were the most precious thing in his world.

Almost every night, no matter how she resisted, she fell asleep thinking about that kiss in front of the bakery. In odd moments during the day, her senses would just curl up in a ball thinking about how she felt. Playing at romance back in

Thorne's Well had served its purpose—but had set her world tumbling in a way she hadn't expected.

Over the last few weeks, Riordan had added more *incidents* to overwhelm her, and always at the most inappropriate times. His kiss in the park, his fingers playing with her hair, images his words painted. . . his insistence that he wanted her for his wife.

And, just as he intended, she'd begun to wonder if by some miracle Riordan was right, that they would be happy together. For the truth was, he was right about one thing . . . the thought of *procreation* with anyone but Riordan seemed utterly impossible.

She hadn't changed her mind. He was a rogue, chasing after what he could not have, no doubt enjoying the hunt as much as the prize he deviously sought. But, it was getting harder to resist . . . to never waver.

Lady Chester's ball was a perfect place to evade Riordan. After last night's sentimental weakening, she'd been canny as a cat all night. Two more dances and she could go home without him touching her or insinuating suggestive thoughts to haunt her half the night.

Riordan moved along the perimeter of the dance floor and found Cambria walking toward her aunt. Without stopping, he pulled Cambria out to the balcony, weaving through couples rushing in at the sound of music.

"Let me go, Riordan. My next partner is waiting for me."

He pulled her down the stairs into the dimly lit garden. "You haven't given me a choice, Cambria."

"A gentleman would take a hint."

He pulled her into a dark corner, out of the light and out of view. "Whoever said I was a gentleman? Certainly not you."

She exploded with fury. Pounding on his chest with her free hand, she growled, "You're right . . . try barbarian. Try deceitful, hateful—"

He caught both her hands and pulled her hard against him. As she fell against his chest, he lowered his face so close he could see the tears welling in her eyes. "Try a man in love, Cambria."

He took her mouth in a slow, savage kiss. She tried to pull back, but he slid one hand into her hair to hold her fast, then softened the kiss as her struggling waned. He lifted his mouth a whisper away. "You want to, Cambria. For once, be honest with yourself. Kiss me back."

A shuddering sigh escaped her. Her hands moved, tightened their grip on the back of his coat. Her swollen mouth lifted to meet his.

Cambria poured all her feelings into the kiss. Once more, she thought, *just once more* she would let herself feel his powerful arms around her, feel his wonderful mouth satisfy this strange need. She let his tongue taste the edges of her lips, then begin a marauding exploration. His mouth invaded, then drew her back, before invading again, sending her whirling into a turbulent abyss of aching pleasure. "That's it, Cambria. Come with me." Tremors swept through her, intense, demanding, pulling her where no one existed except this powerful man.

Finally, he shuddered and dragged his open mouth across her cheek and buried his face in her hair, his chest heaving. "We *must* talk, Cambria. Your birthday is almost here, and this is getting too serious."

His words were like a dash of cold water. "You won't be able to keep me from marrying? Is that what you mean, Riordan?"

"Don't push me that far, Cambria. I'll do what I must."

"You admit it?" she said incredulously. "After all this deception, you admit you want to stop me marrying?"

"Not for your damned land, Cambria. For *you*. You bested my mother. You've won every fight. Desist now . . . please."

Diana's voice jarred them both as she marched up beside them. "I shall call a footman if you try something like that again, Riordan."

Riordan's arms dropped. "Ask your niece if she wants to leave."

Militant, Diana glared at them both. "Cambria?"

As Cambria walked away, Riordan thought, *That's the last time you get a civilized courtship, Cambria.* Her birthday was a week away. He was not letting her stubbornly walk straight into a life of misery.

Hours later, he awakened to a knock on the library door. Struggling out of a deep sleep, he raised his head off a pile of papers on the desk. "Come in, Alistair." He sat upright and rubbed his eyes.

"I brought you the note you wanted from Amelia."

Riordan waved him forward. "What does it say?"

"Tomorrow Cambria's going to visit the Hale's estate on the way to Thorne's Well. Two other coaches are going to Thorne's Well the next day."

Riordan jerked upright, his head swimming. "What? Are they engaged?" His chest felt like it was exploding. Hale and Cambria?

"Amelia's note says it's unofficial. If all goes well, they're coming straight back here to marry. Diana is remaining in London to obtain a special license."

Riordan threw back the covers. "I'm going to Lakeview."

Alistair turned to leave. "I'm coming with you."

Chapter Eighteen

"So, Miss Thorne," Viscount Hale, Anthony Hale's older brother, asked as they admired his duck pond, "What do you think of our little place here?" Considerably shorter than Anthony, Lord Hale exuded a nervous energy that reminded Cambria of an ant who'd lost its way. If his feet weren't shuffling, his toe was tapping as if anxious to be on the move.

"It looks . . . very efficient. I admire a landowner who cares for his property." Everything about the Hale property was trimmed to within an inch. "Your garden, for instance, is splendid."

"My wife oversees it personally." He gave his round little wife an approving smile. The wife in question looked like she could use a good night's sleep, Cambria thought. But there was little chance of that with their six children continually escaping the overworked nursemaid and clinging to their mother's skirts. Anthony, had drawn the younger children to the other side of the pond to toss crumbs. That kindness strengthened Cambria's choice.

Hale's haughty voice interrupted her pleasant thoughts. "How does this compare to your property?"

She knew that was coming and dreaded the inquisition. "We

have a garden as well. We pick our own fruit and hunt game in the rather extensive woods around us.'' *Of course, it doesn't belong to us, but what's a necessary skip over the truth with such an important matter impending?*

"Tenants?" He wanted to know the value as well.

"None, Lord Hale, but we do have a rather thriving establishment on our property." That much was true.

Lord Hale's mouth pursed tightly. "A *business,* you say?"

"Yes. Hot Roman baths. We allow subscriptions to a select few."

Like a hound with the fox's scent, he leaned forward. "Subscriptions?"

Talia joined in. "Like Almack's, only a little more discreet. Havenshire and Ragsdale are on the committee."

Hale's eyes opened wide. "My word."

Cambria could hardly believe the change in the man. To be one of a selected few was a magic elixir to the *ton,* and Hale was no exception.

"I might be persuaded to visit, Miss Thorne."

"Of course. When would you like to come?"

"I don't know," he said with a direct challenge, "I wouldn't want to come without a subscription."

Talia wasn't letting him get away with it. "You may come now as our guest. Family members, of course, need no subscription."

Silence reigned as Riordan and Alistair dismounted and walked toward Lakeview. No noise, no mess, no workman—the house was finished. Inside, men worked only at last minute scraping putty off windows.

Once upstairs, Riordan halted at the doorway to his mother's room, appalled to see that while he'd been courting Cambria, his mother had been nesting here at Lakeview. The walls glowed with ivory brocade panels and blue velvet drapes adorned the windows. She'd filled the room with expensive furniture. An heirloom pier glass from Langcliffe Hall stood in the corner. His mother's clothes filled the wardrobe.

Damn it, Cambria was on her way. She was weakening. A few more days and she would be his . . . or lost forever if his mother had her way.

He went to find Peck. "Where is Lady Langcliffe?"

"Gone to get more furniture. Said she'd be right back."

How exhausting it was, Cambria thought, to remain cheerful for an entire day and a half, especially with Lord Hale, who never stopped *moving.* If it wasn't a tapping foot, his fingers drummed. Talia simply fell asleep in the middle of a conversation, which Lord Hale, of course, found charming. Cambria had tried it once, but Hale simply badgered her with questions until she gave up the ruse. She'd long since run out of evasions and had fallen back on telling ancient tales.

Beside her, Talia stirred. "The village is just up ahead. It's very charming," she said with a straight face, "Shall we walk through?" Talia hated *walking* only slightly less than she loathed the villagers. Lord Hale, however, had bobbed to the top of Talia's aversions, and she wanted *out.*

Lord Hale sent an acquisitive inspection over the village and knocked on the roof. "Ah, yes," he said, "I'd like to see it all."

Anthony leaned forward. "Would you like to walk, Cambria?"

"Yes, thank you." *Dear Anthony,* she thought. So different from his brother. Selfishly, Lord Hale had taken the forward-facing seat and insisted his brother sit beside him. When they stopped for the night, he commandeered the best chamber and let the rest fend for themselves.

Anthony might be grateful to live at Thorne's Well, if only to get away from his annoying brother. The thought of Anthony's happiness in the midst of the pleasure-loving Thornes cheered her.

As the coach stopped by the church, Lord Hale stepped out first and stood stretching while his brother assisted the ladies down.

"This is, as you can see," Cambria said to the gathering

group, "St. John's church, with history going back to ten fifty-three. The lower part of the tower is probably Saxon, the rest Norman. The timber roof is three hundred years old." They sauntered through the building, admiring the late-medieval brasses, then descended the steps to the cemetery.

Anthony immediately held a handkerchief to his nose. "I've never seen a flower garden in a cemetery."

Cambria stared, horrified, as Anthony's breathing became labored and the color drained slowly from his face.

Lord Hale tapped his foot. Still worried, but anxious to keep the peace, Cambria hurried forward. "Our monument beyond the vicarage was raised as a memorial to Henry, Duke of Langcliffe, who fought valiantly with King Phillip at the battle of Crécy and became one of his favorites."

Lord Hale halted. "Langcliffe? Ancestor of *Midas* Langcliffe?"

"Riordan, Lord Langcliffe? Is that what he's called?"

"You *know* him?"

"Yes," she managed, "He is restoring one of his homes nearby.

Just up the footway, two village ladies who'd sided with the duchess strolled toward them. Seeing Cambria, they nodded briefly, but passed beyond without a word. Not knowing she'd been snubbed, Lord Hale nodded in approval. "I see they hold you in proper respect, Miss Thorne."

Talia chuckled and tipped her parasol to hide her face.

Cambria gave Talia a warning scowl and turned away to observe Anthony's harsh breathing. He whispered, "I am somewhat sensitive to flowers, Miss Thorne." Cambria glanced back down the road, horrified at the gauntlet of flowers she had drawn him past. "I'm so sorry . . . will you be all right?" She waved her coachman forward. "Get in the coach, Anthony. We'll go straight to Thorne's Well." *As soon as she got him past her own meadow full of flowers.* Her stomach tightened another notch.

Lord Hale protested. "He'll be fine. Let's see the rest of the village."

Anthony scrambled in, with one cautious eye on his impatient brother. Talia and Cambria followed quickly, leaving Lord Hale no other choice. Huffing like a pouting child, Lord Hale stormed into the coach and folded his arms tightly across his chest.

He glared at Cambria all the way—until they approached Lakeview—then abruptly, he leaned out to gawk at the mansion. "Is this your home?" He pounded on the roof, bringing the coach to a stop.

"No," Talia snapped, "It's Lakeview, Lord Langcliffe's home."

Hale's eyes widened. "Langcliffe's house?" He scrambled out and rushed toward the house. The others followed, Anthony with keen interest, and Talia with the last dregs of patience. Reluctantly, Cambria climbed out, trying to block out feelings that seeing Riordan's house churned up inside her. She only wanted to go home, cast her eyes on the flowered meadow, touch the walls of the beloved old house, and renew her vow to save it.

She strolled slowly toward the trees—and stopped. Off to the side, tied in a shady copse of trees, were two horses, Riordan's and Alistair's. Riordan was here at Lakeview? If she stepped into the house, she would see him? She hesitated, waited while the thought beckoned.

Her feet moved forward. Just *once more,* her emotions insisted. Just *one* more time. before she set her feet on another, irrevocable path.

She quietly stepped inside, her gaze searching. Hale and Anthony were just coming out of the library. Talia was in the hall conversing with Alistair. Scraping sounds in the back identified yet another workman.

She looked up—and the sweetest feeling poured through her. Riordan stood on the landing, looking down at her. Neither of them moved.

Some emotion crossed Riordan's face, something harsh and aggressive . . . possessive as if she had something he wanted, and should she move to leave, he would come after her. She felt no fear, knowing she was safe as long as she did not retreat. Slowly, she could feel her tension unwind. Jarred and jagged edges softened with a calm serenity.

She saw Riordan's chest heave as if he'd just remembered to breathe. He lifted his chin as if to tell her to come up, and he stretched his hand outward . . . and waited. She wanted to go. She was safe as long as she went toward him. Her gaze steadied on Riordan's hand, for that was her objective as she ascended, to put her hand in his. To say goodbye.

His grasp was warm, strong as he pulled her up the last few stairs to stand beside him. His hand loosened, let her go so he could slide his arm around her back, tuck her close against his side. So still, So quiet.

Talia looked upward, smiled, and began mounting the stairs.

Like a hunting dog. Lord Hale's ears pricked up. He pushed his way up past the others. "Lord Langcliffe? I'm Viscount Hale." Langcliffe raised a surprised brow at the man's rudeness, but grinned at some private thought. Anthony smiled up at Cambria as he trailed up behind the rest.

She could feel Riordan stiffen as the approaching crowd separated them, could sense the hunter's instincts aroused. Then his head rose as the sound of coaches jangled into the yard. "More suitors?" Riordan murmured as the young people came pouring through the door. Ellie and Amelia came in first, followed by Lord Marchant. After that, a small cluster came, young ladies and gentlemen accompanied by two starched and proper chaperons. They filled the foyer. A smiling Alistair hurried to greet them, invited them up to meet his uncle.

Riordan changed before her eyes. Donning a smile that charmed them, he took them through upstairs common rooms. He complimented the girls until their cheeks glowed, and quizzed the young men about sports and racing, their homes . . . and their prospects. Her stomach knotted and began to ache. Would he ruin her chances for a match as he promised?

Cambria dawdled on the landing; her nerves rattled as Riordan let the rest go down and stood alongside her. "Charming fellow, Lord Hale."

Cambria couldn't raise even a small protest over Riordan's caustic tone. "You should spend two days in a coach with him."

He reached between them, captured her fingers, pulled their

linked hands behind him to draw her closer. She tugged, but, as usual, it was a waste of time. She looked at the people below them. One wrong move, and everyone would be wondering what the devil was she doing holding Riordan's hand. How could he do this with everyone just inches away?

She shifted closer to Riordan to hide what he had done. Riordan, of course, only chuckled softly, the wretch.

Hale slowed and looked back up at Riordan, while the rest of the company continued downward. "Will you be entertaining here, Langcliffe?" The man was so transparent, Cambria thought, practically inviting himself to dine with the neighbor-duke.

Riordan's hand began a slow, insinuating slide up Cambria's back. "I haven't made any plans, Hale. What do you think? Would it make a good house for guests?" Without releasing her hand, Riordan unfastened a button in the back of her dress.

She inhaled sharply, suddenly afraid to move. Frantically, she slide the button back in place. She could feel Riordan's stifled laughter.

"Oh, yes, it's a wonderful house," Hale insisted, "Are there any other families in the area?"

"A dozen families who would love to meet you," Cambria said, trying for a composed voice.

Riordan stopped. "Who were you thinking of, Cambria . . . Sarah?"

Riordan was a beast to do this. Lord Hale would never allow the blacksmith's wife at his table. Anthony might, but that was not the question. "It's your guest list," she snapped. "Invite Bass, too, if you wish."

Hale frowned. "Bass? I'm not familiar with a Lord Bass."

"He's rather reclusive," Cambria said quickly. What had she started with her runaway temper?

"He gardens," drawled Riordan. "He's something of a collector. Even the vicar has commented on his ingenuity."

A bubble of laughter threatened, but Cambria breathed quickly to keep it from rising. Before she could compose herself, Riordan's marauding fingers made another foray at her buttons, and this time, he undid two. Her laughter died as panic set in.

Did Riordan plan to compromise her right here in front of everyone? She sent her free hand upwards, chasing the errant buttons. Lord Hale frowned at her awkward action, then looked toward Riordan to see if he had noticed.

Riordan immediately took action. "Let me see," he said, dropping her hand to grasp her shoulders from behind. "It's a little flying insect," he said, "He's gone down the back of your dress."

Hale started up to see for himself, but Riordan scowled him away. "Stay back . . . I'll see to it." At Hale's shocked gasp, Riordan drawled, "We've practically been raised together."

Before she could think what to do, Riordan took his own action. He unbuttoned her dress down to her shoulders. She held the dress tight against her chest, while Riordan's fingers rooted around as if looking for the insect. Down his hand went inside her shift, touching her where the Langcliffe devil knew she was ticklish.

She yelped and wiggled, gritting her teeth to stifle any noise, but the most horrible sounds came out of her throat. The crowd downstairs looked up, their mouths open like gaping fish. That struck her funny and hysteria set in. She began to laugh and choke at the same time.

Riordan's hand whipped out and swatted at the imaginary insect, and then began pounding her on the back. He looked down to explain to the company. "She swallowed that pesky bug."

That only made it worse. Tears of laughter streamed down her face while Langcliffe stood by with an innocent expression, pummeling her as if she did this all the time.

She glanced up into his face. While his expression was pure, arrogant boredom for the others' benefit, his eyes were laughing. Devilish eyes full of mischief that met hers as if saying, *Wasn't that fun?*

Then she knew why just the sight of him earlier had given her such peace. Why all her troubles fell away just looking across the room at him.

Despite all, she loved being *with* him.

She was *filled* with love for him.

She dare not let him know.

Her eyes closed with the hopeless pain of it. Still holding her dress against her, she felt herself swaying. His hands tightened on her shoulders, and she heard him say, "She's all right, Anthony. Run down to the kitchen. There's a pump there and a dipper. Bring her a drink, will you?"

He spoke again. "The rest of you run outside while I see to her . . . you too, Hale." Then, calmly, he began to button up her dress.

Riordan smiled in satisfaction. Cambria tried to hide it, but for one brief second he'd seen the truth in her eyes—and the panic. She wasn't going to acknowledge the discovery that she loved him, the stubborn girl. Too bad, for now he had that priceless bit of information.

He turned her around to face him. Lifting her chin, he looked into her eyes. "Don't be afraid of it, Cambria."

She glanced to the side, refusing to return his gaze.

"If you would *talk* to me, Cambria, we could have this all settled. You wouldn't have to look for anyone else." *Please stop,* she thought, keeping her emotions tightly in check.

"All right, then. Be stubborn. But I'll tell you now that I will never let you marry someone you don't love. Your birthday is what? . . . Five days away? Well, you are not leaving this valley without admitting you love me. I have a special license coming. We can marry before your birthday."

She looked up then. "You can't keep me a prisoner, Riordan."

"After today, you think I won't do whatever it takes?"

"You did that for a *lesson?*"

"Would you like a clearer demonstration?"

"No," she gasped.

"Then talk to me. Tell me what the barrier is. Tell me what my mother said. There is nothing that I can not explain."

Anthony came rushing toward the stairs, a glass of water in his hand. "Here you are, Miss Thorne."

"Tonight we'll talk, after everyone's asleep . . . *promise.*"

She glanced down at Anthony. "Very well. I promise."

Riordan smiled at Anthony and sauntered down the stairs.

Strolling to the Hale coach, he waited for Cambria and Anthony to come out out of the house. After they were seated, Riordan slid in beside Cambria. She stared silently but made no objection.

As they began to move, Lord Hale began his inquisition. "So, Lord Langcliffe, where are the property lines between you and the Thornes?

Beside him, Cambria stiffened. Clearly, she didn't want Hale to realize how small her property was. "I have no idea. We've all lived together in this area so long I don't know what the boundaries are."

Hale blinked. "You don't know? What if you wanted to sell it?"

"Where's your sense of history, Hale? We've held this valley together since the crusades. Lakeview is entailed, and, if I remember right, the Thorne property is entailed as well . . . isn't it, Cambria?"

"That's right," she said shakily. "We cannot sell the property."

Riordan patted her hand. "That's what I thought." Anthony's eyes narrowed, but Lord Hale approved of the close connection. *Obsequious toad.*

They drove for a few minutes, then Riordan signaled the coach to stop. Cambria gave him a quizzical glance, but Riordan smiled and shooed them all out of the coach. "I have something to show you. Then we'll walk the rest of the way."

When they stood down, Talia remained inside, "I'll go with the coach on up to the house." Riordan nodded and waved her off. As the other two coaches drew near, he waved them on toward Thorne's Well.

Motioning Cambria and the Hales to follow him, he took down a short embankment where a small stream broke off from the river. All along the stream, thick beds of wild flowers blew in the breeze.

"See those two slabs of rock meeting on the edges of the boulder in the middle of the stream? That's a clapper bridge . . . it's very old."

Lord Hale's eyes glazed over with boredom. Anthony

sneezed and his eyes watered. He slapped his handkerchief over his nose and turned to scramble back up the incline and onto the road.

Cambria looked after him, a worried expression on her face. "He's sensitive to flowers."

Riordan managed to look surprised. "Poor fellow." He then extracted his own clean handkerchief, dipped it into the water, and took it up to Anthony. "Put this over your nose. It will help you breathe."

Cambria touched his arm. "Thank you, Riordan."

"Shall I run ahead and bring back the coach?"

Anthony shook his head. "Absolutely not. I'd like the walk." Riordan had to give the boy credit, but not enough for Cambria to marry him.

Hale pointed up the road. "There's a bridge up ahead . . . the road crosses the river there?"

Riordan strode up to walk beside Lord Hale. "Yes. You can hear the falls from here. It's a beautiful spot, cool on a hot summer day."

"I suppose you don't know who owns the bridge either?"

Riordan laughed. "We don't care, but our servants have a regular war over who has to clear it after the spring floods."

Cambria moved up beside them, "We've done it for twenty years, and now Riordan has promised to take over for the next twenty. Isn't that right?" Lord Hale nodded smugly at so cozy an arrangement. No doubt, Riordan thought, Hale saw himself rising through the ranks of the *ton*.

Riordan slowed down to walk beside Anthony while Cambria answered Lord Hale's endless questions. Strolling two-abreast, Riordan ran a running tally of woodland plant life. "Better keep your nose covered, Tony. All through here we've got pignut, blackthorns, and ramsons—they smell like garlic. Raspberries probably won't bother you, but the cow-wheat might. Do you like birds?" At Tony's nod, Riordan listed the birds— finches, jays, snipes, and woodcocks—hoping feathers gave him fits as well.

They traversed the stretch up to the bridge in relative quiet, Tony somewhat breathless at the steeper climb. They caught up with Cambria and Lord Hale just as they stopped at the bridge.

Tony took deep breaths of the water-cleansed air, eyeing the rest of the road with obvious dread. Riordan felt outright sympathy as Tony trudged past the flower-strewn meadow and up the long driveway.

"It's only like this in spring and summer," Cambria told Anthony.

Inside the house, Riordan guided Tony up the stairs. "Come up and bathe your face, Tony. Talia will have some lemonade waiting and that will make you feel better." Inside Tony's room, Riordan watched with admiration as Tony washed his face. His poor eyes were swollen and his breathing shallow, yet he hadn't uttered a single complaint.

A footman knocked, marching in bearing a tray with a note and a glass. A tonic sent by Cambria, so the note announced, concocted from one of Diana's recipes. Evidently no stranger to tonics, Anthony pinched his nose and drank it down. Riordan's admiration rose another notch as the boy stood there shuddering and swallowing hard, his eyes watering as he grimly made it through the ordeal.

By the time Riordan and Tony joined the gathering in the parlor, the rest of the company had found their rooms, refreshed themselves, and were ready to be entertained.

Lord Hale waited for their return, his smile beyond obnoxious. The house, the land, the company of exotic Talia, and the bounteous refreshments made him talkative and feeling quite Lord of the manor—which, Riordan thought, is exactly what the man had in mind.

The British Isles might sink into the ocean before Riordan would allow it. "Come see the baths," he said, rising to his feet. "Lead the way, Cambria, you can tell Lord Hale all about your business." He bustled the other young people and their chaperons into the corridor toward the baths.

Like a conductor, he carefully shifted he and Anthony to the end of the group. He gave Tony a thoughtful, kindly uncle look. "You know, Tony, a person with your reaction to nature would benefit by taking the baths."

Anthony looked encouraged. Indeed, Riordan thought, the clean air *might* do the trick. He hoped he wasn't outsmarting himself. "After all," he said, "that's what they are famous for . . . making sick people well. If you stayed here a few days, you would see coach after coach of sick people toddling up the road. Even helping the family run the baths would put you near the water."

Anthony swallowed hard. "The family *help* the sick people? They don't touch them, do they?"

Riordan shrugged. "Servants are hard to get in this small town. Everyone does his part."

"Even Cambria?"

Riordan sighed heavily. "Especially Cambria, since it's her land. Of course, it's taken a toll. She seems to get sick a lot. Haven't you noticed how she always wears shawls over her dresses when no one else does?"

Chapter Nineteen

Cambria took one look at Anthony's hopeless expression as he left the baths and knew he'd decided not to marry her. Had Riordan said something to him? Surely not . . . Anthony's flower allergy was enough to deter any man.

"Anthony," she murmured, "Come into the library where we may discuss our situation."

He looked relieved. "As you wish."

As they moved toward the library, Lord Hale's footsteps rushed to catch up.

"Miss Thorne," Hale said, "you must not be hasty in your decision."

"We only want a moment in private, Lord Hale."

He moved to block the doorway. "You're going to end the agreement, aren't you? If you had a man to advise you, he would tell you you're making a foolish mistake." He looked up at Riordan. "Here," he said with anxious relief, "ask Langcliffe if I'm not right."

Riordan gave Hale a look of exasperation. "Right about what?"

"They plan to dissolve their agreement. This is what happens when a female has no man to advise her. Explain to the girl, Riordan.''

Riordan took a long look at Cambria, then turned to Hale. ''On the contrary, Hale, I *am* Miss Thorne's adviser. If she wishes me to be present, then I shall be happy to assist this meeting. If not, then I must insist that we leave them alone. She is of age, you know, and has been managing Thorne's Well for over five years without any male assistance at all.''

Cambria listened with wary relief. His sincere compliments warmed her rather battered confidence. Just when she expected Riordan to pull some interfering trick, he stepped in with fatherly approval and a way out, should she wish to insist on privacy with Anthony.

Which, of course, she did. But . . . looking at Lord Hale's stubborn face made her stop to consider. She and Anthony were perfectly able to manage their own affairs, but upon exiting the library, they would still have to run the gauntlet of Hale's objections.

She dipped her head. ''You're both welcome, of course.''

She opened the subject as they seated themselves at a grouping near the low-burning fireplace. Determined to get right to the point, she sank back into the leather chair and managed a smile. ''I've always thought a courtship *began* with flowers. I never dreamed they would be the cause of its ending. Unfortunately, flowers are an integral attraction of the valley. If we tried to halt their growth, the wind would undo all our efforts.''

To his credit, Anthony forsook false gallantry and followed her lead. ''It's is a beautiful place. I'm sorry I'm unable to enjoy it with you.''

His fingers drumming on the chair arm, Lord Hale snorted. ''You're acting as though the decision were made, Miss Thorne. You can't dissolve an betrothal simply because a gentleman *sneezes.*''

Anthony leaned forward. ''We have no betrothal, George, only an agreement. Miss Thorne is entirely correct. She would end up married to an invalid, or we would have to live apart.''

Cambria nodded. ''We could sit here and argue, but I cannot

think what other conclusions might be reached. Both Anthony and I agree. There's nothing left to say.''

Lord Hale shook his head. Jumping to his feet, he began to pace. ''Let's give it a couple of days. After a good night's sleep, you might change your mind, and then it would be embarrassing to go through all this again.'' He looked at Riordan. ''Don't you agree?''

Cambria sighed, utterly weary, and waited for Riordan's reply.

Riordan stood and crossed to her chair. Taking her hand, he lifted her out of her chair. ''You're right about one thing, Hale. Miss Thorne is on the verge of collapse. On the other matter, however, you must stop badgering her. Let it go.''

Riordan's kindness unnerved her. All afternoon, her treacherous heart had been wondering *what if* over her love for Riordan. Her only hope was to see him as the foe. *What ifs* were for dreamers, only good for muddling the mind. What she must remember was that Riordan had just won a victory of sorts . . . and she had just lost her first choice for saving Thorne's Well.

Riordan looked down at her and, pulling her along to the door, said with a gentle, calm voice, ''I'm sure Miss Thorne will spend the afternoon thinking very hard about her future. He accompanied her to the foot of the stairs. He lifted her hand and, shielding her from the others, kissed it softly. ''Sweet dreams, Cambria.''

Cambria awakened slowly to a dark room, less rested than when she'd stripped down to her shift and climbed under the covers.

She had dreamed . . . *and the dream had broken her heart.*

She'd often had annoying dreams where she was trying to find something and every time she got close, it eluded her somehow. In this latest dream, what eluded her . . . was Riordan.

If she looked in the woods, he disappeared among the trees without knowing she sought him. If she caught sight of him across the river, he couldn't hear her. At the church, she finally got his attention. He was mouthing words across the aisle, but she couldn't make out his message. Finally, in disgust, he left, and after that, she never saw him again.

She'd awakened bereft, a woman at the dark end of hope.

She needed no seer to tell her what that dream meant. The message was clear, clearer than any of her own thoughts.

She was going to lose Riordan forever.

As she looked up at the canopy, the dream kept enacting itself over and over in her mind, and every time, her loss became more real.

"Blast!" Furious with herself, she forced herself out of bed, blinking at the darkness. Glaring at her heavy draperies, she padded to the windows and yanked them open. *What the devil?* It was dark outside?

"Cambria?" Amelia's voice murmured through the door. "Are you coming down to dinner?"

Dear heavens . . . *dinner.* She'd ignored her guests for hours. She hurried to the door and, looking quickly out, pulled Amelia inside. "I fell asleep. Where is everyone? Are they waiting downstairs?" Bubbles of worry danced inside her. All those people . . . so attuned to the drama enacting here. They probably thought she was up here bawling her eyes out over losing Anthony. Or losing her land, which everyone was privy to by now.

"They're starting to go down now. I thought you were already downstairs, but I couldn't find you anywhere." She took a step and stopped. "I'm going to light a candle, Cambria. I can't see a thing."

"Please do. I've got to wash." She rushed toward the washbowl and poured the water. By the time she was through, her shift was wet and she needed to change. She scurried around, finding dry underthings and throwing them on. The wardrobe next. A dress . . . but what? Something special to give her color, to give her confidence. She reached for a dress the color of pale wine. It did wonders for her skin and hair and, as Talia said, made her look like a girl in a Rembrandt painting.

"Button me, Amelia."

Amelia moved quickly. "There," she said. "Where are your slippers . . . in the wardrobe? They both rushed to look, and

Amelia found them first. Cambria slipped her stockinged feet inside and turned to look at her image in the mirror.

"Oh, no . . ."

Amelia pushed her down onto the bench. "It's not so bad, Cambria. Let's just brush it out, and we'll make a chignon at your neck. If I had a face like yours, I would never do anything else."

Amelia wielded the brush with surprising strength, pulling out snarls and tangles with abandon. Cambria gritted her teeth and prayed for an end to it. Amelia's clever fingers twisted the thick hair and fastened it with enough pins to secure it through a raging gale.

Cambria leaned forward to look at her face, then sunk back in despair. She must have been crying in her dream, for her eyes were red and swollen. She was *not* going to go down and face anyone looking like this. Amelia's eyes narrowed. "I'll be right back."

Cambria slumped on the bench. What the devil was she going to do? If she intended to marry one of her suitors, she would have to . . . what? It's not like they would line up at the dinner table and raise their hands for attention.

Marchant was her next choice, of course. He reminded her of Phillip with his zeal for horses and sports. Of course, he didn't have her brother's intellect, but he seemed *harmless*. She propped her elbows on the table and rested her chin in her hands. The girl in the mirror was an idiot. She was choosing her mate because he was a bit dim, but harmless?

She sat back. She could do it. Marchant was so smitten with her—and her thriving business—that one hint would bring him to her side. But would he be willing to marry her in time? Surely he would understand, since the deadline for her saving Thorne's Well had long since ceased to be a secret; indeed, it seemed to be on everyone's tongue these days.

Riordan's face broke into her thoughts.

What about losing Riordan?

She swallowed hard and cursed the devastating loss that assailed her once more. Who was she fooling? Even if Riordan was lying through his teeth, *she couldn't take the chance of losing him.*

She took a deep breath. She would accept Riordan's offer. She would see if he would truly marry her, or if he would wait until the last moment and let her lose her land.

Her stomach tensed at the thought. Steady . . .

Her choice was simple. Not logic, but pure emotion. Did she choose the sure thing—Marchant—and live this afternoon's nightmare the rest of her life? *Live filled with despair?* Or did she choose Riordan and endure the fear that had driven her since John left her . . . until her birthday came? After that, it was out of her hands. Riordan either loved her, or he didn't. At least she would be able to live here at Thorne's Well if he deserted her after the wedding.

Amelia rushed back into the room. "Here. It's Diana's cucumber cream. Put it on your eyes and wait a few moments."

Cambria closed her eyes and rubbed it in. "How do you know about this stuff, Amelia?"

Amelia shrugged. "Oh, you know me. I cry over everything. Diana finally gave me my own pot." She sighed. "I wish I were like you, Cambria. You never seem to get upset."

Riordan watched Cambria come into the conservatory. She glanced his way, gave him an enigmatic smile and stepped forward to respond to her guests' greetings. The crowd was enormous—bath patrons mixing with Cambria's young guests—and Cambria disappeared in the crowd.

The Thorne's Well servants had worked a miracle during the afternoon. Small tables of all sizes were scattered over the room to enable them all to be seated for dinner. Candles were fastened to the larger trees, turning the room into a fairyland as their lights reflected off the dark windows and back into the room.

He'd never seen anything so enchanting . . . except for Cambria. Her face had never been more strikingly beautiful. He'd never thought of her in such a setting, but always striding along at Thorne's Well with all that energy and purpose and strength.

But, tonight, her dark eyes and warm coloring enhanced the richness of her inner beauty. She was a woman who would only improve over the years.

Seated across the room with the Thorne's Well servants' last minute efficiency, Riordan endured the dinner with an increasing irritation. Why hadn't he planned their meeting earlier? He'd managed a private session in the baths and even tried to nap—anything to escape the toad-eating Hale—but what he wanted was this thing settled with Cambria.

The damned puppy, Marchant, touched Cambria's arm, speaking in his usual roar. "Miss Thorne, do you have riding horses in the stables? I wondered if you would consider riding out with me in the morning."

Cambria hadn't been listening, evidently. "What? she asked.

"You could show me your land," said Marchant eagerly. "There must be some great riding trails through the woods."

As Cambria responded politely, Riordan observed Lord Marchant. Having determined earlier that he'd moved up on Cambria's list, he was busy engaging her attention. Riordan had already decided that getting rid of Marchant would be a simple matter of discovering if the boy would sell his interest in Cambria for a pair of matched bays or a hefty bank draft.

Talia and Cambria rose, followed by Ellie and Amelia— letting the other ladies know that they were to leave the gentlemen to their port and cheroots. Cambria spoke to the group. "Our tomato seedlings are sensitive to tobacco, so we have arranged for the gentlemen to retire to the library next door. The ladies will follow me up to the parlor."

Riordan caught her as the milling crowd trooped out of the conservatory. "The gazebo, after they're all in bed." She nodded nervously . . . then took her little flock of ladies with her.

Riordan strolled to the library, then stood near the door while the others went inside. Manners demanded that he join them, so he slipped inside and chose a chair near the door. The moment he sat down, he knew he wouldn't last another hour with this company, especially with the puppy, Marchant, acting like the cock of the hill.

The minute the door closed, the young gentlemen instantly

lost their formal manners and jumped up to fill their glasses at the side table. Boasting began . . . races won, female conquests, admiration received. Marchant pulled a cheroot from his pocket and lit it. Pipes appeared. Soon, smoke hung low from the ceiling. Tony coughed.

Riordan knew if he didn't leave, he would snap at the first man who irritated him. He rose from his chair. "Please excuse me." Protests filled the air, for he'd been the target for half their conversation, a chance to impress the much-admired duke. He couldn't wait to get outside.

He'd barely shut the door behind him before it opened again. Alistair grinned. "Great idea, Uncle Riordan. I'll come with you."

Riordan shrugged and turned toward the front door. Once on the grounds, he took long strides down the road to walk the kinks out of his legs, enjoying the fresh air.

"It's a bright night," Alistair murmured, looking up at the sky.

Riordan looked upward, expecting to see a full moon but only found a hazy sliver resting on its side. As he neared the bend of the road he could hear the waterfall, louder than usual, and . . . *what the devil?* . . . Coming out of the wooded shortcut, a servant ran toward the house without seeing them.

Immediately, Riordan's senses went on alert. Were there other footsteps coming, perhaps someone chasing the lone servant? He wished he'd brought a weapon. "Let's go see what he's running from, Alistair." They veered toward the path and took off at a trot. When they reached the road beyond they stopped in horror.

Alistair gasped. "Fire in the woods."

Flickering tips of flames backlit the trees before him. Riordan began to run toward the glow, with Alistair keeping up beside him. "I wonder if my mother's arrived at Lakeview."

Had his mother arrived early and inadvertently held a candle too close to her new draperies? He sped up, coughing as smoke flowed toward them down the tunnel-like road. He could hear the flames from here. Around the next bend, they stopped in amazement.

The bridge was on fire. Fully engulfed, too late for saving. *On the other side, his own woodsmen stood calmly watching it burn.* In the fierce light, he could see their expressions clearly . . . satisfaction in a job well done. He sent a frantic inspection of the area near them, but no woman stood gloating beside them.

"Is this Grandmother's doing, Riordan?"

"I suppose it is."

Where was his mother? Safe at Langcliffe Hall, ready to plead innocent? Or did she wait at Lakeview, sniffing the smoke and triumphantly watching the glowing sky?

How had she dared to do this after Cambria warned her off?

Damn it, you dolt, it's your own fault. In scolding the duchess over her gambling, he'd dissolved Cambria's threat. And, as for his own warning to his mother—not for the first time—she had simply ignored him.

Sickened, they stood unmoving and watched the fire.

Chapter Twenty

Breathless, Cambria hurried toward the bridge. It was burning, the servant said . . . and Langcliffe's woodsmen started it? How could that be true? Back at Thorne's Well, servants were gathering buckets and shovels to stop the fire before it got too serious.

She rounded the last bend—and stopped. The entire bridge was afire. Riordan and Alistair stood calmly watching, while across the river, the Langcliffe woodsmen watched with them. *No,* Riordan couldn't have done this. But why then, did he and Alistair stand here watching so complacently?

Her brain began to function. This hadn't happened in the last few moments. This bridge would have had to be splashed, *soaked* with fuel to burn with such even consistency, which meant that this had been planned . . . and executed . . . long before dinner. Riordan's warning came back to her. He'd warned her that he would stop her marrying . . . but he could have kidnapped her until after her birthday, absconded to Scotland to force her hand. He hadn't even waited to speak to her, to see if she would give in and marry him. Why burn the bridge?

Dear heavens . . . her business.

Her patrons couldn't leave, nor could tomorrow's group reach Thorne's Well. Her patrons who had come by horse could make their way out the overgrown Pick Hill trail, but not the coaches. She could ferry the guests out over the lake in small groups, but once they reached Thornedale, they could only get out on public coaches, which would take at least three days. She couldn't make it to London in time to reach Diana and her license. Her guests' and patrons' coaches would be trapped inside the valley. They would be furious with her.

Her successful, money-producing business would never survive their anger. Marchant could not afford to take a wife with no dowry. He would probably be on the first boat out.

She stepped forward . . . then saw Riordan and Alistair point down to the river. They moved to the side of the road. Nodding calmly, the pair stepped off the road and tromped down beside the river.

And now, they intended to just stroll down to an easier crossing and leave? Alistair was part of this? Fury filled her. The Langcliffes had lied and cozied up to their enemies to search out weaknesses, then destroyed their last hope of saving Thorne's Well. In one last stroke, days before her birthday, with her suitors and her bath patrons watching.

Maddened beyond thinking, Cambria started after them. Lifting her skirts, she grabbed onto bushes, her evening slippers growing damp on the wet grass. She glanced up just as they approached the last narrow place in the river before it began to form the small lake. Water flowed around large rocks, and if they were agile, they might be able to jump from rock to rock and make their way across. They were escaping . . .

Crazed at that thought, she looked for a weapon to stop them. It was darker down here, despite the blazing bridge on the hill. She finally found a stick lying on the ground. Picking it up, she flew toward her quarry.

Riordan and Alistair turned as she approached. Alistair stepped aside, not saying a word, but Riordan's devious face broke into a mask of concern. "Cambria . . . I'm so sorry—"

She swung the stick and caught him squarely in the midsection, knocking the breath out of him. As he doubled over, his hand snaked out and wrenched the stick out of her hand. "Damn it, Cambria, what's wrong with you?"

"You dare to ask me that? You think you can burn my bridge and just walk away without a backward glance?"

"You've got it all wrong—" He grabbed her hand. She struggled, but he wouldn't let loose. No . . . not again . . . she couldn't stand it. She reared back and punched him squarely in the nose, then as he finally let go of her, she shoved him hard—into the river.

As soon as Alistair dragged Riordan out of the water on to the other side, he began to laugh.

Glaring at him, Riordan lay coughing on the bank, his head pounding and a pain in his side. The damned woman had probably cracked a rib, and if it wasn't so dim on this wooded side of the river, he'd be seeing double after his head hit the river boulder. He pulled himself up to a sitting position, groaning aloud as pain tore through him.

Alistair roared. "Riordan, if you could have seen your face . . . the great Riordan Langcliffe . . . oh, I'll never forget this moment."

"Is she still over there?"

"No, she stalked off toward home. Probably gone to get her musket."

"She didn't even wait to see if I'd drowned?"

"I don't know. I was too busy jumping in after you to look."

"She thinks I burned her damned bridge."

Alistair sobered. "I know."

"Help me up. We've got work to do."

Cambria held her heartbreak at bay all during the long evening. By the time everyone straggled into the house, the kitchen was working at full capacity to feed guests full of energy after their unexpected excitement. In their element, cook and her crew managed to feed them all, enabling Cambria to send them off to their beds in excellent spirits.

Tomorrow, she thought as her head hit the pillow, tomorrow her house would be like one giant birds' nest, with everyone's mouth open, chirping for her.

Riordan squinted against the morning sun and surveyed the crew of men before him. Villagers and farmers armed with shovels and axes. His own men, guilty woodsmen included, looked grim after his private scourging. Wagons stood at the ready, waiting to haul downed trees away.

Riordan spoke to the men. "We're going to build a temporary road down to the river and up the other side to Thorne's Well. I've sent for men from my other estates and sent for a bridge-building crew from London. There's a bonus for each of you. The sooner the road is open, the larger the prize. First, begin clearing the path. Look for the notches on the trees to tell you where to cut."

Riordan flexed his fingers, wincing as broken blisters protested the stretching motion. He and Alistair had taken the woodsmen down to the river, and, by lantern light, they'd spent the night marking a path for the road. He hurt all over, thanks to his ladylove, but those wounds were a small matter compared to the state of his anguished mind.

The sound of pounding hooves turned his head. Alistair came galloping down the road from the village, then stopped a few feet away. "Hello," he called, swinging off his horse. "Your runners are gone with your notes in hand, including the one to Rountree." He watched the men chopping away at trees. "Looks like you've got this organized. What's next . . . Cambria?"

Riordan shook his head.

"You're going to let her keep thinking you burned the bridge?"

"She's not going anywhere, Alistair."

"You may be wrong there. Her servants took four of the bath patrons and all of Cambria's guests—except for Lord Hale and Tony—out through the woods and across the lake on boats. They hired coaches from the inn and sent them back to London.

One lady wrenched her ankle. They were not very cheerful, any of them, by the time they reached the village.''

Stubbornly, Riordan refused to be budged. "Until she gets rid of the rest of them, she'll stay at Thorne's Well, and if she tries to leave, she will be detained in the village.''

"How did you manage that?'' Then Alistair gave a small, disgusted shake of his head. "The notes I delivered to the vicar and to Bass, of course. I'm still asking foolish questions.''

Alistair led his horse to a tree. Tying him to a branch in the shade, he turned to Riordan. "What if she sends for a clergyman from London? Tony's still here. She's bound to marry him now.''

"She'd need a special license to marry without the banns. If she sent a request, the earliest one could return from London is four days, and that's if they drove night and day to get here.''

"Even so, why are you waiting to talk to Cambria?''

"I have to do something else first.''

Alistair leaned back against the tree. "Grandmother.''

"Yes.''

"D'you want me to come with you?''

"I think you'd better. Then, I'll be gone two days, taking her back to Langcliffe Hall. You'll have to stay here in case Peck needs anything.''

"The point is, Riordan . . . will Grandmother go?''

"Yes.''

Cambria joined her family and guests at the enormous formal dining room. Talia had already started the servants serving the meal. A servant stood at her shoulder with a tureen of soup. She nodded, and, as her bowl filled, she looked around the table. Eight bath patrons and her own private guests still waited to be sent safely back to London, leaving their coaches behind with promises to see all restored to them as soon as possible.

She felt weary as she mentally calculated how much must be refunded. All those subscriptions, and they would want them all at once. She would not even have the benefit of her improvement to the old Roman baths but could only let all fall into Riordan's greedy hands.

She had managed to get a third of the guests and patrons out this morning. Marchant and the other young people had been the most anxious to leave. Two more days, and she might be rid of them all. Then two additional days until her birthday.

Lord Hale, who had bullied his way to a place opposite Cambria at the foot of the table, cleared his throat. "I don't know why everyone must all rush home just because the bridge is gone. It's a perfect time for all of us to get acquainted and enjoy a nice little holiday."

Havenshire's cousins, having decided on their first day at Thorne's Well to remain for an undetermined time, nodded in agreement. Hale beamed at such pillars of society in agreement with the future master of Thorne's Well, namely himself.

Talia, who had made Hale her particular enemy, cleared her throat in mockery of Hale's own pompous habit. "We must remember the difficulty of importing supplies without a road."

Hale waved an indolent hand. "Horses, servants' backs, a dog cart."

Talia was adamant. "You have a farm waiting for your attention."

Giving Talia a hard look for her criticism, Hale snapped a finger for the servant to take away his soup. The servants ignored him.

Dreading the commotion to follow, Cambria knew it was time to get rid of Hale for good. "In four more days, I will lose Thorne's Well. You will understand that I have a lot to do before that time."

A cunning smile spread over his features. "I'm perfectly aware of that, Miss Thorne. I sent a note to your aunt, Lady Waterson, to bring the special license to us here."

Talia exploded. "How dare you!"

"George," Anthony said, "You must not—"

"I *must not?*" Red faced and furious, Lord Hale silenced his brother, then turned to Cambria with an arrogant smile. "You mean you would lose your home—this wonderful heritage, living next to Lord Langcliffe—because Tony gets a little summer ague?''

She cut her fish into a crumpled heap, absently pushing the tender flakes into a coffin-shaped mound. ''Your brother is miserable here, Lord Hale.'' She motioned to the servants, and they burst into action, readying the table for the next course.

Hale knew when to retreat. ''I shall, of course, obey your wishes, dear, Miss Thorne. However, just in case you change your mind, we shall remain close by, at your service, until your birthday.''

Riordan ignored Alistair's offer to ride his horse and, instead, walked toward Lakeview. Walking would at least keep all his injuries in familiar places. Atop a horse, he might discover others, and he had surely reached his limit for surprises.

Then, too, he needed a quiet moment to review his decision concerning his mother's actions. He'd checked during the night to be sure that she and her personal servants were, indeed, settled at Lakeview. He'd ordered her coachmen to keep her there until his return later today.

Most important, despite the woodsmens' confessions, he must hear from her lips that she had ordered the burning. She'd had it done, of course. With her gambling secret out, Cambria's threat had lost its power.

All through the last evening they'd spent peacefully together at Langcliffe Hall, she kept warning him of the danger of loving a Thorne. He hadn't really *listened*. His own negligence had actually encouraged this overt violence and, if he didn't stem it now, she might do worse. This wasn't about property and bridges, but about danger to Cambria and the sanity of his mother. Logic meant nothing to her, only her own fierce emotions . . . revenge for her sorrow, fear for his future.

It was time to stop her.

They entered the house. Addressing his mother's footman, Riordan asked, ''Is the duchess awake?''

He bowed. ''Yes, she's been up for some time. I'll tell her that you are home.''

Waving Alistair ahead of him, Riordan stayed back to speak briefly to Peck. After Riordan had clearly stated his wishes twice, the overseer nodded reluctantly and went to speak to his men.

Alistair turned to wait for him. "What will you do, Riordan? If she did it, I mean. Do you know how to stop her?"

Grimly, Riordan nodded. They turned back toward the stairs.

The duchess appeared cheerful as she looked down from the landing. "Alistair . . . Riordan. I thought you were in London. Have you come to check on the house? Come see my room."

Alistair ran up and kissed her on the cheek. "Hello, Grandmother."

She looked down into the foyer. The workers had all left. "Why aren't they working, Riordan?"

Riordan walked slowly up the stairs. "I told them to rest."

She beckoned him to her room. "I brought my own people in to finish my rooms. I'm just too impatient to wait." Her maid, Hettie, smiled at they entered.

"Very efficient of you, Mother." Very politely, he admired what she'd accomplished and what she had yet to finish.

"This is my sitting room. The walls are done, but the drapes aren't ready yet. I brought the furniture with me. It's out in the wagon. Will you ask the men to bring it up?"

"In a moment. First, let's go for a walk, Mother. We have something to discuss, and we'll need some privacy."

Her hand fluttered to her chest. "Never tell me you're engaged to that Thorne woman." Her voice shook.

He stepped out into the hall and waited for her. "No."

"Does that mean you weren't able to convince her?"

"That's correct." He offered his arm. "Shall we go?"

She fell silent as they left the house and strolled slowly up the road. After today, things would never be the same between them. To let her continue in her accelerating reign of abuse would eventually end with her being locked in a house with guards keeping her prisoner. He could not endure letting it go that far.

Steeling his emotions, he was determined to gain the clearest picture of his mother's thoughts. He asked his first question. "Tell me why you want to live here, Mother."

"I told you. "I've always loved this property best. It's closer to London than Langcliffe Hall, and once the Thornes are gone it will be perfect."

"But if the Thornes retain their property?"

"You forget, Riordan. I've seen you when you're after something. You never let go, you always find a way. I'm sure this will be no different."

"Then why didn't you just stay away and wait for that to happen as I asked you to?"

"Because *you* didn't stay away as I asked you. I warned you about the Thornes, begged you to stay away, but you could not resist." Her voice broke. "And, just as I warned you, now one of them has you in her clutches. I cannot let that happen."

His pity stirred. Persist, he thought, stay with her reasoning no matter where it led. "But how does burning their bridge change my falling in love with Cambria?"

Tears were falling now, tears of real anguish. "I can't change the way you feel about her—I tried that with your father—but I can keep her from wanting you."

His heart sank. One more mark against him . . . Closing down those thoughts, he chased the crucial point—one that clanged the gates closed on his clemency. "You admit having the bridge burned?"

"It stopped their nasty little business, Riordan. No more wagons on our road. When you come to your senses, you'll thank me for it."

He gathered the scattered bits of her logic together. "So because I'm bewitched and cannot see the danger I am in from the Thornes, you went behind my back, stirred up the village against her, and, when that didn't work, you burned the bridge."

"I knew you'd understand, Riordan."

"But can't you see where this will end?"

"I do, don't you see? I didn't fight before. I didn't know what to do, so I just left Lakeview, so I *wouldn't* see it anymore. I lost your father here, and now I'm in danger of losing you as well."

His throat ached. "You think I'll stop loving you? That I'll leave you out of my life?"

"I saw your Cambria in action, Riordan. She's just like you, totally ruthless. She would have smashed me like a fly."

"But you had already threatened her, done harm to her. What did you expect her to do?" He sighed in frustration. "I'm wondering how far you will go . . . will you burn their house next? And if that doesn't work, begin murdering them one by one?"

Her hand fluttered to her chest. "You think that of me?"

"Mother, I can't believe you did *any* of this. How far am I supposed to let you go? If you keep on, you'll end up a criminal . . . in truth, you already are."

She stared at him in horror. "But you're a *duke*. You wouldn't let anything happen to me."

"You're right, Mother. I will never let anyone hurt you. And perhaps that's the problem. I have always let you have your way. I don't want to have you restrained, so I must do something to end this before you hurt yourself."

Finally, the severity of his words touched her. "I don't like the sound of that, Riordan. Tell me what you mean."

"This land has been the source of unhappiness to you, Mother, and, with the Thornes living here, it always will be. So," he said, hating to hurt her, "I've decided that the Langcliffes will no longer live alongside the Thornes in this valley."

"But you can't do that, Riordan. I've already moved in. I've hired servants. I even brought one of our cooks with me."

"I'm sorry to hear that, for as we speak, my men are taking your things out of the house. Your servants have been advised."

She wiped away her tears. "I shall just take them back in. Just because you make a decision, that doesn't mean I must abide by it."

He felt sick. "Just so I understand, tell me what will happen if I let you stay? Will you leave the Thornes alone?"

"You expect me to let those coaches run back and forth in front of my house? Heavens, I *know* some of those people."

"You believe I would allow you to continue this destructive spree?"

''Darling,'' she said, sure now that she'd gotten her way, ''I know what I'm doing.'' She marched back to the house and began ordering the servants. Peck sent Riordan a questioning look and, sickened, Riordan nodded.

Alistair looked relieved as the workers began taking the furniture—her favorites—into the house. Moving alongside Riordan, Alistair gave a huge sigh. ''For a moment, I thought you meant it, Riordan. It would hurt her to leave the house now just as she's gotten it back to the way it was. I thought you were going to be stubborn.''

Riordan couldn't answer. Despite Alistair's opinion, *nothing frightened him more than letting his mother go on like this.*

When the wagon was empty, Peck walked over to Riordan. ''What now? Back to work?''

Riordan shook his head. ''Get everyone out of the house.'' Peck halted and looked carefully at Riordan to be sure he understood. Nodding finally, he took off in a trot.

Alistair turned to look at Riordan. ''What are you doing?''

''Bring your grandmother here, Alistair. Do it now.''

''Damn it, Riordan—''

''Now.''

Alistair strode away and came back with the duchess. ''Riordan, darling,'' she said, ''I'm busy. What do you want now?''

''Just a hug, Mother. And to tell you that I'll always love you.'' He pulled her to him, wrapped his arms powerfully around her. Over her head, he nodded to Peck.

In moments, Lakeview was engulfed in flames.

Chapter Twenty-One

Moving quietly, Cambria shifted her cup of chocolate to her left hand and opened the library window. Stepping over the low sill onto damp grass, she shut the window behind her. Beyond the enormous rose garden, the concealing woods waited to welcome her. She hurried along winding, petal-littered paths until she reached the shortcut through the woods.

A few feet into the shady trees, she turned back and leaned against a tree to study the house. No one followed her, no face watched her from a window. Relaxing, she sipped her drink, slowly savoring the warm, sweet chocolate. Servants would be in the kitchen now, preparing an early morning tray for Lord Hale.

Before long, Hale would come looking for her. Would follow her around all day, bludgeoning her with questions, determined to know every detail about running Thorne's Well. Without offering the slightest assistance, he'd already criticized her every action——from the three-day nightmare of implementing her patron-guests' departure to the everyday supervision of the small estate——insisting she should use a better system, namely his own.

She'd refused to respond to Hale's disapproval of her releasing servants as they accompanied her patrons to Thornedale. She ignored his argument that her using stablemen as boatmen showed a kind of "parsimony" that was beneath her class. She deigned to explain that even with a lessened crew of servants, she could barely pay their wages.

Under Hale's barrage of advice, she finally understood why Riordan hated explaining himself. It only opened the door to argument and gave her no room to experiment or change her mind without further critical scrutiny.

She'd endured three long hellish days listening to Hale pontificating as though he were already master of Thorne's Well. Three grim days of watching his brother, Tony, weakening in his resolve until all he could say was, "It's up to you, Cambria." Her cousins wanted Riordan back, and Talia had turned on her, asking why she didn't just evict Hale by force.

How could she? She had no other way to save Thorne's Well except to marry Tony. She'd considered going back to London, but after almost two days travel, she would have only hours to find someone to marry . . . a ridiculous waste of her time. No, she only wanted to stay here and savor the bittersweet pleasure of freedom while she could.

Especially this morning. Diana should arrive today, bringing the license. Before her brisk, no-nonsense manner came to shake up the house, Cambria was escaping, declaring a holiday for the mistress of the house.

Leaving her empty cup near the base of the tree, she walked along the well-trodden path. Sunshine warmed her face as she reached the road, and as she turned toward the river, it soaked into her back, sending shivers of well-being through her.

As she neared the river, she heard voices. Immediately, she slipped into the trees to safely observe. Two men stood at the edge of the turbulent river—*on her side* of the missing bridge. Well-dressed men who pointed with their hands and measured with calculated strides.

Bridge builders. Of course. Skilled craftsmen sent by Langcliffe to replace her ancient wooden bridge. After he took possession of her land, he would need easy access to Thorne's

Well. *Or so he thought.* She marched angrily toward them. "You are trespassing, gentlemen."

Surprised and confused, they glanced at each other, then back toward her. One bowed. "We are here to rebuild the bridge—"

"Hired by Lord Langcliffe, correct?"

Their faces cleared. "Yes. He just got back this morning." Rather urgently, they pointed down-river. "He's down there now, finishing the road."

Road? Riordan was building a road onto her property? She turned and began scrambling down the side of the road, following the same path she'd used the night of the fire. Beneath her feet, the ground had been trampled by many feet, and recently. *How dare he?*

She followed the trail with no hesitation, marching along with only one desire, to confront Langcliffe and throw his failure to seize her home in his face. Typical of a Langcliffe, he didn't wait for legalities before marching triumphantly onto her land.

She walked near the river and found them where she suspected they would construct a bridge . . . the spot where she'd pushed Riordan into the water. She looked for him, thought she'd find him leaning indolently against a tree in the shade.

Instead, shirtless, he was standing thigh-deep in the swift-flowing water, hammering nails into a low, rough bridge. She was shocked to see his broad shoulders bared to the sun, a sheen of moisture delineating his strength with each forceful blow of his arm. He was deeply tanned, she realized, and she remembered his telling her how he liked to work alongside his men.

The laborers facing her stopped working, pointed her out to Riordan. He turned, his eyes squinting against the sun. Immediately, he began moving toward her. Black hair swirled over his heavily muscled chest, and as his powerful legs took him around rocks to the river's edge, he sent his piercing black gaze her way. Tense, resolute.

She'd made a mistake coming here.

She always underestimated Riordan, but never more than

today. She'd allotted him the powerless impact of a self-drawn character, someone who would be shocked at her triumph like a villain in a play, who would display a woe-is-me expression and slump away in defeat. The truth was, he was on the attack. *She'd never been less ready to face him.*

She told her feet to hurry, to retreat before Riordan got any closer—but she could not seem to move. Instead, her stomach tightened and her heart pounded with, of all things, the pain of loss.

Looking at him now, she knew why.

For less than one day, she'd known she loved him. For a few hours, she'd let her mind say *what if.* After her heart-breaking dream, she stopped fighting, let herself hope, plan. And now, still vulnerable, she had no defense against the sight of Riordan striding toward her.

"You've saved me the trouble of coming to get you, Cambria."

She watched his face, prepared for any of his many devious expressions, but found only a solemn, shuttered look. He sent his steady gaze skimming over her, not missing a thing. She knew how haggard she looked, knew dark circles shadowed her eyes, but she didn't care. This was not a social meeting, but one of business, legalities, hard speaking. "Call off your bridge builders. You're not getting my land."

That did shock him. "You've married?" He looked sick.

She started to deny it—then realized how she'd walked into a trap. All he'd have to do is kidnap her, and he'd have her land. "Yes."

His eyes darted to her ringless hand. "Who is the lucky bridegroom?"

"Anthony Hale."

"Who performed the ceremony?"

Dangerous ground. "I'm not here to answer your questions, Langcliffe. I'm here to tell you to leave." She turned to retrace her steps, but he came up fast behind her and seized her arm. "Who married you, Cambria?"

She struggled to get away, but he wasn't budging. "Leave

me alone, Riordan. Or are you going to add assault to your legion of crimes?''

''When you answer me, I'll let you go.''

She raised her chin and prayed she was saying the right thing. ''The vicar. Your own mother's vicar. He came in the night so you wouldn't find out and performed the ceremony.''

He smiled then. A triumphant, exultant smile. ''Liar.''

Shaken, she shrugged as if it didn't matter. ''Believe what you like, but just get off my land.''

He only laughed again, tightened his grip, and began marching them both back toward his bridge. She twisted and struggled, furious with her own foolishness . . . too late. Over the bridge he took her, down the new road and into the woods. Out of sight of the silent, staring workmen, beyond hearing should she scream.

When he freed her hand, she considered running, but knowing how easily he would capture her, she decided to bluff it out. She gave him a caustic look. ''At last, we see the real Riordan Langcliffe, kidnapper, bully.''

He lifted a shirt he'd evidently retrieved at the bridge and dropped it over his head, stretching his arms into the sleeves. ''You've never see the real Riordan Langcliffe, Cambria. Only the ogre you've imagined.''

Backing up, she cocked a disbelieving brow. ''Imagined? Surely you didn't drag me into the woods to tell me more lies. You've burned my bridge and ruined my business. If the Hales hadn't stayed, you would have won. But then, even the great Riordan Langcliffe can't control everything.''

He leaned forward. ''I did not burn your damned bridge, Cambria.''

She tried to step back, but instead backed into a rough-barked tree. ''All right, if you insist, your *men* burned my bridge.''

He grabbed her shoulders and looked into her eyes. ''*Think* Cambria . . . why would I burn your bridge when you'd just discovered that you loved me? If we hadn't waited so long to talk about it, we would have been engaged by now, as well you know. And now, because you're too cowardly to trust me, you're *looking* for reasons to push me away.''

"Looking for reasons? The ground is littered with them, Riordan. "You lied about not knowing you owned Lakeview. The man I sent the reports to—Lord Moulton—is your *uncle.* I suppose you hadn't seen him for twenty years?"

He exhaled sharply. "So, that's what my mother told you."

His jaw clenched, as if every word were being torn from him. "I was only fourteen when my father died, and my mother and uncle were named trustees. It took me four years to wrest control of the estate from them. By that time, they'd lost everything except Langcliffe Hall and the town house. I didn't know this land was entailed. I thought we'd lost it. I didn't know my mother kept the Lakeview papers separate. Not until your brother died and she asked me to foreclose on Thorne's Well."

"Your *mother* hid it from you?" She hated to admit it, but that sounded possible. "But, knowing how she felt about us, you left your mother here in the valley. She turned the village against us—"

"Do I seem like the kind of man who would have his mother do his dirty work for him? If I wanted the villagers to treat you badly, Cambria, I would have done it myself, and far more effectively."

"She said you hated us, that you always had. She said you dropped everything to go after Thorne's Well. Are you going to say it's not true?"

He ran a hand through already mussed hair. "It was true then." His eyes closed for a moment, then pulling himself together, he began again. "I've never seen someone so pathetic, so heart-breakingly fragile as she was when we left Lakeview, or worse, when my father killed himself. When she got the chance to redeem Thorne's Well, it was a wonderful retribution for her. I wanted to see her happy again."

He looked off into the distance. "I couldn't stay away, though. She begged me not to go near the Thorne family, afraid I'd fall under their evil spell. But, did I honor her request? No, off I jaunted to investigate, which made her all the more frantic.

"And then," he said, "not only did I confront her with her gambling, negating your threat completely, but I told her I loved you. She felt free to come back here, but to what? Her nightmare come true. One more attractive Thorne woman up the road, only this time taking her son. She wanted to keep you from believing in me . . . and, when things go badly, she acts without any thought of repercussion or consequence.''

Cambria began to panic. This was all beginning to make too much sense. All her barriers were crumbling, *exactly* what she'd feared. But what if he told the truth? "Then, your *mother* burned the bridge?''

He nodded. ''I got there only minutes before you.''

This was it, Cambria thought. The moment when she capitulated. Something inside squirmed and twisted, tried to get away. What if he lied? What if she was just asking for another humiliation, another dose of pain? What if he were only trying to keep her from marrying?

''So,'' he asked, ''do you have any more questions?''

She searched through her mental list, clutched for one last try. ''The road. Why are you building a road on my property if you aren't planning to take it over?''

He stared at her. ''Idiot children . . . d'you realize that's what we'll be producing? We'll have to tie them to trees for fear they'll wander off and drown themselves in the lake.''

Her face scrunched up. ''What?''

He placed his large hands on either side of her face, his thumbs gently caressing her cheeks. ''Damn it, Cambria, why do you think I'm building a road? It's my responsibility to replace your bridge, but in the meantime, you need to get in and out.'' He exhaled heavily. ''Just for once, give me credit for doing something right.''

She closed her eyes. ''Talk to me, Riordan. I can't stop feeling this way, you know. I only have two days before I lose my land, and all I can think is that you'll say anything to make me believe you.''

Wrapping his arms around her, he pulled her against his chest. ''I know that. I hate this damned birthday of yours. It's given everything a warped sense of value.'' He kissed her hair. ''We'll marry *before* your birthday . . . and in case you still believe *that's* a trick to get Thorne's Well . . . *Think about it.* Thorne's Well might be lovely, but it's a drop in the bucket compared to the rest of my properties. Why would I do such an inane thing for a little plot of land?''

One last grasp for sanity. ''You'd do it for your mother. She still wants me gone so she can live at Lakeview.''

Abruptly, he grabbed her hand and pulled her toward the road he'd built. ''Damned stubborn woman,'' he muttered as they rushed through the woods. At the junction to the main road he stopped and let her look around. Immediately before them, felled trees blocked the way to the dangerous river, and stuck in a dirt-filled pail, an arrowed sign directed traffic down the new path.

She turned slowly . . . and looked toward Lakeview.

The blackened skeleton that used to be Lakeview.

''No . . .'' she whispered, moving toward it. Tears clogged her throat as she surveyed the scene. Brick fireplaces rose from the ashes of the mansion, protesting the loss of their former glory. All gone, the proud tower, the sprawling wings that had housed generations of Langcliffes for centuries. Riordan spent his childhood in this house. Only days ago, he'd brought the young people here to see if it could be saved, and they'd laughed and teased and acted as if he couldn't possibly destroy this heritage of his family. The restoration had begun, been almost complete. Lovely, with new life breathed into the old edifice.

She could barely speak as tears filled her eyes. ''Your mother loved this house, Riordan. How could she do it?''

''She didn't do it.''

''But—''

''I did.''

''Oh, Riordan . . .''

''I was terrified for her, Cambria. She had to be stopped before she did something worse. I told her that I would not rebuild it, that there would never be Langcliffes and Thornes at odds in the valley again.''

''How you must have crushed her.'' She looked into his face. His complexion looked gray, and, for the first time, she saw how helpless he was feeling now, how guilty and unsure he'd done the right thing.

The coldness of his voice told her how strong was his control.

"I took her home to Langcliffe Hall. She's hurt. She thinks I've chosen against her, that you will keep us apart. Now she dare not cross me, but I have no idea if she will ever recover. She's secluded herself in her room . . ." He broke off, denying himself the expression of emotion.

He gave her a gentle look, reached over to wipe her tears away. "I don't want you to carry any part of this burden, Cambria. This was not about Thorne's Well or the past, or even you, except not letting her hurt you. This was about stopping her before I had to take the next step . . . immuring her in Langcliffe Hall with guards to restrain her."

"Riordan, how can you ask me to marry you? Shouldn't you choose another wife, someone your mother can love?" When he remained quiet, she persisted. "She must hate me."

He smiled faintly. "She claims you're a demon from hell."

"Then, how can you bear to hurt her, Riordan?

"Cambria, if my mother were a child, I wouldn't let her dictate my life." Wonderingly, he trailed his fingers over her face, buried his fingers in her hair. "In all these years, I've never even been close to love, and now that I've found it with you, I don't want to spend the rest of my life without it. Besides," he added solemnly, "what about your feelings? Are you to be denied a life with the man you love? Shall we deny life to the children who will come to us?"

She looked up into his face. She did want to be with him, to bring babies into the world with him . . . rowdy little black-eyed children chasing each other through the woods, just as she and her brother had done. And something else. "An end to the feud. I'd like that. It's a terrible heritage for our families to have lived with, for us to pass on."

Riordan's large hands tightened on her shoulders. "Could you just mention the word *love*, Cambria? My ego is taking a beating here, if you hadn't noticed."

She smiled at last. Teasing, she gave him a frown. "Love?"

He reached for her. "Close enough."

Riordan lowered his head and kissed her, then, not satisfied with so barren an embrace, pulled her fully into his arms. Cambria's mouth was hot and giving, as she relaxed against him. Finally, he thought fiercely, she was where she belonged. He pulled out her hair pins and let the long mass loose . . . a glorious mane that fell to her waist. He buried his finger in the thick stuff, pulled her closer, inhaled the fragrance of her hair, her skin . . . flower-scented and womanly. His woman. Tonight this luscious mane of hair would lie on his pillow.

Reluctantly, he lifted his head. "Cambria, my love, much as I would like to pursue this to a glorious end, we have important things to do."

Cambria sank back against him, held him tight. "No. Hold me. Let's just stay here forever. We'll dry like Egyptian mummies and never have to face the world again."

He chuckled. "We had this little scene before, Cambria. You were a bit shorter then, and my own heart was breaking at leaving you."

She leaned back. "I didn't know that . . . you seemed so strong."

He shook his head. "I went into the woods and bawled my eyes out. My world was falling apart, and leaving you . . . Cambria," he said urgently, "I want to marry you today, before your damned birthday. I never used to believe that Thornes and Langcliffes were doomed to be enemies, but every time we become close, something happens to tear us apart."

"Your mother's in bed," she offered. "That should help."

"Perhaps we shouldn't *talk*. Instead, we'll make motions and draw pictures."

She smiled eagerly. "Declare a day of silence. For my family, too." Then her face crumpled. "I'm scared, Riordan."

Riordan looked down at her flushed face, her lips swollen from his kiss, and her hair loose and wanton. A torrent of love, *lust,* poured through him. "If we stand here much longer, I'm going to carry you into the woods and anticipate our marriage vows. You'd be mine then, carrying my child, perhaps." As the words fell from his lips, the idea possessed him. He watched her eyes to see if he'd frightened her. They turned dark with desire to match his.

He caressed her face, ran his fingers slowly over her eyes, watched them droop closed, curved his palm over her cheek, brushed his thumb over her parted lips. "You'll like love-making," he said softly, letting his thumb caress the tip of her moist tongue. A soft moan issued from deep within her, the sound of surrender.

He leaned down and let his mouth rest on hers, touching the tip of his tongue against hers. She stirred against him, edgy, wanting what she didn't understand yet. He let his tongue lave her lips, then come back to mate lightly with her open mouth. He ached all over, needing her.

He spread his fingers across her back, slid them slowly down to curve at her hip. "You'll like my hands on your skin." Her breathing changed. Soft, fluttering . . . with tears slowly creeping down her cheeks. She was so ripe, so ready for him.

He wiped her tears away with his thumb. *What if,* he wondered, what if something else happened to part them, and he left her ruined, never knowing that *he loved her more than he wanted her.* That he honored her even now as his own wife.

He leaned his face against hers. "I can't dishonor you, Cambria." A soft laugh escaped. "Much as I want to, more than you can imagine."

"Nor can I," she admitted. She sighed shakily. "This thing between us is so powerful, isn't it, Riordan? Almost as if all the emotions of our ancestors were still battling within us. Making us want each other more than life itself, yet still trying to tear us apart."

She rested her head against his chest. "Sometimes I think I never stopped loving you. That's the reason I hated you so—because deep inside me, that childish love refused to die. And sometimes I wonder if the reason I'm so scared of loving you again is fear of having that precious little hidden kernel of love finally die and leave me all alone without *any* of you with me." She shook her head lightly. "Did that make any sense?

"Probably not, but just the thought of that love dying within you, never to give me another chance, fills me with terror." A dark shiver went through him. "We won't let it happen, Cambria. When my messenger gets here, we'll stop everything we're doing and end this waiting."

"In the middle of dinner?" She grinned. "You must love me, indeed, Riordan, if you would risk insulting my cook."

He grinned back. "The final test . . . I think I can do it."

Cambria stepped back. "I don't want to go back home. Let's marry first and tell the people at Thorne's Well after."

He slid one arm around her and slowly started them back down the rough-hewn road through the woods. "You can't do that to your family."

"You don't know what it's like there now."

"Tell me—" Suddenly, Riordan stiffened. Quickly, he pulled her off the path. "Someone's coming."

She frowned. "Why should we hide?"

Grinning, he lifted her loosened hair. "Your reputation."

Frantic, she slid her fingers over the mess. "Where are my pins?"

Wincing guiltily, he confessed. "On the ground back at Lakeview. Can you braid it for now?"

He pulled her back behind a bush. "Let's see who it is." A coach slowed down at the main road, and voices argued over turning into the path. Finally, a whip snapped and they crept slowly closer. It was a large coach, barely able to pass through.

"It's Diana." Cambria whispered as it went past them. "Hale asked her to bring a special license. She's come for the wedding."

He looked incredulous. "You were really going to marry Hale?"

She lifted her chin. "Of course. What did you think I would do?"

He took a wary look at her face. "I had hoped you would realize that I couldn't have done such a terrible thing as burn your bridge." He mused, "I think you might be right about one thing, Cambria. We need to marry now, before you think of something else to be angry about."

"I won't," she promised, moving into a clearing to braid her hair.

"What will Hale say when you tell him you've changed your mind about Tony?"

She looked down. Digging a hole into the soft dirt with her

booted toe, she mumbled, "I didn't exactly tell him I *would* marry Tony."

Grinning, he leaned over to see her face. "Why not?"

"It's hard to explain," she said, pushing her hair back out of her face. She braided it quickly, then ripping a ribbon off the bodice of her dress, she handed it to Riordan. Turning around, she ordered, "Tie this."

As Riordan complied, he asked, "Are you going to answer me?" He flipped her braid over her shoulder to show it was done.

She turned back. "I have a better idea. Come with me now. Remain close to me all day. Don't argue with Hale, just observe." She grinned. "We won't tell them about us, so he'll still think he's going to be telling his brother how to run Thorne's Well."

They strolled toward the bridge. "That bad, eh?"

"Yes. I dreamed last night that I'd dumped him out of a boat in the middle of the lake, but he wouldn't sink. He just kept floating on his back—his neckcloth wasn't even wet— and he just kept pestering me with questions about how many fish were in the lake."

He chuckled. "Poor Cambria."

"That's not all," she said woefully. "I shoved my oar into his stomach to push him down, but he'd just folded up so that his nose touched his knees . . . and kept on talking."

Riordan laughed. "At least when you attacked me, I sank."

She touched his sleeve. "Are you sure you want to marry me, Riordan? I'm not very lady-like. I have this temper—"

"I love you, Cambria Thorne. I wouldn't change a single thing about you." He pulled her close. "Let's take you home. When my messenger arrives, we'll marry at once. Nothing's going to separate us."

Chapter Twenty-Two

When Riordan strode ahead and carried on a long, intense conversation with Alistair at the new bridge, Cambria assumed he was making her apologies for snubbing his nephew. But when Alistair rushed past her with no more than an apologetic wave, she couldn't help wondering why the secrecy. Watching Alistair disappear in the direction of the main road to Thornedale, she frowned as she crossed the bridge. "Where is he going?"

Riordan turned to walk along the river. "To get the vicar."

"It took you all that time to tell him that?"

Frowning, he dipped his head to look into her eyes. "I know that look, Cambria. I thought you trusted me."

"I'm sorry" she said. "I won't ask."

He looked relieved. "Good."

She give him an innocent grin. "I won't ask why you rushed ahead to talk to Alistair privately."

"Then," he said in kind, "I won't tell you that he's gone to get the vicar and watch for my messenger. And I won't insult you with my foolish worry that if my license doesn't show up today, your suspicious little mind will begin concocting nefarious schemes where there are none."

"I'm glad we didn't have to waste time on such a foolish conversation." She sighed. "Just don't keep things from me, Riordan."

Once on the road, he slipped his arm down around her waist. "No more secrets, I promise. Now," he said, smiling once more, "tell me what the drill is for the day. Will someone have missed you already?"

"Not my family. They've all begun taking trays in the morning just to avoid Lord Hale. I don't believe Talia has spoken to him except at dinner, and last night, she pled a megrim and stayed in her room. Amelia and Ellie have taken Tony under their wing, set up a card table in the baths where he feels better. They're teaching him the game of brag."

She leaned against him. "When they learn you're here, they'll all come out like curious mice."

He didn't smile. "If you didn't tell Hale you'd marry young Tony, why didn't they leave with the rest?"

She turned off on a path through the woods. "No matter what I said—that I'd released Tony, that I was going to lose Thorne's Well—Hale insisted on staying. Hale knew I had no choice."

"But, after you'd seen what kind of life you'd have with them, you'd still have married Tony?"

"Either that or lose my home."

"You'd be a lot happier doing that than handing yourself over to Lord Hale and his weakling brother."

She took a moment to stifle her anger. "Since I'm no longer suspicious of you, I won't mention that you sound like a rich aristocrat who thinks nothing of *other people* losing their homes."

Riordan looked confused, then his face cleared. Assuming a bored expression, he murmured, "So glad you understand, my dear."

She had to laugh. "Wait until you see the marriage settlement I shall demand, Riordan. You'll be the one squirming, then." She snatched up the cup she'd left behind earlier and, stepping out into the sunshine of the rose garden, moved quickly out of his reach.

Riordan frowned. "Cambria," he said, moving slowly toward her, "If we marry today, there won't be time for settlements. Do you want to wait until Mark Glendover can draw one up? Will that make you feel more secure? Or can you trust me to see it done afterward?"

Stopping, Cambria suddenly felt ill. He was right. If she married him now, she would have no guarantee. She'd be stepping off a cliff with no assurance Riordan would catch her.

"Miss Thorne!" Cambria looked toward the house. Lord Hale came rushing out of the front door. "I've been looking for you. You should really tell people when you are going somewhere."

Riordan growled, "Pompous ass . . . let me tell him you've been busy getting engaged."

"Not on your life, Riordan. I want you to see what I've been going through. We'll tell him when your messenger gets here. Or, better, when the vicar does the deed."

His eyes shone. Moving around to shield her from Hale's view he grasped her hands. "You'll marry me without a settlement? . . . With no reservations?"

Cambria looked into his face. Love was not a safe place to be, but she could not forever deny herself the joy because of the inherent danger. She nodded. "I had decided to marry you the afternoon the bridge burned, but I fell asleep until it was time for dinner."

His eyes darkened. "I'm glad to hear that."

"Is that you, Lord Langcliffe?" Hale called. Riordan turned, shading his eyes as Hale traversed the lawn beyond the rose garden.

Riordan nodded. "Hello, Hale."

Hale snagged his sleeve on a rose bush. Working it loose, he frowned at the two of them. "Have you two made up your quarrel?"

Riordan grinned. "You mean my burning her bridge?"

Hale gave an uneasy laugh. Turning back toward the house, he strolled alongside Riordan. "I never believed it, of course. A great man like you wouldn't stoop so low. If you wanted to ruin Miss Thorne, you could have done it a dozen easier ways."

He was so absorbed with cozying up to Riordan that he didn't even acknowledge Cambria.

Watching Cambria's temper heat up, Riordan mocked Hale's arrogant tone. "Just so, Hale. And, why should I fuss over such an insignificant piece of land when I'm so wealthy, right?"

"Absolutely right." Hale rubbed his hands together. "We must get together now that we're to be neighbors, so to speak. You could give me some guidance. I've a little money set by that I'd like to invest. My wife's money, actually, but what's it for, if not to advance her husband, right?"

"Just what I've been explaining to Miss Thorne. A woman's first concern should be to trust her husband to do the right thing while she busies her inferior mind with the house and the children . . . *ouch!*"

Alarmed, Hale cried, "What's wrong, Langcliffe?"

Surreptitiously, Langcliffe rubbed his ribs where Cambria had twisted a bit of flesh. "Just a Thorne in my side."

Hale nodded absently. "Your aunt arrived a while ago. She's been waiting for you. Shall we go inside?"

"After you," Riordan said, waving Hale ahead of them. To Cambria he whispered, "The devil with your dream . . . let's take him down to the lake tonight. We'll drown him right this time."

Cambria surveyed the parlor, slowly filling up with her family and the Hales, with whom she'd been caged far too long. Once she and Riordan were married, she intended to leave them all behind. Let Talia have the pleasure of chivying Hale out of Thorne's Well and facing Diana's indignation.

When Diana and Ellie entered the parlor, Cambria stood up to kiss Diana's cheek. "How are you feeling, Diana? When I came home, you were asleep. I didn't think you would awaken until morning."

"Nonsense," Diana said, returning the kiss. "I didn't want to miss the festivities. That is," she said with a frown at Cambria, "if there is going to be a wedding. Talia tells me it's all up in the air now—after Havenshire went to a great deal of trouble to obtain the license for you.''

Ignoring any possible response Cambria might have, Diana turned to Tony next. As he made his bow, she gave him a concerned frown. ''Are you ill?'' Her face softened with motherly concern. She raised her hand to his flushed cheek to test for fever.

Before Tony could respond, Hale stepped up beside them. ''Merely a summer cold, Lady Waterson. He's been spending time in the baths and he'll be just fine.''

Diana wasn't having it. Without apology, she pulled down Tony's eyelid, then sent prodding fingers down the side of his neck. ''Cambria, this boy needs a tonic. Did you give him one?''

''Every morning and every night, Diana. He's sensitive to flowers, though, and with the entire valley in bloom, he's not improving.''

Diana stepped back. ''Do you feel well enough to eat, Tony?''

Tony blinked his swollen eyes. With a nasal croak, he replied, ''Of course, Lady Waterson. Please don't worry about me.''

Diana sent Cambria a stern look of disapproval. ''Cambria, do you think this marriage is wise?''

''The very thing I've been asking her,'' Riordan said as he and Alistair entered the room.

Diana whirled. ''Riordan?'' She immediately scowled at Cambria. ''What is going on here?''

Lord Hale laughed heartily, giving no one else a chance to reply. ''Oh, you mean that business about the bridge. No one really believes a duke would do such a thing. We've invited Langcliffe to dinner.''

Diana went quiet, clearly not quite believing what she'd just heard . . . a guest declaring the enemy, Langcliffe, innocent in one breath, and in the next, issuing invitations for the house.

Talia slid an arm around Diana's waist. ''Come meet the vicar who's just arrived, then we'll go in to dinner. You can resume your inquisition after the food's been served.''

The vicar seemed prone to blush every time anyone looked

his way. Eager to please, Cambria thought, easy to coerce his approval, a perfect weapon in Lady Langcliffe's hands. He blushed through introductions and then moved quickly to Amelia's side, the safest, kindest haven in the room.

Hale did a little dancing scramble to offer his arm to a very confused Diana as the rest trickled along behind, casually as was the usual Thorne's Well manner. Hale frowned at Riordan's drifting over to chat with Amelia and Ellie on the way in. Cambria held back a laugh. Hale had been trying to get them organized into marching grandly into dinner by rank since his arrival, and no one would cooperate. Now he had a lordly duke in company, and even he would not cooperate

As they drifted aimlessly to the table, Riordan managed to flank Cambria on her right as Hale pushed Tony toward the chair at her left. Riordan's brow rose sharply as Hale took his chosen place at the foot of the table. Diana's eyes narrowed, and, had she been a tea kettle, Cambria thought, a high squeal would have been issuing forth by now. Talia, for the first time since leaving London, wore her old lazy smile of amusement.

As the footman began serving, Riordan leaned toward Cambria, his knee touching hers. "Riordan," she warned softly, but he didn't budge. Instead, below the table, Riordan's hand found hers as he murmured, "Will you give me leave to announce our betrothal?"

She grinned. Riordan's mood had been deteriorating all day. His messenger had not arrived, and each hour with Hale had pushed him closer to the raw edge of civility. For her part, she found his misery vastly amusing, and it could only get better as Diana continued to search for any possible threat to her family's happiness. "Did your messenger come?"

"You know he didn't, brat."

"Well, then, we shall not disturb dinner with an announcement." She reached for her spoon. "Eat the soup while it's hot."

Diana did justice to the first course, but once the second began, she began demanding answers. "Riordan, did you or did you not burn down the bridge?" Amelia gasped, but Ellie grinned and leaned on her elbows to hear the answer.

Giving Diana a closed look, Riordan replied simply, "No."

"And your house?" Diana asked in a softer voice.

"What's this?" demanded Hale, ignorant of Lakeview's sad fate. The rest looked curious, but Diana leaned back, her intelligent gaze fastened on Riordan. "We shall speak of this later," she said firmly.

Her gaze switched to Cambria. "Now explain what you plan to do about this wedding. Your birthday is in two days."

Hale nodded as though he and Diana were sage adults explaining options to a dull child. Cambria could feel Riordan's anger rising. Quickly, she replied. "I shall announce my decision tomorrow, no sooner."

Again, Diana considered the matter. "That's all very well for you to make your decision, but what about poor Tony?"

Anthony stiffened. "I am pleased to be of service to Miss Thorne. I want everyone to understand that."

Diana's eyes widened with respect, but her protective instincts were still dominant. "Nobility is fine, Tony, but living in misery most of the year is not wise. What will you do when Cambria wishes to spend time in the valley with the children, and you must choose between months of illness or letting them go alone? If that's the kind of marriage you have in mind, I must tell you that—"

Hale rang his fork against his glass, silencing the room. "I, too, have given this some thought. What I propose is that since Tony's childhood home—where I now reside—seems far more healthy for him, that I will turn over that property to him."

Nobody spoke. Tony's shoulders hunched as if expecting a blow. Impervious, Hale's chest expanded in his munificence. "I shall give him the larger property to manage, and I shall bear the burden of Thorne's Well."

The only sound to be heard was Riordan's harsh, "The hell you will."

Shocked out of the rosy picture he'd painted for himself, Hale stared at Riordan. "I beg your pardon?"

"Thorne's Well always belongs to a Thorne, Lord Hale. If the heir is a woman, her husband must assume the Thorne name, did you know that? It can't be sold or given or even loaned to another. It can only revert back to the Langcliffe family.''

Hale didn't like being corrected. "That archaic law? Surely in today's modern world, who would keep track of how it's managed?''

Talia jumped in. "Now, look here, Hale—''

She stopped as the door opened, and a footman strode quickly toward Riordan. "A messenger, your grace.''

Riordan sent Cambria a triumphant, possessive look and rose from his chair. "This concerns you, Cambria. Come with me.''

The footman leaned forward. "If it pleases your grace, the gentleman insisted on seeing you alone. He sent his card.''

Frowning, Riordan took the pasteboard—then turned a ghastly white.

Cambria touched his arm. "Riordan, what is it? Your mother?''

Riordan placed a heavy hand on Cambria's shoulder. "No. Another matter entirely. Stay here. I'll be back in just a few moments.'' When she tried to rise, he shook his head. "Please, Cambria.''

She watched him go with a great deal of misgiving. What could possibly cause such a reaction in a man so strong, so impervious to the emotions that dismayed most normal men? She tried to remain in her seat, to honor his request, but she kept seeing the color drain from his face. Before she knew it, she was on her feet. "Please excuse me.'' She hurried out to the hall and skipped quickly down the stairs.

When she reached the foyer, she found it empty. She turned toward the library, the most logical place to conduct a private conversation, wondering why the room reflected no light. She stepped inside. Empty. Where had Riordan gone? Not outside, surely?

Back in the foyer, she moved toward the front door—and heard voices, clear in the damp evening air. Now what should she do? She couldn't eavesdrop, for that smacked of the very distrust she'd forsaken earlier that day. No, she had only two choices—to retreat or step outside.

Then a voice spoke. "Sorry, Lord Langcliffe. I was afraid

a messenger would somehow be delayed, and I would get here too late to stop your marriage."

"Just give me the facts, Rountree."

"You cannot marry her now. Miss Thorne must lose the land first, then the claim must be made. After the court has given its verdict and Thorne's Well is yours, then you may do as you wish."

Cambria gasped. Surely, she'd misunderstood those words. Sickened and disbelieving, she opened the door and joined them on the steps.

Both men turned. Riordan moved to block her sight of the visitor, and the stranger tipped his hat down to hide his face.

Too late.

In the light of the open door, she could see the tinge of red in the stranger's beard, recognized the face, the glasses. She'd seen this man before. In the foyer of her betrothed, John Adley. The man who enticed John out of the country, the man who represented a wealthy gentleman who'd taken up the charity work of sending *single* men to India.

Riordan was that *wealthy gentleman.*

Pain tore through her. She leaned back against the door and a dark, wailing cry burst forth from deep within her, sounding like nothing she'd ever heard before. Humiliated, unwilling to bare her sorrow, she tried to halt this abhorrent thing happening, but her body was in revolt against such common sense. One after another, the sobs erupted, as if she were bleeding to death, hemorrhaging from a heart torn asunder.

Riordan's arm swept around her, but with every bit of strength, she repulsed him, pushed him away. He fell back, but ignoring her blows, he gathered her up into his arms, tight against his powerful chest. Into the library he strode, and carried her to a worn, leather settee. Never letting her go, he sat down carefully, silently, his own chest heaving with every breath.

Nearby, his man lit a candle, but she could feel Riordan's hand wave, and it was pinched out. Blessed, blessed darkness. Her sobs slowed, leaving her empty, sore, hurting, lost in some other place. Inside her head someone was still screaming *no, no, no . . .*

Talia came with a warm shawl, then Diana with her remedy bag. A drink was poured, a spoon rattled. Coaxing voices, a nasty taste. Even as oblivion came to draw its black curtain, the last thing she remembered was finally, *finally,* Riordan released her from his smothering hold.

Chapter Twenty-Three

Cambria awakened at dawn, wretchedly thirsty, feeling like she'd run all the way to London pulling a carriage with the strap tied around her throat. A glass of water sat on the bedside table, and she quickly reached for it. Two swallows later, she repented her eager haste and reverted to tiny sips, wincing as the water trickled down her raw throat.

She stared at the fire. Not the usual banked embers, but a well-kept fire, a luxury usually allotted to the sick and elderly. Worse, Talia lay asleep beside her. Shame filled her. She'd been so hysterical that they feared to leave her alone? Well, after her disgusting display, she deserved to be in pain, and she deserved the indignity of a watchdog.

What she couldn't understand was why she'd fallen apart like that.

Suddenly, Riordan's image filled her mind . . . and tears filled her eyes and overflowed, wetting her face and soaking into the pillow. Blast, she thought, sliding out of bed, what was wrong with her that the mere image of Riordan's face could do this to her? She would go for a walk, she would conquer this thing in privacy. She quickly made her ablutions and donned a dress, a comfortable old thing that could withstand woodland branches or sitting on a leaf-covered ground. Boots next. Grabbing them, she sat on her dressing stool.

Talia stirred and bedclothes rustled. Raising up on an elbow, she squinted at Cambria. "What are you doing?"

"Go back to sleep, Talia. I'm going for a walk." She picked up a boot and slid her foot into it. She reached for the other one.

Talia sat up. "Then I should warn you that Riordan is sitting outside your room. He says he's not leaving until you listen to him."

Cambria straightened up, one boot in her hand. "He's been there all night?"

"He says he can explain, whatever that means. Will you listen to him, Cambria? He looks like a man on his way to the gallows."

She couldn't *think*. She dropped the boot and frantically pulled the other one off, tossed them both into the corner. Like a hunted animal, she'd been run to ground.

Talia padded across to her. "Darling, you don't have to make up your mind this very minute. I'm going to my room to dress now. Lock the door behind me if you wish. Climb back in bed and go to sleep." She put her arm around Cambria and pressed her toward the door. The key was in place, ready to be turned. Talia slipped out into the hall, and Cambria swiftly locked the door. Then she stood there and stared at it. Backing up, she made her way to the bed and climbed under the covers.

There, she was safe once more. She could sleep for days if she wished. As peace filled her, she marveled at how simple that was. She would sleep as long as she wanted, and when she was strong enough, she would listen to Riordan. Only this time, a very cold, clear-thinking mind would make the decision. Gratefully, she closed her eyes.

Coward.

Her eyes blinked open. She couldn't hide here in bed. Tomorrow she turned twenty-five. Whatever she was going to do, it had to be today. Once she left the room, Riordan would pounce on her, pleading his excuses for sending John to India. She supposed if he'd sent Mark and Anthony off to India as well, he could spin a trio of tales . . .

Taking shallow breaths, she pulled herself upright, afraid if she moved too quickly, her train of thought would disappear, and this was important.

Riordan had intended to leave . . . but he stayed. He offered his expertise, secluded himself with her day after day. *Bringing Alistair to keep Mark with the others . . . with Ellie.* Oh, yes, he'd seen Mark and Ellie laughing together and seen at once how yet another suitor might be enticed away. And all that time while he was planning to deal her another dose of rejection and pain, she'd been falling in love with him.

And Anthony? She didn't know how, but as certain as the sun set every night, Riordan had put his fatal touch on her third suitor as well. Remember Anthony's face as he left the baths?

And then after that, he cut off her last hope of finding yet another suitor—Marchant, perhaps—with the debacle of the bridge, a lethal end to her dowry, infuriating the *ton* patrons, making sure her welcome among them was fragile at best.

As for the burning of Lakeview, he'd somehow twisted the story to fit his purpose. How ruthlessly efficient he was.

The man she'd fallen in love with wasn't real. The true Riordan had two sides, one a dark shadow whom she'd finally seen last night with his skulking henchman.

Dear heavens, she could not afford to *listen* to Riordan ever again.

But how could she stop him?

Reluctantly, Riordan let Talia coax him to his room, offered his stiff muscles a hot bath, promised that Cambria would not escape. As he sank into the hot water, his mistakes came back to haunt him.

He should have told Cambria about her wedding present— that he was trying to give her Thorne's Well. He should have never risked speaking to Rountree where Cambria could recognize him. He should have gotten the license long ago, should have had it with him, and *then* when Cambria asked to marry him *before* returning to Thorne's Well, he should have married her on the spot.

Because the fact was that *now* she would marry Tony.

He stood and quickly rubbed his body dry with a thick towel. Cambria might *try* to marry Tony, but he would not allow it. If he had to drag Tony away kicking and screaming, he would do so. Better yet, he thought, donning fresh clothes from the bag Rountree brought, he would send the vicar away. The man was in his employ, what could be simpler?

Just let her try to get out of the valley. If he had to surround her house with an army of his servants, he would prevent her escape.

He wrapped his neckcloth with a simple knot, then reached for a brush on the dressing table. A swift run-through was good enough. He rose to leave the room just in time to hear the soft knock on the door.

"Come," he called, hurrying to the door.

Talia stood in the hallway, a paper in her hand. "A note from Cambria." Riordan looked out into the hall, but only a maid worked down the hall. Disappointed, he ripped the missal open.

> *"Riordan,*
>
> *I am sure you have an explanation for last night, indeed, for all that comes to my mind after seeing the man I met at John Adley's house. I understand now your interference with John and Mark, but my one curiosity is what you might have said to Tony.*
>
> *However, I shall forsake hearing that answer, since my most fervent wish is to never hear your voice again. I know how it is with us, having played the fool so many times. Somehow, you would find a way to spin your tale, and, inevitably, I would listen and believe. Therefore, I must take desperate steps to prevent that very thing.*
>
> *I am going to tell you a story, Riordan, a true one that in their generosity and kindness, my aunts have kept from you, often to their own detriment, and certainly to the suffering of their reputation. They were not only pro-*

tecting you, but your mother as well, from the cruelest of news. You may not believe this, but that is no matter.

    Your father did not lose your inheritance. Instead, your mother did that with her unrestrained gambling. Even after his sternest efforts, she would not cease, but like a spoiled child, she became hysterical over his attempts to restrain her.

    You may think me indelicate to tell the rest, but I must. After years of these troubles, your father lost his ability to function as a man functions with his wife. He came to the baths, hoping to remedy that situation. For some reason, he could not confess this to his wife, and she reacted in her usual unrestrained manner—wildly jealous, vindictive, spreading her tales about my aunts throughout the ton.

    Your father confessed his dilemma then, but, still angry, she took you away, turned you against him. He began to drink, and that sent him into the deepest depths of depression, which in turn led to his death.

    I cannot be sure how hearing this would affect your mother. Perhaps not at all, for she only listens to her own voice. But as you told me, she is now at a fragile time in her life, so perhaps my threat to you will carry some weight. I cannot help thinking it will be painful should she discover that she, in effect, killed her own husband.

    These are my terms. You and Alistair will leave immediately, within the hour, leaving the vicar at Thorne's Well. If you ever interfere in my life or attempt to speak to me, even send messages with someone else, I will give Diana permission to carry this tale to your mother. She longs to do so.

    Heartless cruelty seems to be the abiding link between the Thornes and the Langcliffes, does it not?

Riordan stood silent as the import of the paper hit him. Somehow, he knew Cambria told the truth. Had he not seen his mother in action? And remembering his kindly father, how he always gave in to his mother's demands, how helpless he must have felt.

How *hopeless* he must have felt.

Riordan wanted to go home and throw this letter in his mother's face, demand . . . what? Punish her for destroying his father?

Right, Riordan, you would have to drag a beaten woman out of her bed . . . and destroy her with the truth of Cambria's letter? He'd already burned her beloved house. He had been the first person in her life to stand firm and stop her. Anything more would be like kicking a beaten dog.

What if, in her despondent mood, she actually *listened and understood.* Would she follow his father's footsteps?

But . . . oh, the other truth . . . that his father had *not* pursued an affair at Thorne's Well, he had not gambled his wealth away, nor chosen the Thornes over his family.

Riordan bowed his head. All those years when Riordan had been busy hating his father, that honorable man had been grieving for the loss of his family. And all that time, his son had been forcing himself to hate his blameless father.

What mistakes he'd made, both with his father and then with Cambria. Cambria who now would marry Tony . . . Riordan crushed the paper in his fist. "Have you read this, Lady Maxwell?"

"Unfortunately, yes."

Riordan nodded at Cambria's door. "Will she do this?"

"I'm afraid you must believe her, Riordan."

"And now, I suppose she's going to marry Tony."

Talia's lovely face crumpled. "I cannot talk her out of it."

"I won't allow it . . . I'll kidnap her. Hell, I'll kidnap Tony if I have to. I'll keep my mother at Langcliffe Hall and won't let anyone in."

"If you make a move against anyone, the maid outside will call for help. Every servant in the house will come running and carry you and Alistair off Thorne's Well property."

Hoarsely, he said, "I can't leave her like this . . ."

Tears in her eyes, Talia moved forward and wrapped her arms around him. "This time you're going to have to walk away from what you want, Riordan. I think this land is cursed, and you never had a chance.''

Cambria sat unmoving before her window, long after Riordan and Alistair made their way to the stables and down the road. Diana had ordered the Hales to remain in their rooms until they were called, at which time luncheon would be served. They waited for her now.

Finally, Cambria stood and turned away from the empty road. It was time for her to take the last step. She crossed to the door and signaled to the maid. ''Call everyone to table, please.''

Closing the door, she changed to one of her favorite dresses, a soft cream silk with embroidered roses at the hem and neckline. Soft leather slippers finished the ensemble. She hesitated at the thought of wearing the matching shawl. After all, one did not wear a shawl to her wedding, did she? She headed for the door, then paused once more. She was cold, cold to the bone and feeling very vulnerable. Sighing, she went back, snatched the warm shawl, and wrapped herself in it. A flimsy protection against the choices she had to make, but at least she would be warm.

The Hales were waiting for her in the hall. Tony offered his arm. ''The maid told us you hadn't gone down yet, so we waited for you.''

Behind them as they descended the stairs, Lord Hale began his litany of disapproval. ''Strange way to manage a household, Miss Thorne, telling guests to stay in their rooms until they're called.''

Hoping silence would end the conversation, she did not reply. Still, her skin tingled unpleasantly, and she could feel her shoulders tensing in anticipation of his next thrust.

Lord Hale's fingers grabbed her arm, stopped her on the stairs. ''I think an explanation might be in order.''

Tony looked at his brother as Lord Hale stepped down beside them. ''As guests, we must be amenable to the workings of a house, don't you think, George? Miss Thorne doesn't have to explain.''

That slowed Lord Hale down only for time to catch his breath. 'You're going to have to be more forceful than this, Tony, if you're going to keep a wife in her place.'' Then, he gave Cambria a condescending smile. ''Of course, your place will always be on a pedestal, Miss Thorne.''

''As your wife's is, Lord Hale?''

Too dense to feel Cambria's pointed thrust, Hale's face relaxed. ''Exactly.'' He took Cambria's other arm and moved the party forward. With every step, Cambria's breathing became more labored as the world seemed to close in around her. She needn't allow Hale's bullying, but for some reason, she thought she wanted to test herself to the limits. The walls felt closer, the air thicker, but she made it down to the formal dining room.

As her family took their places, a sense of peace flowed through her. This was why she was marrying, she thought, to save this inheritance for her family and for her own children.

Riordan went as far as the Rose Thorne Inn and could go no further. ''Alistair, you may take the coach wherever you want. I'm going to stay here and speak to the vicar when he returns to the village.''

''Aren't you just going to make yourself more miserable hearing about Cambria's wedding?''

''I have to know for sure, Alistair. Nothing could be more agonizing than my thoughts right now.''

Alistair sighed. ''D'you mind if I stay with you? There's something awful about wondering.''

''Stay, then. I'd like the company. We'll go inside and sit by the window, and when the vicar comes out on the lane, I'll stop him. We'll leave then and reach Langcliffe Hall before morning.''

''Riordan,'' Alistair ventured as they entered the inn, ''how did this all go so wrong? I keep thinking back, wondering what we could have done differently, and, given the information we had at the time, I can't think what we would have changed.''

They took places at the window table. "Feeling guilty, are you?"

"Aren't you?"

Riordan looked out of the window. "Remember the lecture you gave me coming home from Thorne's Well one night?"

Alistair blushed. "Vividly."

"Well, Alistair, you were right. I had no right to do what I did. Even more arrogantly, I had no right to pursue Cambria without telling her who she was falling in love with . . . all the facts."

"So you lost all the way around."

"Not entirely. He reached inside his coat. "Read this."

Alistair skimmed through it, then read it once again. Looking up, he looked stunned. "If we'd only known, Riordan."

Riordan nodded. "Cambria had no idea she was giving me a priceless gift. My father was an honorable man. He never threw me away for something he wanted more. He was just a man in love who didn't know what to do."

"Lord Hale," Talia drawled, "don't you think since Tony is to be the head of this house, you should relinquish your chair at end of the table?"

Cambria felt badly she hadn't thought of it. "Yes, Tony, please change places with your brother." Tony flushed and looked at his brother. She could see him doing the same thing she did, bracing himself for his brother's reaction. She turned to watch Hale's face. Neither king nor country was going to budge him out of the place of honor.

She opened her mouth to insist, when Amelia interrupted. "When you're visiting your brother, Lord Hale, will your wife have Cambria's place?"

Hale looked like he'd like to swat Amelia. "As head of the Hale family, I think that would be the proper protocol."

Ellie jumped in. "Did you know that Cambria booted Lord Langcliffe out of the house this morning?"

Hale's eyes fairly bulged. "What idiocy is this?" To Cambria, he growled, "Isn't he coming to the wedding today?"

Ellie wasn't letting go. "You'll never see him here again."

Diana frowned at the girls. "This is a private matter, girls. Change the subject."

Hale seemed consoled at Diana's tone. "Just so, Lady Waterson. I'll speak to Langcliffe myself. He'll see reason, I'm sure. Langcliffe's not a man to take umbrage at a female's eccentricities."

Diana didn't particularly like his response, Cambria could tell, but her aunt was a stickler for harmony in the house— except when it involved Langcliffe. "Let's talk about the wedding, Cambria. What music shall we play? The servants are decorating the parlor, and cook has been working since dawn on a wedding supper."

"Lord Hale," Amelia asked, "why didn't you ask your wife and children to come when you sent for the special license? Or your sister?"

Cambria frowned in confusion. Why were the girls belaboring over Hale's behavior? All during the past few days, they'd been quietly keeping Tony busy and comfortable and seemed pleased with him as a friend. Now they were definitely up to something quite, quite different.

Hale waved his hand in dismissal. "She's needed at home. She'll understand."

"Amelia," Diana said tightly, "desist now."

Ellie pushed harder. "Is that what you'll expect of Cambria . . . to stay home, never invited to festivities? Especially" she said with a pointed look at Cambria, "if she's living at your farm and you're living here?"

Looking somewhat harried, Hale sent Diana a look that demanded she control the saucy young misses. Diana's mouth was still open when Amelia kept going before anyone could stop her, "If you're living here, Lord Hale, does that mean when we want to visit Cambria, we have to go to your farm? Or will she be allowed visitors at all?"

Ellie leaned forward. "How long since your wife has been to London, Lord Hale? Or anywhere, for that matter?"

Talia drawled, "If you keep this up, girls, Cambria will be seeing so unpleasant a picture of her life that she won't marry at all."

Diana's fist hit the table. "Talia!"

"Well," Ellie said flatly, "I'm not coming back here. I couldn't stand the company."

Diana gasped.

Amelia stood up. "I can't stand it now."

Ellie stood as well. "Nor can I."

Talia looked at them with pride. "You can't hide from the truth forever, Cambria. Better face it now than after it's too late."

Cambria's heart began the slow, steady thud of a funeral dirge. For the first time, she saw the picture they were desperately trying to show her. Once married to Tony, her relationship with her family would change, and for the worse. She'd been blind to such a possibility.

She looked at her future brother-in-law. "What do you think about this, Lord Hale?"

Hale rolled his eyes. "Silly girls' tantrums, Miss Thorne. They'll come around."

Cambria looked at Diana, who'd gone suspiciously silent; Diana who was Hale's strongest supporter. "And Diana? Do you think I'll be happy? Will we all stay close after I marry?"

Diana's eyes narrowed, but her lips quivered with emotion. "I think you should come home with us where we can take care of you."

Amelia and Ellie linked hands, then turned to look imploringly at Cambria.

Talia shook her head. "Sit down girls, this is not our decision to make." Amazement flitted over the girls' faces, but they sat, quietly, knowing that they'd gone as far as they could, that Cambria might yet choose Thorne's Well.

Talia said softly, "This is not about lost loves, Cambria, or triumphing over a foe."

Cambria and Talia shared a profound look of understanding. "Talia's right," Cambria said to the silent table. "Someone said recently that my birthday has given everything a warped sense of value. He should have added that it gave *me* no value at all, that I believed my only value was Thorne's Well."

As Talia sighed contentedly, Cambria stood up. "So I've decided to do something of even greater value for the Thorne family. I'm going to be the one to end a very long, painful war.'' She looked at the dear faces of her family, now all grinning and wiping at tearful signs of their approval.

She turned to the vicar, sitting so timidly through her family's great drama. ''Reverend, there will be no wedding, but I would like you and the Hales to stay for luncheon. Cook would be insulted if we did not do it justice.'' Turning to Tony, she said, ''Tony, I'm sorry, but we must not marry. Neither of us would be happy, and I don't want either of us to be miserable for the rest of our lives to save a piece of land.''

Hale jumped up. ''You can't do this.''

Anthony rose slowly and looked down at his brother. Placing his hand on his shoulder he shoved him back to his seat. ''Shut up George. If you don't, I'm tossing you out of the room.'' Then Tony raised his glass with a sweet smile. ''A toast to Cambria. The loveliest flower in the valley.''

Then he sneezed.

''She's a strong woman, Lord Langcliffe. I don't know anyone, man or woman, who would have been so courageous.''

Humbled and elated all at once, Riordan replied, ''You're a wise man to recognize that fact, Reverend.''

Alistair grinned as the vicar left the inn. ''So what are you going to do, Riordan? At least you have a chance now.'' Then, his face clouded. ''Except for all Cambria's rules.''

Riordan reached for his coat. ''You know, Alistair, I haven't prayed for years, but when I left Thorne's Well, I struck a bargain with God. If she would just *not* marry Tony, I'd do what I could to make it right for her, not asking for anything else for me.''

''You're not going after her?

''No. Some day she'll find a man worthy of her.''

Alistair eyes widened. ''What are you going to do?''

''The honorable thing. Something my father would endorse if he were here. Cambria deserves the freedom to do what she wants with her life. I'm going to make that possible for her.''

Chapter Twenty-Four

"Talia, this is absolute foolishness," Diana exclaimed, smoothing down the heavy velvet dress. "I'm too old for this nonsense. Why couldn't we have just eloped like you and Havenshire?"

"Because Ragsdale has never been married, and he wants to see his bride dressed in her finery, not dragged into a church with a five-minute warning as I was."

"I think it's romantic," Amelia said loyally, fastening the back of Diana's dress. "He probably didn't want you to change your mind."

Talia laughed. *"That* wasn't what he was afraid of."

"What, then?"

"He was afraid *he* would change his mind. He got the license yesterday and then came by this morning to take me driving before I was even awake. I thought he looked ill and I told him to go home, but he wouldn't budge. Then he drove straight to the church and pulled me inside while his tiger held the team."

Ellie threw herself into a chair. "This is unfair. Everyone is getting married while I have to wait for years and years!"

Diana sighed, a long-suffering, well-practiced response to

Ellie's dramatic lament. "I told you I wouldn't let you marry a poor man, Ellie."

"Well, Langcliffe's dismissing Mark didn't hurt him. His own business is flourishing. Every day, someone else comes to solicit his services."

"It's only been five months, Ellie. I'm not leaving this to chance."

"Riordan's not going to turn on Mark, Mother. He's the one sending the clients over."

"Well," Diana muttered, "that's the only reason I let Ragsdale talk me into inviting Riordan to the wedding." As the others gasped, she scowled fiercely. "He and Riordan are friends. What could I say?"

Talia studied her sister's crimson face. A mocking smile played at the corners of her mouth. "Forced you to invite Riordan, did he?"

Diana slid her feet into her wedding slippers. "I had to do something, Talia. Cambria's become an absolute hermit, and she's not eating. She'll lose her figure if she gets any thinner."

"And Cambria didn't get upset?"

"She doesn't know."

Cambria eyed the package on the bed with loathing. What was wrong with Mark that he would send yet more of his horrid papers for her to sign on Diana's wedding day? Bad enough that she must sign anything concerning Thorne's Well—which she usually did quickly, like taking a wretched tonic—but not today.

The box just sat there like a bit of spoiled fish. She didn't want it near her any longer than necessary—certainly not waiting for her all through Diana's wedding party. Gritting her teeth, she untied the string and took the top off the box. With distaste, she turned it upside down and shook out its contents. Leafing through quickly, she looked for the place where Mark usually had her sign. First page, second, third . . . she couldn't find it anywhere.

She went back to the beginning, running her finger down

the lines of writing . . . "Plaintiff, Cambria Thorne, vs . . ."
What the devil? She read on, sure this was some mistake, then
went back to the top of the page and read again. Mark had
sued Riordan on her behalf? *Sued Riordan for attacking
Thorne's Well . . . a provision provided for just such a viola-
tion?*

She slowed her perusal. Langcliffe admitted burning the
bridge? He admitted deliberately interfering with her inheriting
Thorne's Well? She read the items, one by one. It sounded
more like a deathbed confession than the powerful man she'd
known.

She stared off into space. Why would Riordan do such a
thing?

Turning the page, she read the next document, her mouth
dry and her heart pounding. Oh heavens, if she wasn't misread-
ing the wording, she'd been granted ownership of Thorne's
Well *and Lakeview.*

"This can't be right," she muttered, turning to the last document.

A deed. *Her deed* to both those properties, with Havenshire
and Mark as trustees. "I'm dreaming," she muttered, lifting
the last document.

And a bank draft for fifty thousand pounds in damages?

*And a note that Mark was waiting downstairs to speak with
her.*

Stuffing the documents back into the box, she scrambled off
the bed On the way downstairs, her treasures in her arms, she
thought of Riordan and how furious he must be. She wished
she could see his face.

"Mark," Cambria exclaimed as she hurried into the parlor,
"I got your note that you wanted to see me." She put the box
down on a table and, sighing, asked, "How did you ever think
to do such a wonderful thing?"

"Cambria," he said gravely, "perhaps you'd better sit
down."

She sobered immediately. "Something's wrong?"

"Nothing's wrong with your papers, but something is definitely wrong, and that's what I have to tell you. But, first I

must have your promise you will not invoke your threat on Riordan if I mention his name.''

She sat down on the edge of the settee. ''He hasn't sent you with a message, has he? Some threat of his own, now that he's lost?''

''No. May I have your promise?''

She slid back into the corner. ''Very well, you have it.''

Mark turned sideways on the settee, facing her with his arm draped along the cushioned back. ''You asked how I ever thought of challenging the will, winning Lakeview for you? Well, I didn't, Riordan did that, and he'd slay me if he knew I was telling you this. That's why he severed our business relationship, so it could be done legally.''

Cambria's eyes closed as the room began to swirl. ''I don't want to hear this, Mark.''

''I know you don't. I was worried when I saw you falling in love with Riordan. Not because he was after Thorne's Well, but because of the kind of man he is.''

''Ruthless, I believe you said.''

''Yes. Because he's rather like a powerful invading army when he wants something. His hellish life made him that way— just as your own rather ill-fated life made you the way you are.''

''What do you mean 'the way I am?' ''

Mark hesitated. ''Part of the reason you've fought loving him is a matter of trust . . . but there's more, you know.'' He watched her closely. ''I wonder if you're afraid of him, Cambria. If you don't want a man who will overpower you in any way.''

''You're wrong, Mark. I'm not afraid of anyone.'' *Only how badly he can hurt me . . . has hurt me.*

He sighed gently is if she hadn't replied. ''Loving someone means granting him the power to hurt you in ways of the heart, and, for a woman, it means giving the man the power to control every part of her life, from the purse to the nursery to the bedroom.''

She gasped. ''Mark!''

''If Phillip were here, he'd be giving you the same lecture,

Cambria, otherwise I wouldn't have to do it for him." His fingers tightened on her shoulder. "There's no safe place in life, Cambria, not really. But fortunate people like you have family to keep danger at bay, a place to hide when you're frightened."

"You think I'm hiding?"

Mark sighed and looked down where her fingers were tracing the pattern in the tufted velvet. "I'm just trying to keep a very great injustice from happening when it might be averted if the facts are placed in the open. Facts can't hurt, Cambria. Only our response to them."

Cambria fastened on a particular phrase. "A great injustice?"

"Yes. An injustice to a man who has made recompense in his own way, a man who deserves a hearing."

"Riordan."

He nodded. "After he read your note, he not only believed you about his mother, but he and his solicitor investigated it, proved the truth of it even though it broke his heart. He does not hide from the truth, Cambria."

"He manipulated you, Mark. Doesn't that make you angry?"

"Of course it does . . . or at least it did."

"Then, how can you be pleading his case for him?"

"I'm not pleading his case for him, Cambria. I'm pleading it for you. One of these days, it's all going to make sense. You'll understand him when you let the facts settle into place. You might even see the humor of how crazy you made him, popping up with new suitors every few weeks, making him chase you all over . . . while in the background his mother was destroying everything he tried to build with you."

Mark smiled. "He didn't want to fall in love, either, Cambria, but when he did, he faced it squarely and tried to make it work despite all his secrets, all his problems, and a woman who did not truly want him."

"How can you say that? I did love him, Mark."

Mark caught her glance and held it with a tender look. "Answer honestly, Cambria. When you saw Rountree out on the step, weren't you just a little bit relieved?"

"*Relieved?* How can you think that of me? No, I was devastated. How many times had I trusted him and then found out he was lying? Every time was more painful than the last. I was *relieved* when I decided to send the note, relieved to find a way to never *listen* to him again. Mark," she said with a broken voice, "I've loved him since I was a child, and I don't think I shall ever stop loving him. But *trusting* him . . . the price is too high to be made a fool again. I can't do it again."

Mark shook his head and went doggedly on. "Stop and think. He'd just explained everything to your satisfaction . . . *everything* . . . and yet when this last secret came to life, something that was started before you even met again, you sank your teeth into it and hung on. Cambria," he said softly, "you did have the truth, several times, but you always *chose* not to believe. You reacted to the pain and hit out at him when *you should have asked for his side of the story.*"

She leaned forward, her arms crossed over her middle. "Why are you doing this, Mark?"

"Because I'm the one in the middle. I see you becoming a faint whisper of your old self, and I see Riordan closing himself off from every bit of human warmth in his life. He'll never reach out to you again, Cambria. Probably not to anyone."

Dear God, she'd never imagined . . .

"He blames himself for everything. His father, his mother, you . . . he hatched this scheme to give you the land, to give you control of your own life. He thinks of himself as unworthy. That's why he admitted to all the crimes in those documents. To make it easy for you, so you could keep hating him and make a new life for yourself. It's *all* to make you happy."

He stood up. "He's coming to the wedding today, Cambria. Not to try to make up with you, but because Ragsdale wants him to stand up with him and wants him at the wedding party."

His jaw tight, Mark said awkwardly, "Forgive me for being so presumptuous, but it's nothing Phillip would not have said. I think now I have done what I can to repay Phillip as a friend. And as your friend, I'll not speak of it again." He leaned over and kissed her cheek. "I have to go now." Then he strode out of the parlor, closing the door softly behind him.

* * *

On the way up the wide church steps, Riordan pasted a solemn expression on his face, determined not to give away his churning emotions.

Cambria. *Dear Lord . . . Cambria.*

Why was he doing this to himself? He wasn't even going to speak with her, not even look at her if he could manage it. And the damned party afterward. He'd go in long enough to let Ragsdale see him there, then leave. He had work waiting for him, and after this, he would need the soothing solitude.

Cambria forced herself to look at Riordan's broad back during the wedding, forced herself to dredge up every conversation they'd ever had, from the moment they'd met in the woods until that last painful moment at the house. When she finished, she reviewed Mark's condemning rebuke, determined to exonerate herself. She *wasn't* a coward, hiding behind her family's skirts, hiding from the facts. She was a woman lied to, tricked, betrayed. A logical woman who had only let love overcome her common sense, and upon seeing damning proof, quickly ended that particular fiasco and sent the blackguard on his way.

She watched Riordan's back as he shifted from one foot to the other, every movement signaling his impatience to be somewhere else. When he turned around, she would drop her eyes and never look at him again.

When he turned around, she looked up, straight into his face.

She need not have worried about their gazes meeting, for he kept his own firmly locked on the back of the room, far above the heads of the wedding guests.

But his eyes . . . were so *blank*.

People swirled around her as they exited the church. She let herself be stuffed into a carriage and assisted back out as they arrived at the hotel where the celebration would be held. As they stood in the receiving line—with Riordan on one end and Cambria on the other—her mind began to see how truly slanted was her perspective. *She'd been so busy defending herself from*

Mark's criticism that she'd essentially confirmed everything he'd said.

Back in the town house were documents, money even, made possible by Riordan Langcliffe. Tangible proof that made everything else shift into place. Riordan's lifeless eyes told the rest, verified all Mark said.

Or, *almost* all.

She didn't like hearing that she'd never *truly* wanted Riordan. She'd always been attracted to him, indeed loved him. He'd always charmed her. Invoked her sincere admiration. Made her laugh. Made her long for the pleasures of the wedding bed.

But he also panicked her. Made her clutch for any excuse to deter him, to send him out of her sphere.

No, that couldn't be true.

Think. At Lakeview, Peck—acting as Riordan's representative—stood up to the duchess and granted Cambria all she wanted. But did she give Riordan a chance to explain, did she grant a fair hearing? No, she chose to believe Lady Langcliffe's vitriolic slurs.

Her blood began to surge through a heart long frozen.

She'd done well to trust her wary intuition, to suspect him at first. But just as she was falling in love, *so was he.* Just as she had been appalled, *so had he.* They were each fighting their emotions, each trying to cling to the truths they'd started out with. Somewhere in the middle of it all, love had grown between them, entwined them so thoroughly that *apart,* they each must wither.

Riordan had understood this, for what had he asked from her? *What about her feelings, was she to be denied a life with the man she loved? . . . Would she deny life to the children who would come to them?* He'd enticed her with those words, with his concern over her happiness. All through those golden moments together, he had been concerned that she would not trust in his love . . . in her own love. Indeed, she'd been afraid of the same thing.

Yet, what was her first response to his evening visitor? Rather than fight for love, she'd curled back into her cocoon in

Thorne's Well. She'd been clinging to that childhood sanctuary all along. *Mark was correct.*

What had she done?

More to the point, what was she going to do about it?

As the receiving line broke up, Riordan escaped to the balcony overlooking the garden, leaving behind the stifling ballroom with its glaring chandeliers and noisy people. *His head was pounding as if a spiked ball were banging back and forth between his temples.*

Well, what did he expect when he'd ground his teeth for two hours while the entire *ton* trooped past, expecting him to *chat* with them. Idiots all. He would never attend another social event in his life . . . never.

"Ah, there you, Riordan." Talia leaned forward and kissed him on both cheeks. "I wanted to get your promise for a dance. I know we don't have dance cards here, but you waltz so beautifully. Would you please promise me your first waltz?"

What could he say? "I'd be charmed." As she drifted away . . . or should he say, sensuously twined herself between the others on the cool balcony . . . he kicked himself for staying even this long. When, he wondered, would the first waltz occur? The sooner the better.

"Lord Langcliffe . . . we hoped we'd find you here." Ellie and Amelia fairly flew at him, ignoring his bow and throwing their arms around him. Something inside him winced at that unabashed affection. It was the last thing he wished.

"We wanted to waltz with you," they said together, then looked at each other and laughed. "Will you?"

He couldn't do this. "I've promised my waltz to Lady Maxwell."

"Oh, don't worry," Ellie said. "We're paying the band, and they're going to play *lots* of waltzes tonight because this is such a romantic occasion. So, I'll take your second waltz and Amelia will take your third."

"Bye," Amelia said as they turned to leave, giving him her

sweetest smile. He couldn't bear to hurt her, that much he knew, but how much more could he endure?

Riordan leaned over the railing. Down below, there was a cool pond and a small waterfall. Perhaps, if he could just dunk his head in that cold water, he might be able to make it through three waltzes. All that whirling would surely kill him.

"Riordan Langcliffe, what are you doing out on the balcony when you're part of the wedding party? Everyone is asking for you."

He turned. "Hello, Lady Waterson . . . oh, that's right, its Ragsdale now, isn't it?"

Diana moved closer and leaned forward to buss his cheek— but never completed the move. Stopping to look into his eyes, she scolded, "Why didn't you say you had a headache, you foolish boy?" She waved at a waiter, and the uniformed man hurried forward. "Get me a glass of cold water and a soft cloth . . . hurry!"

Riordan spoke his thoughts aloud. "Ragsdale is a lucky man."

She sighed happily. "I'm the fortunate one. I never wanted a man who was so terribly noble, though. They all seem so very boring."

The servant came running at a trot. Diana bade him follow her down the stairs, then motioned Riordan to a high-backed bench near the inviting pool. Once she had him seated, she poured a bit of icy water over the cloth, squeezed it, and lay it over his forehead and temples. "Lean back, dear. Close your eyes while I get a powder out of my reticule."

He leaned back. The instant the cold cloth hit his skin, the pain began to recede. Relaxing added its own bit. For once, he didn't mind her managing ways, her bossy mothering.

He felt a spray of water on his arm and opened his eyes. Diana had her hand over the top of the glass and was shaking her concoction, completely ignoring the fact that her sleeve was getting wet. "Here you are, Riordan. Drink this quickly before it settles on the bottom."

Tamping down on the emotion clutching his throat, he obeyed without question. Any man in pain was bound to be grateful for relief, he assured himself. Just because it was Diana . . . treating him as one of the family . . . didn't really mean anything at all.

"I hear you have given away your first three waltzes, Riordan."

He sat up and caught the cloth before it plopped onto his lap. "What?"

"I shall settle for your fourth if I must, but after making me take last choice, you must sit beside me for the wedding dinner." She took the cloth from him and waved it in the air to refresh its coolness. "Here, let's put this on the back of your neck, Riordan. In a few minutes, you'll be back in fighting shape."

With those enigmatic words and a swift kiss on his cheek, Diana glided across the dark garden and up the balcony stairs.

Wrapped and delivered, he had to stay for the party.

He could have wept.

Chapter Twenty-Five

Talia found him as the first waltz began its prelude to signal dancers onto the floor. "Riordan, darling, Havenshire begged me for this first waltz, so do you mind dancing with Cambria?" Before the words made any sense, she'd pushed Cambria into his arms.

Like a loon, he just stood there and stared at Cambria, wondering why she'd allowed herself to be thrown at him like that. She wore a dress of soft ruby silk and around her neck she wore the famous Langcliffe ruby necklace. "The others are taking the floor," she said calmly, "I'd hate to miss the first waltz, wouldn't you?"

His feet moved. The music set the beat, and he swept her onto the floor, all the time wondering what he was supposed to do next. She'd specifically said she didn't want to hear his voice again, yet she'd asked him a civil question. Which, for the life of him, he could not remember.

"The wedding was lovely, didn't you think, Riordan?"

"Uh . . . yes. Splendid."

"Did you know that Havenshire dragged Talia off to the church this morning, had a clergyman waiting with a special license?"

A smile flew onto his lips. "Havenshire?"

She smiled dreamily. "So romantic. He married her, and then dropped her off at the town house so she could get ready for Diana's wedding."

"You call that romantic?"

She nodded. "He just swept her off her feet."

Riordan bit the inside of his lip to see if he was dreaming this, to see if he'd gone unconscious with Diana's tonic and was still in the garden. *No, he was wide awake and confused as hell.* "You're looking lovely, Cambria." Great, Langcliffe, whip out an inane courtesy as if she were a stranger.

"I've lost weight. Diana thinks I'm losing my figure."

He sent a quick glance over her. "Not from my viewpoint."

Smiling, she examined him in return. "So have you . . . lost weight."

Riordan's brain finally quit spinning. Taking stock of the situation, he decided that he'd accept this fluke, this moment out of time. He didn't dare attempt any more conversation; he was incapable of anything intelligent at all. Pulling her closer, he finished the rest of the dance in silence. Hell, things could not get worse.

Ellie came rushing up, Mark in tow. "Mark wants this waltz. Do you mind? I asked Cambria to take my place." This time Cambria moved into his arms without a push. He wasn't stupid. For some reason, Cambria's relatives were pushing them together, and on both her aunts' wedding days, she was willing to behave. Smiling distantly, he nodded at Ellie and whirled Cambria onto the floor. "You're being very civil, Cambria. I suppose because it's a special day, you're willing to call a truce between us."

"No, that's not it, Riordan."

"What's not it? The truce, the special day . . . What?"

"That's not why they've given me their waltzes."

"Surely, you don't believe this is a coincidence."

"No."

He danced around the floor in silence, cursing the day he'd

ever gone to Thorne's Well. He used to be sane. He used to
be able to think at lightning speed, calculate a dozen possibilities
at once, and make decisions in a moment's time. Now he
couldn't even think of an intelligent question.

"The lawsuit," he managed finally. "You got the papers
and now it's time to be pleasant to me." Although he'd done
it with the purest of motives and wouldn't change his mind for
any reason, this cat-and-mouse dialogue didn't sit well with
him. "Don't strain yourself to be polite, Cambria. The court's
decision is final, and you can go on your way without this
insincere pleasantry."

A spark of anger danced in her eyes, but before he could
exult in having stirred her out of her bland facade, a contented
smile spread over her face. "Thank you, Riordan. That's very
kind of you." She moved closer to him and finished the waltz
in serene silence.

Riordan saw Amelia coming, Alistair's hand in hers. "Do
you mind, Riordan? Alistair and I have just declared ourselves
friends again, and I don't want to let him get away just yet.
Will you dance with Cambria instead?" Cambria gave him an
innocent smile and moved into his arms.

Riordan exploded. "Damn it, Cambria, what's going on?
Why didn't you tell them this wasn't necessary?"

She tipped her head to the side. "Mark told me I was afraid
of you, Riordan. Do you think I am?"

"What?" He halted for a second, then stumbled around
getting back the rhythm. He looked around at the other dancers,
not surprised to see them all watching him and Cambria. Blast,
just what he wanted, to make a total ass of himself the last
time he appeared in public.

He dipped his head toward Cambria. "What did you say?"

"Mark said I was afraid to be in love with you. That you
were too powerful for me."

"What the hell . . . I'm too powerful for you? You made
mincemeat of me, Cambria. You chased my mother out of
town, got a thumb-lock on me at the dance, socked me in the

nose—that's after you beat me almost senseless with a stick the size of my leg—and pushed me in the river.''

"So you don't agree with him?"

He raised a cynical brow. "If you'd like to refresh your memory on the little love letter you tossed me out of Thorne's Well with, I'd be glad to send it over to your house."

"Actually," she mused, "I tend to agree with him."

"Well," he said grimly, "I hope you don't intend to try to even us up anymore. I'll declare you the winner if you wish. I'll tell Mark Glendover to keep his damned mouth shut lest you send me to an early grave."

She smiled. "That's very sweet of you, Riordan." Dreamily, she danced the rest of the waltz in contented silence.

When Diana sidled up to him with Cambria in tow, he just took her onto the dance floor in total defeat. "After this, I'm leaving," he declared. "My poor ancestors, trying to battle the Thornes. I'm surprised they had a single brain left to hand down to me."

She reached up and ran her fingers down his cheek. "Poor baby."

He recoiled. What was wrong with her? Had she been at the punch bowl once too often? Horrified, he glanced around the room to see if anyone had observed her intimate caress—and blinked at the strangest sight. Many of the dancers had stopped dancing and stood watching them with identical beatific grins.

Grimly, he looked back at her. "Don't look now, but everyone is staring at us, Cambria. What the devil did you do that for? You know how these people twist everything."

She ignored him and looked around the room. Dipping her head at them in a rather royal manner, she smiled back up at him. "They're just staring at you being so friendly for a change, Riordan. Usually, you growl around the dance floor, steal my waltz and the dinner dance, and leave for the night."

"Well, at least I'm not stealing the dinner dance tonight," he murmured.

"Oh, but you are. This *is* the dinner dance, didn't you know?"

Stunned into silence, he finished the dance a half-beat out of tempo.

Havenshire stood as they approached the dinner table reserved for the wedding party. "Langcliffe, may I have a word with you? Bring Miss Thorne, if you will, please."

"Certainly," Riordan replied, wondering if they were going to get a dressing down for Cambria's behavior on the dance floor. He and Cambria walked around the back of the table to stand near Havenshire, who didn't mince words. "As Miss Thorne's guardian—as stipulated in your recent court case— I must ask you if you wish me to announce your betrothal or if you wish to do it yourself."

He was losing his mind. "Betrothal?"

"Surely you don't think you can dance with a well-bred girl four times and not do the right thing?"

"Four times?"

Havenshire frowned. "What's wrong with you, man? Have you been drinking? You danced with her four times. *Three* would have done the job, but *four* doesn't leave you any choice."

Riordan shifted his attention to Cambria. Surely, her temper would explode any second now. She looked back at him like the cat who got the cream. "You did this on purpose, Cambria?"

Havenshire growled, "Lower your voice, Langcliffe."

"Why?" he bellowed, watching Cambria's face for some clue to this stratagem. "Everyone is listening, anyway. Better that they get the story straight."

As he watched, her innocent smile changed. Her lips twitched and a grin danced just beneath the surface. "Are you going to answer Havenshire?"

"You want to marry me?"

"Oh, yes."

He stilled. His chin came up, and his eyes narrowed. "This was your plot? To compromise me?"

Biting her lip, she nodded solemnly.

"It's not a joke, some little revenge you've been planning to humiliate me?"

"No."

Glendover handed him a heavy piece of paper, a special license, signed and sealed. "I got this just an hour ago. Damned hard to do at such short notice."

Riordan glanced at it briefly, checking the date and names inscribed. He looked back at Cambria. "If there were a clergyman here, I'd wipe that smile off your face."

Glendover spoke up. "There is, Riordan. The one who married the Ragsdales. Shall I get him?"

His gaze steady on Cambria, he said, "Yes. Now."

Her smile fading, Cambria backed up a step. "We can't do it now, Riordan. I was just sending you a message. We need to talk, first."

"Marry now, talk later. You begged me to do that once, and I didn't listen. I'm not taking any chances this time."

She backed up a few more steps, the light of battle that he loved fading from her face. "Absolutely not. I'll need a dress, Riordan. Flowers, music, bridesmaids. You can't just commandeer a wedding, you know."

He moved forward. "I think your family can organize something.

"Diana," he called over his shoulder, "D'you suppose you can be ready when I bring her back from the garden? She wants to *talk.*"

Diana laughed. "Hurry back."

He took two long strides forward, slid his arm around her waist, and whisked her outside. He took a deep breath as strength poured through him. Cambria Thorne was going to marry him if he had to gag her to get the job done.

Then he'd take her home to Langcliffe Hall and see how she fared with his mother. That ought to be interesting, he thought, just the thing to get his mother out of bed and onto her feet. After he let them battle it out for an hour or so, he'd take Cambria home to Thorne's Well and keep her speechless for a week.

Once down the stairs, he pulled her into his arms. His lips close to hers, he said, "This is it, Cambria. No more chances."

She tipped her head back, putting more space between them. "That's what we need to discuss, Riordan. You can't just have your way all the time, charging ahead like a maddened bull—"

He reached down and, with an arm under her legs, hauled her tight up into his arms. Cradling her against his chest, he kissed her with all the raging love pouring though him. He caught her surprised gasp in his mouth, and while her lips were parted, he deepened the kiss. Without prelude, his tongue began a mating dance, teasing her lips, leaving a forceful trail of possession as he made his way inside. Sighing, she fell limp against him, raised her mouth to get closer, her hands clutching his shoulders as she gave him what he wanted.

"I'm going to make you so damned happy," he murmured, moving his mouth down her neck, nuzzling, soothing. The taste of her skin went to his head, the feel of his love in his arms, when he thought he'd lost her, hardened his resolve not to lose her again.

How much love he had waiting to give to this woman, this maddening woman who never backed down! But here, in his arms, the Thorne warmth shone through, the generosity, the limitless giving . . . here in his arms, she surrendered her will and offered her love. And here in her arms, his own will became one with hers.

She tipped her head back and, still resting against his chest, looked up. She caressed his cheek. "I hurt you so . . . I'll never do it again."

He kissed her nose and began his trek back to the ballroom. "Yes, you will. When I tell you all my sins in detail, you'll be furious."

"No I won't, I promise. Tell me now, you'll see."

He started up the stairs. "Not now, Cambria. Later. Maybe one each year." He stopped just outside the door with her still in his arms. Leaning back against the wall, he said, "Before we go in, kiss me, Cambria. Put your heart into it."

Cambria looked into his dark eyes and met the challenge

sparkling in his eyes. "Tell me one sin and I will. Tell me what you said to Tony." She grinned, daring him to trust her.

He grinned back. "I told Tony you were sickly, and that's why you wore those old-lady shawls."

"You *what?*" she sputtered, her eyes flashing. "You told him I was—"

He pulled her tight for another long, surrendering kiss, all the while moving into the ballroom toward the wedding guests waiting for him. He dropped her on her feet, her eyes fluttering as she tried to figure out where she was.

"I think she's ready," he told the clergyman. "but make it quick."